SHE WAS LOST
WHENEVER HE WAS NEAR.

Being so near Garrick made Dawn feel dizzy, so much so that she clutched at his shoulder for balance. Slowly she was bound by the music's spell, a fragile silken thread that was woven about them. For just a moment she allowed herself to forget who he was, what she had been, what could happen if she allowed herself to love him and gave herself up to the moment. The look of passion in his eyes made her believe herself to be all the things she'd longed to be. Beautiful. Proper. Alluring. Desired. The kind of woman a man like Garrick Seton could love.

Also by Kathryn Kramer:

SIREN SONG

DESIRE'S MASQUERADE

UNDER GYPSY SKIES

Lady Rogue

KATHRYN KRAMER

A DELL BOOK

Published by
Dell Publishing
a division of
Bantam Doubleday Dell Publishing Group, Inc.
666 Fifth Avenue
New York, New York 10103

ISBN: 0-440-20934-X

Printed in the United States of America

Published simultaneously in Canada

July 1991

10   9   8   7   6   5   4   3   2   1

OPM

To my nephew, Aric Wesley Hockett.

And to the children of the world in hopes that someday mankind will learn the futility of greed, and that there will be no such thing as poverty.

Across the gateway of my heart
  I wrote "No Thoroughfare,"
But love came laughing by, and cried:
  "I enter everywhere. . . ."

— Herbert Shipman,
  No Thoroughfare

Author's Note

The early to late 1800s more than any other period in English history have been associated with elegance, propriety, the pursuit of ideal beauty, social poise, and distinguished achievements in literature and art. It was an era of opulence: the furniture of Chippendale, Sheraton, Hepplewhite, the interior decoration of Robert Adam, the china of Wedgwood. Even silverware and book bindings were chosen with the object of beauty and harmony. Men wore well tailored frock coats and carried gold pocket watches. Women donned dresses that flowed with the natural lines of Grecian art. Horses were carefully groomed, carriages such as phaetons and landaus were designed for speed and grace. Architecture knew a resurgence and came to fruition in stately English mansions and tall colonnades.

Abroad, Nelson and Wellington brought victory and heightened self-assurance to complement artistic achievements at home, yet the age that produced Byron, Shelley, Beau Brummell, and Jane Austen had another aspect as well. Side by side with the aristocracy and beauty there was an urban underworld of thieves, gamblers, and rogues.

Historians have often neglected this other world, but life on the streets was as unique and colorful as it was full of sorrow and travail. Boisterous pleasure seekers and stealthy pickpockets rubbed elbows on crowded streets. Public buildings of importance were situated in the middle of steamy districts. Magnificent shops and houses were surrounded by badly lit alleyways swarming with thieves. As a thriving international seaport, London offered rich pickings for everyone from guttersnipes to hardened veterans of Newgate. London surpassed the rest of England in crime and vice.

Wealth and poverty existed side by side in early nineteenth-century London: two different worlds in the same sphere. Even so, it was not impossible to raise oneself to a higher standard of living, nor was it forbidden by law to dream. Hope is a sustaining human gift that grants to a young, parentless girl the strength to endure a harsh environment and the courage to envision new beginnings. In the midst of squalor and despair an act of kindness sparks a flame of love and brings a young pickpocket into the arms of a handsome, determined young architect.

Prologue—1800

It was dark in the prison cell. Dark and eerie. Huddling against the hard stone wall, her legs drawn up to her chest, Dawn Leighton fought against the fear that enveloped her whenever she heard a sudden sound or caught sight of a shifting shadow. When was this horrid nightmare going to end?

Three weeks and still the high-pitched shrieks of the rats as they scurried about in the night made it impossible for her to sleep. The mumbles, mutterings, and groans of the other prisoners unnerved her. The ghostly clang of closing gates, the rattle of keys, the heavy tread of footsteps were constant reminders of her family's shame.

It was a mistake! It had to be. They had done no wrong. Her beautiful, gentle mother was no criminal; her brother was full of mischief but neither he nor she had done anything amiss. If only everything could be just the way it used to be. But no! Things would never be the same again.

Dawn could hear the drip, drip of water as it fell from the ceiling above to the stone floor, the mumbles and murmurs of the other inhabitants of the cell. How quickly happiness could turn to tragedy. Her eighth birthday: She remembered that day vividly. The sky had been a bright blue canopy overhead, putting lie to the lips of those who had promised rain. It had been a perfect day, all the more so because her father had proclaimed it to be *her day* and had promised to buy her the china doll that sat so prettily in the toy store window in Bloomsbury.

"You will look just like her when you become a young lady, Poppet," Howard Leighton had said, kissing her on the brow. "Her eyes are just as green as yours, her curls just as shiny dark brown." He had promised to take her to the puppet show that night when he came home from work. "Until then, be a good girl and mind your mother."

"I will, Papa. I'll even see that Robbie behaves. He'll have to or I won't give him any of my cake." She had smiled angelically, relishing the thought of taunting her brother with her birthday confections. Robbie always thought himself so superior just because he was a boy, but today belonged to her and the thought had filled her with heady pleasure.

Dawn had watched with pride as her father climbed into the family carriage. He was one of the most prestigious merchants in town. Leighton's China and Glassware was the largest shop of its kind in the city. A wooden sign bearing three painted goblets hung high over the door beckoning the most important people in London to enter and buy. Her father even leased two large ships to bring the finest glass from Venice and hand-painted china from Holland.

How lucky she was to have such a father, she had thought. Indeed to have two such doting parents. Both Howard and Elizabeth Leighton lavished affection on their children. Her mother was the most beautiful woman Dawn had ever seen. Certainly no one had such lovely clothes or dressed so elegantly. Dawn was determined to be just like her mother when she grew up, to find a man just like her father to marry.

Passing a long gilt mirror on her way back inside the house, Dawn stopped to study herself. She had most certainly felt grown up in her white muslin dress with lilac-colored dots. The rounded neckline and short puffed sleeves were patterned after a dress her mother favored. She had promised she would not get the dress dirty, or scuff up the toes of her new black slippers. Carefully she had positioned herself on the green velvet settee, her hands folded in her lap, until Robbie sneaked up behind her and pulled one of her long dark braids.

"Ouch! Stop that!" Robbie goaded her into a playful scuffle. Dawn held her own. "Today's my birthday, you goose. How can you be so mean?" she reprimanded him, annoyed that he did not remember.

"Your birthday? I nearly forgot," he teased. Robbie's smile was pure mischief. Taking her by the hand, he had led her to the hall closet. Opening it with a wink, he revealed his present, a large red ball decorated with a bow. The temptation to try it out was too much for Dawn. Before she could nod her head, he whisked her out the door in to the cobbled street.

"Bet you can't catch this . . ."

"Bet I can!"

Bending, standing on tiptoes, reaching high, she struggled to catch every throw, basking in the warmth of his surprised praise. Forgotten was the promise to act like her mother's "proper little lady." They were both laughing when Elizabeth Leighton called to them from an upstairs window, beckoning them inside.

"Look at you. Both of you. You look nearly as dirty as the urchins who beg on the street." She sighed.

"I'm sorry, Mama." Dawn brushed her dirt-smudged dress and tugged her hair bows into place.

"Only hoydens frolic about so. For shame!" Though

her tone scolded, her mother's lips held the hint of a smile. She wasn't really angry. "Brush yourselves off! I'll try to repair the damage—" A knock at the front door interrupted their mother's careful ministrations. "Now who could that be?"

All too quickly they found out. A stern-faced beadle, his hat in his hands, had given them the tragic news. Dawn knew if she lived to be a hundred she would never forget his words.

"There's been an accident! Are you Elizabeth Leighton?" he asked.

"Yes."

"Wife of the merchant Howard Leighton?"

"I am." A look of fear and apprehension replaced her mother's lovely smile. "Why?"

Shifting nervously from foot to foot, the beadle went on with the dreadful news. A wealthy young rogue, driving his phaeton at a furious pace through the streets had collided with her father as he stepped out of his carriage. Howard Leighton had been crushed mercilessly beneath the wheels.

"No!" Dawn cried. How could that be? Only moments ago she had watched her father leave for his shop. "Not my father . . ."

"I fear you'll have to come with me, Mrs. Leighton," the man had said, ignoring Dawn's outcry. "I need you to identify the body." The *body*. Such a cold word.

"No-o-o!" Her mother's wail echoed Dawn's own. Always the one to seek haven and comfort in her mother's arms, now it was Dawn who gave solace. The shock of her husband's death was too much for Elizabeth Leighton. She wept and shrieked hysterically. For the first time in her life Dawn was called upon to be the strong one, to make decisions. Somehow she calmed her mother, but the days that followed still hovered nightmarishly in Dawn's thoughts. She had been forced to grow up very quickly.

Because her mother had taken the news so badly, Dawn was forced to put her own heartache aside. Over and over she repeated soothing words to her mother, reminding her that the man they had so loved was now in God's hands. That was how her mother had always explained death to her; what other explanation could there be for such a loss?

"Somehow we'll get through this, Mama. . . ." And somehow they did, though the repercussions were more grave than they ever could have imagined. Always generous to a fault, oftentimes careless in money management, Howard Leighton had left a mountain of debts, more than it was possible to repay. Dawn tried hard to understand. Money seemed to be far more important than she had ever dreamed. In the next few days she came to see that it was *everything*. Those without it were severely punished.

Dawn, Robbie, and their mother watched helplessly as the furniture was taken from the house. Elizabeth Leighton sold all her possessions, even her wedding ring, but the stack of bills was bottomless. In the end they lost everything but the clothes on their backs. But the worst was yet to come. Though Elizabeth Leighton had tried hard to find help, had sought work, intending to make good on her husband's remaining debts, it was an impossible task. When one of the leased ships returning from China was lost in a storm their financial ruin was complete. Like leeches Howard Leighton's business associates clamored for restitution. The family was taken to debtor's prison.

The Fleet was one of three prisons administered by the Royal Courts of Justice, as Dawn's mother called them. Justice? As the prison cart rumbled over the cobbled streets, Dawn bitterly reflected that it seemed hardly that.

Impassive as he selected a key from the giant ring he wore tied to his pants, the gaoler had shown no sympathy. Slowly the door was opened. Dawn, her mother, and her brother were thrust inside. Now ruined, humiliated, they found that a stone-walled room had become their home.

"Oh, Daddy. Daddy. How different our lives might have been." Dawn whispered aloud to herself mournfully. Her father had been a very clever man. Somehow he would have found a way to pay the money he owed. Now there was no hope. Though Dawn's mother had scraped together every bit of money she owned, it had not been enough. It appeared the family would spend a long time in their present surroundings.

Dawn watched as her once beautiful and elegantly attired mother gave in to despair. Hour after hour Elizabeth Leighton sat staring at the bare stone walls, growing thinner and paler, no longer caring how she looked or what she did, seeming to age overnight.

Attuning her ears to the night sounds, Dawn listened to her mother's rasping breath, her dry cough, her moans.

"Mama? Mama, are you all right?" she asked. A fierce convulsion of coughing shook the silence.

"Yes . . . yes. Go back to sleep. . . ." Her mother's voice was so weak, it could barely be heard.

"Mama . . ." Dawn reached out to stroke her mother's face, then recoiled in shock. Her mother's forehead was hot. Fevered. Dawn had heard her mother caution against such things often enough to know there was danger. "Mama, you're sick."

"No . . . no, I'm . . . I'm not. It's hot in here, that's all."

"I wish there was a window to open." Indeed there

was not even one small crack to let in fresh air. Dawn had been told that they lived in much better circumstances than some of the prisoners in rooms below. The debtors had privileges not granted to ordinary inmates. At least they were allowed to stay together and had beds instead of straw pallets. The food they ate was more appetizing, the cells larger and not quite as dirty. Even so the large room had a nauseating odor: a mixture of sweat, rotting food, and decay. Dawn wondered if she would ever grow accustomed to the smell.

"We had windows once. . . ." Her mother's voice was wistful.

"And we will again. So many windows that we'll be able to see the whole city. You'll dress in silks again, Mama, and have a dozen or more fancy hats, just like before." She was fiercely determined to give her mother hope, to make her smile again. "But first you've got to get well, for me and for Robbie. . . ."

"I will." It was a promise Elizabeth Leighton could not keep. Fragile and gently reared, she lacked the stamina to survive the harsh environment. Her condition quickly deteriorated, hastened by the onset of gaol fever. Though Dawn did her best, Elizabeth lay on her bed in the dark corner, hardly moving, never eating, rapidly wasting away.

Though Dawn pleaded with the warden, it was several days before a physician was called. Something in the old man's eyes alarmed Dawn and told her it was too late. In two days' time Elizabeth Leighton was dead.

"Mama!" Dawn loved her mother desperately. Now she wept agonized tears. First her father and now her mother. It wasn't fair! Why? How could she survive the loneliness?

A debtor was allowed no coffin, no name-stone; thus Dawn and Robbie bore the added grief of seeing their mother buried in a pauper's grave. It was as if the beautiful woman they had known had never existed except in their memories. Almost overnight, Robbie changed from a laughing, teasing boy into a grim youth seething with defiance. Dawn became a solemn child filled with bitterness. *Orphan.* That's what people were calling them. With no relatives to claim them they would be put into an orphanage.

"Not me! I won't go." Restlessly Robbie kicked out at one of the rats before it could steal his supper. Chattering, scolding, the rodent slithered away. "They use a paddle on you if you don't behave. Make you work all the time. I've heard the talk. It's even worse than here. I won't go, Dawnie."

"Then neither will I." Dawn quickly made up her mind. Slapping each other's palms twice in their childhood gesture of agreement, they made their plans. Though they appeared acquiescent when the gaoler came to fetch them, they were merely waiting their chance. It came the moment they were outside the Fleet. Pushing free of the guards, they broke into a run. Never had a race been held for such high stakes.

The children were fleet of foot, agile. Dodging the guards, racing through the narrow alleyways, they soon left their pursuers behind. Taking refuge behind a large rain barrel they giggled softly in triumph.

"No orphanage for us!" Dawn crowed.

"We're free as birds," Robbie agreed, taking her by the hand. "No more stone walls, nor locks . . ."

"No more gruel. Ugh!" Dawn made a face.

"We'll go anywhere we like, do anything we want. It will be a frolicsome life, you'll see."

They spent the day exploring the city, from the docks to the gateway, from the highest point atop London Bridge to that point on the quay where the bank sloped down. For a time they were content, until their stomachs began to rumble with hunger. They hadn't so much as a farthing to spend for food. Neither Dawn nor Robbie had ever gone hungry. Food was something they had always taken for granted. Even in prison they had been fed, though they had grumbled about the fare. Now they were faced with sudden reality. The streets were filled with vendors and tradesmen, but not a one was willing to part with his wares for nothing.

"Go on with ye. Don't be begging here!" they scolded.

"Tattered little sparrows, I daresay. Aye, that ye be. But I have no meat pasties to spare," insisted a frowning pieman.

"Ye be overbold. Get out of here before I call the night watchman," threatened another.

Dawn and Robbie retreated to Billingsgate, clinging to the shadows, hoping for a more charitable attitude among the fishermen and cod sellers. But their dirty clothing brought scorn, not sympathy. The people of London had hardened their hearts against those in need. Perhaps because there were so many, Dawn reflected. They were not the only children wandering the streets in search of food.

"They don't care any more about us than they do the rats!" Robbie snarled, breathing in the scent of fish, potent yet strangely appetizing.

"They do! Someone will give us food, you'll see. They won't let us starve, Robbie." Remembering her manners, Dawn approached a fishwife, asking politely for something to eat. An upraised broom and a barrage of curses were the response. That night, frightened and alone, they slept in a doorway, huddled together, sharing the misery of their aching stomachs. Both swore it was the last time they would ever go hungry.

Prowling about for nails, old metals, twine, paper, or broken glass to sell to the rag-and-bone man for a few pennies, Robbie and Dawn fared better the next few days. When they could not find anything to sell, they stole their dinner. Desperation had its own lessons to teach.

Life might have continued in the same pattern had not fate taken a hand. Going about their daily routine, scrounging for odds and ends to sell to the ragman, they suddenly came face to face with a band of young ruffians. Urchins, her mother had called them. Now those rowdy and ragged beings came after Dawn and Robbie, assaulting them with obscenities as well as fists. Coming to her brother's aid, Dawn fought furiously, until one eye swelled shut and her lip was split open. In the end they were defeated, pushed and shoved along the cobbled street, barely managing to avoid the open gutters of filth at their feet and slop from pails being emptied from the windows above. They soon learned that they had unknowingly encroached on the territory of one of London's boldest and most powerful thieves. Now they were dragged trembling into his presence.

Black John Dunn greeted the two trespassers with a dark scowl. Dawn looked into the black-bearded face with awe, certain she had come face to face with the very devil. "B'God!" he thundered. "Wot 'ave we 'ere?"

"Caught 'em pilfering, we did, John. Staking 'emselves in our territory. Brought 'em roight away to yer, we did." The boy who spoke flashed Dawn a wide-gapped grin, obviously pleased with himself.

"We weren't *pilfering*, merely gathering a few discarded things so that we could make our way." Holding her head up, trying to mask her fear, Dawn stepped forward. "Please, sir, we didn't mean any harm. It's just that we have nowhere to go. Selling things to the rag-and-bone man seemed to be the only way."

"Did it, now?" Black John Dunn crossed his thick arms across his massive chest. Thick brows pulled together in a vee as he questioned the feminine new-comer in their midst. Dawn answered every inquiry with a truthful reply, pouring out the entire story in her need for comfort.

"Orphans ye be?" The mouth beneath the mustache twisted into a grimace "Wi' no plaice to go. Such a pity."

Dawn saw the wink he gave the others but didn't grasp its meaning. All she knew was that suddenly she and Robbie were being welcomed into the little band. There was no retribution, only generosity. He gave them food—carrots and ham—and told them to make themselves comfortable. His was the first mea-sure of kindness they had been granted since their father's death. Was it any wonder they capitulated to his churlish charm?

"Ye 'ave an 'ome wi' us fer as long as ye loike. All that I ask is that ye do as I want. Cooperate wi' me, ye might saiy. We're all one big family 'ere, ain't we, Tweezer?" The gap-toothed boy nodded his head.

"Family . . ." The word sounded wonderful to Dawn. To belong once again, she and Robbie.

"Would ye loike to stay?" A grin slashed its way across Black John Dunn's face as he asked the ques-tion.

"Yes. Oh, yes." How could she say otherwise? Searchingly she looked over at Robbie, relieved when he agreed.

"Good. Good. Now there's a little matter of yer schooling. Just 'ow much do yer know?"

"Robbie and I know how to read and write. How to do our sums." A chorus of giggles answered Dawn's statement but she was undaunted. Making a face at the youth called Tweezer, she continued. "Mama taught us how to do the latest dances, so that we would know them when we got older." Again the laughter. Only by biting her lip did Dawn control her temper. What boorishly rude oafs these boys were. Urchins. Her mother had been right about them.

"At's all very fine." Black John silenced the guffaws with an upraised hand. "I 'ave it in mind ter teach ye about other things, 'owever," he said. "Skills, 'at will 'elp yer to survive. Lessons 'at will 'elp yer cheat the 'angman."

Dawn and Robbie didn't grasp the full import of the robber-chief's words then, but in the coming days they would come to understand. By then it was too late. Those whom Black John Dunn took under his wing he never let go. True to his word he schooled them in the art of thievery. They had found a home and lost their innocence forever.

I

A Thief's Angel

LONDON
1810

He that prigs what isn't his'n,
When he's cotched'll go to prison. . . .
—"Happy" Webb
(quoted by Lord William Lennox)

1

Rays of brilliant sunlight danced down on London's church spires and rooftops, giving promise of a scorching July day. Even so, Dawn Leighton kept her white mobcap pulled down tightly over her raven-black curls. Blending in with the servants, workmen, and day people of the city, she assessed the pickings of the day. From the corner of her eye she watched her brother Robbie merge into the crowd, moving cautiously yet effortlessly so as not to attract attention.

"Dust ho! Dust ho!" Ringing a bell, the dustman called out as he tried his best to clean the streets of litter and grime. Coughing and choking on the powdery dirt stirred up by his broom, Dawn rubbed at her eyes, narrowly escaping the rumbling wheels of a market cart as it clattered over the rough cobblestones. Forgetting herself, in her anger she raised her fists, giving vent to a curse that inspired an ostler's stare. Much to her dismay, the man fell into step a few paces behind her. Pretending not to notice, she strolled along, feigning interest in the shops until she outdistanced him.

"Pancakes!" cried a shrill voice.

"Dumplin's! Dumplin's! Diddle, diddle, dumplin's ho!" called another, vying for her trade. The city never slept. If the nights were filled with those seeking adventure and gaiety, the days were for those who chose a more regulated existence—the workers of London.

"Hot baked warden pears and pippins!" A hopeful little man in a white apron stepped out in front of her, nearly colliding with Dawn as she passed his way. Though she was hungry, she shook her head, determined nevertheless to taste a delicacy the moment the vendor's back was turned. The appearance of another customer gave her her chance. Her nimble fingers captured an apple and carefully concealed it in her apron pocket.

"Looks like it's gonna be an 'ot one, it does," she said with an angelic smile.

"Hot as hades, I would imagine." He eyed her suspiciously but Dawn retreated quickly down the street. Taking refuge behind the corner of a building and scanning the street for any sign of trouble, she relished the tartly sweet fruit with a chuckle, threw the core over her shoulder, then continued nonchalantly on her way.

London's tradesmen and wealthier merchants were opening up their shutters, briskly setting up shops and stalls to display their wares. Passing by a window showcasing china and glassware, Dawn felt a prick of sorrow, remembering those days long ago when she'd helped her father with his morning routine. It seemed a lifetime ago. Now she and Robbie stole from men like her father. Any twinge of guilt she might have felt was washed away, however, by terrible memories of the Fleet and days and nights spent wandering the streets. No one had offered her comfort. It was just as Black John said: "Every man for 'isself!"

Thievery and trickery was the life she'd become accustomed to. True to his word Black John had tirelessly trained Dawn and Robbie in their new vocation. But Dawn still remembered the fine manner in which she and her brother had once lived, and she could never quite seem to push her dream of being a lady permanently from her mind. Someday, she knew, she'd be just like one of those brightly dressed peacocks she saw strutting around on the arms of handsome young dandies or riding in shiny black landaus. Now those so-called *ladies and gentlemen* carefully avoided her, but she knew one day she'd see looks of admiration replace their expressions of scorn. Until then she'd have to make do. Above all Dawn was a survivor. Experience had taught her that she had to be.

"Here's yer rare holland socks, four pairs a shilling!" The cobbled streets were slowly becoming crowded with tradesmen, hawkers, and shoppers. Dawn's specialty was handkerchiefs, a skill she'd been taught right from the first. Satin and lace confections fetched a moderately decent price at the rag fair in Rosemary Lane or at its rival, Petticoat Lane, where second-hand clothing was bought, then sold again. Robbie's skill lay in filching purses and pocketbooks. In their thieves' circle both were credited with having a touch as light as the stroke of a butterfly's wing.

I oughtta be able to find me quite a lot of fancy wipes among this bunch, she thought, eyeing each person that passed with a calculating eye. Adroitly she wove in and out of the crowd in search of prizes to be plundered. She did not see the tall chimney sweep until she ran headlong into him.

"Oomph . . . !" Black soot and ashes smudged her clothing from head to toe. Grumbling, she brushed herself off. "Watch where yer goin', ya blinkin' arse!" she scolded, even though the accident had been her fault.

"Sorry, miss!" He grinned, dabbing at her soiled

gray cotton dress with his large-boned hands. Dawn uttered a string of swear words, gave him a look of contempt, and crossed the street. "I sweep yer chimneys clean O, sweep yer chimneys clean O," she heard him warble wistfully.

Suddenly a hand reached out and grabbed her shoulder. Frightened, Dawn whirled around, expecting to be accosted by someone taking her to toll for her thievery a couple of blocks back. Instead she found her brother's deep blue eyes appraising her.

"Ya looks as if yer was out fer a bleedin' stroll. Step lively, sister dear. Surely there mus' be some bloke wot looks profitable. It's not me intent to roam the bloody streets all mornin'. I got better things ta do wi' me time. Can't be watchin' o'er you every minute."

"Watch over *me*? Ha!" Indignantly Dawn put her hands on her hips. "It's *me* wot watches over *you*. Makin' certain ya don't go lurkin' all bloomin' mornin' in Weasel's tavern."

"And if I does?" Robbie's brows danced up in question.

"I'll box yer ears, I will! I won't lose me bro' to the likes o' gin." Her frown softened. "I love ya, Rob. I'd protect ya wi' me life if I had ta. Jus' you and me. 'At's all wot's important. As long as we got each other, we don't need nobody else." Though Dawn was younger by two years than Robbie, she guarded him. Since the death of their mother it had always been that way.

"Yeh? Well . . ." Robbie caught his thumbs in the waistband of his patched trousers. "But ya ain't me mum. I want t' get meself a staike in a card gaime, I do. Profit twofold offen me skills." His pouting mouth challenged her to tell him nay. Instead Dawn merely sighed. "I only answers to meself."

"Do wot ye will, Rob, but be careful, I say. If ye ask me, yer gettin' a bit too cocksure, and one o' these morns it'll do ye in, it will! Weasel is not to be trusted. E'll fleece ye. Just wait and see. His flash house is the devil's own lair." She snorted disdainfully. "Even a thief must 'ave some honor. Besides, it ain't good ter steal more than we need plus Black John's share. It wouldn't do ter get caught."

"Caught? Me?" Holding up his hands, he wiggled his fingers, proving his dexterity. "No one can 'old a candle ta me. Fastest fingers on Fleet Street, I 'ave."

"It taikes more 'n speed, I daresaiy." She threw up her hands. Black John had turned Robbie's head with his abundant praise. "The truth is a thief needs luck as well."

"Luck? I got 'at in abundance, I do." He nodded in the direction of a rotund man dressed in tan pantaloons, cambric shirt, and dark brown velvet frock coat. "E 'as the look o' wealth about 'im, I daresaiy. I wager I can lift 'is purse afore 'e can blink an eye. Watch."

"No, Robbie . . ." She might as well have been whistling in the wind for all the attention he paid her. Robbie always taunted Dawn for her caution, and she was the one Black John took to task for not filching enough goods.

"It's beneath 'er dignity," he would growl disparagingly. "She thinks she's a blinkin' laidy, she does. A laidy in a rogue's court. Laidy Rogue, she is." It was a nickname that had endured, though Dawn had come to feel pride in it.

Now Dawn wished Robbie had just a bit of her reserve. She watched uneasily as Robbie approached the preening, top-hatted man. There were too many people around. It made her fidgety. Robbie was taking a risk. One toff's purse was not worth hanging for, nor even going to prison for. There wasn't enough money in the whole wide world worth a man's freedom.

Quickly she inched her way forward, watching as Robbie slashed the strings of the man's money pouch with a deft flick of his wrist. His eyes were sparkling with triumph and a grin cut its way from ear to ear as he winked in her direction. Taking the bulging pouch in one grubby hand and hefting it confidently in his closed fist, Robbie strutted back across the street. He didn't realize that he had been observed, but Dawn saw a cadaverously thin man dressed in black move forward.

"Robbie!" Dawn gasped, gesticulating wildly. The man had the stealthy look of a Bow Street Runner. Now he was following her brother step by step. "Robbie!"

"Thief! Thief!" The cry rang through the air. "Catch him."

"Bloody damn!" Dawn's warning had come too late. Now she watched in helpless horror as a crowd of blue-suited men closed in. Dear God, Robbie was cornered! "Robbie!" she shouted again. Visions of his capture assailed her, but her brother was as agile and as cunning as a cat. Pushing into the pudding-and-pie man, he overturned the cart, vaulting over it to safety as he threw the pouch Dawn's way. The money bag sailed over the heads of Robbie's pursuers and landed in Dawn's outstretched hands. With reflex action born of years of practice she juggled it like a hot potato, then clutched it to her bosom, watching as Robbie sprinted down the street, vanishing into the crowd.

"To the Dial!" she heard him say. He was heading to Seven Dials, that haven of safety amidst the rookeries, where seven streets intersected. Usually no one could tell down which street a thief had fled.

"That young woman has your purse, sir!" A bootblack boy added his voice to the tumult, pointing unflinchingly in Dawn's direction. Like a tide the throng of pursuers changed course in midstride as she took to her heels. From the looks on their faces, she'd get no mercy from anyone in the square.

Purposefully Dawn followed her brother's example and tipped over a fruit peddler's cart, scattering apples, oranges, and pears all over the cobbled street. The men following after her, slipping and stumbling, gave her at least a head start. Flitting across the road on legs made agile by desperation, she used her wits to avoid capture. Changing direction several times, she confused her pursuers. The ominous shadow of Newgate goaded her even when she was too winded to go on. How much longer could she outdistance them?

Dawn's eyes darted from one side of the street to the other as she frantically sought a place to hide and catch her breath. The open door of a shiny black carriage offered haven. Her wish had been granted. A *toff's* carriage, the last place her followers would think to look. Scrambling inside, closing the door behind her, Dawn shrank back into the shadows, throwing herself to the soft rug on the floor. Anxiously she counted to ten, listening as the sound of clomping feet stampeded past.

"Go on, ye blighters," she breathed, feeling much like the fox at a foxhunt. This time she had bested the hounds and she felt exhilarated. "Let them run their bloomin' legs off—they'll never catch me now."

Lifting her head, she peered cautiously out the window as the swarm of men moved off in the distance. They looked like a group of angry ants, she reflected, stifling a triumphant giggle with the back of her hand. With avid interest she watched until they were out of sight, then leaned her head against the padded leather seat and closed her eyes.

"What the devil!"

Dawn's head snapped around to look at the man

who owned the rich baritone voice. Bloody hell! She
wasn't safe yet.

"Well . . . ?" With a snort of exasperation a tall
man jerked the door open and eyed Dawn with obvious irritation. "Who are you?" Seeing surprise and
fear clearly etched on her face, he guessed the answer. "You're the one they were looking for."

"No . . . no!" Dawn stared back into the bold blue
eyes. She was apprehensive, but even so a spark of
defiance lit her eyes. "Suppose 'at they were? Wot's it
ter ya?" *Bloody bastard,* she thought. He was probably afraid she'd soil his fine carriage. Oh, she knew
the type, all right. His well-tailored garments, the ar-
rogance in his manner, and his precise manner of
speech proclaimed his wealth. A rich bloke.

"Just curious." He quirked a brow, clutching a
stack of papers as he took a step closer. "Were they?"

She felt the effect of his potent stare all the way
down to her toes. "Were they wot?"

Self-assurance was etched all too plainly in his unwavering gaze and the stern set of his jaw. Not a man
to be trifled with, she reflected. He looked to be a
dangerous gent if crossed. Stubborn, more than
likely. Daring. Unafraid. Realizing at once that here
was a man who was more than her match, Dawn
eased towards the door, her thought now of escape.
The man blocked her way.

"Were they . . . *are* they after you?" he asked, his
tone of voice seeming to hint that he was losing patience.

Clenching her hands into tight fists, heaving a long
drawn-out sigh, Dawn lowered her eyes. Though
schooled in the art of telling vibrant lies, she found
herself telling the truth. "Yes . . . yes . . . they . . .
they are."

"Aha!" It was an easy conclusion to come to.
Dawn's gaze traveled from the toes of the gentle-

man's well-shined black boots to the top of his head as she tried to assess the situation. What to do? Tussle with him? No. Elegant clothes could not hide his masculinity. His shoulders were broad, his thighs well muscled. He would be more than a match for her. Were he to live in her circumstances, he might even be more than a match for Black John.

"They are after me. . . ." she said, watching him warily, "but . . . but it's a *mistaike*. . . ."

"A mistake?" Now he seemed doubly interested. Damned if she didn't detect a note of compassion. "How so? Speak up, child."

Child? Dawn brushed nervously at the skirt of her dress. The drab frock had been purchased from a vendor in Petticoat Lane and more than likely had been stolen from a gentlewoman's servant. A maid, perhaps. A woman obviously much larger than Dawn. Undoubtedly, hiding her bosom as it did, the dress made her appear much younger than her years. She decided to play upon his error. If he thought her to be a child, he wouldn't turn her in; he might even be inclined to help her.

"They . . . they think I did somethin' I didn't do, sir."

Slowly she looked up, studying him intently, and her breath caught. Oh, he was a fine-looking bloke, he was. His nose was straight, proud, and well shaped, his cheekbones high, his jaw strong with a determined set to it. Despite its grim set his mouth had an interesting fullness that spoke of lips pleasant to kiss. Her eyes traveled to his hair—brown with unusual golden highlights, thick, and vibrant. Combed back in the fashion she'd seen the wealthy wear, it brushed his collar as if he hadn't taken time for a recent trim. Neary as long as Robbie's. From the top of his golden-brown hair to the tips of his black boots, he was awesomely handsome. It was his eyes, however, that fascinated her. Startlingly blue. Every instinct within her was vibrantly awakened as she gazed into those eyes.

"You have been wrongly accused. Is that it?" Something in the depths of those eyes, a measure of kindness, gave her a faint glimmer of hope.

"Yeah. Yeah. Wrongly." Though she wanted to look away, his eyes held her captive.

"Just what is it they think you did? Tell me, girl." Before Dawn could answer, the leather pouch broke through a hole in her pocket and plopped to the floor of the carriage. "Aha!" All trace of compassion evaporated from the gentleman's face as he folded his arms across his chest.

"It's . . . it's a gentleman's purse, it is. But *I* didn't steal it." There was an earnestness in her voice that couldn't be practiced. She was telling the truth. "I swear it, sir. I didn't."

The answering silence was unnerving. Why didn't he say something? Anything. By now any other gentleman would have peached, that was for sure. And yet he hadn't. She looked up through her fringe of dark lashes at him, taking in his broad shoulders again, the elegant cut of his dark blue coat. Though he was a toff, he didn't seem a bad sort when all was said and done. In fact, he seemed a bit of a noble bloke. So far he hadn't even called a beadle.

"Another 'un filched it, 'e did." She failed to mention the close relationship of the scoundrel. Handsome he might be but obviously he was also gullible, easier to fool than she could have suspected.

"Someone else stole it. . . ." There was just a trace of a mocking smile on the gentleman's lips. "It just fell into your hands, is that what you would have me believe?"

"Yes . . . yes.' 'At's 'ow it 'appened, it did." She answered his smile, the corners of her mouth trembling. "Fell into me 'ands."

"Interesting. Care to tell me the details?" His voice was husky with a trace of anger as he moved closer. It was clear that he didn't believe her as he climbed into the carriage, and pulled her up on the seat beside him. The door closed with a clank, and a shiver of alarm ran down Dawn's back. She was a mouse, trapped by an unrelenting cat. He was not as gullible as she had so foolishly supposed. He knew exactly what she had done. Even now he watched and waited for her to confess.

"Well-l-l?" Dawn felt the strength of his hand on her shoulder. His hard fingers exerted pressure. She would never escape. A quivering tension coiled in her stomach. She had to convince him of her innocence or all was lost.

Burying her face in her hands and pretending to give in to tears, she wailed, "Ooh, it was terrible, it was. I nearly died o' fright." Groping for his hand, she clutched it tightly, her fingers trembling. "'E . . . 'e came wit'in an 'air's length of getting caught, 'e did. It was then 'e . . . 'e threw the purse at *me.*" She sniffed in feigned indignation. "Tryin' ta cover 'is own tail, 'e was."

"And you didn't steal it?" His eyes were hot blue coals that seared her.

"No-o-o! Oh, please believe me. I'm a good girl, I am." Peeking through her fingers she was overcome with relief. It was working. She could tell by his expression that his sympathy had been piqued.

"Hmm." The gentleman's eyes narrowed speculatively. She was so petite that he judged her to be still of tender years. A homeless waif, by the look of her, but not a hardened criminal. Perhaps then her story was true. He would give her the benefit of the doubt.

" 'E ran for 'is life, leavin' me be'ind to answer for

wot 'e done. . . ." Clutching again at his hand, gazing into his eyes, she whispered, "Please 'elp me, sir."

The enormous green eyes with their long, thick, dark lashes were his undoing. She looked as guiltless as an angel. How then could he refuse? He wouldn't want to see the girl put into prison, especially if she had done no wrong. Perhaps even if she had. He was hardly one to judge another's sins or failings. God knew he had enough of his own.

"All right." His thumb rubbed over the back of her hand in a strangely tender manner. "I'll give you a ride back to your home. That should get you there safely. Will that do?" He held out his white cotton handkerchief to her. "Now, blow your nose and dry your eyes."

As she took the offered cloth she noticed his hands. Large. Strong. His hands confounded her. The knuckles were scarred as if he'd been in several fights, belying his elegant attire. Well, she wasn't going to ask. She dabbed at her eyes, then looked in fascination at the initials so carefully embroidered on the fine cotton. G.F.S., it said. She raised her well-arched brows in question.

"Garrick Frederick Seton is what those letters stand for. My name." He had been holding a bundle of papers and now plopped them down on the seat. "I'm an architect by profession." When she didn't answer, he added, "I draw the plans for many of the buildings being erected in the area."

"Oh!" Dawn was clearly impressed. "An artist of sorts."

"In a manner of speaking." This time his smile had no trace of scorn. "When so many men and women decide to live in the same area, things are bound to happen. Growth. New roads. Sturdy new buildings." He leaned out the window, motioning to his driver.

"Where to? East or west?" He guessed the answer before she said it. The poorer districts were to the east.

"Ah . . . ye don't 'ave to taike me all the way, sir. Jus' to the Red Feather Inn will be far enough." She had her pride. The thought of this fine gentleman seeing the squalid conditions in which she lived filled her with shame. Her back stiffened as her resentment returned. It was the cruel indifference of his kind that kept her languishing in such circumstances.

"Not a one o' 'em rich blokes cared a fig fer the likes o' us," Robbie was always reminding her. "They think about us as if we was bugs crawlin' on the wall."

"The Red Feather Inn?" Garrick was dubious. Even in the daylight hours it was a dangerous part of town. "Are you certain? I can take you all the way home. It would be no bother. Really. I'd like to make sure that you are . . ."

"Don't trouble yerself." Something in her eyes stilled his protests.

"The Red Feather Inn it will be." He watched her trace the outline of his initials with her fingertip, relishing the handkerchief as if it were something precious. Then she handed it back to him. "No, you keep it." He smiled. "A memento of our meeting. It isn't every day I have such an auspicious meeting with a pretty little girl."

"Keep it . . . ?" Dawn blushed to the roots of her hair, her antagonism momentarily held at bay. He'd called her pretty, as if he meant it. She'd received few compliments. Not since her father died had a man shown her real kindness. "I'd be 'onored, I would. I've never been given a gentleman's 'ankie before."

"Think of it as a token of friendship. Everyone has need of friends, don't you agree?" At the moment she looked so small and forlorn huddled upon the seat.

Sympathy welled up inside him. He wondered if anyone truly cared about this girl. "Do you have someone to look out for you? A mother? A father?" he asked.

This time the sudden tears that blinded Dawn's eyes were real. Oh, how she hated to cry in front of him. "My . . . my father was killed in an accident and my . . . my mother is dead, too . . . but . . . but I have a brother. An older one. 'E taikes care of me, or rather we taike care of each other. 'E says I cluck over 'im like a mother 'en."

"A brother? Good!" Her answer relieved him. The girl had at least one member of her family to look out for her. Strange how the little waif tugged at his heart. As the carriage rattled on down the road, he was tempted to find out more about her, perhaps even to ascertain some way of seeing her again, but at last he thought better of it. Mind his own business. That was good advice. Besides, they came from two different worlds, across a gulf impossible to cross. He could tell by the wistful look in her eyes that she knew it too. She was much like a stray kitten, but he was not the one to take her in. Nevertheless, he was strangely unnerved when the large wooden sign of the Red Feather Inn came into view.

"Here we are."

Dawn was so warm and comfortable that she was reluctant to leave the confines of the carriage and the soothing charm of his company. There were so many things she wanted to tell him. How could he ever understand? Her heart hammered painfully in her breast, and her tongue seemed frozen to the roof of her mouth. She stared at him mutely, at last managing a strangled "Thank you." Then she was climbing down from the carriage, glancing over her shoulder as she waved good-bye. On a sudden impulse she grasped his hand, relishing the firm, strong grip of his handshake. His touch evoked a longing deep within her. She was genuinely surprised by the jolt of sweet fire that swept through her veins at such a chaste and common gesture. She had the crazy impulse to throw herself into his arms, to cling to him for comfort, a temptation that was definitely alarming. Was that why she suddenly fled, running as if the very devil was pursuing her? Only when she was safely within the confines of the Red Feather did she dare to look back, to watch the carriage pull away. It was then that Dawn made a startling discovery. She'd left the coin-filled leather pouch behind! In spite of her dismay, she laughed at the irony of it all. Then, picking up her crumpled skirts, she made her way towards Seven Dials to find her brother.

2

The stench of the narrow cobbled street assailed Dawn's nostrils as she hurried from the Red Feather Inn. After the clean leather-and-tobacco-scented carriage, it was one more harsh reminder of the differences between herself and the fine gentleman. Now she was doubly glad she had declined his offer to take her all the way home. St. Giles was as different from Mayfair as night was from day.

"Blimey," she whispered, "but 'e would 'ave 'ad apoplexy for certain if 'e caught sight o' these digs." It was hardly a part of town a man like G.F.S. would frequent. With a sigh she paused to glance down at the handkerchief he had given her, then put it to her face. The linen smelled pleasantly of leather and spice, his scent. Closing her eyes, she conjured him up: his thick brown hair, brilliant smile, and piercing blue eyes. He was the kind of man a girl could dream about. *But never 'ave!* she warned herself. He was as far from her reach as a star. Shaking her head, scolding herself for such fanciful thoughts, Dawn thrust the handkerchief back in the folds of her bodice and continued on her way.

Dawn passed by a pawnbroker's shop, a second-hand clothing store, two gin shops, and assorted decrepit dwellings, many with rags or papers stuffed in the broken windowpanes. It was a stark contrast to the gentleman's side of town. Dicing, whoring, and guzzling gin were pursued here with a passion and if any men in suits were to be seen, it was certain they were indiscreet young gents flitting about on the fringes of the underworld to indulge in vice. Thieves preyed upon these noble rakes. It was a haunt for hunters looking for quarry.

"Just think," Black John Dunn always told her, "what good we be doing these blokes. Turning them to a more diligent and 'onest waiy of life by teachin' 'em a lesson. A good bop on the 'ead, the loss of their purses will maike 'em quit their philandering waiy of life. They'll be upstanding citizens, they will. And it's all due to us. . . ."

Indeed, Dawn thought, any man who dared walk this main avenue ran the risk of being robbed of his handkerchief, pocketbook, or watch. Those who put up a squabble often lost their lives. It was a harsh reality, as much a part of life as hunger and poverty. That was the way of the world, or so she told herself over and over.

Black John Dunn had a network of contacts to ensure his own safety—unscrupulous parrish beadles, prison turnkeys, greedy magistrates who helped him thwart those who would see him brought to justice. In return he gave them cash, liquor, or favors in one form or another. Trading justices, he called it. Even so, a body had to be careful. Every now and then a rare honest toff could be found, endangering the thieves with demands for a hanging. That was why she worried so. Robbie's life wouldn't be worth a shilling if a thieftaker got him. That's why Seven Dials was so important.

Seven Dials was an irregular square from which streets and alleys ran in every direction. Seven to be exact. Here a thief or miscreant could vanish into the unwholesome vapor of fog and smoke that enveloped the city. The tenement Robbie and Dawn shared with a band of pickpockets was located nearby.

"G'daiy, missy . . ." A short, tattered man, tipping his hat in the manner of a gentleman, greeted Dawn with a grin as she turned the corner.

"G'daiy, Jamie." Deformed at birth, abandoned and left to die, Jamie, affectionately called "the monkey," had been taken in by Dunn and his clan. Now he was one of the very finest pickpockets around, watches and fobs his specialty. Jamie had never come close to being nabbed. Built low to the ground, swift on his short bandy-legs, he was difficult to catch. "Is Robbie about?"

"Got 'ere less than five minutes ago. Mumblin' under 'is breath." He nodded in the direction of the tallest of the buildings. "Went inside, 'e did. By the looks o' 'im, 'e wasn't at all 'appy."

"No . . . most definitely not." Dawn let out her breath in a long sigh, thankful that Robbie was safe. "Nearly got caught todaiy . . ."

"No!"

"Yes!"

"Got to taike care. Gettin' more and more dangerous it is, workin' in the light." The little man's thick brows drew together in a scowl. He tugged her sleeve, wanting to hear the story, but Dawn shook her head. She was tired. All she wanted was a cold glass of cider and a place to rest her aching legs.

"I'll give it to ya in detail when we sup." Jamie was one of the fourteen in their group who slept, worked, and ate together. He was an odd sort of guardian. Of all the thieves he had been the kindest, taking them under his wing right from the first.

"Awroight, 'en." With a smile he tipped his hat again then merged with the crowd.

There was a cold air of desolation on the shadowed street. Human forms in various shapes and sizes littered the curbs. One man staggered drunkenly about, roaring a bawdy ditty. A small crowd had collected around a trio of giggling women, imbibing the contents of a bottle of gin and bitters. A few lost souls loitered about the gin shops, squabbling in the center of the road. Every lamppost supported a figure, leaning against it as if in fear of toppling into the dirt face first. Gin was the misery of both rich and poor. Indeed, more than half the grain sown in England was used to make some kind of liquor. Like poverty, it was just something a person soon got used to.

"Any shillings, Dawnie dearie?" A bleary-eyed man blocked Dawn's way, holding out his hand.

"Not a farthing, Will. I've come back empty 'anded."

"More's the pity. Black John is in a surly mood. You'll be addin' to it." Shrugging his shoulders, he took a step back, allowing Dawn to step by. His words were only too true. When Robbie revealed that she had held such an amply coined pouch and let it go, she would be in for certain trouble. Nevertheless she hurried on. She wasn't a coward, wasn't afraid of a licking. Over the years she'd toughened her sensitivity, indeed her very hide, to such things. Besides, Black John was oftentimes "more blow than go," as Robbie said. A whirlwind of bluster.

"I'm not afraid of Black John!" she said under her breath a dozen times or so. And yet when a cat suddenly pounced down beside her, she jumped. "Shadow! Silly cat, ye scared me within an inch o' me life." The gray tabby greeted her with enthusiasm, rubbing against her, entwining itself between her legs as she tried to walk. "No, I 'aven't been to Billingsgate todaiy. No fish." Reaching down, she scratched the cat under the chin. "But if there's any bacon left from sup', I'll give ye a bit." Bounding atop a water barrel, then to a windowsill, Shadow meowed his approval. With a leisurely stretch, he jumped back to the ground to follow her up the steps and through the doorway.

The large tenement room was dirty, and in a shambles of disrepair. Plaster had fallen from the walls, windows were broken and stuffed with rags, straw mattresses lined the walls with not even a partition between them. Clearly, privacy was at a premium here. The women slept on one side of the room, the men on the other, but it was not unusual to hear sounds in the night that told very plainly what was going on. Indeed, Dawn had been accosted in such a manner until she had learned how to defend herself. Now she was a scrapper, known to have the claws of a lioness and to pack quite a punch.

In the corner of the smoke-filled room stood a woodburning stove with an iron frying pan atop it. The smell of frying bacon scraps and cheese mingled with the aroma of onions. A single candle on the wooden trestle table in the middle of the room lighted the gloom of the interior. Cracked plates, cups, and several burned-out candle stubs littered the planked table where several of the tenants had already gathered, anxious to get their share of food.

"Farley . . ." Dawn nodded in the old man's direction. " 'Ow was pickings todaiy?" His lay was stealing luggage by cutting the ropes that bound traveling chests to carriages. Beside him sat Murdock, who had apprenticed himself to be trained in the same skill. Murdock's specialty was waiting in innyards, offering his service to carry baggage, then stealing it.

Each of Black John's people had a specialty. Dawn's eyes scanned the group. Newton was a rat-catcher, sent aboard cargo ships to get rid of the destructive vermin. Little did the ships' captains know that he carried the same live rats from vessel to vessel, creating the opportunity to steal as he went. She shuddered to see him playing with two of his caged creatures. Rats! How she abhorred them. She'd befriended the gray tabby cat, allowing it to sleep on her bed of rags, just to keep the rats away.

Three of the women and two of the children were mudlarks, or scuffle-hunters, as some called them. They would wade in water, lurking in the silt beneath moored ships, waiting to catch packages thrown to them from those aboard who were in cahoots. For Black John, that was the most profitable bit of trickery.

Taddie, pretending to be blind, robbed her unsuspecting victims. Doris used her beauty to lure men, then stole the poor blokes blind. Dawn's favorite of all, however, was a newcomer to their group. A poet by trade, he supported himself by his verses. Rhymes were a ha'penny, longer poems a shilling. Sensitive and vulnerable, Arien had been friendless and in dire poverty when he met Black John. Now he was the heart and soul of their little group.

"Ah, fairest flower. Come, sit beside me," he said now, nudging Taddie aside. "I'm writing a sonnet to a lark. A gentleman on Bond Street gave me three shillings for inspiration."

"A lark?" Smiling, Dawn took a seat next to him, wondering how he could possibly get any inspiration from these surroundings. It was almost as if he could actually see things the others could not even imagine. Flowers where there was only rags and refuse. Stardust where there was only dirt and grime. Diamonds where there was only tears and raindrops.

Once again Dawn looked around her, trying to see the room through Arien's eyes. The floor was strewn with all manner of debris. Heaps of rags, old jackets, shawls, and coats made up the beds. The walls were dirty and cracked, the ceiling was lopsided due to a leak in the roof. The stairs leading to the room were old and rickety. In truth, it was merely a place to sleep and eat, hardly fit as living quarters, certainly not a real home. And yet to Arien it had become special.

"Listen . . ." Uncrumpling the piece of parchment, Arien began. "High above the blue canopy of the sky a white bird wings his way. Gliding, soaring, flying like . . ."

"Enough! I have other things to say to her." Black John's booming baritone shattered the spell as he came to stand behind the poet. He pinched Dawn as he grasped her shoulder. "Robbie tells me ye filched a purse together, you and 'e. Ye knows the rules. Goods before food." He held out his large, thick-fingered hands, hands that were nevertheless agile for thievery. "Give!"

"I . . . I don't 'ave the purse." Dawn watched a nervous tick set the scars on the swarthy man's face dancing. It was a dangerous omen and proved his agitation.

"Don't 'ave it! Bloody damn! Ye'd best 'ave a reason."

"I lost it in flight, but . . . but it might 'ave been much worse. Either Robbie or I might 'ave been nabbed."

"Gruh!" Running a hand through his coal black hair, he grumbled. "Times is gettin' 'ard. Pickin's meager. We'll all starve if it don't chainge." He was a large-boned, stocky man. His protruding belly told clearly that *he* was in little danger.

"I'll give Dawn my share!" Arien was quick in his generous offer, though he had the least of all.

"Argh . . ." Folding his arms across his massive chest, Black John tapped his foot, eyeing Dawn up and down with annoyance. "Todaiy the little laidy 'ere didn't pull 'er proper weight. 'At cain't be allowed. Leavin' the pickin's behind is nigh on to a sin.

Nor is she ter get special treatment. A mistaike is a mistaike. . . ."

"It really wasn't 'er fault, John." Bounding into the room, Robbie came to stand between his sister and Big John. "I was too cheeky, I'll admit. Nearly got us both caught, I did. Blame me if ye've got ter blame anyone."

"Yeh?"

"Yeh!" Like two hounds about to fight they circled each other, but just as suddenly Black John broke into laughter.

"Ah, 'at's wot I likes about ya, Robbie. A spunky lad ye are. But we got us no need to quarrel. My pride and joy is wot ye be. Come, sit down. Sit down. It's the first time ye ain't brought somethin' back. I can forgive ye."

"Oh, but I did." With a mischievous grin, Robbie reached in his pocket, bringing forth a fat bulging pocketbook. "Got this down by the docks, I did, and it got me to thinkin'. Ye talk 'bout slim pickin's, but there's a world o' wealth down 'ere."

"Ha! That's where the whores 'ang about the sailors. Ain't interested in startin' no 'ouse." Black John puffed out his chest. "I runs a decent business, I do."

"As clean as a dishwasher's 'ands. I'm not proposin' anythin' lewd. Why, 'ow could I when I got me own sister in mind?"

"Me?" Dawn shook her head violently. "Oh, no! I won't have no dealin's wi' that kind." She looked imploringly at John. "I'll get me fingers workin' faster. If I tries, I might be able to bring in five or six 'ankies daily. I will. You'll see."

" 'Andkerchiefs! Bah! They're 'ardly worth the bother. What I 'ave in mind will maike us all rich." Leaning forward, Robbie outlined a plan. Dawn would be the lure. All he needed was the chance and the right gentleman. "A wealthy toff. One wot enjoys a bit o' dalliance, if ye knows wot I mean."

"No!" Dawn stamped her foot vehemently. "I wouldn't even know 'ow to begin."

"Doris can teach you." Stretching out his hand, he yanked the mobcap from Dawn's head, sending her long brown hair tumbling in wild disarray about her shoulders. "She's a beauty, if I does say so meself. Don't ye agree, John?"

"Mmm. She could be, in the right duds. A red satin dress, perhaps. A little rouge, a little powder." Black John raised a brow as if really noticing her for the first time. "She ain't a child no more, I can see. Skin like alabaster. Hair like the night. But it's 'er shape wot counts." Much to Dawn's mortification he pulled her to her feet, probing her young curves with bruising hands. "Nice! Like ripe peaches." He ran his hand down the curve of her waist. "Slim, wi' hips jus' the waiy I likes 'em."

Dawn sprang into action, putting up her fists. "Ye get yer 'ands off me, John Dunn. Don't be gettin' any ideas. I wouldn't put up wi' the likes o' yer pawin' me."

"Business is all I gots in mind. Jus' business." With a disappointed shrug he stepped away. "Blimey, wot a temper." He patted Robbie on the back, however. "Looks to me as if she'll do roight fine. Roight fine. 'Sides, wi' wot happened todaiy, they'll be keepin' an eye out fer ye. Might be a good idea to work the night. Different blokes and all."

"I won't do it! I won't stand fer some bloke, toff or not, fondlin' me. I got me pride! Being nimble-fingered is me lay. I'll stick to it." Dawn was adamant.

It took a long time to cool her down, even longer to convince her, but in the end she grudgingly gave in. She didn't want Robbie to get caught. Perhaps if she worked with him she might still keep him safe. In truth, it seemed a sound plan. She would flirt outrageously with the chosen mark, keeping the gentleman occupied and distracted while Robbie stole his purse. If there was any sign of trouble Robbie would act the enraged husband and frighten the poor fool off with the threat of a beating. It seemed harmless enough.

"And there will be benefits, me dear girl." Robbie winked conspiratorially as he put his foot up on a chair. "A chance to get out o' those duds wot makes ye look like a scullery maid and into finer garments. It's time ye showed off yer beauty." Lowering his voice, he added, "and mayhap someday we'll get ourselves out o' 'ere. 'Ats me wish, Dawnie dear. Indeed it is."

How could she refuse when he put it that way? "All right. I'll do it, but I want ye ta use care. . . ."

"I'll be as cautious as a banker wi' 'is 'and in the till. Aw, Dawnie, it'll be all roight. Ye'll see 'at it will. Don't worry." Taking her hand, he squeezed it affectionately. "We'll make a perfect team."

She hoped with all her heart that he was right. But even so, she could not deny the feelings of foreboding that swept over her like the tides of the Thames.

3

Garrick Seton drummed his fingers on the large mahogany desktop, squinting against the dim lighting of
the room as he concentrated on the drawing that lay
spread out before him. He was so close to accom-
plishing all of his dreams. The plans for this new
building might well establish him as the next Robert
Adam, and oh, how he wanted to take London by
storm.

Stroking the paper proudly, he thought of his long
struggle. He had proved beyond a doubt that he
could make it on his own, that he had no need of his
wealthy widowed mother's influence. Indeed, he had
boldly unleashed the collar from around his neck
and launched his own career. That in itself was an
accomplishment.

His mother had wanted him to seek a law degree,
but at Oxford Garrick had gone about his own pursuits. He would not dance to another's tune like a
trained bear, not even if that someone was the
woman who had borne him. More than anything else
in life he valued his freedom, no matter what the
price. His mother had retaliated by cutting him off
without a farthing. Instead of giving in, however, he
had stood firm. By working nights penning ledgers,
he had been able to keep himself in school. He had
joined the East India Company, in whose service he

had traveled to China, making his own way. With good business sense, hard work, and determination, he had prospered. When he had accumulated a goodly sum of money, he had decided to make a thorough study of Italian architecture. On his return to England he had blended the art of the Renaissance with a style uniquely his own. Taking on a partner, a man a few years younger than himself, he had opened an architectural firm that could rival any in London. He was quickly establishing himself as one of the most gifted architects of his time. Now at last all his efforts seemed ready to come to fruition.

Clutching his pencil, Garrick carefully drew in the final details on his drawing. It was an eight-room, two-story plan, embellished with an elliptical projecting bay that gave distinction to the style. Simple, yet elegant. A flawless retreat for the Prince of Wales's latest mistress. Portico and classical colonnades completed the sketch.

"Perfect!" There was no trace of modesty in the tone as Garrick whispered the word to himself. Indeed, he was the sort of man who knew his worth and saw no reason to hide it. It was a lesson his teacher, James Burton, had taught him. The world was like a farmyard with all the animals clucking, growling, and voicing their own opinions on every matter, Burton had said. A smart man took the example of the rooster and crowed as loud as he could.

So far Garrick's work, his diligence, and, yes, his firm assertion of confidence in what he could do made the future look bright. The wealthy were building luxurious homes to glorify their power and prestige. Prosperous merchants were building tasteful town houses to flaunt their newfound riches. Not since the aftermath of the great London fire had there been such a surge of construction. Garrick had designed various public buildings and institutions as well, including a Navy House, Ordnance Office, and Royal Academy. He had been commissioned to assist in the task of designing new military headquarters for the Horse Guards, houses in Piccadilly and St. James's Square, and office buildings alongside his own office on Bond Street. But it was coming to the Prince of Wales's attention that had opened a new door for him.

"Work, work, working again, eh, Gar?" Garrick's thoughts were interrupted as the office door flew open and a tall, flame-haired young man stepped briskly into the room.

"Yes. I have a job to do. Unlike *you*, I'm not in a habit of turning my bills over to someone else to pay." Garrick smiled in greeting at his partner even as he voiced his admonition. There was just no changing Ollie no matter how hard he tried to instill a sense of responsibility in the young man. Affectionately but critically known as a rake, Oliver Howard Chambers was a man who didn't hesitate to indulge himself in the pursuit of pleasure.

"But all work and no play makes for a very dull gentleman. You don't want to become *boring*, do you?" Oliver threw up his arms in mock horror.

"No, but neither do I want to become *poor*. I was reminded this morning of just how distressing that kind of life can be." Garrick put down his pencil, staring for a moment out the window, remembering the young waif he'd encountered that morning. Even now he could not forget her haunted, tearful little face.

"You poor? Never! If you would only show some concern for your mother, you could be as carefree as I am. Poor? Ha!" He gesticulated with a sweep of his hand towards the opulence of the office—the heavy crystal chandelier that when lighted twinkled with flames, the lush Persian rugs, the velvet- and leather-upholstered chairs. "This is hardly the office of a beggar."

"And yet there have been those who have gone from splendor such as this to debtor's prison or ended up in Bedlam because of too much gin. The streets are crawling with unfortunates, I daresay." Deciding that he did not like one of his sketches, he crumpled up the paper and tossed it at the wastebasket, but the basket was filled to the brim with discarded ideas, and the parchment fell to the floor. Usually Garrick was a meticulous worker, but today papers, pens, and pencils were scattered haphazardly across the polished desktop, and books on architecture were strewn around the room.

"My, what a wet blanket you are today, Gar." Plopping down in a leather chair, Oliver sprawled comfortably, concentrating his attention on his fingernails. They were badly in need of a manicure. He wondered how on earth Garrick could actually involve himself in boxing. It was so dastardly damaging to the hands. "What in the bloody hell is eating you? Loosen up a bit, old sport."

"A little incident this morning set me thinking, that's all. I had a little beggar girl take refuge in my carriage to escape the runners." Leaning back in his chair, closing his eyes, he briefly described the morning events.

"So? There's rich and poor and a few people in between. That's the way it's always been and always will be." Oliver clucked his tongue in annoyance. "You're too ambitious, Gar. You want it all now. Relax. Have a bit of fun now and then." Holding out a pearl-and-silver snuffbox, he grinned. "Have some?"

"No, thank you." Snuff, he thought, was a foolishly foppish habit. Instead he took out a thin brown cigar and lit it.

"London is gossiping about the sexual prowess of a

certain virile young architect." Taking a pinch of the brown snuff between thumb and forefinger, Oliver Chambers sniffed it, covering his sneeze with his handkerchief. "Of course I know just *whom* they mean."

"We all have vices, Ollie. Yours are drinking and gambling. Mine is women." Garrick shrugged his shoulders. Since he'd first come to manhood, he'd attracted the feminine sex very easily. It was something he just took for granted. Surely he had never had to work at it.

"Beau Brummel himself could envy your success with beautiful women." Both brows shot up in question. "Why then have you so suddenly cloistered yourself away?"

"Something important has come up and I don't have time at the moment for women. That's all." Garrick knew that when he decided he did have the time there would be some young woman or other awaiting him. Right now securing his future was uppermost in his mind. He'd learned at all too early an age just how important money was. Money was power, bestowing on him who had it anything his heart desired. That included a lovely woman on each arm if that was the inclination.

"Don't have time? Bah! We could go to the square with a bottle of gin and have a riotous time." He snorted disdainfully as Garrick shook his head. "As you will. Work yourself into an early grave. I've done with you." With an expression of peevishness he rose to his feet.

"I'm sorry. I didn't mean to be short with you, Ollie." Another day, another time, and he might have agreed. Why then did he say no? The beggar child. It had emphasized how precarious one's fate could be. "It's just that seeing that little girl made me realize how it is outside my crystal shell. Children like that little green-eyed girl, struggling . . ."

"A little thief is most likely what she was." Ollie took another pinch of snuff. "I wouldn't trouble my mind with her." Cocking his head he thought a moment. "And yet it is most unusual to hear you preach on something besides architecture. Perhaps you have a heart after all. Am I to believe you have decided to quit this pursuit of capital gain and throw yourself into philanthropic pursuits?"

Garrick shook his head. "No . . . I . . ." He could see by the expression on Oliver's face that he just wouldn't understand. Seeing the tattered girl had caused him to look deep within himself for just a moment. "It's just that I couldn't help thinking that if not for all the greed in the world, there needn't be people in such dire circumstances."

"Greed!" Oliver threw back his head and laughed. "You're a fine one to talk. To you money is *everything*, Gar. Sun, moon, and stars. I can't see you giving up your share to the paupers of London." He sniffed disdainfully, his words coming out with his sneeze. "And neither would I. Neither would *anyone* of right mind, I daresay. Poverty is the way of the world, but luckily so are riches."

"I suppose it is impossible to right the injustices in the world." Garrick clutched at his pencil. In his own callous way Oliver was right. Since man's expulsion from the Garden of Eden there had been those who had and those who needed. "But perhaps at least I can make it a more beautiful place in which to live." Work was his escape. It made him feel valuable and needed. Oliver didn't understand: more than money, creating beautiful things was Garrick's driving need. "Now if you'll excuse me, Ollie, I have a deadline to meet. . . ."

Oliver looked at Garrick in silent mirth, then broke

out in laughter again. "That's the old Garrick Seton I know so well. Which leads me to the point of this visit." Toying with his cravat he avoided Garrick's eyes. "Will you be a good sport, old boy, and do me a favor?" Before Garrick could answer, he put up his hand. "Business, I assure you. Something for the good of our partnership."

"Such as . . . ?" Garrick prepared himself for what was coming. Oliver had incurred a gambling debt again and wanted him to loan him money until he could convince his parents to come to his rescue. Oliver was always piling up such liabilities. "How much this time?"

Oliver stiffened, making a great show of being offended. "Why, Gar, you wound me to the quick. I don't want money. All I want is a bit of your time."

"My time?" A commodity nearly as valuable as money.

"I made an appointment at the waterfront tonight to meet with that tiresome cloth merchant who has it in mind to build a palace. Something else came up and . . ."

"If you made an appointment, by God, you will keep it." Garrick's irritation was fueled. "I won't be as foolishly manipulated as your mother and father are, Ollie. I have my own customers to please. If you're off to lose at cards or dally with some bit of fluff, I won't save your butt for you." He pressed so hard on his pencil that he broke the lead and swore angrily. "Besides, the waterfront is dangerous. If he wants to meet, have him come *here*."

"Ah, he claims to be a busy man. He has to see to the unloading of some silks from China. I can appreciate his predicament. What with so many ships in the harbor it takes so long to unload them that thievery is rampant. He claims he's lost a fortune, and I find myself believing him. It's not the first time I've heard such a story."

"I'm just as busy a man as he is." Garrick emphasized his declaration by slamming his fist down on the table. Truly Oliver could be annoying. "I repeat. If you made the appointment, go yourself!"

"It's Mother's birthday. I forgot that I promised to attend the little gathering she's having tonight. Please, Gar, you know how sensitive she is." A smile trembled at the corners of Oliver's mouth. He knew already that he had won. Garrick was too much the gentleman to risk disappointing a lady. "Would you want me to break her heart? Nor can we risk losing the coinage that a rich old client can bring in. . . ." He shrugged his shoulders helplessly, watching the emotions that flitted over his friend's face. From anger to resignation. "It won't take you very much time. Please . . ."

Garrick knew he had lost the argument. He did not want to lose the merchant's business or take the risk of angering him. There were other merchants who might decide to go elsewhere if word was spread that they had carelessly kept one of them waiting.

"All right! You win." Pushing his papers aside, he threw up his arms in frustration. "Bring me your drawings. Tell me what you want said to him. And wish your mother a very happy birthday for me. I hope that I have not let myself in for trouble by giving in to your whim."

Bounding to his side like a frolicsome puppy, Oliver pounded Garrick on the back in gratitude. "Thank you, Gar. Thank you. I knew you wouldn't let me down. I owe you one."

"And I intend to see that you pay up!" Carefully rolling up his own drawings, Garrick pushed them aside with a sigh. He'd just have to see to his own sketches later, as soon as he returned. Hopefully, this business of Oliver's could be settled quickly and he would find himself back behind his desk before another hour was out.

4

A cacophony of voices and sounds rose from the waterfront, a blend of peddlers' chants, the drunken singing of sailors celebrating their stay in port, and the chattering of dock workers and passersby. The exotic mix of tongues and dialects reminded Garrick that the unfortunates of the city spoke a language all their own.

"Would you like me to wait, sir?" Garrick's young carriage driver cocked his brows hopefully as he opened the door. The new cravat he was wearing and the cologne gave proof that he had made plans for the evening and was anxious to be finished with his duty.

"No, I don't know exactly how long this meeting will last. I wouldn't want to spoil your plans, Vinnie." Garrick patted the youth on the shoulder with a smile. "Is it Rowena who is waiting?"

Blushing to the roots of his dark brown hair, the young man nodded. "Yes, sir."

"Then I must say you've got an eye for beauty." The young woman was one of the prettiest ladies' maids in all of London and conveniently in the employ of Garrick's neighbor. "Enjoy your night off with my blessing. I'll hire a coach when I'm finished here."

"Thank you, sir!" With a sudden bounce to his step the youth hurriedly bought a bouquet of violets from a flower girl standing nearby, then jumped back upon the seat. He was off like a shot, leaving a chuckling Garrick behind. Garrick made it a practice to treat his servants kindly. Besides, the young man had served him well these last months.

Ah, young love, he thought. *Love.* That was something he'd had no time for. *Love.* It was a weakness. An insanity. He was sensible. He would never allow himself to be entrapped *again.* A bevy of lovely women paraded through his life and shared his bed. But Garrick had always made certain that his women understood the rules. He had no immediate plans for marriage nor any intention of aiding any aspiring female in her upward social climb. When an affair ended, that was that. In turn he played fair, lavishing his current paramour with gifts and attention while their passion flamed high.

And yet long ago he had been naïve and vulnerable, and his heart had been bruised. He only hoped that young Vinnie would have better luck than he'd had. Garrick was disillusioned enough to shy away from serious entanglements, yet he was not so jaded that he did not realize that there were women worth giving one's heart to. Precious jewels among women. Warm, loving, loyal females whose hearts were steadfast and unwavering. That was what he wanted for his young carriage driver. Something he'd never had the good fortune to experience himself.

Garrick had been just about Vinnie's age when he'd fallen under the spell of wide hazel eyes and curly dark hair that framed a pertly pretty face. Like a man consumed by a fever he had fallen for Anne, a barrister's daughter, who had sworn undying love. Garrick had made plans to marry her, thwarting his mother's plans, ignoring his friend's warnings that the seemingly gentle miss was not all that she seemed. He had been captivated by the young woman, but his mother interfered. Giving the young woman money, she stip-ulated that Anne Hyde stay out of Garrick's life. It had been a cruel lesson. So much for avowals of love.

When the Prince of Wales had turned his eyes in Anne's direction, the foolish girl had given in to the Prince's urgings, hopeful of furthering her ambi-tions. It had earned her a town house, an elegant wardrobe, and acquaintances in all the right places. For a time it seemed like a fairy tale until the prince tired of her. Working her way down among the gen-tlemen of her crowd, Anne slipped drastically from favor, only to end up as a whore parading up and down in St. James's Park.

Nor could he put his own mother's tawdry past completely behind him. Garrick's mother had used her considerable charms, first enticing his father to marry her, then going on to yet another advanta-geous marriage two weeks after James Seton died. Garrick had never completely forgiven her. It had been a source of contention between them for years. That his mother took lovers much younger than her-self was common knowledge. While her old, befud-dled husband lay abed suffering with apoplexy, Mary Seton Charing indulged herself with ostlers, butlers, or handsome young servants who caught her eye. Her lascivious behavior had hardened Garrick's heart. He would never be so vulnerable as to let such a woman use *him*. A scheming woman of easy virtue would never get past the cold, protective shield he wore around his heart.

"Coo, ain't yer the fine one." A brightly painted and feathered bawd accosted him now, startling his thoughts to the present. "Will yer buy me a bit o' gin at the Cap 'n' Crown, lovey? I'll maike it worth yer while, I will."

Garrick avoided such women as if they had the plague. Indeed the disease they carried could be just as injurious. "Most definitely not!" Without even a grimace of pity Garrick strode on by. He felt deeply moved by urchins, waifs, beggars, and the like and showed them generosity whenever he could, but he was bitterly contemptuous of women who strutted about the streets and sold themselves to any available man.

"Clean yer boots, sir? Shoeblack, yer honour! Black yer shoes, sir!" A boy stepped out from the crowds carrying his three-legged stool and a pot of blacking. Clutching his brushes, he looked so forlorn that Garrick paused to let him black his boots though they needed no such tending.

"A hurried shine is all that I need." Garrick was no true dandy though he thought of himself as fashionable. A true dandy spent too much money, time, and trouble for his liking. All out of proportion to sensibility. Unlike Oliver, Garrick could not spend hours discussing the shape of his cravat, nor did he shrink with horror at sight of a badly cut coat. Even so, he was an elegant sight in beaver hat, tan breeches, and square-cut black coat, double-breasted and long in the lapel. He carried a cane which he planned to wield, should a cause arise, and a large leather case stuffed to capacity with Oliver's drawings. He would guard the plans as diligently as if they were his own.

"There ye be, sir. Maide yer boots look as good as new, I did."

"So you did. Here, take this shilling in token of my gratitude." Bending down, Garrick pressed the coin into the boy's hand. It was the payment for at least ten shoeshines or more.

"Blimey! Thank ye, sir!" Biting the coin to ascertain that it was real, the bootblack beamed his gratitude, then hurried off down the quay just as an approaching night watchman announced the time.

"Nine o'clock and all is well. Bit o' fog a-comin' in."

The watchmen, affectionately dubbed Charleys, had several duties besides announcing the time. It was their business to guard the streets and waterfront and take charge of the public security, as well as to give information on the weather.

Nine o'clock, Garrick thought. He'd arrived fifteen minutes early for his meeting. Even so he hurried to the appointed spot, anxious to meet the merchant, perhaps have one ale at the nearby tavern, and then be on his way. Since it was summer, it wouldn't get dangerously dark for another hour, but nevertheless, he was fidgety. He wanted to be about his business and then return home. Already he could feel the dampness of the approaching fog, mingling with the brisk sea air. The Thames was crowded with barges and ships, all laden with goods from faraway places.

Gazing out over the water, Garrick remembered his own sea-going adventures. For a time he'd even toyed with the idea of becoming a sailor, but common sense had rescued him. Still, whenever he smelled a salt breeze or caught sight of white billowing sails, he was touched by his boyhood dream. Gliding about like swans on a lake, the ships were an inspiring sight. The farther downriver his eyes scanned, the more closely packed were the vessels on either side, a visible sign of how quickly London was growing.

Taking out his pocket watch, he noted the time. The merchant was late. Trying to calm himself, he gazed out at the forest of masts that loomed on the horizon. A stray flag fluttered in the breeze, a sailor hung on the spars of a ship, another sailor, agile as a monkey, skylarked on the topmost crosstrees of a vessel anchored at port. Sailors strolled the docks, making their way to the tavern. One entertained Garrick with a sailor's hornpipe and a "double monkey" somersault before moving along. Even so, Garrick's irritation increased with each passing minute. As the shadows lengthened, he instinctively clutched his leather case closer and secured his watch in an upper coat pocket. Each moment that ticked by increased his annoyance. He always made it a point to be prompt; why couldn't others? Watching the fog drift in, he wished he had not been quite so accommodating to Oliver. Well, at least *he* was enjoying the evening. Garrick hoped that when at last this night was over, he could say the same.

5

 ∽ ∾ ∽ ∾

It was a dull, murky evening. A light fog now covered London in a wispy shroud. The streets swarmed with hackney coaches and carriages. Silk-lined leather sedan chairs transported splendidly dressed men and women to various destinations; theatres, taverns, cozily lighted inns, or more intimate rendezvous. *The nobs*, Dawn thought, and among such as these she was to find a likely pigeon.

Leaning against a large rain barrel, hiding in the shadows as she tried to gather her courage, Dawn peered anxiously at the throng of people who rode and walked about the cobbled streets. Nabbing hankies was her special lay, and she had no liking for this new task. None whatsoever. Dealing with the swells always brought a body close to trouble. Black John's greed and Robbie's overconfidence were sure to be their undoing. Hopefully it would not be hers as well.

"All we'll get for this is a one-waiy journey to New South Wailes," she mumbled under her breath to Robbie and Black John, who followed close behind. "Or a necktie maide o' twine."

She felt devastatingly self-conscious in her high-waisted, low-cut gown, which showed much more of her bosom than she thought proper, though her careful stitchery had made it more decent than had been originally planned. The satin gown with a matching train attached to the back of her shoulders had once been pearl colored but had lost its original luster. Still, it was far more beautiful than anything she had ever hoped to wear. And still stylish too, she thought. Grecian, some called it. The low bodice and short sleeves were bordered with narrow net frilling of gold.

The dress was a purchase Robbie had made for three shillings from the rag fair in Rosemary Lane, a bargain he was quite proud of himself for making. Under different circumstances she might have felt some pleasure in wearing it. As it was, the only emotion she could muster was fear.

"Come on. Come on. We ain't a-gonna gi' our toff if we 'ide 'ere in the shadows all noight. Git it going." Black John offered a well-aimed poke to Dawn's ribs, pushing her out of her hiding.

"It's jus' that I feels nervous, I do." Tugging at Robbie's shoulder, she had a sudden change of heart. "I ain't ready, I'm not. Let's do it another time. Tomorrow. Next week . . ."

"Roight now! I didn't part wi' me shillings jus' fer the fun o' it. I expect ter maike a profit, I do." In a sudden, rare show of affection Robbie pinched her cheek. "Besides, ye look lovely, Dawnie. I swears 'at ye do. Don't she, Johnnie?"

Dawn thought that on the contrary she looked horrid. Her hair was parted in the middle and worn in a tight bun at the back of her head. Covering her hair was a hat of gold-and-black satin with three large ostrich plumes protruding. The one that was broken kept falling haphazardly over Dawn's left eye, and she had to blow on it to keep it from blocking her vision. Her cheeks and lips were smeared with scarlet rouge, her green eyes outlined with kohl. Why would any man even want to give her the time of day? It was a puzzlement, though Black John smiled and told her she looked very appealing.

"There be a ripeness 'bout yer mouth, a huskiness in yer voice that will soon have the toffs eager ta sample wha' ye offer, Dawnie, me dear." Much to Dawn's dismay, he punctuated his words with a pinch on her buttocks. She shrieked indignantly, raising her fists in warning.

"Keep yer 'ands te yerself! I'll poke ye in the nose and march meself back 'ome if ye do 'at agin, I will."

"Now, now . . ." Black John threw up his hands in defeat, agreeing to do as she asked. As they proceeded on their way, he was whispering a tally of what he hoped to gain from the night's pickings. "We'll get 'is watch, a' course. Any money. Rings and stickpins, all fetch the 'ighest price. And if we're lucky 'e'll 'ave a silver snuffbox. Might keep that, I might. Always wanted to set meself up loike a gen'leman."

Dawn sniffed in derision. "Taike more 'n a snuffbox ta maike a nob outta you, Black John, I daresaiy."

A bell from a tower somewhere tolled nine times. Even so, there were still a few vendors out and about. The baked-potato man, the kidney-pie man, the cheesemonger—all hoped to arouse the gentry's appetites with their singsong chanting.

"A pie. A pie have I, meaty and tantalizing."

"Potatoes. Hot baked potatoes. Eat 'em wi' the skins or peel 'em. Potatoes."

Seeing that the crowd had seriously dwindled, the cheesemonger drew in his blind, eyeing a small group of ragged boys warily. The boys crouched in little knots in the projecting doorway, holding out their hands in supplication for a small piece of cheese. Indeed the red, gold, and pale yellow cheese did look appetizing.

"Go on with ye. Get, or I'll bring the watchmen down on yer head," the proprietor threatened. Without another blink the children took to their heels. No doubt they would either find a way to steal what he denied them or go to bed hungry. Dawn remembered when she had been in the very same depths of destitution before she'd met Black John and softened her anger towards him. Robbie was right in what he said. Those that had didn't give a farthing for the poor who had not. It was obvious by every look, every gesture. Why then should she regret what she was about to do? No doubt the toff they picked would have watches aplenty. He'd merely deck himself out with another, meanwhile telling the story of his fortitude in surviving his unfortunate experience. The rookeries were, for a fact, the topic of many a conversation in alehouses and taverns, or so Robbie and the other men declared.

From out of the fog a mournful voice keened a song. A ragged woman with an infant in her arms was attempting to earn a penny or two. A pitiable sight, thin, pale, her eyes dark and sunken, she tried to cover her child's nakedness with a remnant of her own scanty shawl as she whimpered her tune. Brutal laughter was all she received for her efforts. Reaching into her pocket, Dawn took her last penny and placed it in the woman's hand.

"God bless ye." The woman's eyes shone with gratitude.

"She'll soon be goods fer the body snatchers," Black John grumbled. "Why waste yer coins on 'er?"

"Somethin' 'bout 'er reminded me of me mum, it did," Dawn replied, taking a last look at the wretched sight over her shoulder. "Wish I could 'elp 'er more, I do. Somedaiy I will. I swear 'at somedaiy when I'm a grand laidy I'll not pass 'er kind by wi' out being generous." Rollicking laughter was her answer.

"Dawnie a laidy. 'At's a good one." Black John slapped his thigh.

"Somedaiy I will be. Ye'll see." Lifting her chin proudly, Dawn affected a graceful walk as they trudged over the cobblestones. It was a dream not even the London streets could take away. In truth it was all that kept her going from day to day. Someday the life she was living now would be just a memory. Someday . . .

The stench of the river told Dawn that they had almost reached the docks. The garbage and refuse that was dumped into the waters gave forth a terrible smell. It was even said that those who made their living rowing boats on the Thames grew ill if once they fell into its rancid depths. Strange, Dawn thought, for on those nights when the moon illuminated the waters they looked deceptively inviting, even magical.

"Oars! Oars! Will you have any oars?" Mistaking Dawn for one of the gentry, a small group of watermen came running towards her, only to shrink back and erupt in ribald laughter.

"Oars. Ha, ha. It's an oar she be, all right. Well, take ye along with yer lass unless ye've a mind to give us a free sample." Raising a dirty lantern one tried to get a look at Dawn's face. "This one don't look so bad. Maybe even could be called pretty." They spouted off a long list of vulgarities, greeting passengers in all the passing boats with outlandish, fanciful insults and derision as was their custom. It was custom to respond in kind, a good-natured bantering which all but the hopelessly inarticulate returned. Raising her fist, Dawn uttered a stream of swearwords. Call her a whore, would they! And yet that was what she was pretending to be. The notion pricked her. This time when Black John took her to task for loitering, she hurried along, anxious to get this bit of business over so she could return to the security of Seven Dials.

The Thames was at high tide, the waters lapping loudly over the quay. Even with the fog Dawn could see the sails of the ships that lay at anchor in the open river. As thick as flies, the ships were forced to stay there, sometimes for weeks at a time, because movement was restricted. London had become the largest trading center in the world, yet there were no proper docks. The quays had not been enlarged for more than a hundred years, Black John Dunn had said. It was not unusual for ships' crews to be discharged before cargo could be unloaded. So much the better, John proclaimed, for it enabled his mudlarks to have an easier time of it.

Even at such a late hour there were men walking along the wharf side with ropes swung over their shoulders. At first glance they looked respectable, but Dawn knew differently. River pirate was their real profession. It was a known fact only to those of the underworld that there existed a labyrinth of secret passageways and concealed trapdoors beneath certain taverns through which smuggled goods could be transferred. The docks, as a matter of fact, had several rookeries, criminal districts, and flash houses, pubs frequented by criminals.

"Come on. Come on, Dawnie, there mus' be someone 'ere who is a likely mark. Pick a bloke and be quick about it." Black John Dunn readied his cloak for the proceeds. It was a specially tailored though tattered mantle lined with pockets.

"Don't 'urry me. Don't be impatient! I wants te taike me time." One tavern seemed to have attracted a crowd of frock-coated, top-hatted men. It was an anthill of activity, with men of all sorts going in and coming out. Dawn peered in at the window to see the patrons elbow to elbow as they lifted their tankards high. "There's a likely one 'ere, I'll wager." Cautiously she scanned the crowd.

"Forget the pub. I see jus' the one." Tugging at her arm, Robbie pointed to a man pacing back and forth in the shadows. "Whatever 'e's got in that satchel must contain a great prize. Look at 'ow 'e guards it. 'At's yer man, me girl."

"I don't know . . ." Now that the moment had come she was filled with apprehension. What if something went wrong, as it had this morning? Besides, if the leather case was so valuable, the man would certainly put up a fight for it. "Robbie . . . ?" She stood there indecisively, wishing she could tell Robbie that she had changed her mind. She wasn't afforded the chance, for his firm hand propelled her forward.

"Go on!"

Taking a deep breath, Dawn walked forward, exchanging her graceful gait for the exaggerated sway Doris had taught her. Holding her hands brazenly on her hips, she smiled.

"Ev'nin', luv . . ." she crooned. Though she had practiced the strut and the smile for several hours, it still didn't feel quite right, but it was much too late to back out now. "Nice ev'nin', ain't it. 'Ows 'bout you and me 'avin' a bit o' fun?" To her dismay she could see that he was intent on ignoring her. Looking over her shoulder at Robbie, she shrugged, but his annoyed gestures urged her on. Unlike some of the other men she had passed, this man did not smell of gin or rum. Warily she eyed him. A sober toff might well pose a danger. She could see only a silhouette and thus took a few halting steps closer. "I was sayin' 'ow you and me ought ter get ter know each other better and . . ."

In that instant the man turned his head. "I beg your pardon, miss, but I'm here for a very important reason that does not include dallying with such as your kind. Excuse me, if you please."

Gasping in surprise, Dawn was dismayed to find herself looking into a face she recognized. How could she ever forget that face, handsome as it was. It was the very same man who had rescued her this morning. Now her face burned under the scrutiny of his gaze, expecting him to recognize her too. Mercifully he did not. The gown and the rouge had aged her.

"B-beggin' yer pardon s-s-sir. I'll be goin' on me waiy."

Backing away, all she could think of was flight, but it was dark and she stumbled on the slick, uneven boards of the quay. Long, firm hands gripped her, breaking her fall. Suddenly she was closer to him than even Robbie might have schemed. Her breasts were lightly brushing against his hard chest and a heady warmth enveloped her, a quivering tension as taut as a bowstring. Her hand trembled in his as he helped her to her feet.

"Are you hurt, miss?" His voice was a soft, deep rumble sending a shiver all the way from her head to her toes.

"I'm fine. Really I am." She wanted to tell him who she was, but his impersonal manner, the disgust in his expression at the thought of what she was, strangled her words. Her eyes darted to and fro, seeking an escape, and it was in that instant that she saw Robbie coming up from behind. Dawn shook her head violently, trying to give him a sign. She could not, would not steal from *this* man.

But Robbie was upon the gentleman before she could blink an eye. She saw him extract a heavy gold watch from the man's pocket. With lightning speed he found a stickpin and a pocketbook. However, it

was not until Robbie reached for the leather satchel
that the gentleman sprang to action.

"Oh, no, you don't, you young scoundrel!" The gentleman she knew as G.F.S. lunged out with a punch
that landed squarely on Robbie's jaw, sending him
squealing. Effortlessly he pushed her brother against
the wall of the quay, cutting off any chance of his
escape. "You'll not be getting these."

"Please, sir. 'E didn't mean any 'arm, 'e didn't."

"Don't plead for him. You're in on it too. I know
your game. Well, we'll see what the law has to say. I
have a particular loathing for women who use their
. . . uh . . . charms to lure a man on, only to send
him to his death in the Thames. I'll see that both of
you are apprehended. It's one thing to steal, quite
another to . . ." With a groan he slumped forward
and Dawn stood in frozen horror, feeling his pain as
if it were her own. Black John had come upon the
gentleman from behind and hit him on the head with
a large wooden club.

"Ye've killed him, yer 'ave!" Dawn's eyes were
fiercely accusing as she bent down to wipe the blood
from the man's head.

"If we 'aven't, we'll bloody 'ave to now. This is the
kind o' toff wot won't rest until 'e sees us all 'ang."
Black John fished in his coat for a knife, wielding it
with deadly intent as he crouched down.

"No!" Stealing was one thing, murder another.
Dawn would have none of it. Besides, this man had
shown her kindness when she had been in a pickle,
had even given her a ride in his carriage. With reckless daring she threw herself in the way of John's
knife.

"Get out o' the waiy! I'll gi' yer the back o' me 'and,
I will!" He brandished his fist threateningly, used to
being obeyed.

"No-o-o! I won't go. And wot's more, if ye 'arm 'is

one I'll peach on yer, Black John. I swears I will."
Clenching her jaw, determined to stop at nothing,
Dawn held her ground. "Awaiy wi' yer now."

"Argh . . ." In vexation John threw up his hands.
Dawn's outburst was attracting dangerous attention.
Several heads were already turned their way. Thinking quickly, John picked his victim up and slung him
over his shoulder. "Never could 'old his whiskey, this
'un. Nothing fer it but to take 'im 'ome," he said
loudly. To Dawn he bristled, "Yer've won, at least fer
the moment. Come on." Moving into the shadows,
John trudged along the docks with Robbie and Dawn
following close behind.

She had held Black John at bay for the time being,
Dawn thought. But how long would her obstinence
grant G.F.S. his life?

6

~~~ ~~~

Dark clouds covered the sky. The small procession moved stealthily along the quay in misty darkness. Dawn followed close behind Black John as he headed towards a deserted warehouse. Usually that dilapidated old building sheltered his ill-gotten gains, but tonight it would serve a more ominous purpose. Dawn shuddered to think of it. Somehow she had to stop Black John and find a way to set the gentleman free before the night was over.

"Come on! 'Urry up. 'E's heavy. Move yer feet!" John Dunn struggled under his burden as he issued the order. "Stop yer doddling, for if we're caught I promise ye I'll maike yer pay."

"I'm 'urrying as fast as I can!" That was a lie. In truth she was moving as slowly as she could, hoping for the first time in her life that they would be intercepted by a beadle or a night watchman. If that happened, John would be so interested in saving his own skin that perhaps he would leave his victim behind.

"Hurry, Dawnie!" Robbie added his voice to the command.

"I am! I am! But it's slippery, it is." That much was true. It was high tide and the waters of the Thames sloshed over the wooden boards of the walkway. Worse yet, in the fog she couldn't see where she was going. Nevertheless they arrived at the warehouse sooner than she liked.

"Don't just stand there loike a statue, me girl. Open the door!"

Realizing that there was nothing to be done but obey, Dawn made as much noise as she could going about the task. The hinges were rusty, the wood warped from the constant damp; the door creaked and groaned. Grumbling, Black John pushed past her.

"Loight the lamp, Rob! Be quick about it."

Noises in the dark—a shuffle of feet, a loud muffled thud, swearing, the scratching of a match. Dawn squinted as the black void was suddenly disturbed by light. The lantern cast a soft glow on the large wooden beams of the low ceiling and on the bales, barrels, and bundles crowding the room. Black John was accumulating quite a profitable hoard, Dawn thought sourly. She watched as he dropped his human bundle on the planked floor.

" 'E's still out loike a light, 'e is. Yer must 'ave given 'im quite a knock to 'is noggin', John." Robbie sounded a bit wary. Like Dawn, he wasn't one to commit murder. "Do yer think 'e's . . ."

Dawn held her breath, her blood chilled as she looked down at the still form. Oh, she didn't want him to be dead! She rushed forward, but John blocked her way.

"If 'e is, so much the better for us. Trouble with a capital *t* is wot this one spells, ye blokes. Let me see . . ." John prodded him none too gently with his foot. A muffled groan put an end to the suspense. " 'E's alive. Tie 'im up before 'e waikes up!"

Dawn helped Robbie in the task, mainly in hopes that she could somehow keep the knots from being tied too tight. When that was done she gently prodded the bump on G.F.S.'s head. The bleeding had stopped, a clot plugged the wound, but a large lump was forming. Tearing off a strip of her gown, dipping it in the cool water of an old rain barrel outside the door, she carefully tended him.

"Poor bloke. If only I'd known it would be you . . ." Her eyes swept over him as she gently probed his injury again. He was such a strikingly handsome man, even when unconscious. Just looking at him was strangely exciting. It was as if for the moment he belonged to her. "That bump is as big as a goose egg, it is," she whispered in sympathy. But at least he was alive, for the moment at least. Warily she looked over her shoulder to ascertain John's whereabouts. As she might have predicted, he was sitting with Robbie, scrutinizing their newly acquired treasures.

"Ack! After all we went through there ain't nothin' in this satchel except some silly pieces of paper with drawings on 'em," John was saying. "Not worth a farthing!"

"Worthless and here I'd thought we'd found something really valuable." With a snort of disgust, Robbie crumpled the drawings and tossed them to the floor. "But look at 'is watch. Solid gold, it is." Robbie turned it this way and that in the lantern light, admiring the workmanship.

"Everything about 'im speaks o' quality, and they can be dangerous, they can. 'At's why I know we got to do 'im in." John's eyes were slits of anger as he turned towards Dawn. "Ye 'ear 'at, ye silly twit! He's a rich toff. Who knows, 'e might even 'ave ties with the Prince o' Wales. If so, 'e's the kind who will squeal, who won't rest until we're 'anging! Do ye want yer fine bro' here to swing?"

He knew he'd touched a soft spot, but still Dawn

was unrelenting. "I'll 'ave no part in murder, John! Nor will Robbie. We'll taike our chances. If the bloke meets 'is end, ye'll 'ave to pay the consequences. I don't want it on me conscience."

"Ye'll think conscience, me girl. They won't care none about 'at when 'e tells 'em wot we done. All they'll think is 'at yer a menace. They'll get yer off the streets, all roight. They'll put yer in prison they will. *Newgate!*"

Dawn tried not to flinch as she answered, "Better 'at, I'd saiy than going straight to 'ell when I die." Still the very idea of Newgate set her hands to trembling. It was the very place that every thief feared.

"Argh . . ." Black John grumbled but it seemed despite his bold talk he too was loath actually to do the deed, now that his temper had cooled a bit. Sighing with relief, Dawn settled down to watch over her charge. Defenseless, he brought out all the protective instincts within her. She promised him silently that she would do everything in her power to keep him safe.

" 'E's got to be rubbed out," she heard Black John say to Robbie behind his hand. "For some reason yer sister's sweet on 'im. Threatened me, she did, if I silenced 'im. Said she'd peach! But it don't maike a pauper's pinch o' difference. If 'e leaves 'ere alive, if 'e opens 'is mouth, 'e'll 'ave every Bow Street Runner, beadle, and watchman on our trail like a pack o' 'ounds. Do yer get me meaning?"

"Aye." Robbie folded his arms across his chest. "But I ain't gonner be the one ter do it, Johnnie. I gots me principles. Are you of a mind to raise yer 'and to 'im?" Robbie laughed at the answering scowl. "No, I thought not."

"It's one thing ter kill a gent in the 'eat of an argument but while 'e's 'elpless is a different thing. There is, 'owever, those wot ain't so squeamish who we could 'ire to do the job."

"Someone else to slit 'is gullet?"

"Aye! Shall we taike ourselves to the Devil's 'Orn and find us such a bloke?" With much guffawing and backpatting they decided on just that, thinking to have solved their problem.

"We're going to Will Neb's flash house, to . . . to celebrate our fine catch," Robbie announced to Dawn, thinking to hide his true motives behind a smile.

"Oh?" *Let them go*, Dawn thought. She'd welcome the relief from their chattering presence, and while they were gone she'd free their prisoner. That thought caused her mouth to tremble in a smile. Her expression was quickly read by unwelcome eyes.

"Wipe that smile off yer faice, Dawnie me girl. I'm not fool enough to leave yer behind. I'd 'ave to be the village idiot to gi' yer a chance ta free 'im. Ah, no, me girl. Come on, yer going with us, that ye are."

"No!" She quickly hid her disappointment. "We can't leave 'im behind. All alone."

"We can't leave 'im all alone," John mocked. "We can and we will!" As she cast a worried glance at their captive, he added, "I doubt the toff will be going anywhere. 'E'll be roight there ter welcome us when we return. We'll maike sure of that. In the meantime, I'll be watching you." He guffawed again, giving Dawn a push, then said to Robbie, "Tie 'im to the support beam, Rob me boy, and we'll be off. We'll settle our little *problem* when we get back." With an exaggerated wink he opened the door and the little group was off.

Well, let him think he's bamboozled me, Dawn thought. *Let him think he's won.* Dawn knew that at the first opportunity she would be back, and when she returned she'd set G.F.S. free. No matter what the consequences, it was a thing she had to do.

Pain throbbed unceasingly through Garrick Seton's head, tormenting him back into consciousness. Slowly opening his eyes, he was startled to find himself in unfamiliar surroundings. His pulse quickened and he stiffened as he tried to get his bearings. Where the devil was he? An old cracked oil lamp cast an eerie glow, bouncing slivers of light off the splintered walls. A windowless dwelling. A storehouse of some kind, he thought hazily. In an effort to accustom himself to his whereabouts, he let his eyes wander over the room.

"What the . . . ?"

As he turned, another stab of pain shot through his head, and he tried to move his hands with the intent of massaging his temples. He gave an outraged cry when he realized they were tied together. A tall support beam ran from ceiling to floor, and it was to this that he was securely connected. So he was a prisoner, then.

Little by little the events that had brought him to this end formed in his mind. Memories swirled about as he pieced together the events of the night. He'd been *robbed*! There was no other word for it. He'd been set up by that painted little strumpet who'd batted her eyelashes so artfully. He'd been conned by a painted little tart practicing the world's oldest profession. He, who always kept such trollops at great distance! He'd been trapped. It didn't matter that he'd become her victim unwillingly.

"Bloody damn!" He was coldly furious with himself. He'd always been cautious with women of her kind. Now he was here, trussed up like a Christmas goose, and all because of some thieving little strumpet. He was in a murderous mood that was not helped the least by the meanness of his surroundings.

Lying sprawled on his back, he wondered what the hour was. Late enough no doubt to have missed his meeting. Gad! After all his admonitions. Now they would lose the merchant's business for certain. Not that he wasn't thankful that he was still alive! He'd read in the papers about those who were not so fortunate.

From the corner of his eye he could see his satchel and raised his head for a closer look. When he moved he felt as if twenty hammers were pounding simultaneously in his head. In frustration he lay back down but not before he glimpsed the crumpled drawings littering the hard planked floor. Ollie's architectural drawings. Scattered about like so much trash. It fueled his outrage and made him all the more determined that he would make the blackguards pay.

When I get my hands on those scoundrels. . . . His head felt as if they'd split it wide open. Perhaps they had, he mused. He tried to rise to his feet, balancing against the pillar, but dizziness rendered him helpless. In frustration he slid back down.

The flames of the oil lamp sputtered and sparked and threatened to go out and leave him in total blackness. His life wafted just as precariously before his eyes. What were they going to do to him? Set him free? Ha! He sincerely doubted it. They'd tied him up for some ominous reason. More likely they had it in mind to kill him when they returned. Well, he'd see about that. If they thought they'd chosen a lamb who would go peacefully to the slaughter, they were dead wrong! He'd fight like a lion with every ounce of strength he possessed. Aye, he'd give them a fight, but first he'd play possum. When they came back from wherever they were now, he'd pretend he was still unconscious. He wouldn't blink, wouldn't move an inch. Hopefully they would untie him before they slit his throat, and he would have the chance to retaliate for what they had done to him.

Have patience, he scolded himself. They'd reappear eventually, and when they did he'd be ready for them!

7

The Devil's Horn Tavern smelled of sweat, grease, smoke from the kitchen stove, stale wine, and ale. All these odors assailed Dawn's nostrils as Black John pushed open the heavy door and she followed him inside. Being a frequent guest at the tavern, he was welcomed with open arms.

"Lord love a duck, if it isn't John! I was 'oping ter see ye tonight, mate." The proprietor scurried from behind the counter to greet him personally, slapping John on the back. "My best customer, 'at's wot yer are."

"And I'll continue to be, but . . ." Putting his mouth to the man's ear, Black John buzzed his secret.

Customer indeed, Dawn thought. Dutton was Black John's partner in crime, more often than not his contact in selling stolen goods. No doubt it would be he who'd provide an executioner for the poor unfortunate toff John had bonked on the head. Dawn had little doubt they'd soon find someone to do the task. The Devil's Horn was one of the most notorious flash houses in the district and catered to their kind. Dawn eyed it now with trepidation, knowing what Black John meant to do.

"Come on, come on . . . loosen up a bit. Try ter smile. We're 'ere to celebrate, not to 'ide in the corner." Brushing at the legs of his pants, Black John affected a jaunty air. " 'Ave a drink, Dawn, me girl. On me."

Such generosity was rare and Dawn looked at him askance, knowing full well his intent. Such bribery might work with Robbie but not with her. Even so, she forced a smile. Her own plans would fare better if Black John thought he'd won her over.

"I'll 'ave a bit o' wine!"

"Wine . . . ?" Robbie laughed. " 'At's me sis. She's got hoity-toity tastes, all roight. Gin for me, Johnnie."

Firelight danced and sparked, illuminating the scarred wooden tables, the uneven plaster on the walls, and the bowed beams of the ceiling as she walked into the largest room. The plank floor was sprinkled liberally with a mixture of rushes and sawdust and was badly in need of a sweep. The taproom had seen better days, though a few hundred years ago it might have been grand, Dawn thought.

The tavern was crowded to overflowing with hardly enough elbow room to lift a tankard. The sound of strange babbling could be heard, for London was a city of many nationalities. Many of those assembled had turned to crime for want of a better vocation. The laughter and chattering was deafening, so much so that Dawn could barely overhear the conversations bouncing about the room. Ah, well, it didn't matter. She'd have little time to socialize tonight, she thought.

"I needs a plaice to conduct me business, I do. Too noisy, eh, Robbie, me lad?" Black John winked at the younger man as if they shared a secret, as if they thought Dawn didn't know what deed they planned. "Let's seek out the private quarters."

There were eight drinking-rooms for semiseclusion, each one provided with screens so that they could be divided up into partitions for those who re-

quired privacy for business or matters of a more amorous nature.

The west wall was stacked with large barrels that
wobbled and swayed precariously as they passed by.
Dawn found herself hoping one would fall and crack
Black John on the head, for it seemed the only way to
evade his ever-watchful eye. She had no such luck.
She'd have to find another way to get back to the
warehouse.

"What can I get for you two gents and the laidy?" A
tavern maid bent over to give Robbie an extensive
view of her enormous breasts as she asked the question. She looked at him with an appraising scrutiny,
then smiled, showing her dimples. She cooed and
flirted to be rewarded by a winsome pinch on her
well-rounded behind.

"Two gins and a wine, me good woman." Robbie
cocked his head, grinning at the tavern wench as
they all sat down. "And Black John will paiy. Come
into a small fortune we 'ave, and we wants to celebrate." Taking out his newly acquired gold pocket
watch, he made great show of looking at the time in a
move to impress her, then slipped it back in his
pocket.

"Maike 'at three gins. . . ." Black John's smile was
toothy as he nodded, greeting a tall, cadaverously
thin, red-haired man who joined their small party.
Dawn recognized the man at once, for he had an unsavory reputation as one who would do anything for
a shilling, including robbing graves for bodies to sell
to anatomists. She shuddered as he sat next to her.

"Dutton, 'e says yer might 'ave need o' my services . . . ?"

"I might. . . ." Black John broke into a rasping
conversation of double-talk, a way of communicat-
ing he often used when dealing with others in his
profession. It was a conversation of rhyming slang

that gave him protection in case there were any un-friendly ears eavesdropping. "There'll be bees and honey fer ye. . . ." Bees and honey was a code for money.

"How much?"

"Tom Nicks." Dawn knew that to be six, most likely shillings.

"Not enough."

"Cock and hen?" That meant ten.

"We'll talk about it o'er our gin." As the barmaid brought back the full tankards, Black John raised his in a toast. "To the future."

"To the future . . ." Robbie echoed.

Future, Dawn thought. There wouldn't be any fu-ture if she couldn't slip free of John. She had to find a way to get out of his sight without raising his suspi-cions. Raising her own glass, she sipped the wine ea-gerly, hoping it would give her courage. She had al-ready outlined her plan, knowing as she did of the trapdoors concealed in the tavern's floor to allow smuggled goods easy access into London. If she knew Robbie and Black John, they'd soon be in their cups, and when they were, she'd use those secret en-tranceways as an escape route, slip out of the tavern, and take the handsome gentleman to a place of safety. She had to be patient. In the meantime she contented herself with eavesdropping on the conver-sation taking place at the table. Just how much was a man's life worth, she wondered, and was chillingly given the answer. Eighteen shillings. That was the sum agreed on for the murder. The very thought sick-ened her, though John seemed to feel proud of him-self and the bargain he'd struck.

"Let's drink to it!"

Dawn's fingers trembled as she raised the glass to her lips. Though the wine was sweet, she couldn't get it down. Dear God, she had to find a way to free the gentleman before it was too late. The walls seemed to be closing in on her. The room was hot and stuffy. The rattle of pewter tankards against the table as the tavern maid brought the second round of drinks caused her to jump. Suddenly it seemed so quiet, with an oppressive silence that unnerved her, as if everyone had stopped talking all at once. In that moment it seemed she could even hear the ticking of Robbie's pilfered watch as it measured the passing minutes. *Please . . . let there be a way!*

Her prayer was answered in the strangest manner. While making eyes at Robbie, the tavern maid jostled Dawn's arm, spilling the contents of the wine glass down the front of Dawn's oyster-colored silk gown. "Oh!"

"Oh, miss. I'm sorry. 'Tis such an awkward one I be." Trying to give aid, the buxom young woman moved closer, brushing at Dawn's dress with the hem of her apron. In so doing she sloshed even more of the red liquid on the already ruined gown.

"Ye've spoiled me gown! Ye've spoiled me gown!" Dawn pretended more outrage than she actually felt. "I'm soaked to the skin, I am."

"Now don't get in a snit, Dawnie. Accidents 'appen, they do." Robbie hastened to make peace between the two women. "Anger won't 'elp." He turned to the tavern maid. "Do yer 'ave something me sis could wear until 'er gown dries off?"

"I do and I'll gi' it to 'er most gladly. She can hang 'er dress in my room to dry."

"There, yer see!" Robbie patted the woman again on her plump behind. "She's a generous one, she is, as well as being lovely."

Dawn's heart was beating so loudly she was certain everyone at the table could hear, yet she forced herself to rise from the table slowly. She must not let John guess how eager she was to be out of sight. Nevertheless, he grasped her wrist as she pulled free of the table.

"Remember, Dawn me girl, I'll be watching the door, just in case . . ." Dawn nodded silently, glancing at her escape route from the corner of her eye. The trapdoor to the underground tunnels was behind the large barrels. Could John see it from here? She decided he could not.

"I ain't goin' nowhere, Black John. Specially not in me shift. I'll be back down, I will. It wasn't my fault she's clumsy!" Looking at the poor unfortunate girl, Dawn pretended anger. "Ooh, and such a lovely dress it was. . . ."

"I'll get yer another one, twice as pretty," Robbie promised, adding, "Leave Dawnie be, John. She'll be back. She'd ne'er desert her bro'. She knows which side her bread is buttered on, I'll wager."

"Argh . . . Go on then," John retorted, "but if yer ain't back in fifteen minutes, I'll come after yer, I will."

Somehow Dawn managed to walk away without stumbling over her suddenly unmanageable feet. She followed the tavern maid up the stairs and into her tiny chamber. Accepting the plain dun-colored cotton gown, she nodded to the girl to leave.

"Just 'ang yer dress over that wooden chair and the fire'll 'ave it dry in no time. . . ."

"I will . . . and . . . and thank you." *For more than you will ever know,* Dawn thought. It seemed to take forever for the girl to leave, but as soon as she did, Dawn followed at a safe distance. Stealthily she worked her way across the taproom, hiding in the shadows. Passing a shelf, she grabbed a kitchen knife. She'd need it to slash the twine that held her gentleman captive. Hiding the utensil in the folds of her skirt, tugging the trapdoor open, she did not even pause once as she made her way down the narrow, rickety flight of stairs that led to the tunnel.

The air was chilly and damp. The water of the Thames was an ever-present danger, for at high tide it often flooded the hidden passageway. Dawn wrapped her arms protectively around her body as she fumbled through the darkness, bumping into obstacles and brushing against spider webs. She was at last rewarded by the sight of a light at the end of the tunnel. Dragging herself up the steps, she didn't even pause before she broke into a run, putting the Devil's Horn and Black John Dunn far behind her.

8

⧼≈⧽

The warehouse was in semidarkness, the sputtering
oil lamp creating shifting shadows. Dawn hesitated
for a moment in the doorway. If she freed him, he
might send them all to Newgate. Was she prepared
for that? But if she did not free him, his fate was
sealed. That was a *certainty*. Above all she could *not*
live with being an accomplice to murder. Never!

Chiding herself for her hesitation when time was
so precious, Dawn hastened forward. She had to set
him free and return to the Devil's Horn before Black
John or Robbie realized she was gone. Striking a
match, she turned up the wick and relit the lamp.
Her eyes scanned the room for the object of her concern. He was still there, right where they had left
him, so immobile, in fact, that it caused one more
worry. He was as still and silent as a corpse. What if
John had killed him after all?

Kneeling beside him, Dawn stretched out her hand
and touched his arm, feeling for a pulse. It was there,
giving proof of a strongly beating heart. Dawn
rubbed her cheek against his shoulder and listened to
the reassuring rhythm. Thank God! He *was* alive.
Lifting his hand to her face, she kissed his bruised
knuckles. He'd proved himself a fighter, that was certain. Had he not been attacked from behind, he
would have been unbeatable.

With deeply felt concern she ran her hands over his muscled shoulders, marveling at his strength. Black John had toted him to the warehouse like a sack of grain. She wanted to make certain no bones were broken, or so she told herself. Carefully she lifted the hair that lay on his temple and examined his head wound, watching his face for a sign that she was hurting him. He didn't as much as flicker his eyelids. There was a huge knot, proof of the blow that had rendered him senseless. Nevertheless she had to wake him up somehow, for how was she going to get him away from here if he couldn't move on his own strength?

"Sir!" Oh, how she wanted to see his lips spread in a smile, wanted to gaze into his bold blue eyes again. She shook him gently, the pressure of her hands somehow changing into a long, leisurely caress as her hands followed her eyes. It was pleasant to touch him. Oh, what a fine man he was, broad shouldered, long limbed, and as elegantly dressed as a fashion plate, those colorful drawings she remembered so vividly from her childhood that always showed the latest styles. A gentleman was what he was, just as her father had been.

Her fingers touched his arm and moved to wrap around his hand. Deftly she struggled to untie the knots at his wrists, pausing only when she heard a noise beyond the doorway. Could Black John have noticed her perfidy so quickly? If she were caught in the act of freeing John's "pigeon," there would be hell to pay. Rocking back on her heels, seeking the shadows, she remembered the kitchen knife and clutched it for security. She waited cautiously but no one entered, much to her relief. Turning back to her work, she was able to tug the last knot free without need of the knife. Leaning closer, she chafed *her* gentleman's wrists in hopes of bringing back the circulation, willing him to open his eyes.

"Wake up! Oh, please!" Pausing just a moment, she buried her face in the hollow of his neck fighting her panic. He was much too large a man to drag from the warehouse. What was she going to do? "Wake up!" Again she shook him, shifting her position as she did so, wishing he would move. When he did, she wasn't prepared for the suddenness of his movement. All at once she wasn't holding him anymore, he was holding *her*, grasping her wrist so unexpectedly that she gasped. She tried to jerk free, but his long, strong fingers held her fast.

The fluttering flames of the oil lamp lit his features, casting a red glow in his eyes, eyes that were wide open and staring at her. "You're not going anywhere." His husky voice was rough with anger.

"I . . . I came to 'elp you," she stuttered. She looked up into that perfectly chiseled face so near her own. His thick eyebrows curved sardonically over deep-set sapphire-blue eyes. The mouth beneath the slightly flaring nostrils was set in a grim line. Hardly an expression that boded friendliness.

"Into the next world?" he asked dryly.

Before she could answer, he flipped her onto her back and was rolling over on top of her, pinning her down. He wrested the knife from her hand. It clattered to the floor, leaving her helpless. Such a frightening feeling.

"What are ye doing?" The hard length of him was pressed into her softness. "Get off o' me!" Dawn's voice was shrill, a squawk of protest.

"Be quiet, or you'll rue it. I don't intend for you to call your companions, by God, I do not!" The musky masculine scent of him teased her nostrils as he tightened his hold. Dawn found herself held captive by strong, well-muscled arms that encircled her waist. It was frightening yet also stirring to be held so.

"I came to set ye free, I did. Truly . . ." She was all too aware of the way they were entwined, her hip pressed intimately into his groin, their legs entangled. She could feel the muscles of his body as he held her close against him. Her full, firm breasts were crushed against his hard chest. It was a semblance of an embrace that left her trembling, though he seemed not to be affected in the least.

"Set me free? Ha! A likely story. Is that why you were holding a knife?" he returned gruffly. "But then, what should I expect you to say?"

Dawn bristled but ignored his words, not deigning to comment. She couldn't expect him to think the best of her when she had been pretending to be a doxy. Her eyes locked on his lips, and in that moment she wished fervently that she could wipe away his frown. Oh, how she wished he would kiss her! Just the thought caused her throat to go dry. A breathlessness assailed her, a sense of expectation that was cruelly shattered by his contemptuous look.

"I'm telling yer the truth," she whispered. His body was heavy, his hold on her so tight it left her breathless. Her head was thrown back, her mouth wide open as she gasped for air. Her nails dug into his back.

Garrick was infuriated with himself. There was something sensual about the woman. Their struggle was actually arousing him. Damn it! That thought enraged him, and he took his anger out on her. She was the cause of his peril. "You and your kind, you're all alike!" he snarled. With that said, he pushed away, his fingers accidentally brushing the tips of her breasts, leaving a tingling trail of fire. Slowly he rose to his feet.

Dawn flushed but looked unflinchingly into his angry gaze. "As are you and yer kind. Uncaring. Unfeeling. Walking about as if ye owned the world. Passing judgment when ye don't 'ave a wit. Looking down yer aristocratic noses at those ye think are dirt beneath yer feet! Well, I'm human too!" Squaring her shoulders, she stuck her chin up. "One who's down on 'er luck through no fault o' 'er own, but a person just the same. Did ye ever think there might not be 'my kind' if blokes like yer kind showed at least a thimble's worth of empathy or kindness! Selfishness is all ye know. Feeding off o' our poverty to benefit your hoity-toity selves like . . . like leeches!"

"That's quite enough." He ought to strangle her, he thought. He might have, if he were not such a gentleman. Murdering women just wasn't in his nature. "Quite!"

She bit her lip to keep from crying as she stood up. Here she had risked Black John's punishment, had tried so diligently to protect his life, and all he could do was think the worst of her. *Black John!* How could she have forgotten? Foolish chit of a girl, there was something far more important at stake than her pride. Think what he might of her she had to get this arrogant toff away from the docks quickly.

"Go on! Get yer arse outta 'ere!" she railed, waving her hands in the air.

"I beg your pardon . . ." For a moment he wasn't certain he had understood her.

"Ye heard what I said. Git!" She mumbled a string of angry oaths. *Obstinate, unappreciative bloke. The devil take him.*

"Just like that?" Garrick didn't trust her. His left hand tightened compulsively on her shoulder. "What's the game this time?"

"No game!" Pain throbbed in a wave from her chest to her throat as she fully realized the loathing he felt for her. There was no use in arguing. The hard glint in his eye proved he would never believe her if she spent eternity pleading her innocence. "The others will return sooner than yer know. And if ye are still here, ye'll be fare for the body snatchers, ye will."

Garrick eyed her warily. Whether she was telling the truth or not, there was no reason to stay. "I'll consider your warning." Bending down, he picked up Ollie's drawings, groaning with dismay as he tried to smooth out the wrinkles. He'd have a tough time explaining this one. All he'd garnered from the night was a lump on his head and a headache. So much for favors.

" 'Urry!"

She didn't have to warn him again. The thud of Garrick's heels sounded his retreat. He paused at the door only long enough to bend forward in a long, mocking bow. "Good night and good-bye!" Then he vanished into the gloom of the night.

"Aye, and good riddance!" Dawn spat the words, fighting tears of disappointment and humiliation. Leaning against the wall she shuddered, letting out her breath in a long-drawn-out sigh, trying to quiet her pounding heart. The touch of his hands had set her blood afire. It was a truth that shamed her. By his every expression he had shown his contempt for her, but though she wanted to feel hatred for him, she could not. The truth was she would have given anything in the world to see a different look in his eyes. Perhaps she would one day. Someday when she was a lady. Someday. It was a thought that gave her comfort as she spun on her heel and retraced her steps, running all the way back to the tavern.

The opening to the dimly lighted labyrinth yawned behind Dawn as she climbed the last step and shut the trapdoor behind her. The noises of the tavern clamored in her ears as she stepped through the secret entranceway. It was smoky in the taproom. The coal stove belched noxious clouds and she fought the urge to sneeze. From her place of concealment behind the wine barrels she surveyed her surroundings from a safe distance.

The majority of the men—louts, thieves, and river rats—were already precariously close to being in their cups if they weren't already. Ribald songs and obscene oaths fouled the air with words Dawn had heard a thousand times before. But now the words stung her ears as she contrasted these men with the man she had just set free. Like comparing gold to lumps of coal, Dawn thought with a long-drawn-out sigh.

The sordidness of her surroundings, the humbleness of her existence, were impossible to ignore, and though she tried to push the actuality from her mind with the usual toss of her dark curls, she saw herself through the gentleman's eyes. Was it any wonder he had looked down his aristocratic nose at her? Oh, if only there was some way that she could escape this squalidness as easily as she'd freed him of his bonds. Run away? To what? London and its mean streets were the only world she knew. Reality pushed away any dreams Dawn might have had. Besides, she couldn't leave Robbie. He was the only family she had left.

Blinking back tears Dawn stepped from her hiding place only to collide with the tall, ghoulishly thin man Black John and her brother had hired tonight. His long bony fingers dug into her shoulders as he regained his footing. "Ah, 'tis you! Yer brother 'as been looking for ye!"

Dawn's heart skipped a beat, yet she maintained her composure. "I was seeing to me person, I was."

"Oh, ye was?" His probing gaze seemed to strip her

naked. Thin lips pulled sideways into an ugly leer, revealing several missing teeth. Dawn tried to sidestep him, but he blocked her way.

"If Robbie is looking for me, I'd best let him find me." She couldn't hide her revulsion for this creature.

"Don't be so haisty now. I'd loike to get ter know ye better, if ye knows what I mean." His fingers brushed her arm suggestively, pinching and patting the soft flesh, but Dawn slapped his hand away.

"Ye'll keep yer paws to yerself if ye knows wot's good!" Bracing herself, hands balled into fists and poised to strike, Dawn affected a stance to protect herself. She'd never abide such an odious wretch as this molesting her.

Piercingly dark eyes fixed on her in a cruel stare. "Miss 'Igh and Moighty, ain't yer? Well, I'll see that yer is brought down from yer 'igh 'orse. Just wait and see." His tone of voice held warning, and Dawn knew she'd made a serious enemy.

"Here ye are, Dawnie. Where yer been?" Robbie's voice had never been so welcome. "Black John's been in a huff, certain ye'd run off."

"Suffering this one's unwanted company, among other things, 'at's wot," Dawn responded, taking hold of Robbie's arm. She couldn't repress a shudder.

" 'E's been bothering you?" Folding his arms across his chest Robbie glared a warning. "Stay awaiy from me sis! Besides, ain't it 'bout time yer was about yer *work*?" Raising his foot, Robbie sent the man about his business with a well-aimed kick, then burst into drunken laughter. "Oh, 'e's a ghastly soight, 'e is. Ole Johnnie sure knows 'ow to pick 'em."

"Yer 'ad as much ter do wi' it as John," Dawn scolded, "and somedaiy ye'll rue it! Somedaiy we'll all 'ave to paiy for wot we've done. Oh, Robbie, isn't there a way we can get free of John? Go to the country and change . . ."

"Afeared we'll 'ave to paiy the piper?" Robbie shook his head. "We'll let's 'ope that day is a long, long waiy off. No 'angman's going ter get me no matter wot I 'ave ter do." He hiccupped loudly as he tugged on her arm. "Come on. John's fit to be tied. When yer wasn't up in the serving maid's room, 'e was certain ye'd gone off to free that lordly bloke wot 'e bonked on the head."

So they had noticed her absence, Dawn thought. She had come back just in the nick of time. "Free 'im? Naw . . ." she answered, averting her eyes. "I felt cooped up in that tiny little room, so I came back down 'ere. I caught sight of a fine 'ankie, I did, and was trying ter get me 'ands on it when that evil scum cornered me."

"I tole Johnnie he'd pegged yer wrong." Robbie guided Dawn back to the tiny partitioned cubicle where John was pacing up and down. "I stuck up for yer, didn't I, John? And I was right. 'Ere she is."

"Argh!" Guiding his girth back to his chair, Black John took a swill from his tankard, eyeing Dawn up and down. "Aye, so she is, and it's 'ere she'll staiy until *I* say!" A basket of scones sat in the middle of the table. John pulled forth first one of the triangular-shaped fried bread slices and then another, stuffing his mouth full. "Keep 'er in sight, Rob, me boy, until our little . . . er . . . uh . . . errand is accomplished." Taking an intricately decorated stickpin from his pocket, he examined it carefully, then used it to pick his teeth. "And for God's sake, sit down."

Dawn sat next to Robbie, intertwining her fingers tightly together as she waited anxiously for the inevitable. It was only a matter of time before she was found out. From time to time she craned her neck, watching the door for the ghoul's return. He'd come back when he couldn't fulfill his errand and reveal that the rich toff had broken free. When he did, Black John would be suspicious.

Leaning back in her chair, she mulled over all the things she might say. Batting her eyelashes, she'd affect the very picture of innocence, melting even John's hard heart. Prepared for the worst, Dawn braced herself when, at last, the tall, skinny, red-haired man pushed through the door. Though others in the tavern paid scant attention, her eyes were riveted on him as he made his way to Black John.

"Awroight, I done me duty. Pay up," he said, holding his hand out, palm up. Dawn's eyebrows shot up in surprise. What was this? A numbing fear spread over her. Had her gentleman not gotten away quickly enough? Had he been captured again, only to meet his death?

"Yer . . . ?" Sliding his index finger across his throat, Black John made his meaning all too clear.

"Aye. I found him roight where yer said he would be. Tied up as snug as a Christmas goose." The raspy voice lowered to a whisper. "I done him in, I did. And threw his body in the Thames. He won't be squawking. Now I wants the rest o' me money."

Tied up? Right where he said he would be? The weight of the world was suddenly lifted off Dawn's shoulders. He was lying. He was pretending to a deed he had *not* done just for the money. Thank God for the man's greedy, lying, evil nature; it had saved her this time. The haunting depth of the passion she had felt for the handsome gentleman had nearly been her undoing, but now as she left the Devil's Horn with Robbie and Black John, she crossed her fingers, hoping against hope that all would be well.

9

BOW STREET OFFICE, the sign read. It was the home of the Bow Street magistrate and his staff of sixty Bow Street Runners, so-called because of their fleetness of foot. Garrick had wasted no time in seeking them out. Crime was reaching epidemic proportions. His own encounter with thieves and brush with death was evidence of it. Accordingly, he meant to be instrumental in putting a stop to it. That black-bearded, amply girthed rogue would be the first to be targeted, and if everything went as it should, he'd see that the younger man and the young doxy got their punishment as well.

It is a matter of principle to put such wrongdoers where they can do no more harm, Garrick thought self-righteously, reaching for his watch out of habit. *Stolen, by God!* Like his money pouch, stickpin, and other valuables, it had been forcibly taken last night.

The thought angered him still, but not half as much as the memory of that painted little strumpet. She had actually tried to make him believe her intent was to help him. Ha! He'd be a damned simpleton if he imagined for one minute that she cared about his fate. She was a thief and worse. Women like that had no hearts! Ah, no, it had been naught but a ploy. There had been something up her tattered sleeve, all right. And yet for just a moment he *had* read a softness in those kohl-darkened eyes. Well, no matter. The Bow Street Runners would soon put end to her game.

Garrick had not come to his decision lightly. After returning to the safety of his home, he had tossed and turned in bed all night long, furiously pondering the matter. At first he'd wanted to pursue his assailants himself. That was the kind of foolhardy thing Ollie might do. But he was far more practical. Taking the law into his own hands could have dire consequences. What then?

The very thought of those rogues going free set his jaw ticking in anger. But it was the way of things in London. Methods of law enforcement were slow, cumbersome, and appallingly outdated. Why, there hadn't been much of a change since the time of the Great London Fire, Garrick thought with scorn. Justice was all too often thwarted because of ineptitude. Obviously there was a need for something more formidable than old men running about the town carrying their lanterns. Night watchmen, indeed! Charleys, so named because they'd been instituted in the reign of Charles II, by God! They were frightfully unsuited to thwart crime and no match for those whose profession was thievery and murder. London had grown too big for that.

Something had to be done, however. If necessary, he would have every street in London searched until he found the man responsible for his unsavory experience. If he had to walk, nay, even run down every street in Lon—run—runners . . .

It was then he had happened to remember an article he had read in the newspaper about the Bow Street Runners. He recalled that they were employed to catch the most daring and successful criminals and were held in awe by the general public. Sitting bolt upright in bed, he had known at that moment

he'd found the answer. The best known Bow Street
Runners were often hired by private citizens as well
as by banks to protect or restore their valuable property. At the crack of dawn, he had decided, he would
seek them out.

Now pushing open the door, Garrick scanned the
interior of the Bow Street Office. It was much like
any other place of business. There were chairs and
desks and people milling about. An iron banister outlined the perimeter of the large room, acting as a
barrier to keep unwelcome stragglers out. A chandelier hung from the elongated ceiling, and Garrick
could not help thinking how the architecture was all
wrong. He would have done the floor plan much differently, the space a bit more oblong, with more windows, another flight of stairs, perhaps, one on each
side to keep the flow of people coming and going at
an even keel.

Over the fireplace hung a portrait of someone
whom he supposed to be either Henry Fielding or his
brother Sir John, who had in essence started the so-
called Bow Street constables. Garrick would have
placed that painting on another wall and positioned
it higher. Ah, well!

Garrick elbowed his way through the throng and
stood in front of a large oak desk. Two men were
preoccupied with a poor ragged creature whom they
were pushing and shoving through the doorway. It
was obvious that the woman was inebriated, for she
kept ranting and raving about having the runners
track down her errant husband in exchange for the
apples she was selling. The Bow Street Runners were
far more expensive than the poor woman could af-
ford, thus she was soon forcibly evicted from the
premises.

Garrick was ignored at first, but after clearing his
throat a number of times, he attracted the attention

of one of the three men sitting behind the desk, a short, rotund, balding man with a gray moustache. Between puffs upon his pipe he questioned Garrick as to the reason for his presence in the office. His attitude made Garrick feel more accused than accuser.

"I was robbed last night and I wish to have my assailants apprehended," Garrick answered, running his fingers through his slightly tousled hair. He winced as he touched the bump on his head.

"Robbed? Explain," the man said without a flicker of expression on his face.

Garrick did, in very vivid detail, even to the color of the woman's gown. "I was set upon from behind. A most cowardly act, for I daresay I could have protected myself had I been allowed to fight man to man."

"Mmm." The man's piercing brown eyes scrutinized Garrick, taking in his height, wide shoulders, the strength of his hands as they gripped the rail. "It would seem so."

"But I didn't get the chance. I was hit on the head, and when I opened my eyes I was in a warehouse." Garrick's voice was a growl as he related his experience. "My watch, stickpin, money purse, and satchel had been stolen."

"I see. And just what did you do after this so-called robbery?" The tone of voice was impersonal, as if the man didn't really care.

"So-called?" The man's manner infuriated Garrick. He had been set upon and his possessions taken from him. He might even have been murdered had he not gotten the upper hand. "Not a so-called robbery but one of *fact*. If you want proof, just take a close look at the bump on my head." Garrick pointed to the offending lump, trying to maintain his calm. No wonder London was crawling with vice if this was the attitude the so-called law keepers affected.

"Mmm." Taking out a pair of spectacles, the man put them on. "It appears to be a nasty blow." He eyed Garrick suspiciously. "What did you do after your . . . uh . . . unfortunate experience?"

"*After?* I went home to bed."

"And then?"

"Went to sleep, woke up this morning and had breakfast." Garrick's jaw tightened. He didn't like the man's manner. One would have thought *he* was some sort of culprit. "I suppose you'd like to know what I ate," he added sarcastically. "Buttered toast, tea, pork chops, and eggs! Then I made straight for here."

"Do you frequent the docks often?" There was insinuation in the man's tone of voice, as if to chide Garrick for his lack of discretion.

"No! I'm usually wise enough to avoid the type of people who mill about there. However, in this instance my business . . ."

"Which is?"

"I'm an architect! Garrick Seton by name." It seemed the man had heard of him for his eyebrows shot up as Garrick spoke. "My business dealings drew me there to talk with a merchant. Needless to say, I never saw him. For all I bloody well know, he might have been set upon by thieves, too."

"It's entirely possible." The man's brusque manner immediately became more deferential. "Gads, the thieves seem to be everywhere. But little by little they're coming under control."

"I hadn't noticed," Garrick said sarcastically.

"These things take time. The West India Dock in the Isle of Dogs with its high walls and armed guards is giving the blighters a devil of a time. Now there are other enclosed docks planned."

"I know about the docks. I've studied the plans."

"Mmm. Architect, you said. I seem to recall hearing about you. But what did you say you were at the docks for?" He seemed preoccupied by other musings.

Garrick's patience was waning. He was in a hurry to get this matter settled so he could move on to his office. Ollie had to be told what had happened. "I had an appointment with a merchant to show him some plans . . . but now see here, my good fellow . . . I haven't the time to stand here jabbering all day. A crime was committed, and if you will not aid me in finding the culprit and seeing that he is punished, I will go elsewhere!" To emphasize his determination, Garrick turned his back and started for the door, but before he could take hold of the knob the man called him back.

"Don't leave, sir. You have come to the right place if it's thieves you are after." The hint of a smile softened his visage. "Sorry for the delay, but I had to make certain that you were . . . well . . . sincere in your reasons for coming here. Sometimes the underworld sends spies to flush out our doings." He got down to serious matters. "I assume you have money."

"I can pay your price, and I assure you I am no spy." Taking out his money pouch he hefted it temptingly before the man's greedy gaze. Bow Street officers were known to be a closely knit caste of speculators, self-seeking and unscrupulous, but also daring and efficient when daring and efficiency coincided with their private interest. Money, it seemed, talked everywhere. This time when Garrick told his story, he had the man's undivided attention.

"They sound like a devious and dangerous trio, all right. The London robber *is* like a venomous snake with his hideaway in the dark holes underground, in hidden back rooms of dirty houses or on the gloomy banks of the Thames. The females that follow them are in most cases even more devious than the males. Ferocious." He punctuated his sentences by puffing on his pipe and blowing the smoke out in a series of small bursts. "And if he is father to a child, he molds it at an early age to the muddy whirlpool of the town, there to beg, steal, and then to perish. I loathe them all, but there is little we can do if they have, as many of them do, acquaintances in high places. Bribery can be very profitable, dear sir."

"Yes, I suppose it can," Garrick said dryly. Certainly he had little doubt that this man had his price.

"Well, you did come to the right place. We bloody well can catch them, and we will. We don't call ourselves thieftakers for nothing. I have just the man for you. Townsend is his name." Picking up a bell, he rang it until one of the runners appeared.

"Yes, sir!" The man wore a dun-colored coat and trousers and a yellow vest with a row of nearly thirty small buttons which threatened to pop each time he took a deep breath. He was corpulent and heavy of jowl and was tight-lipped when he tried to smile. He had a prominent nose and bushy brows. Charles Townsend was his name.

"Charles has the nose of a bloodhound. Quite! He'll bloody well soon find your attackers. Just leave everything to him." Holding out his hand, palm up, the man at the desk demanded half the fee of twenty shillings to be paid in advance. Granting Charles Townsend one of these coins, he nodded his head, taking leave of Garrick.

"Leave the matter to me!" As if to reassure Garrick, Charles Townsend patted him on the back. "Before the week is out, we'll have them locked up. It will be my pleasure." As if savoring his victory, he licked his lips. "The whole of London is ringed by the thieves' kitchen, but I've got those who'd peach on their own mothers for . . ."

"A thieves' what?"

"Thieves' kitchen. An unpatroled criminal area into which those who steal have been drilled from childhood to make their safe escapes. Seven Dials is one! A place where several streets intersect each other. Blimey, what a mess it is to try to chase a brash young fool down in that area. There's a large clock there, or at least there used to be, with large dials. That's how the area got its name, you see, but as I was saying, I have ways of making even the most loyal of those blokes sing. I'll find your black-bearded robber king, all right. Upon my oath, you'll see him decorate a cell at Newgate or my name isn't Charles Thompson Townsend, which it *is*. Your thieves, all of them, will soon find themselves caged birds."

Throwing back his head, the Bow Street Runner laughed, but Garrick didn't share in his mirth. As he left the Bow Street Office he felt strangely unnerved, a feeling he quickly shrugged off as his own office came into view. He'd done what was necessary. He'd be a damned fool to feel pity. A crime had been committed, and for that the culprits must pay. It was the way of the world; a man, or woman, must pay for their sins. He would not allow himself any regrets.

10

Snuggling against her pillow, Dawn gave herself up to the same dream that had dominated her sleep since the night at the docks. Music drifted through a mist, intensifying her dreamy languor. She was dancing, whirling round and round in the arms of her handsome gentleman.

The heat from his body enveloped her. She was close to him, her breasts lightly brushing against his hard chest. His height made her feel feminine and fragile. Looking up at him, she watched that chiseled mouth smile with honest affection and no sign of scorn. Oh, how she loved his mouth, its sensuality. As if reading her thoughts, his blue eyes twinkled at her from his mesmerizingly handsome face.

"You are the most beautiful woman here," he was saying, his arm tightening around her waist as he pulled her closer. The rippling muscles of his thighs moved sensually against hers as they moved together in time to the music. Her senses were spinning. The way he was looking down at her made her feel cherished. This time there was no scorn in his gaze, only admiration.

The music reached a crescendo as he spun her around, then dipped her over his arm with a husky laugh, drawing her closer still. His warm, hard lips caressed the soft curve of her shoulder where her skin lay bared. She clutched frantically at his shoulder for balance, joining him in laughter, feeling wonderfully carefree and gloriously happy. He wanted her. The thought was as intoxicating as gin.

Her hair slipped loose from its pins and hung down her back. "That silvery gown brings out the dark luster of your hair, the pink softness of your mouth. I'll never let another man claim you, Dawn." She shivered at the intensity of his voice. "Never! You belong to me . . ."

His fingers tightened on her shoulder, his mouth hovered only inches from her own. Molten heat flowed through her, surging in a restless tide as he bent closer. Taking a deep breath, she awaited his kiss . . . but the kiss never came.

The light illuminated his face and he was no longer smiling. There were tense lines on either side of his mouth. His eyes had changed from a soft blue to a darker, smokier sapphire. He raised one eyebrow as his insolent gaze wandered over her face. Suddenly she felt as if her very soul was exposed to his stare.

"You!" he exclaimed. Suddenly he was pushing her away and she was falling . . . In desperation she reached out, but instead of steadying her fall, he was joining her in her descent, pinning her down with his body . . .

Dawn was rudely awakened as a strong hand held her back upon the bed. Her head thrashed on the pillow. "No!" Dear God, *he'd* suddenly realized who she was! He was angry. He loathed her, just like before. "No . . ." Remorse and fear pulsated through her veins as she awaited his torrent of fury. He'd send her to Newgate or worse. "No, I didn't . . ." Where was Black John? He would beat her for setting his quarry free! Didn't the man know that? Pushing at the hands that held her prisoner, she struggled, but before she could give vent to an oath or a scream her brother's chuckles sounded in her ear.

"Don't squirm so. It's yer birthday, sister dear."

She squinted up at her brother with heavy-lidded eyes. "Robbie?" It had only been a dream, and yet so real. Even in a dream he had the power to stir her. Running a hand through her tangled hair, she tried to put it out of her mind.

"You know our tradition," Robbie was saying with a grin. A generous amount of cool, slick butter was liberally applied to the tip of Dawn's nose amid her sputters of protest. "There ye be."

"Oh, Robbie!" She pursed up her lips in mock anger but joined him in laughter. As Robbie said, it was a tradition they'd followed since childhood, but from whence it had come no one was really sure.

Bending down Robbie licked the butter off her nose, then planted a greasy kiss on her cheek. "Mmm, yer taste good. Like a fresh muffin. I loves ye, sister dear. I do!" Birthdays were the only time he ever espoused such tender feelings. Any other time Robbie hid behind his facade of plucky bravado.

"And I love you!"

" 'Ere! I got a present fer ye." With an impatient grunt, he handed her a package wrapped in old newspapers, which she quickly opened. Inside was an object she most certainly remembered. Her gentleman's watch, the same one Robbie had taken the night at the docks before she'd set that man free. "I ain't blind to the way yer keep lookin' at it, Dawnie, as if it's somehow special. It's yours. Part of the spoils, ye might saiy."

"I couldn't!" There were too many memories attached to it. She thrust it back into Robbie's hands.

"Of course yer could!" His smile set his eyes dancing sparkles of light. "I can get another. Yer knows how easy I can. I want yer to have it, I do."

He was expressing his love by the gesture, and she was deeply touched. How could she refuse? Besides, somehow just touching the watch made her feel lighter of heart. It was something that had belonged to *him.* She did want it. Perhaps someday she might even give it back. It might be an excuse to see him again. Just one more time. "All right, I will take it. And . . . and thank you, Robbie."

Under the scrutiny of her grateful stare he blushed, and for just a moment the years were washed away. He was a boy again, taking her by the hand to show her the brightly painted ball he'd hidden. How could they have ever imagined then how different their lives would be? Dawn's birthday was a day of mixed emotions, one that always brought back memories of her father's death no matter how she tried to put it from her mind.

"Now maybe ye'll be on time more often and not raise Black John's ire. 'E's still angry, 'e is, 'cause yer won't go to the docks again."

"That one time was quite enough, it was. I'll . . . I'll never forget wot 'appened." Burying her face in her hands, she feigned tears. "That poor bloke. I knows wot yer 'ad done. Yer killed 'im, ye did. No, I'll never go there agin."

"Wots 'at? Tears? Me girl can't cry, not on the anniversary o' her birth!" Offering the tail of his coat to dry her eyes, Jamie clucked his tongue as he came to her side. "Shame, shame on ye, Robbie, ter maike yer sister cry."

"He didn't." The matter at the docks was a secret so she couldn't explain her emotions. "It's just . . . just that I remember how it was once when Rob and me 'ad family," she whispered. This time the tears were real.

"Family? Yer got one now." Like a mischievous elf Jamie grinned, summoning the rest of the group with a crook of his finger. "We can 'elp yer celebrate yer birthday wi' the best o' 'em."

" 'Appy birthdaiy!" they all chorused as they came closer.

Farley held his hands behind his back. With a grin he brought forth his surprise, a small piece of leather luggage that he'd taken. "An 'at box, Dawn, me girl, for 'at time when yer 'ave an 'at wot doesn't 'ave a broken feather."

Taddie gave Dawn a length of lace she'd "picked up." Doris made an offering of a silver chain. Mary pulled a length of periwinkle-blue satin from her sleeve. The straw mattress groaned and creaked as the three sat on the edge of Dawn's pallet, eagerly awaiting her reaction to their presents.

"I feel as blessed as a queen to 'ave such loyal friends, I do!" Throwing her arms around each one, Dawn expressed her gratitude. It was Arien's gift, however, that touched her the most. He had written a poem just for her.

"The moon hovers in the darkness, lighting up the
   dreary night,
Hiding his face with wistfulness as he glimpses the
   glowing sight,
Of beauty, grace and all things perfection that are
   Dawn.
The flowers in the garden sigh with envy, giving free
   vent to their jealousy,
Unfurling their petals to full bloom, futilely compet-
   ing, they try to be,
As resplendently colorful as the fragile young woman
   who shares our hearts.
Dawn, now and always, as precious to us as a summer
   sunset, a sky filled with rainbows.
May this day and all the days of your life be happy
   ones!"

Taking off his hat, he bowed.

"Oh, Arien!" Dawn's heart was filled with a special warmth as she smiled, but her smile soon faded when Black John burst into the room.

"Still abed, are we, me girl?" Pulling back the covers, he grabbed her roughly by the arm. "Get up!"

"It's 'er birthdaiy, John. Wot kind o' blackguard be yer to treat her this waiy?" Jamie sought to protect Dawn from John's growling anger but was swatted away like a bothersome fly.

"Now see 'ere, Johnnie . . . I won't 'ave yer manhandle me sis!" Robbie's jaw ticked warningly as he put up his fists.

"Relax, Rob, me boy. I don't aim to 'arm 'er, but birthday or no she'll not be lying about loike a queen. Nor will the rest of yer. On wi' yer now." He scattered the group with a fretful wave of his hand. "A new daiy is blinkin' and a lot o' blokes are just ripe for the pickin'. We need an *arvest*!" Tightening his tie, he motioned one of the younger men to his side, whispering, "Murdock, come wi' me down ter the warehouse. I need 'elp in distributing a 'eap o' goods the mudlarks brought in yesterdaiy. Got ter strike while the iron is 'ot, so ter speak."

John's manner was cocky as he strode across the room, and Dawn could only suppose why. Black John was certain he was about to come into some money, an amount which she doubted he would share with the others. Robbie's frown confirmed her suspicions. It seemed that there was a one-sided code that said that while the whole group shared their takings with John, it wasn't the same with him. Whenever he was able he kept the lion's share. Robbie had long suspected that Black John was cautiously stashing all his profits away somewhere. What Dawn wouldn't have given to know just where! More than anything she wanted to get far away from the grime

and foul odor of the city and start a new life with
Robbie. But for now she'd do as Black John said.

Slipping on her faded gray dress, mobcap, and
wooden clogs, Dawn stifled a yawn and listened to
the sound of John's footsteps as he plodded down the
stairs. One hanky, that's all she'd nab. It was her
birthday! She wouldn't let Black John bully her today. "To work, me laddies and ladies!"

"We'll 'ave a real party tonoight, we will," Jamie
promised behind his hand. "A surprise party, if yer
will."

"I'll filch a chicken, I will, for stew!" Taddie exclaimed. "Maiybe we'll even have dumplin's."

"Everyone get their fingers busy. Hup! Hup! Hup!"
Robbie flashed Dawn his toothy grin. "Tonoight we'll
'ave quite a gathering."

Like a flock of scattered sparrows they all went off
in different directions. Black John had divided London into various sections for picking pockets. Dawn's
new "walk" was Covent Garden, the chief market for
fruit, vegetables, and flowers in all of the city. Arien
had told her that it was named from an old garden
that belonged to the monks of Westminster Abbey
long ago, before the eighth Henry had sent them
packing. Since the market days there were Tuesday,
Thursday, and Saturday, and today was Thursday,
she scurried on her way.

As usual the streets of London seethed with traffic,
wagons, carriages, and coaches sending the pedestrians fleeing as they rumbled down the road. Streets in
Dawn's area were in such deplorable condition that
ruts and holes were filled with sticks and straw and
the streets were so narrow that only one vehicle
could get by at a time. Was it any wonder the drivers
swore such violent oaths? Dawn was forced off the
street time after time, narrowly escaping serious
harm to her person. Even so she much preferred

working the daylight hours to the night. That one experience at the docks had been enough for a lifetime. She'd take her chances in the light no matter what Black John advised or how Robbie cajoled.

It was a pleasant summer morning. Men were shouting, horses neighing, dogs barking, cats fighting, piemen calling, donkeys braying, market carts stirring up dust as they rattled by. Dawn listened to the din of the women chattering as they walked down the street, their straw baskets bulging with fruit balanced on their heads. Everywhere Londoners were going to and fro to earn, or steal, their daily bread. Cheerfully she merged with the throng.

Advertising was everywhere, even on the sides of vacant houses or scaffolding, and as she walked along, Dawn read the handbills, thankful that her mum had taught her the skill. The printed pieces of paper acted as roadmarks to lead her on her way and assure her swift return when the time came.

Covent Garden hummed with voices. Wagons and carts had been arriving for some time. Porters were busy transferring their contents to the different stations of traders called costermongers and setting up displays. Produce was assigned to one area, flowers and plants to another, hens and chicks to still another. Carts and wagons of vegetables—fresh cabbages, onions, leeks, potatoes, clean-washed turnips, carrots, and cauliflowers—were drawn up close together on three sides of the market. They brought to mind Taddie's promise of a stew. Perhaps she'd pilfer a few of the more appetizing eats.

The west side of the square was covered with all sorts of plants in bloom. Cut flowers for bouquets and tiny buds for nosegays were artfully arranged. Such a gay, beautiful, and fragrant display they made, Dawn thought.

Little tables were set out with refreshments by vendors of tea and coffee. Dawn's first filch of the day was a hot brimming cup, artfully hidden in the folds of her dress until she could safely savor its contents behind a pillar of the piazza. Peering out, she scanned the gathering crowd for her target. So far only the workers had turned out and she would not steal from *them*. Only from the nobs. She'd have to wait a bit then.

That's all right, she thought. The air was filled with the fragrance of flowers, and she sniffed with a contented sigh. If ever she took up honest work, it would be as a flower seller, she thought. Sweet briar and roses gave out such a delicious aroma. Closing her eyes, Dawn whiled away the time daydreaming. She was in a garden dressed all in satin and lace, surrounded by suitors, as *he* walked by. Coolly, calmly, she turned her head and offered him a smile. Would she take a walk with him? Perhaps . . .

A new hum of activity disturbed her reverie as the business of the day began in earnest. A young swell moving among the potted plants offered Dawn an easy target. As he busied his hands carrying his newly purchased heliotrope, she busied hers taking his handkerchief, a lace confection she knew would fetch a good price. Though she'd told herself just one, another tall, foppishly dressed young man with bright red hair seemed a good pick. Stealthily Dawn moved forward, her hands itching to get hold of the linen that poked from his pocket. Two handkerchiefs were better than one.

"This one will be perfect for the office, don't you think, Gar?" he was saying as he hefted a huge potted plant. Dawn reached out, but before she could even touch the handkerchief she caught sight of his companion and froze for just a moment in her motion. It was her handsome gentleman!

"Blimey!" she breathed, stepping back into the

shadows. Her heart leaped into her throat and she was certain that its loud and rapid beating sounded like a drum to passersby. A rush of emotions flooded over her, from joy to fear. She'd thought never to see him again.

"Get anything you think suitable, Ollie, I really don't care. Besides, it's your office too." The deep masculine voice gave added proof that her eyes were not deceiving her. She would never forget that voice. How could she when it haunted her very dreams?

"Well, I daresay, you're not much fun, Gar. Usually you're just as elated as I to brighten up our office. Ever since your little incident at the docks you've been as grumbly as an old bear. I was just trying to cheer you up by making the office a bit more pleasant."

"I'm sorry if I didn't sound appreciative, Ollie. I've got a lot of things on my mind."

He sounded deeply troubled. Was it possible that he regretted the way he had treated her? Her heart swelled with the hope that now, after thinking the matter over, he realized she had never meant to harm him. Perhaps there was hope after all.

"A lot on your mind. Like that Bow Street Runner you mean. Unpleasant fellow, if you ask me. By Jove, what a common sort he is. But then I suppose chasing after thieves and the like would not be a prudent occupation." He struggled for a firmer hold on the potted tree. "Do you really think he's telling us the truth when he says he's closing in on the leader of that pack of rats, or do you suppose he only wants our money?"

What's this? Dawn thought, *Bow Street Runners?* She was poised in stunned surprise, frightened by the very thought of the men who were death to her kind.

"He tells me he's traced that black-bearded knave down, had him followed from that warehouse to his living quarters, as it were. He promises to have the whole gang of them taken in today. He seems so confident that I believe him."

Dawn's entire body tensed. Three facts pounded over and over in her brain. He'd enlisted a Bow Street Runner to find them. That man had followed Black John from the warehouse to their living quarters in Seven Dials! Dear God! Dear God! He had said he'd have them all taken in today. All of them! Robbie. Arien. Taddie. Doris. Jamie. All the others. Not just Black John. Oh, what had she done? In freeing one man she had sealed all their fates.

"I don't mean to appear grouchy, Ollie. In fact I do like that plant. The leaves are just the right size and color."

Dawn didn't hear another word. She set her feet flying over the cobblestones. Robbie and the others had to be warned! There was no time to waste. Every single minute spelled danger.

"Wait! You! Ollie, I recognize that girl." The stones clattered with the pounding of feet as Dawn was pursued. "Come back! I won't harm you."

Wouldn't harm her? Ha! He already had, Dawn thought as she darted in and out between the various wagons. As she headed back toward the seven intersecting streets that marked her home, she whispered a silent prayer that God in his forgiveness would spare them all.

11

❧❧

The twisting streets of Seven Dials welcomed Dawn like familiar friends. Still she moved cautiously, stealing a quick glance up and down the labyrinth of merging roads. Two men lurked near the doorway of her building immersed in conversation. From their fine garments she could tell at once that they were not local denizens. *Who are they?* she asked herself.

One man in particular drew her eye. He was walking briskly in front of the door, pacing back and forth like a fat cat ready to pounce. Her heart leaped as she suddenly realized she'd seen this man before, pulling a shackled man along behind him. He was a runner—she was certain of it. She'd arrived too late to warn the others.

Damning the brown-haired gentleman with every breath, she thought of how he'd brought them to this sorry end. He'd rewarded her kindness with treachery. Putting the Bow Street Runners on their trail was unforgivable. Anger boiled in her blood, but a voice whispered in her ear that she was as much to blame. *She* had set him free, ignoring Black John's warning.

Foolish snip of a girl, what 'ave ye done?

Slumping against the brick wall, she tortured herself with musings of her perfidy, feeling more alone than she had since her parents had died ten years before. Her stomach churned at the thought of what she had brought about. And all for what? Because he had a handsome face? Because she hated to see him close his eyes forever? As if he would care a whit for the likes of her or for the lot of them. He was a toff without a thimbleful of pity. How could she have been so totally witless, so disloyal to those whose misery she shared?

I'll never forgive myself if . . . Trembling, Dawn pressed her forehead against a broken windowpane; then from the safety of her haven across the street she watched the heavyset man strutting about as he carefully laid his trap. How was she going to warn Robbie and the others? She had to think of a way. Her insides lurched every time she thought about the consequences. Newgate! The very name inspired stark terror. She couldn't stand being cooped up again, nor could Robbie!

Dawn jerked away from a hard poke in the ribs. Whirling about, she found herself nose to nose with a teetering old man in his cups. Lurching from the ginhouse, he reeked of drink. Their collision hurtled her into the unexpected glare of the sun, just as a magistrate's wagon thundered by, coming to take them all away, no doubt. Above the thud of horses' hooves, rattling wheel rims and cracking whips, she heard voices from inside.

"Townsend says this is the place, all right. See, there he is."

"He's got that surly black-bearded bastard already in hand. Now we'll just wait and hope we can catch the others."

"Have to catch them before they go inside, for you know how silly the law is. As if thieves have any rights. Ha!"

"Don't fret, Bill. We'll catch them red-handed, and

then they'll rot in that stinking hole of a prison. Serves them right, I say."

"If it were up to me, I'd hang the lot of them."

Somehow Dawn managed to get back to her hiding place without arousing any undue attention. Shivering and fighting a surge of panic, she darted like a rodent from shadow to shadow, avoiding the circles of sunlight that threatened to give her presence away. Like a pack of hounds, the armed foot patrol was closing in. How could she live with herself if her brother, Jamie, Arien, and the others were sent to that terrible rat-infested prison because of her? She couldn't.

Calm yourself, Dawn, ole girl, she advised breathlessly. That was easier said than done. For just a moment she panicked. Robbie and Jamie were walking up the street, heading for the doorway. They'd be caught! She had to head them off. There was only one way. She would make herself the target. It would be her penance for what she had done.

Reaching down she pulled at a loose cobblestone, aiming it right at the stout Bow Street Runner's head. She tensed, holding her breath as she flung it. A horrified shudder coursed through her as she heard the sickening thud, but she somehow forced herself to remain clearheaded. This had to be done.

"I knows who yer are, I do. Runners yer be! You've got Black John, but yer won't taike me!" she taunted, picking up another stone and hefting it threateningly in her hand. She tossed the second cobble just as the heavyset man barked his command.

"After her!"

Dawn bolted for an open window, evading the arms that reached out to take hold of her. Her only satisfaction was in knowing Robbie and Jamie had heard and understood her warning and were now in flight.

"She went into that building across the street. The ginhouse. Don't let her escape!"

Banging into tables, bumping into drunken pa-trons, Dawn stumbled only once as she chanced to look back. Pushing through a back door, she chose her avenue of escape, then was running for her life with the pack of human hounds at her heels. Up one street, down another, ducking behind barrels, slipping through open windows, she was fortunate that familiarity with her territory gave her the advantage. With a gasp she flattened herself against the cold stone of a building, listening cautiously. The din of heels and voices passed by her, but even so she remained in her hiding place for quite a long while, then shakily she emerged.

"Ahhh!" She breathed as something touched her shoulder. Soft fur brushed her face. "Shadow!" A loud meow greeted her. The cat rubbed up against her neck affectionately. "So you too have been spared." But what of the others?

Clinging to the security of the shadows, Dawn sought them out and found them in a chandler's shop a half mile from where the chase had begun. A bell jangled over the door as she entered; the scent of warm tallow filled the air. Pushing past a row of molds, Dawn joined the others.

"Thank God, Robbie! Thank God!"

Dick Boothington, the candlemaker, had once been Black John's boon companion in crime, until he'd bettered himself. Sympathetic to their circumstances, or perhaps because he was on John's list of those to be bribed, he often gave them safe haven. Now he looked at her over the top of his spectacles.

"Yer out o' breath, missy."

"I should think so! I came within an 'air of being caught, I did."

"Ah, but yer were marvelous, Dawnie, me dear!"

Jamie hugged her close as he exuberantly heaped praise upon her head. "If not fer ye we'd all be gibbet bait."

"Aye, sis, me dear, yer were grand." Robbie squeezed her hand. "But 'ow did yer know who they was?"

"A little bird told me," Dawn answered, averting his thankful gaze. Her guilt, despite her heroics, tweaked her still.

"A pigeon, no doubt!" Jamie guffawed loudly.

"Is . . . is everybody here?" Hurriedly Dawn gave count. Taddie. Doris. Arien. Farley and the others. Just as she supposed, however, Murdock was gone, in addition to Black John Dunn.

"John's been taiken," Taddie answered, her voice quivering with emotion. "Or so we've heard."

"Oh, has he?" Dawn pretended surprise. "How . . . how do ye know?"

"Willy was on the docks and saw 'im being hauled awaiy. In one o' them big carts that strikes fear in me 'eart whenever I sees 'em pass by," Doris answered.

"You're . . . you're sure?"

"As sure as I am that I'm a thief!"

"And . . . and Murdock?" Crossing her fingers, she hoped beyond reason that somehow he might have escaped.

" 'E was wi' John, 'e was."

"Oh . . ." If the truth were known, Dawn held little sympathy for John, though she did not wish him any ill. Murdock was another matter, however. He was scarcely older than Robbie. So young to be condemned to a prison cell. Tears blinded Dawn at the thought.

"But 'ow did they know about us?"

"Who peached?"

"We've all been so careful. Not a one o' us has been followed."

Dawn wiped at her eyes, focusing them on her clogs, fearful that guilt might be clearly written on her face. She was the one! Inadvertently her good deed, her show of humanity, had cost dear.

"Ah, yes, Black John and Murdy 'ave been taken in by the Thames Marine Police," Dick Boothington announced. "Look! Yer can see 'im from here. Clutching to the bars o' the wagon, 'e is."

Hiding behind the shade, several of those gathered peered out, staring as the wagon rumbled by. There was such a look of hatred on John's face that Dawn winced. If he ever found out what she had done, if her actions were ever revealed to him and he somehow caught her in his grasp, she knew her life would be forfeit.

"There's no 'ope for 'im now. 'Is goose is cooked!"

"But wot o' us?" Taddie asked mournfully. "Wot will we do wi'out him?"

It took only a few moments for Robbie to step forward. Though he was one of the youngest of the men, he was also the most daring. "We'll need a leader, we will. I appoint meself that man. Unless yer 'ave any objections." There were none, for no one else wanted so great a responsibility.

"Yer it, Robbie, me boy!"

" 'E can 'andle it."

"Robbie, no!" Dawn alone was vehemently opposed to the idea, but there was no arguing with her brother. He was intoxicated by the thought of his power, drunk with the idea of being a robber-king.

"I can 'andle Johnnie's job. Just wait and see."

"And suffer his fate too?" A premonition of trouble tickled at Dawn's spine, but she was powerless to dissuade him.

"Smile, Dawnie dear, and kiss yer brother's cheek fer luck." Standing on tiptoe, she did just that.

They'd have to lie low until the furor died down

and then seek out other lodgings. They were free for the moment and that was the important thing for now. Pushing her fears aside Dawn tried to count her blessings.

12

≈ ≈

The great scarred doors of Newgate prison clanged
shut behind Garrick. Uppermost in his mind was anger that such a place was necessary, but his anger
was tempered by a twinge of sympathy for those who
dwelt within. *What a horrible place,* he thought, eyeing the rough, heavy walls, the massive doors plated
with irons and mounted with spikes. Starkly impressive in a sinister way but a good place to avoid.

"I got two of them for you. I think you'll be
pleased." Charles Townsend held up his head and
thrust up his chin proudly. "Just come along with me
and identify them and they'll be on their way to the
judge and the hangman."

"Lead the way." The stale odor of rotting straw and
other unpleasantries assailed Garrick's nostrils, and
he flinched. Had there been any alternative, he
would never have condemned another man to this.
He grumbled against the Bow Street Runner's cheer-
fulness. He found no joy in this matter, only a sense
of duty.

"Oh, this smell is terrible!" Ollie coughed and stifled a sneeze with his linen handkerchief. "I said I'd
come with you, old boy, but let's identify your blackguard and be quick about it. I daresay the stench in
here is enough to gag a swineherd!"

"I'm as anxious to be away from here as you, of

that I assure you," Townsend shot back with a wry smile, "but once set into motion these things must be completed. It must be on record that there was positive identification. And you must agree to be called as a witness."

"Then lets be quick about it," Garrick said brusquely. He wanted to put this matter behind him and get on with his life. The rogue had set upon him, robbed him, and thought to have him killed. Now he must pay his dues to society.

"Come, come!"

Garrick and Ollie followed the swaggering runner into the depths of the prison. The nauseating reek of Newgate assaulted them all the more the farther they went and pressed upon them like an enveloping cloak.

"What is that horrible odor?" Ollie covered his nose with his handkerchief.

"The smell of death," Townsend answered over his shoulder. "The inmates call it 'Newgate perfume.' The hangman leaves his 'gibbet fruit' swinging all week before he cuts them down, as a special lesson to those inside here. A way of frightening them into abandoning their life of crime, ye might say."

"Dear God!" Garrick exclaimed. It seemed a most hideous thing to do.

"Does . . . does it . . . it work?" Ollie looked over his shoulder as if fearing something or someone might suddenly pop out at him. An angry ghost, perhaps.

"I suppose it does. Sometimes. The Chaplain of Newgate, the Ordinary, as we in the business call him, seems to think so. In addition, he preaches a traditional sermon to those who are under sentence of death, as if that would do any good." Townsend chuckled. "Oh, they group around a coffin as he rants and raves and some of them goes into fits of trembling. Serves as a warning to their fellow prisoners, at least."

"I daresay!" Ollie touched his neck, loosening his cravat. "I . . . I never really realized." He stayed close to Garrick as they moved along.

"Though you'd be surprised at the bravado some of these lads express. Masking their despair behind a show of courage, I might suppose. They laughingly speak of 'dying dunghill,' expressing contempt for authority as if that would do them any good." Townsend clucked his tongue. "Make what you will of it."

Garrick had thought himself prepared for what he'd find behind the prison bars, but he was wrong. The noisy, clamorous, pathetic creatures who shuffled along with a length of chain between their ankles, or hovered behind the grating, striking at the iron bars with spoons, made his stomach lurch. It was like glimpsing purgatory. There was a look of hoplessness in the staring eyes that touched his soul. For the first time since he'd visited the Bow Street Office, he felt a flicker of remorse, a sentiment that vanished the instant he entered the huge stone cubicle that held the glaring, black-bearded ogre.

"Argh!" Clutching at the bars, the man hurled vile epithets at the guards, threatening them with retribution. "I 'ave friends in 'igh plaices. They'll see that I get out of 'ere. And when I do I'll cut off yer ears and boil 'em in oil! I'll geld yer . . . I'll . . ." Catching sight of Garrick, he ceased his tirade and stiffened. "You!"

"Yes, me!" Seeing him again, Garrick felt a storm of anger, yet he managed to keep it coolly under control. "That's him!" he said icily.

"So, yer ain't dead!" The beady eyes that appraised him reflected the dozens of devious thoughts whirling through that shaggy-haired head.

"No, I'm among the living, as you can see. No thanks to you."

"Yer was supposed to be d—I was told that . . . Argh!" In a frenzy of anger the bearded robber leader shook the bars that held him captive.

"You were told . . ." Garrick misunderstood, thinking the man to be talking about the young prostitute. So she *had* been sent to kill him. The murderous little trollop! "Your little doxy must have gotten cold feet. Oh, she came back, all right, knife in hand, but she slit my bonds instead of my throat."

"Oh, she did, did she?" The flesh that showed around the beard turned bright red. The man's eyes nearly popped out of his head as he bared his teeth. He reminded Garrick of a snarling animal. His anger was a terrible thing to see. "She put me 'ere! Well, I'll repaiy 'er, I will. She'll wish she was never born!"

"You won't be having revenge on anyone. Not where you're going, which no doubt will be straight to hell after you're hanged!" Charles Townsend nudged the mumbling man back from the bars with the tip of his quizzing glass, a monocle with a handle attached, such as the young dandies often sported. "And hang ya will. Now get back!"

"No. I don't want him hanged!" Garrick was emphatic on that fact. He'd not have another man's life on his conscience, no matter what the reason. Besides, in some ways being imprisoned was worse than hanging. It gave a man time to think about his past sins.

"What?" Townsend stared at Garrick in amazement. "Don't want him hanged?"

"That's what I said." Garrick explained solemnly, "If I am the cause of his death, I will be no better a man than he." He shook his head. "No, I will not be responsible for another man's demise. Hanging is a barbaric custom which clearly reveals us to be uncivilized." Garrick remembered the times he'd witnessed such punishment aboard ship, that and the equally savage discipline of keelhauling, dragging a man beneath the ocean the length of the ship. It had made his blood run cold. Life was too precious a gift for any man to take.

"You must be daft!" Oliver gasped. "This man is a thief and mayhap worse. He tried to kill you, Garrick. What can you be thinking?"

Townsend eyed Garrick up and down through his spectacle. "Don't be fooled into thinking *he* would do ye a like turn. He has the look of a killer. Believe me, I'm an authority on such matters." Folding his arms across his massive girth, Townsend was steadfast. "I say he deserves a hanging. Besides, it won't be up to you but to the judge."

"Then I'll tell him my views on the subject as well," Garrick retorted, determined to have his way.

Townsend snorted his disdain again. "Bloody hell you will! Never mind. Your views won't be worth a tinker's damn. This one should and will hang."

"No, I won't. I'll escape the noose some'ow. Meanwhile, I'll wring yer neck if yer don't shut up, yer little pig!" Black John growled. Throwing himself at the bars as if hoping to break through, he swore a multitude of oaths.

"See! He's dangerous. Barely human." Townsend was smug in his opinion.

"I repeat, I want it set down for the record that I don't want him hanged." Turning his back on Townsend, Garrick was firm on the matter. "Keep him here or transport him, I care little which."

"It's not for you to say!" Townsend started to argue then threw up his hands. "I'll talk to the judge and see what I can do, but it's against my better judgment." Mumbling beneath his breath he led them on to another cell. "Here's the other one."

Garrick peered into the gloom at the figure huddled on the straw. Just a boy really. The young man
was sobbing, his shoulders quaking. The very sight of
the pathetically frightened youth touched something
deep within Garrick, dissolving his anger. "Son . . ."
he said gently. The young man turned his head, peering at Garrick from tear-reddened eyes. Something
about the young man seemed all wrong. "I don't believe that's he." Garrick gazed intently at the frightened youth, determined not to make a mistake.
"Bring him into the light so I can be certain."

"You heard him. Bring the lad up to the bars." A
turnkey obeyed Charles Townsend's command, un-
locking the door and pushing the young man forward.

Studying every angle and line of the prisoner's
face, Garrick said at last, "It's *not* the one!"

"Are you certain?"

"Very." The image of that young thief was embla-
zoned in his mind. "I remember the lad who accosted
me. His hair was darker." At Townsend's doubtful
expression he reiterated, "Believe me, I remember
the scoundrel."

"But he was with—"

"I don't care! He's not the one who picked my
pocket." Garrick was secretly pleased with the
youth's innocence in the matter. Now he could see
that the boy was sent scurrying from this dreadful
place. "Set him free."

"Set him free? But he was with that black-bearded
giant."

Cocking one brow Garrick looked down from his
lofty height at the runner. "My dear sir, if we were all
judged by the company we've kept we'd all be behind
bars. I know I've made a mistake now and again. Can
you say that you have not?"

"No, but . . . but . . . well, I have it in mind to

catch them all!" Townsend jabbed his finger towards the cell where the robber leader was secured. "I've had my eye on that one and his den for a long time. Before you came along." For just a moment he seemed to be talking more to himself than to Garrick. "There are so many thieves in London. Thousands, in fact, and my reputation demands that I play my part in ridding the city of their evil."

"Did the young man do anything unlawful?"

"No!" He knew the law to be imperfect. Even when someone was known to have a criminal past, it was difficult to make a verdict stick without either evidence or an eyewitness to the deed. "All right!" Grumbling, Charles Townsend gave the order.

"Thank you, sir! Thank you!" As the turnkey opened the door, Murdock knelt and took Garrick's hand. "I'll do yer a like turn somedaiy, I will!" As he was hustled off he looked over his shoulder and his eyes shown with gratitude.

"Well . . . so much for that!" Townsend was clearly perturbed, but he bowed his head politely. "I have done what you paid me to do. My part is finished, at least for the moment." He held out his hand for the remainder of his fee.

"Come on, Gar. Let's get out of here." Oliver tugged impatiently on Garrick's sleeve.

Watching until the young thief vanished down the corridor, Garrick at last turned towards Oliver. "All right, we're finished here." Actually Garrick was disgusted with the entire matter and anxious to put it all behind him. The young man's plight only reminded him how helpless he was to right all of the wrongs in the world. In his youth he had tried, only to know the taste of defeat and disillusionment. "We've got drawings to do." As he'd said to Ollie, at least he could help to make it a beautiful city, if not a truly just one. "I haven't lost hope that your merchant will give us a second chance."

"That old tightwad? He'll make me get down on my knees, but I'll do it." Ollie prodded Garrick down the hallway. "He's threatened to deduct fees for the time he wasted waiting on the dock. Shall I allow him such liberty?"

"Most definitely not! Had he been on time in the first place, I might never have suffered this knob on my noggin." Garrick ran his fingers through his hair, touching that still sensitive spot, wincing from the memories it still brought forth. Well, at least one of the villains had been apprehended. Now that he knew for certain that the young doxy had meant to be his executioner, he'd see that she was found as well. "But come along, we'll discuss this when we get back to the office."

Garrick and Oliver left the walls of Newgate, thankful that they were free to leave its doleful memory behind.

13

Through the tiny window of the room she shared with Taddie, Dawn could hear the sounds of Soho: the clatter of the carts, the barking of the hounds, the din of pedestrians as they wound their way past shops, the voices of peddlers hustling their wares in strange chattering tongues. Soho was a bustling district of narrow dowdy streets, the principal foreign quarter of London, where thousands of French Protestant refugees had once fled to avoid persecution. Now other peoples were represented as well. It was here, where Soho and Bloomsbury merged, that Robbie and his band had sought shelter.

The group had lodgings in the front one pair—the front rooms up one flight of stairs. A group of jobbers lived in the back: carpet beaters, chimney sweeps, dustmen, who seemed content to mind their own business. Recently gas lighting had been installed on a few of the streets in Soho. To deter crime, Robbie had said, annoyed and apprehensive lest it become a trend. He abhorred the lamps which interfered with his profession, though he insisted that the cleverest thieves could always find a way to lure their victims into the shadows.

Soho was an interesting area. Many of the local brigands pretended to be foreign or had actually come from distant shores. Robbie advised Dawn to watch them closely. They were well trained to leave no traces, to be clever in avoiding arrest.

Smokestacks from factories, church spires, and steeply pitched roofs rose in a hodgepodge against the sky. A dark cloud hung over Soho as smoke from hundreds of chimneys, forges, and furnaces mingled in a thick suffocating fog. Clouds of sulphur, full of stink and darkness, often left clothing covered with soot. But Dawn ignored the smoke as she leaned over the sill. There was a lining to every cloud if one just looked hard enough and today promised to be a bright, sunny day.

She basked in her contentment. Now that Robbie was the leader of their small band, life was more peaceful. Whereas before she'd been forced to share a sleeping room with several of her gang, now she relished her semiprivacy. Though the glass windowpanes of the building were broken and patched with rags, the walls chipped and peeling, the floorboards cracked beyond repair, she hardly seemed to notice.

And Murdock had returned with his tale of the elegant toff who had set him free. It softened Dawn's heart to know that he had shown the lad some measure of kindness. Perhaps his heart was not as hard as she supposed.

"Gor, wot a fine one 'e was! Ordering the turnkey to let me out. I'd loike ter be jus' loike 'im somedaiy," Murdock had said upon his return.

"A gentlemon?" The other thieves roared with laughter, but Dawn had staunchly come to Murdock's defense.

"And why not?" she asked peevishly. "Everyone needs 'is dream. Is it really so farfetched that any one o' us could be 'quality' if we tried?" With her nose stuck haughtily in the air she affected the strut of those aristocrats they often saw strolling the markets and gardens. "Wot separates us from them, eh? Money, 'at's wot. And circumstance."

"Luck, sheer luck, 'at's wot," Jamie countered. "Some o' 'em was born into their fortunes, though they don't do a lick o' work. Any more than we do . . ." He guffawed loudly, striking Farley on the back.

"They talk differently, dress differently, and turn their noses up at us," Taddie exclaimed. "As if we was jus' little worms crawlin' underfoot."

"Aye, but underneath their skin they bleed jus' the same as us," Farley grumbled. "They breathe the saime air, walk the saime streets and the loike."

"There ain't a one o' us who isn't just as good as any o' them. I truly believes that, I do. If Murdock wanted to become a gentlemon, I think 'e could, just as I could become a laidy if I set me mind to it." Dawn punctuated her sentences with a toss of her dark curls.

"Ooh. Laidy Rogue!" The men all bowed mockingly in unison, except Murdock who had a thoughtful expression.

"Laidy? They'd squash yer loike a bug if yer was to even try," Jamie said earnestly. "They want ter keep us roight where we are, Dawnie, me dear. They loikes ter look down on us. Our poverty and grime maikes 'em feel lofty."

"Aye, they don't care if we starves. They don't see us as human. Oh, I tried to plaiy it straight, I did. Tried to get me a job once." Farley crinkled his brow as he remembered. "Twelve hours a daiy I toiled at that factory, and for what. I barely made enough to strike two coins together. I maike far more now."

"They'd never accept ye into their social circles." Jamie was protectively adamant. "All ye'd get fer yer efforts is a broken 'eart! Better to make do wi' yer life 'ere, as dismal as it is at toimes."

Dawn's optimism was overruled by the others in a cacophony of voices, but still she held steadfastly to her dream. Why was her notion foolish? Once she and Robbie had been on the opposite side of the social scale, living in a fine house, wearing finery, even talking differently than they did now. If not for ill fortune, they might still be there. Why couldn't she cross back over if she tried? Why should she shrug off the idea as impossible?

Dawn couldn't push away her dreams. Now that Black John was no longer there to goad her on, Dawn had lost her incentive for thievery. She hated it! As the days wore on she pilfered fewer and fewer hankies. Her thoughts soared beyond her sordid surroundings, and she found herself fantasizing more and more that she was a great lady, the toast of London. At the center of every dream was her handsome gentleman. Oh, how she longed to become a lady!

Despite the danger of lurking runners, she visited the old quarters every other day to see her cat. She'd brought Shadow home to Soho, but the puss had a mind of its own and kept returning to its old haunts. Dawn vowed she would not interfere with the cat's freedom. Independence was a precious thing. Shadow was a skilled mouser and had managed to get along quite well before she had adopted her. A visit now and then to scratch the cat's chin and keep her company was all she would ask. Just like Shadow, she wished for her own independence.

"If only I 'ad a means of saving me shillings, I could use them to further meself. Learn how to talk like me mum used to. But how?" The very thought made her feel guilty, for just as it had been in Seven Dials, the rule here was to look after your own. Thieves had a code of honor. Yet she couldn't get the thought out of her head. If she made a good living honestly, the next time she came in contact with her gentleman she could hold up her head proudly.

Black John had stashed away his profits, that she knew, and she sensed that it was hidden somewhere in that old, dingy, dirty room he had called his own. It was Dawn's hope that somehow she might stumble upon his treasure, that she and Robbie and the others would benefit. Oh, how lovely it would be if she could be the one to bring them all out of poverty!

"Dawnie? Wot ails yer?" Taddie came up behind Dawn, startling her out of her daydream. "Yer keep wiping at that saime spot on the windowsill. It must be clean by now."

"Clean?" Dawn laughed as she turned around. "As clean as it could possibly be." Seeing a concoction of flowers on Taddie's head, she moved closer for a second look.

"Ooh, I knows it's frivolous, me buying this 'at wi' me hard-earned shillings and all, but it maikes me feel pretty, it does. I don't think there's a woman alive 'oo don't loike a new 'at."

"An 'at!" A seemingly preposterous idea was taking form in Dawn's mind. Hadn't Petticoat Lane become a thriving business, selling used dresses, handkerchiefs, and other wearing apparel? What if she were to do the same thing, only specializing in hats?

When she was a little girl her father had always told her she was good with her hands. How disappointed he would be to know the use to which she had put them. But remaking old hats into new fashionable creations might be an answer. And it was honest work.

"I could saive me shillings and use them to further meself."

"Do wot?"

"Never mind . . ."

It was an intriguing idea. Pulling her mobcap over her hair, Dawn hurried from the room. "I'm going out!" She'd go to the toffs' area of town, look in the windows, and get some ideas for her own creations.

14

A gleam of perspiration shone on Garrick Seton's bare chest and arms, emphasizing the rippling muscles that made him look more gladiator than architect. His golden-brown hair was tousled as he got up from the mat. "I'm said to be handy with my fists, but you're a match for me, Richard," he said, running a hand over his jaw. "You pack a mean punch."

"As do you." Wiping his bloodied nose, the other man stuck out his hand, grasping Garrick's in a firm handshake, appraising him with admiration. "I'd call this one a draw."

"Unless you want to go on until there is a win." Garrick grinned, daring the other man to continue. Not until there was a knockout could a man be credited with winning the match.

"Do I look like a fool? No, I'll just thank my lucky stars that I'm still on my feet and let it go at that. You were fighting like a man possessed today. I've been boxing for ten years and I've never faced a more fearsome foe." He gave a pained groan, then playfully slapped Garrick on the back to show that there were no hard feelings. "One would never believe you make sketching your life's work. You seem to have the soul of a veritable pirate at times."

A grimace flickered over Garrick's face. "A characteristic I try to subdue, old man." He was not always as well controlled as he might have liked, and he considered that a flaw. Perhaps that was one reason he had taken so quickly to boxing. It allowed him to vent his pent-up, turbulent emotions. God knew he'd been like a boiling kettle since that night on the docks. "Trying to unleash some of my own private demons, I suppose. Sorry if I took out my frustrations on you, Rich."

"I threw a few wild punches too. But then we're not playing tennis, Garrick. Scuffing up our chins, noses, and knuckles is the name of this game. You were only responding to my punches." He reached for two towels hanging on a peg nearby and threw one to Garrick, watching as Garrick wiped himself off. "Next time, however, I won't be so gentle."

"Gentle?" Garrick chuckled as the two men walked back to the washroom. Stripping off his trousers, Garrick bathed himself by pouring a basin of cold water over his head and letting it run down over his body. His thick brown hair curled rebelliously about his face, and he tried to groom it into some semblance of order with his fingers.

"Is it a woman?"

"What?" Understanding what Richard was alluding to, he shook his head. "Not the way you mean it." Drying himself off and putting on his shirt, breeches, and boots, he revealed not only the story of the docks but also spoke of his encounter with the girl who had taken refuge in his carriage. "I suppose until one has dealings with people in such circumstances, it's easy to put it out of mind. Now I can't seem to forget."

"Well, I have no doubt but that the next time you meet such blackguards *you'll* win the day." Richard flexed his arms, making great show of his aching muscles. "Aye, that you will."

"Will what?" Ollie swept into the small room looking from one to the other, obviously curious about their conversation.

"Beat the devil out of any ruffians I meet, Ollie," Garrick answered. "And if you were wise, you'd take up boxing, too. One never knows just whom one might meet."

"Me? Box?" Oliver's horrified expression made the other men laugh. "It's barbaric. I'll just make do with the runners, if you please."

Richard winked at Garrick. "Why, it's an enjoyable sport, Oliver. You might be surprised."

"Ha! Acting like a heathen, you mean? I'm surprised that old Gar here indulges. Besides, life was meant to be enjoyed. Why, just look at all there is for a man to amuse himself at."

It was true. In London the activities for those of consequence were many and varied, from prizefights to opera. For those whose only problem was to amuse themselves and defy boredom there were entertainments for the day as well as the night. In addition there were clubs, clubs, clubs. London was full of private clubs for this and for that.

"You should join a club, Gar." Taking out his snuffbox, Oliver opened the lid and stared inside.

"It wouldn't be worth my while, Ollie."

"I know. You're a busy man." Partaking of the snuff, he sneezed. "As for me, it gives me a place to escape from Mother and Aunt Margaret. They're always badgering me. Heaven help us all if women are ever allowed inside."

"They want what is best for you, Ollie."

"They want me to be 'sensible' like you." Leaning against the wall, Oliver wrinkled his nose. "I wonder if they would consider you such if they could see you now, fighting like some naughty schoolboy."

"Boxing. There's a difference. It's a gentleman's sport, Oliver."

"The closest I ever get to boxing is putting money on the outcome. Which reminds me . . . there's a game of whist going on in the back room of my club. I was hoping you'd join me." Oliver's principal pastime was gaming, that and frequenting the races at Newmarket to place his bets.

Garrick shook his head. "You know how I feel about gambling." It was an opinion formed from experience. Garrick himself had once been bitten by the "bug" and had only narrowly escaped ruin. He realized that Oliver was ensnared the moment he picked up his first deck of cards. He hoped it wouldn't bring his friend to financial calamity.

"That's because you just don't understand! You, Aunt Margaret, and my mother. Pooh!" Holding his hands together at chest level he lapsed into a falsetto tone, mimicking his female relatives. "Gambling is a villainous chaos of dice and drunkenness."

Garrick threw back his head and laughed uproariously for it was a perfect imitation of Oliver's mother. "Ollie, you are incorrigible!"

"Yes, I am, and damned proud of it." The sudden burst of bravado faded and an embarrassed flush flooded his face. "But I seem to be a bit short of cash. Of course, if you felt in a benevolent mood, you might make me a loan. You always carry that blasted money pouch with you and I've never seen you take out even a farthing."

"That money belongs to someone else." A faraway look came into Garrick's eye as he remembered the girl who had left the purse in his carriage. It had been stolen, to be sure, but since he couldn't locate the owner, he wanted her to have it. Certainly she had looked in need. That was why he had chased her the other day at Covent Garden, but she had run as fast as if the devil himself were at her heels. Strange little waif—and yet she tugged at his heart.

"You don't even have a shilling you could loan me?" Ollie had the expression of a woeful hound.

"Ollie!"

"All right! All right! You are so tight sometimes, Gar, that I fear you might squeak."

"It's not that . . ."

"I know. I know. You don't approve. But you don't realize how exciting gaming can be. Women, wine, fame, even ambition sate now and again. But every turn of the cards and cast of the dice keep the gamester alive. It's much like having sex with a stimulating woman and coming to climax a hundred times in one night."

"I doubt that, my friend!" Richard broke into gales of laughter. "If you think that, you haven't met the right woman."

"Pooh!" Ollie answered defensively. "One can game longer than one can do just about anything else. Eh what?" A mischievous gleam came into his eye. "I'll tell you what, Richard, old boy. I'll toss a coin. I'm willing to gamble, you see. If it's heads, you can stake me to a game; if it's tails, I'll . . . I'll listen to one of your lessons on boxing."

Garrick shook his head. There was no changing Ollie. He gave Richard a look of warning but saw that the other man had succumbed to Oliver's challenge. With a shrug of his shoulders he walked to the door, leaving the two men behind to work out the wager. Pushing the thick wooden portal open, he walked out into the sunshine. He'd best enjoy the day, he thought, for sunny days were all too brief. Soon there would be fog and rain and muddy streets. Oh, how he hated summer to end. There were only two more weeks left. Perhaps he'd indulge himself. A carriage ride with a beautiful woman would be a pleasant way to spend a day.

"Sir?" A sad-eyed flower girl crossed the street, giv-

ing Garrick a hopeful smile. "Vi'lets, penny a bunch."
In a generous mood, he bought two tiny bouquets.

Engrossed in the beauty of the day, he walked
along, coming to an area where elegant shops lined
the street. It was then he saw her, peering intently
into a milliner's window at a row of hats. Hurriedly
he crossed the street.

Dawn was so preoccupied that she didn't see the
tall shadow fall across her path. Glancing up she
found herself suddenly staring into her gentleman's
deep blue eyes. "Blimey!" In fear she broke into a
run.

"Wait!" Narrowly escaping the wheels of a carriage,
Garrick gave chase. She was as quick as a rabbit and
as agile as a cat, eluding him skillfully. He ran a full
ten blocks before he closed the distance between
them, and that only because a conglomerate of wagons blocked her way.

"I didn't do anything! I didn't!" she yelled at him.
"Go awaiy!" Dawn was still edgy because of Black
John's fate. Surely hers would be a like fate.

"Of course you didn't. I just want to talk with you,
that's all." He tried to allay her fright with a smile.

Seeing his expression, she slowed down just a bit.
Could he be trusted? She wasn't certain. Certainly the
last time she'd been in his company he had been hostile, hurling all sorts of foolish accusations. What did
he want from her this time?

"I was just looking in the window, I was . . ." she
threw over her shoulder.

"I know I saw you . . ." He was out of breath.
She'd led him on a merry chase. "I have something
for you. Please, stop."

"Something for me?" She eyed him quizzically, allowing him to catch up. He didn't recognize her,
didn't connect her with the woman on the wharf.
That was a relief. Breathing in deeply, she let out a

sigh. Oh, he did look so fine. No coat this time, the collar open to reveal the light brown hair on his chest. Such a handsome bloke. Enough so as to turn her knees to jelly. "Wot?"

Garrick held out the nosegays. "These, for one thing."

"Violets? For me?" No one had ever given her flowers before. She was deeply touched and giddily conscious of the warmth of his hand as he gave the bouquets to her. Just the touch of his fingers evoked a deep longing within her. Why did he always make her feel all tingly? "They're . . . they're lovely. The fragrance tickles me nose!"

Garrick laughed softly. She was surely the most exquisite little creature he had ever beheld. "Yes, I suppose it does. I've always been partial to violets." His expression sobered. "I've been worried about you." The thought that she might come to a bad end haunted him. Strange, how she brought out his protective instincts.

"Worried?" Dawn stiffened. What did he mean? "I can taike care of meself," she said, bristling.

"I'm sure you can, but I've been thinking a lot about you, nevertheless." In spite of her tender years, her loveliness drew him. She should be dressed in silks, not rags. Beautiful was the word to describe this little urchin. Her skin was soft, unblemished, her cheeks like the petals of a pink rose. Eyes as green as a new leaf stared back at him. He found himself wanting to pull off her mobcap and appease his curiosity about her hair. What color was it?

"Thinking about me? Yer was?" She stared at him openmouthed, her astonishment obvious. "Gor, I don't know why ye'd do that." The very thought pleased her, for the dear Lord knew she'd spent enough hours dreaming of him.

He was intrigued by the look of tender passion so

innocently revealed in her eyes. The child could certainly steal his heart if he gave her half the chance. "I wanted to return this," he said gently. Reaching inside his coat pocket, he pulled forth the leather money pouch. "You seem to have left it behind when last we parted. That's why I was running after you, to give it back."

"Give it back?" She flushed hotly. Again she adopted a belligerant attitude. "It isn't mine as well yer know." Oh, if only he realized what the loss of that purse had nearly cost her.

"I know it's not yours." He had wrestled with the situation and had come to a decision. He wanted to do something for her. Something that would not injure her pride, for he could tell by the set of her chin that she had that in full measure. "But since I haven't a clue as to its rightful owner, and since it most definitely is *not* mine and *you* left it behind, I consider that you should take it." It would insure her well-being for a little while, he thought. "Please . . ."

It was much too tempting. It was like the answer to a prayer! She'd have enough to begin making her hats. Even so, she eyed him warily as she took it, fearful that there were strings attached to his generous offer.

"There, you see. I won't take it back." He found himself wanting to take her in his arms, to give comfort, but held himself back. She would misunderstand. "It's yours."

Dawn felt a rush of heat flush her face. If she hadn't known it before, she realized it now. She'd fallen in love with the bloke, of that there could be no doubt. Otherwise he wouldn't affect her so strongly each time he gazed into her eyes. Yet it was a love that confused her and left her feeling empty and achingly sad. There was no hope for a happy ending.

"I'll taike it, if 'at's wot yer want . . ." She swallowed nervously, guilt tugging at her conscience. What would he think if he knew she had been with the men who robbed him on the quay? Would he be so generous then?

"Good!" He smiled. It was the beginning of what he hoped might become a friendship of sorts. He certainly did want to see her again, just to make certain she was safe. "My carriage is several blocks away, but if you'd care to walk with me I'll give you a ride back to your lodgings."

She gazed at him blankly for several seconds before she blurted out, "No!" Suspicion clouded her eyes again. Was he more cunning than she had realized? Did he recognize her? Was he trying to find the gang's new digs?

Her sudden hostility stung him. "I'd enjoy the company."

She looked at him with uncertainty, her heart at war with her reason. Circumstances had made them enemies as sure as if they were on two sides of a war. Indeed, in some ways they were. And yet at that moment all she wanted was to be with him. "I . . . I can't. . . ." she answered fiercely. She just couldn't be so selfish as to take a chance with her friends' fate.

"Are you certain?" She reminded him of a spitting kitten, but he sensed a vulnerability in her nonetheless. Living as she did was a horrible existence. No wonder she reacted as she did. "It would be *no* trouble, and I'd enjoy the conversation."

His warm smile nearly made her change her mind. "Well . . ." What harm would it do? A great deal of harm if she drew the others into danger, she told herself. She just couldn't take the chance, no matter how she craved his companionship. "No! I 'ave some errands to do." She forced a smile. "But . . . but thank you."

"Some other time?" He was determined to see her again.

"Some other time."

Reaching into his vest pocket, he pulled out a pencil and scrap of paper. He wanted to keep in contact with her somehow. "If ever you have need of me . . ." Scribbling down his name and address, he handed it to her. "You can reach me here." Oh, how Ollie would chide him for what he had just done. It was an invitation to have his house robbed, but something prodded him to take the chance.

"Garrick!"

"Yes?" He was surprised that she could read. So many in her circumstances couldn't. He'd thought perhaps she'd have to get someone else to read it for her if she were in trouble, but so much the better.

"Garrick. Your name. I like it." Garrick Seton, the piece of paper said. It suited him. Garrick Seton. She remembered that he'd told her once before. G.F.S. Garrick. It sounded lordly.

"You never told me your name."

Dawn started to tell him but doubt still nagged at her. "Poppet is what my father used to call me," she said, breaking out in a run, lest he become too inquisitive.

"Poppet." A strange name. It didn't suit her, Garrick thought, wondering if she had told him the truth. He watched her disappear into the crowds of passersby. He'd done all he could. Still, as he looked after her retreating figure, he couldn't deny that the little waif had touched him deeply.

15

Rain tapped at the windowpane, sending a spray through the cracks. Summer was taking its leave with a ghastly storm! Finding an old rag, Dawn stuffed it into the offending hole, then stepped back, brushing several strands of damp hair from her eyes. Drops of rain glistened on her thick dark lashes and she quickly wiped them away. Such a storm! As if God was emptying all of heaven's buckets.

"Poor Robbie and the others, to be caught in this." Suffering a bout of sniffles, she'd stayed inside. "They'll be sopped as mops by the time they gets back."

Not only the rain would pester them. The filth in some parts of town collected in pools on the pavement and would be washed down the streets, bringing along garbage and other offending muck. Overhead waterspouts would pour down on heads and hats.

"A pity." There was a bright side, however. When the weather was bad, it seemed to spark the purchase of clothing, scarves, coats, muffs, mittens—and *hats*. Dawn had ideas for several designs which would shield their owners from the rain. Taking a seat at the small table in her room, she made a few sketches, feeling inordinately pleased with herself.

Indeed, the money Garrick Seton had given her

from the stolen purse was a godsend, enabling her to begin making her *chapeaux*, as those in Soho called them. She had been quite fortunate, as a matter of fact, selling her creations at the markets in Rosemary Lane, saving each and every shilling she could. She gave Robbie a share of her profits, preferring merchandising to thievery. The coins she stashed behind a loose brick in the wall were steadily increasing.

Dawn was becoming quite skilled at keeping ledgers. Robbie made use of her knowledge to help him keep track of the goods and monies his thieves brought in. They made a perfect team, for Robbie had a good business head, even if the others insisted he was a bit stingy. It was Dawn's hope that eventually she could dissuade her brother from his life of crime. Certainly she had a greater feeling of self-worth since she had begun using her clever fingers for something besides snatching hankies.

Absently tapping the pen she held in her hand against her fingers, she made her plans. When she had saved enough money, she would seek out a teacher, someone who could help her with her speech. One could hardly think of being a lady if one spoke like a guttersnipe. Jamie and Farley were right about that. People were pigeonholed by the way they formed their words. Robbie made a game of guessing where people came from, judging by the words and phrases they used or their accents. One had only to open one's mouth and his place in society was marked forever.

Her brow puckered with determination. *I'll learn to talk just like me mum used to, and then I'll seek out Garrick Seton again,* she thought. Even the man's name set her heart pounding in a lively rhythm. And yet she didn't even exist as a woman in his eyes. A child was what he thought she was. A child or a whore, depending on which of their meetings came to mind. Hardly the makings of a romance. Even so, she couldn't banish her dreams. She'd become a lady for herself and for *him*. Then perhaps her pride would be real when next they passed on the street.

Garrick Seton meant trouble, but her heart refused to obey the dictates of common sense. A few days ago her curiosity had gotten the better of her, and she had sought out his address. Along the roadway were glorious stucco-faced homes, a row of fine shops, offices, a concert hall, restaurants, coffee shops, and two churches, one with a tall spire. His house was a two-storied brick structure with colonnades, perfectly landscaped with a garden and trees. Just as she had supposed, he was a member of the so-called *ton*, the elite of the city who lived a life of vibrant opulence and excitement. No doubt he was out every night. He must know dozens of beautiful women, all clamoring for his attention. The very thought caused a pang of jealousy. In her dreams he belonged to her. *But we will meet again, Garrick Seton, that I vow.* And when they did he'd take notice of her, just as he did in her dreams. Until then she would just have to content herself with watching him from afar. Folding and unfolding her drawing, she was pensive as she turned towards the window to watch the rain, wondering just what he was doing now and where he was at the moment. If he was enjoying the company of a woman, Dawn hoped she was not too beautiful.

Garrick was at the moment dining with Ollie, dabbing at his mouth with a napkin as he smiled. "I'm glad I let you talk me into this 'little lunch,' as you call it, Ollie." It had been a grueling week of long hours and severe eyestrain, a successful week in which Garrick had acquired two new clients. When Oliver had suggested for the fifteenth time that month that Garrick accompany him to his club, he had surprised his friend by accepting the invitation.

"My pleasure, old boy. My pleasure." Covering his mouth with his hand, Ollie gave vent to a belch. "Although you might not thank me in an hour when you have heartburn."

Garrick pushed away his empty bowls and plates, wondering how he'd ever been able to eat so much. He'd dined on turtle soup, scalloped oysters, a saddle of mutton, stuffing, boiled potatoes, pickles, tarts, jellies, and assorted vegetables. All washed down with a fine claret.

"If I didn't know better, I'd say you were bribing me. Are you, Ollie?" Garrick arched a brow.

Oliver grinned from ear to ear. "Not really. I just like to see you enjoy yourself. You rarely do. You drive yourself unmercifully. It's hardly sporting and most definitely depressing."

"I've turned our little venture into a huge success. That's what is important to me. A man never obtains his goals without hard work." Garrick's tone held a warning for Ollie.

"Pooh, I don't go along with your philosophy. I'm not made of your cloth, old boy. But tell me all about these two new clients of *ours*."

"One is a banker, Mr. Troley, for whom we're designing a building on Bond Street. The other is a Miss Stephanie Creighton, who has it in mind to build an exclusive home near Marylebone Park."

Oliver sat upright in his chair. "A *Miss* Creighton, eh? Heh, heh, heh! Is she pretty?"

"Now, Oliver! Don't get any ideas. I'm doing the drawings for her house and *that is all*." The matter was a sore spot to Garrick, for it had been obvious right from the first that the aristocratic Miss Creighton had set her beribboned and flowered cap for him. Although he staunchly believed a man should take the initiative, she clearly thought otherwise. She'd boldly asked him to accompany her to the theatre tonight but he had not refused.

Oliver threw up his hands. "All right! All right! Keep your amorous conquests to yourself. I'll speak no more about it, but we'll just see what develops. Ever since the Garden of Eden, you put a man and woman together and romance is the usual consequence." He winked at Garrick. "I'll wager my money on seeing Miss Stephanie Creighton on your arm from now on. Just wait and see. Miss Creighton has her eye on you, Gar."

Garrick's mouth trembled in a smile. Ollie meant well. "We'll see." They watched as the dishes were cleared away, then Garrick stood up.

"You are going so soon?" Oliver was clearly disappointed. "Without dessert?" When the waiter brought the bill he laughed nervously. "Oh, dear, I seem to be a bit over my limit and it seems I haven't brought my wallet with me. Of course, if you felt in a benevolent mood . . ."

"Ollie!"

"Well, you wouldn't want your partner to end up washing dishes. Such an embarrassment to the firm." His cajoling struck home and Garrick lent him the necessary funds. Amiably they took leave of each other, going their seperate ways, hopeful the storm would not linger.

"It will be over before the hour is up," Ollie predicted. Much to Garrick's annoyance it lasted all afternoon and into the evening. Now he was patiently waiting for Stephanie Creighton to come down the stairs and make her entrance. On the pretense of discussing the house plans with him she had wheedled him into taking her to the opera, Purcell's *King Arthur.*

"Garrick . . ." Resplendent in a white gown

worked with threads of silver hemmed by a floral
border, she swept down the stairs. The soft muslin
dress clung to her body, making superfluous any undergarments that might spoil the natural outline and
hide her willowy figure. Her hair, the palest shade of
blond, was parted in the center and caught in a snug
chignon. Her eyes were gray, her features sharp and
well defined. Stephanie Creighton looked as if she
had been chiseled from a block of ice. "You're here
already. My abigail didn't tell me you were waiting.
I'm dreadfully sorry." Her eyes burned with an un-
natural brightness as she turned to him. A feather fan
was attached by a ribbon to her wrist and she fluttered it briskly as she gave him a view of her profile.
She was not beautiful, but she knew how to make the
most of her physical assets.

"It's no problem. I haven't been waiting long."
Fumbling in his pocket, he took out his new watch.
"It's barely six o'clock. We have plenty of time, that is
if you even want to go out now. It's raining cats and
dogs out there. Your new gown, I fear, will get dreadfully wet."

"Raining?" Her thin lips formed a pout as if angry
that nature had ruined her plans. "How unfortunate!
I can't take the chance of ruining my dress. You
know how perfectly terrible the streets are when it
storms." She remained silent for just a moment, then
brightened. A speculative gleam danced in her eyes.
"I guess we'll just have to stay here." With a casual
gesture, she summoned her maid. "Have Toby prepare the dining room. We will be entertaining a very
special guest."

"Stay here? It seems like a very good idea." He took
the gloved hand that she offered him.

"Quite! You don't realize just how long I've wanted
to have you all to myself, Garrick Seton."

Perhaps he had realized, for she made no secret of

the fact that she was pursuing him, like a princess searching and trying to snare the perfect consort. It was very gratifying to his ego, though he didn't intend to let the relationship become serious just yet. Companionship was one thing, a serious commitment another. They hardly knew each other. Besides, he was not looking for a wife and that was certainly what Stephanie Creighton had in mind. Marriage.

"If we cannot go to the opera then the opera will come to us!" She laughed huskily. "The opera director is a very dear friend of mine. As a matter of fact, I put up a goodly share of the capital needed. We can have a few of the singers not engaged in the current production come to give us a private performance. I'll send Jamison out with an invitation." Her tone of voice made it clear she expected that her wishes would be obeyed.

She behaved as if the whole world were at her beck and call. "No." Garrick was adamant. "I wouldn't ask anyone to come out in this storm just for my own selfish whim. We'll attend the opera some other night when the weather is more favorable. For tonight I imagine we'll just have to make do with a deck of cards, or conversation. Despite the time we've spent together, I know very little about you, nor do you know much about me. Perhaps this would be a good time to delve into the past."

"As you wish." She seemed annoyed but carefully kept any sign of emotion from touching her brow. Taking his arm, she forced a smile as she led him into the drawing room. Pulling him down beside her on the settee, she leaned against him, allowing her eyes to roam freely over his face. She felt her blood quicken. He was a handsome devil and just the kind of man who would give every woman in London cause to be envious of her.

Oh, she wanted him all right, she thought to herself. She wanted him with an intensity that was alarming. Was he obtainable? She made up her mind that he would be. There wasn't anything on earth that didn't have its price. Garrick Seton was a flawless specimen, a devastatingly handsome man. The only problem was his cursed independence. He wasn't interested in her money. He appeared to be comfortably fixed for finances on his own. A self-made man, though his mother had opened herself up to quite a fortune. Just how was she going to get him under her spell?

The foolish young man who was his partner and companion might be his Achilles' heel. It was rumored that he had a penchant for gambling. How tragic if his weakness endangered Garrick's little enterprise. But then, of course, she would quickly come to the rescue. That idea pleased her. It was certainly worth a little more thought.

16

~~~

Petticoat Lane, Rosemary Lane, Holywell Street, and Monmouth Street were the centers of the old-clothes trade and the markets frequented by Dawn during the month of September. Since central London was the older part of the city, everyone passing from one district to another had, at some time or other, to go through the rundown areas frequented by thieves. Thus she was strategically placed not only to sell her hats to those of her own kind but to sell them to a few of the "swells" as well. Dawn felt inordinately proud of herself today, having turned discarded flowers, ribbons, and lace into dainty confections which three elegant ladies had promptly purchased.

Hats, it seemed, were becoming more and more elaborate, and Dawn's inventive ideas pleased those with daring. Having seen several of the hats worn by foreigners, she had even adapted berets and turbans into fashionable creations. Her most popular hat, however, was the hat that could be worn in the rain. It was a wide brimmed bonnet of natural straw which she had trimmed with row upon row of silk ribbon, a rainbow of hues which complemented any outfit. Unlike feathers and flowers, ribbons were hard to ruin. Her secret of making the hat weatherproof was simple. She covered the straw with a coating of tallow from candles her friend the chandler had given her.

As she began coming into her own, Dawn discarded her mobcap and loose-fitting dress for something a little more stylish. She owned two dresses, which she alternated as the mood suited her. Today she wore a lavender linen with puffed sleeves, filled in with a tucker to hide the low neckline. If it was patched and torn in a few places, well, it was still fashionable. She had also taken to modeling her own hats. Her choice for the morning was a poke bonnet with a soft crown and rigid brim which held her curls tightly to frame her face.

Bending over, Dawn sorted out her ribbons, preparing herself to replace the hats she had just sold. She jumped as a well-aimed pinch caught the flesh of her buttocks. "You!" She shook her fist at the offender, rattling off a string of swearwords at the grinning buffoon. Throwing his hands up in the air he pretended innocence, but she wasn't fooled. "Overbold blighter!"

She kept her eyes on the rogue as he walked along, troubled by the feeling she had seen him before. What was it about him that made him seem so familiar? Dawn moved closer for a better look.

"Tweezer!"

Oh, she remembered him well, the brash young rogue who had made her life so miserable when she first came to Black John Dunn's lair. He and John had had a falling out and the younger man had gone his way. How she detested him! His departure had given her at least a measure of pleasure. Now their paths crossed again. Had he come into his own? Was he a gentleman? No. His stealthy movements put her on guard, and she recognized him as one of the swell mob, a gang of thieves who dressed fashionably in order to escape detection. They were considered first-rate in the thieves' profession.

Moving amid the crowd, he seemed to have his eye on a lavishly dressed elderly woman in a wheelchair who had not an inkling that she was about to be robbed.

It's none o' yer business, Dawn. Giving herself some good advice, Dawn turned away, busying herself with her hats, but she couldn't still the voice that whispered in her head. *An old woman! A rich one to be sure.* But the thought of a helpless old woman being robbed pricked her. And to be victimized by Tweezer, no less. Waging a battle with her conscience, Dawn at last decided to thwart him. Tweezer stole the poor woman's reticule, but Dawn sauntered up behind him and craftily stole it back again. She pushed through the crowd and came to the old woman's side.

"Excuse me!"

"Yes?" The hazel eyes that met Dawn's seemed to stare into her very soul.

"Yer . . . yer reticule. Ye seem to 'ave dropped it." Biting her lip nervously, Dawn handed it back. "If . . . if I was you, I'd keep a tight 'old on it, I would," she whispered behind her hand. "Thieves lurks 'ereabouts."

"Thieves?" The old woman clutched the drawstring bag to her ample bosom.

"The 'ole plaice is crawling with 'em. Put yer bag somewheres saif," she said protectively. "And if I was yew I'd tell that gent' wot's pushing yer to move on along." That tall, dark-suited, haughty man turned up his nose at Dawn.

"Thieves I'm sure. I wouldn't doubt that she is one of them by the looks of her."

"Hush, Douglas!" The woman's eyes held a sudden kindness. "Thank you, young woman. I do appreciate your honesty *and* your timely warning." Dawn started to walk away, but the woman reached for her hand. "My name is Mrs. Randolph Pembrooke."

"Dawn. Dawn is me name."

"Like the sunrise! Lovely. And you are very pretty." She patted the hand that she held. Her eyes roamed over Dawn, but not in an appraising manner. "I'd like to offer you a reward for returning my reticule."

"Reward?" The offer was tempting, but Dawn shook her head. "I didn't do anything. Really." In fact it made Dawn feel a bit cocky to have bested Tweezer. She wished she could be around to see his face when he realized the bag was gone. Oh, what a laugh that would be.

"Isn't there anything I can do? Anything at all?"

Smiling, Dawn made a suggestion. "Yer could buy one o' me 'ats!"

"Of course! And such charming hats they are." She looked over her shoulder at her servant. "Douglas, I want all seven! See to it!"

"Seven? Madam, you're not serious." He eyed the creations with distaste.

"You heard me!" She handed him her reticule. "Give her the price she wants and then guard this for me. If I lose it again it will be your head. Do you understand?"

"Yes, madam." With a grumble he transacted the exchange, much to Dawn's astonishment. Was the woman serious? Did she really want all seven hats?

"Yer don't 'ave to taike them all . . ."

"Oh, but I do. They are exquisite! I intend to give them to my friends as birthday presents. Don't you think that would be a good idea?" Douglas started to say something, but she nudged him in the ribs. "You fascinate me, child. Starting your own business is very admirable. Just how did you come to be a milliner? And why?"

"To earn me own waiy." Dawn blushed, feeling suddenly shy, but she confided, "I want to earn enough money to learn to talk all properlike. So's I can talk like yer do. Me mum spoke like that once. She was a laidy and I want ter become one too."

"A lady?" Douglas looked down his nose at her.

Stiffening her back, raising her chin, Dawn glared up at the servant. "Yes, a laidy! And I'm going to be one too! No one is going to keep me down!"

"Bravo! Bravo!" Margaret Pembrooke clapped her hands. "I admire your spunk, child." There was something about the pretty young woman that reminded her of herself once. She too had struggled to make her way in life after fate had given her much heartache. Certainly this Dawn was very likable. Despite her tattered garments there was a certain grace in the way she held herself, a loveliness that even poverty had not been able to steal away. In another setting this dark-haired girl could well be a jewel.

"I'm going ter be a self-made woman, I am. People will look up ter me." Standing up on tiptoe, Dawn tried to match the servant's lofty height. Look down on her, would he? She'd show him.

"I think they will." An idea was forming in Margaret Pembrooke's mind. Of course, the young woman was too proud to take charity, and yet she did so want to help her. "Suppose I aid you with your phonetics and diction in exchange for more hats?"

"More hats?" Douglas was aghast. "Are *you* going to become a milliner, madam?"

"I might. I certainly don't have much to amuse me, seeing that my nephew scarcely visits me these days. Unless he wants money, that is. And my sister and brother-in-law are caught up in their own social world." She looked Dawn squarely in the eye. "Would that be agreeable to you? Hats in exchange for my teaching you how to speak like an aristocrat? You wouldn't be afraid that I might give you some competition here? With your hats?"

Dawn laughed merrily. "No, I wouldn't be afraid. And I . . . I would so much like to learn. Seems I might just kill two birds wi' one stone that waiy. When shall we start?"

"Right now seems appropriate. Don't drop your *h*'s, child. It's not 'at, it is *hat*. Huh . . . huh . . . hat! That will do as starters. When you get home, practice saying your *h* words with a candle in front of you. The flame must flicker as you speak. Next week Douglas will meet you here at this same time and bring you to my house. There we will begin your lessons in depth. Once a week we'll meet. Agreed?"

"Agreed!" Dawn couldn't hide her gratitude. It shone clearly in her eyes. "And I'll bring me 'ats."

"Hats!"

"Huh . . . hats!"

Dawn watched as the servant wheeled the old woman through the crowd. She felt lighter of heart than ever before. Everything was going so well that she wanted to pinch herself to make certain it wasn't all a dream. First her successful enterprise and now Mrs. Pembrooke was going to teach her how to talk like a lady. Though storm clouds hovered on the horizon, it seemed a perfect day and only the beginning of the new life she so wanted for herself and for Robbie.

17

The candle's flame flickered and fluttered as Dawn diligently practiced her diction lessons. For three weeks now she had obediently waited for Douglas at the assigned meeting place and gone with him across town to St. John's Square. Praise had been her reward. Margaret Pembrooke lavished compliments on Dawn for her quick learning. Now hope glimmered bright as the fire which warmed Dawn's face as she stared at the tallow candle.

"*How* 'appy . . . er . . . *h*appy the little *h*en will be when she 'as . . . *h*as *h*er chicks back in the blinkin' nest." She spoke the same sentence over and over, forcing herself to remember the *h* was not silent but spoken. There were other rules as well, things she remembered when she closed her eyes and thought of her mother reading her a bedtime story. Things like not leaving off her *g* 's and *t*'s at the end of a word. "Not blinkin' but blinking."

"The letter *a* has many pronunciations. For example, the short tone, 'ah' as in the words 'father' and 'rather.' There are also times when it takes on a long tone"—Margaret Pembrooke had advised sternly—" 'ay' as in 'day' or 'pray.' "

"Daiy. D . . . ah . . . ee," Dawn uttered, unnerved by the woman's suddenly clucking tongue.

"No, no, no, no. Not *'die.' Day!* It will take time, my

dear, but I know you will do just fine. Now practice your *h*'s. I'll expect you to have them perfected the next time we meet." Dawn was determined that today when she met with Margaret Pembrooke, she would have her *h*'s mastered.

"How h-happy the little hen will be when she has h-her chicks back in the nest." The flame danced merrily with each correct sound. "How happy the little hen will be when she has her chicks back in the nest."

"Gor blimey! Yer must be daft, Dawnie, ter be talking ter yerself." Standing in the doorway, Robbie eyed her warily. "Are yer fevered? It's all them rainedrops, it is. Yer've caught a chill!" Coming quickly to her side, he put his hand on her forehead. "Don't feel 'ot."

"*H*ot, Robbie. Not 'ot, but *h*ot. That's the proper way to speak. Mum talked like that." Oh, how she wanted to share her new learning with her brother so that perhaps he could escape this hellhole too. Margaret Pembrooke had been extremely sympathetic, explaining to Dawn that when people were crammed together in an area, such as those who lived in the East End were, their speech flaws were repeated and intensified.

"Lord love a duck! If yer ain't gettin' hoity-toity all of a sudden." He roared with coarse laughter when she revealed her aspirations. "Moonstruck fantasies, Dawnie, me dear."

"The waiy we talk marks us, Rob."

"We talks jus' fine, yer and me, for wot we needs ter do to keep food in our mouths." Crossing his arms across his chest, he was sullen.

"Oh, Robbie, *listen*. I met a woman in the lane and she promised ter teach me how to say me words, just loike those in the West End. If she teaches me, then I can teach *you*."

Robbie patted the concealed pocket beneath his

coat where four coins nestled against the hardness of his chest. "This is all we need. Money. It talks, Dawnie dear. Loud and clear. And it don't care a jot about how we trill our words."

"The waiy we speak is coarse and vulgar. Mum would roll over in her graive if she could 'ear . . . *h*ear us."

"Mum can't see or 'ear us." Clenching his jaw he looked out the window. "They killed 'er, they did, and I'd be willin' ter believe that even tho' she was a damned fine woman she was kept out o' *h*eaven by the loikes of all the toffs. Must be jus' like it is 'ere in the afterlife. I imagine an East End in 'eaven and a West End where all those of consequence reside. If there is an 'eaven, that is."

"There has to be Rob! Mrs. Pembrooke says . . ."

"Mrs. Pembrooke. Mrs. Pembrooke. I don't know 'oo she is, but I'm gettin' tired o' 'earin' 'er naime." Bending down, he met her nose to nose. "I'm your bro'. Remember me!"

"Of course I remember. And I love ye, I do." Hoping to soothe his ire, she revealed to him the story of how she had bested Tweezer by taking back the reticule, how she had given it back to the woman in the wheelchair, and how they had struck up an acquaintance.

"Is she rich?" His eyes sparked with sudden interest.

"Very. Oh, Rob, yer should see where she lives!" Dawn would never forget her first sight of the place. She had hesitated to follow Douglas up the walk at first, certain the two carved lions would pounce, they looked so real. Douglas had prodded her along, however, and suddenly she had found herself in a room so large she was certain she must be in the King's palace. She had stared wide-eyed at the imposing interior. "Marble steps, Rob, veined wi' gold, that led to a huge oak double door. There were carpets on all o' the floors and curtains of blue-and-green velvet. The ceiling was as 'igh as the sky and there were . . ."

" 'Ow often does yer go there?"

"Once a week. I'm to meet Douglas in about an hour. Why?"

He tried to hide his scheming smile. "Just curious, me dear. Don't want this learning o' yers to interfere wi' wòt needs ter be done."

"It won't, Robbie, I promise." Leafing through a stack of papers, she held up the ledgers she had kept so carefully. "See!"

Patting her on the head, he made his plans. He'd follow her to this blooming palace and look it over. Why spend his life scrounging for farthings when there was a larger piece of the pie just waiting for his itching hands? "Ah, yes," he chortled. When a door was opened, only a fool stood idly by. Dawn's acquaintance might very well be the opportunity he was looking for.

18

The midafternoon sun slanted down, cutting through the mists of fog, showing murky yellow through the grim haze. London appeared ethereal and eerie, nearly ghostlike. Autumn had settled over the land. The days were bleak and rainy with heavy fog which often eclipsed the sky. Only the spires of the churches rose above the fog, like needles through a tapestry. The two occupants of the carriage looked out their respective windows as the shrouded scenery passed by.

"By God but I hate to see summer end, Gar. It's on days like this, with the warning they bring of winter, that I begin to think of warmer climates. Italy. Spain."

"If you are so inclined, why don't you go, Ollie? I'm not such a cruel taskmaster that I would not give you a few weeks to warm your bones." Turning from the window, Garrick pondered his friend's sour expression. Perhaps he had been too hard on him lately.

"Money, that's why," the other man grumbled. "It seems to slip through my fingers like sand." His long-drawn-out sigh sounded mournful.

"You need to manage your finances more carefully, Ollie. You—"

"Please! No lectures. I'm privy to enough of those lately." Peevishly, Oliver turned his back.

The carriage jolted over the rutted cobblestones until it came to that part of town where the streets were beginning to be smoothly paved. Garrick saw the rejection of cobblestones as a final break with the lingering medieval past. It was about time. It was progress, and he wholeheartedly approved. In 1733 the renovation had begun. The smelly Fleet River had been covered at last. Raised pavements for pedestrians were becoming usual and gutters were being built on either side of the roads. One by one, the large signs were being taken down; houses and shops were being numbered.

"Now if we could only do something about the crowded streets!" Garrick muttered under his breath.

The streets were always crowded. Every year there were more vehicles on the roads. The congestion was appalling. In addition to the 750 public hackney coaches, or hackney hell carts, as they were commonly called, there were, according to rumor, as many as 5,000 privately owned coaches. Add to that the butchers' wagons, brewers' drays, dung carts, the ducks, swans and geese and grazing sheep, and the sum was a bothersome jumble.

Oliver muttered a loud oath as their carriage nearly collided with a milk wagon. He leaned his head out the window, chastising the coachman. "Watson, mind your eyes. We don't want to end up in an accident. Aunt Margaret would somehow blame me."

"Sorry." The balding, lean-framed driver gave his full attention to the horses and reins, skillfully maneuvering the carriage down the crowded road. At last they came to the exclusive area of the city where the congestion lessened.

"Gar, I'm sorry I was so grumpy a while back, dear fellow." Oliver pounded Garrick on the shoulder. "I can't thank you enough for agreeing to come to Aunt Margaret's with me. The old harridan frightens the tar out of me at times, and I know I am prime for a scolding this time, elsewise she wouldn't have summoned me so sharply."

At the risk of starting an argument Garrick said, "She is as worried about your gambling as I am, Ollie. It's put many a man in dire straits. You wouldn't be the first."

"Oh, bother!" Oliver was defensive. "I've had a bit of bad luck, that's all. A change is right around the corner. You'll see, I'll win back all the money I've lost and have a fortune to spare."

"I doubt it!" Garrick shook his head. "Oh, Ollie, aren't you ever going to change?" He'd always felt like a big brother towards Oliver, but what could he say? Sometimes a man had to learn certain things for himself. He had.

"Change. Of a certainty. I'll change the subject." The old familiar grin sliced across Oliver's face. "How is your Miss Stephanie Creighton? Are there wedding bells in the future?"

"No!"

Oliver was surprised by the suddenness of the reply. "Just like that? Without your even giving it a thought? My, my, my!"

"There's something about Stephanie Creighton that bothers me, though her manners are impeccable." Leaning back in the leather-upholstered seat, he tried to think of just what was wrong with the lady. Her haughtiness, perhaps, the way she looked down at those whose circumstances were less fortunate than her own. She seemed callous in her treatment of her servants, for one thing.

"Something?"

"All right, she's a snob!"

"With all her wealth, she has a right to be."

"That's where you are wrong, Ollie. Those who are truly aristocratic do not flaunt their riches. They have grown used to money. It is the *nouveau riche,* as the French call them, who are intolerably conceited." Stephanie Creighton's fortune was recent, inherited from a father who was a shipping magnate. Taking advantage of England's trade with India, China, and other faraway empires, he had acquired wealth. She did not come from an ancient landed family but from a dubious eighteenth-century fortune.

"Perhaps you are right, but by the look on her face whenever she has you attached to her arm, I would say you're going to have a merry time unhooking that one." Oliver turned again to the window, watching as the border of his aunt's estates came into view. "That's strange! My, my, my, but that one is out of his element. I wonder who *he* could be?"

Garrick was not particularly interested, but he asked anyway, "Who?"

"That young man there, loitering about my aunt's property. His sort usually roams Soho or the streets by the docks. Do you suppose he's actually working up the nerve to ask the old harridan for employment, or has he something more sinister in mind?"

"Let me take a look." Garrick slid to Oliver's side of the carriage. If there was any mischief afoot, he would soon chase the young scoundrel off.

"Look at him, the way he keeps staring in the direction of the house. Bold fellow, eh what?"

"Very bold!"

Unaware of the eyes that watched him from the street the tall figure darted out of the shadows. Wisps of fog surrounded him. Turning his head, he afforded Garrick a clear view of his features.

"Upon my word! It's he!" That face was etched forever in Garrick's memory.

"Who?"

"The young ruffian who stole my satchel at the docks. The one who was in league with that black-bearded scoundrel we put behind bars at Newgate. I'd remember his face anywhere."

"Are you certain?" Oliver stared through the window in fascination. "He looks like a thief. Didn't I tell you?" The carriage rumbled on.

"I do believe he means to rob your aunt's house. Well, I'll soon put a stop to that!" Garrick grabbed the handle of the carriage door, his intent obvious.

"No, Garrick! He might be armed. You'll get yourself killed." Grasping his arm, Oliver tried to keep him inside.

"Let go, Ollie! If you want to help, take the carriage directly round to Bow Street and summon Charles Townsend. Tell him I've got the scoundrel cornered. I'm sure he'll be enthused by the idea of earning the rest of his money." Then he was gone, sliding from the moving carriage, to pursue the young thief whose apprehension had become an obsession to him.

Margaret Pembrooke's keen eyes softened as she gazed at the young woman who so eagerly awaited her in the drawing room. She was much like a rose exposed to the frost. Margaret Pembrooke hoped most sincerely that the warmth of her kindness might revive the girl's tender beauty. The child had already revealed surprising aptitude. Why, she could read, write, and do her sums. These were not skills she had learned in Rosemary Lane. Somewhere in the girl's background was a respectable heritage.

"Good afternoon, Dawn, my dear."

Dawn turned slowly towards the sound of the voice and curtsied in the manner in which she'd seen the maids greet their formidable mistress. "Good afternoon, ma'am."

Strange, Margaret Pembrooke thought, how she could look so lovely in such plain attire. If only she could convince the pretty child to live with her here.

Her presence brightened up the house. Even Douglas was coming around, though he would not admit actually to liking the girl.

It had been unbearably lonely since Randolph died. That devastating experience coupled with her carriage accident a few years ago had nearly been her undoing. Somehow she had managed to survive. Now for the first time she felt a glimmer of hope. She would enjoy life again, seeing all the things she'd become so accustomed to and taken for granted, through this young woman's eyes.

Oh, how I wish she would stay with me, would take advantage of everything I could give her, she thought. She'd posed the proposition, but Dawn had staunchly refused. She had a brother, she said, who needed her protection.

"Come in, child. I'll have Anne fix us a spot of tea. I believe Cook has baked some crumpets. Would you like some?"

Dawn's face brightened. "Oh, yes!" She was coming to like the unsweetened bread. She'd asked about it and learned it was cooked on a griddle, then split and toasted. Today she'd pilfer a few and take them back to Robbie. She regretted some of the things she'd said to him. No matter how he talked, she would never be ashamed of him. He'd always be her bro', and she loved him.

She moves so gracefully, Margaret Pembrooke thought. Despite the dreadful way she slaughtered the English language, she had a tone that could be very pleasant if cultivated. Dressed in the right clothes, she would dazzle the *ton*. Oh, yes, she was a little bud just waiting to be nurtured so that she could come to full flower. But unfortunately the girl had repeatedly refused anything but the lessons.

"I has me pride," she had said.

So a streak of stubborness ran through her. Ah,

well, there was a kind heart beneath those rags. Perhaps she could help the girl, and with a little luck . . .

Margaret Pembrooke led the way, manuevering her wheelchair towards the settee, pleased when Dawn took hold of the handles of her conveyance. "*H*ere, let me *h*elp you." She smiled proudly at having remembered to say her *h*'s.

They settled themselves by the window, talking pleasantries. If the young woman slurped her tea and dunked her crumpets, Margaret Pembrooke didn't say a word. Time enough to teach her manners later. For now it was enough to learn to speak the King's English correctly.

"I been practicing. Can yer tell? How happy the little hen will be to have her hens back in the nest."

"Very good! Now I'll give you another lesson." She stifled a chuckle as Dawn lost her crumpet in the tea and fished for it with her fingers. "We'll concentrate on 'ing.' Hopping and skipping, the frolicking . . ." She broke off as a sudden commotion outside disturbed the quiet. "What on earth?"

Dawn ran to the window. "Two gents is fighting on the lawn, they are."

"Fighting? Upon my word! Brawling in this neighborhood?" Margaret Pembrooke shouted at the top of her lungs, "Douglas! Douglas, come here this instant!"

The fog embraced the two figures but Dawn still recognized her brother. Indeed, he was wearing the scarf that she had bought him last Christmas in Petticoat Lane.

"Rob!" Tearing through the room, she flung open the door and ran as fast as her legs would carry her.

19

Dawn came like a thunderbolt out of the fog, kicking and scratching at Robbie's attacker. In the scuffle her hat came off and tendrils of dark hair whipped at her face and into her eyes.

"Leave 'im be, ye bloody bastard!"

"By God, what is this? You little hellion!" Where had the hellcat come from? Garrick didn't know and didn't have time to wonder. He was more than a match for the boy, but fighting two of them complicated the matter. He could only hope that Ollie would hurry before they both got away.

"Get yer paws off me bro'!" She connected a well-aimed punch to his stomach, chortling triumphantly as he doubled over with pain. In retaliation he lashed out at her with his fists and sent her flying. In a sprawl of arms and legs she fell to the ground, her face pressed into the mud of a recent rain. Even so she came up sputtering. "Yer scurvy . . ."

Taking advantage of the distraction, Robbie looped his elbows through Garrick's arms and held him immobile. "Get 'is money pouch, Dawnie! Then we'll run."

"Oh, no, you don't!" With a lunge Garrick pulled the other man off his feet. Relentlessly he advanced on him, remembering his boxing instruction as he closed in. Balancing his weight on the balls of his feet, he swung and connected a fist with the rogue's nose. The force of the blow knocked the lad to the ground. Garrick's hand came away bloody.

"Rob! Oh, Rob, 'e's killed yer, 'e 'as." Dawn came on the attack again, struggling until she was winded. The man was certainly a strong brute, she thought. She could feel the muscles of his body even through her coat. Strong and mean. Taking hold of his shoulders she screamed obscenities, and it was in that moment their eyes met. Dear God, no! It couldn't be. Not him! The world was a huge place with hundreds and hundreds of people. Why did he turn up everywhere? Hastily she turned away, not knowing what to do.

"Dawnie . . ." Robbie's tone was scolding. "Wot are yer doing? Give 'im a bump on the head, grab 'is purse, and let's be goin'." Brushing himself off, holding his nose, he rose to his feet as voices floated through the fog.

"Over there. Hurry!"

"Gutter rats, that's for certain."

Dawn hesitated, then yelled, "Run, Robbie!" It was the runners. Like an ominous cage their wagon poked out through the mist.

"We'll teach them to accost their betters." Angry faces loomed up through the fog. Robbie broke into a run but being unfamiliar with the area was soon cornered. Cursing and kicking, he struggled but was soon forcibly subdued.

"Let 'im go, yer blighters!" Dawn screamed as loud as she could, hoping to unnerve them and give Robbie a chance. A heavy hand clamped down bruisingly on her arm in answer, the pudgy fingers biting into her flesh. She felt herself being dragged along. Only a well-aimed kick to the groin freed her. She didn't want to leave Robbie, but she had no choice. *Get help*, she thought, taking to her heels. It was the only way. *Quickly!* But from whom? They were in hostile territory. She looked frantically over her shoulder, but it was as she supposed. Not one tattered inhabitant roamed this street. Though thieves helped their own, she could not find one soul who was of her kind.

Circling around she viewed the scene of the scuffle from the safety of a grove of trees. They were taking Robbie away! "Bastards!" They chained and manacled him like the bulls and bears that were baited for amusement!

"No! No!" she whimpered, clutching a tree trunk for support. They were taking her brother away. To Newgate!

Bitterly Dawn looked towards the man who had held such sway in her dreams. His fault. He had been lurking outside. But how had he known Robbie would be there when she hadn't known herself? It didn't matter—all that was important was that because of him her brother was a prisoner.

20

❦ ❦

Dawn wandered the foggy streets of London like a lost soul, not knowing what to do, which way to turn. She tortured herself, reliving the moment when Robbie was shackled, trying to think of a way she might have been able to save him. She cried silent tears, her grief welling up inside her like a dam, ready to burst into an uncontrollable flood at any moment. Robbie was the only family she had left. They'd been through so much together. Now he had been taken from her. It seemed to be nearly more than she could bear.

Brave, yer 'ave ter be brave! she told herself, but it proved to be a difficult task. Little by little she felt as if she were falling apart.

She should not have left him. It was cowardly. Yet what could she have done against the runners? Still, if he had been taken to Newgate, she should have gone with him. But what good would that have done? He had yelled out to her to run. It was insanity to dwell on such thoughts. She wanted to fade into the fog and disappear. Would she find peace then?

She wandered aimlessly for a long while, lost in her painful thoughts. Robbie had hated prison. Now he was condemned to stone walls and prison bars. Or would his fate be worse? Passing by Newgate she stared in horror at the grotesque body of some poor unfortunate hanging from a gibbet, seeing Robbie's face upon the victim.

"Hang 'em. Hang all thieves, I say," said a voice.

"And we'll have another holiday, says I."

Shuddering, Dawn put her hands over her ears to block out the men's words. A hanging day was a public holiday. The scene around the gallows was always a lively one, with orange-sellers yelling at the tops of their voices, ballad-sellers warbling new tunes, pickpockets jostling their way through the crowds to take advantage of the distraction to filch a purse or two. Sometimes the body hung for days as a gruesome example; other times the body was cut down at once and sent to Surgeon's Hall for dissection.

"No-o-o!"

Blindly she ran down the streets, colliding with a rotund woman. "Watch where you are going!"

Footsteps pounded through the fog. In panic she fled, certain the runners were giving chase. Crouching behind a large hawthorn hedge, she waited breathlessly for the running feet to pass. Peering through the foliage, she saw it was just a group of children trying to catch a runaway dog. Slipping from her hiding place, she darted in and out among wagons, carriages, and carts; then, changing direction, she ran the other way.

Brambles clutched at her skirts; roots and branches seemed to reach out to trip her. Once or twice she turned her ankle on the rough and stony ground, only to get up again and renew her flight. Where was she going? In truth she didn't really know, she who knew London's streets so well.

At last Dawn found herself headed for Weasel's tavern. Perhaps she could drown her sorrow in gin. It was musky and smoky inside the Rose and Thorn. The stink of whiskey and ale mingled with the odors of sweat and leather. Though she tried to interest some of the patrons in a rescue attempt, not a one would brave Newgate's walls.

"We'd 'ave ter be crazy!" Weasel exclaimed. "I love Rob like me own son, but I wouldn't do it e'en for 'im. I'm too young ter be pushing up daisies!"

Dawn returned to her gin, gazing into its depths as if perchance to glimpse the future. It was her third glass and it hadn't yet begun to numb her pain.

Oh, Rob! She was beginning to feel a bit lightheaded. Closing her eyes, she tried to muster up her strength. *Robbie, Robbie, Robbie!* Was it her imagination or were her fingertips growing numb? Suddenly the room seemed to tilt and sway, yet she beckoned Weasel to fill up her glass again.

At last, staggering through the door, she wandered back into the streets. For some reason unknown to her she returned to the scene of her greatest unhappiness, the lawn in front of Margaret Pembrooke's house. Crumpling to the ground in a heap, she surrendered at last to the darkness that hovered before her eyes.

"Upon my word. What is this?" Seeing the wretched sight, Douglas moved closer, recognizing Dawn at once. Bending down, he gently prodded her, but she was frighteningly still. For a moment he feared she might be dead, but the soft moan that escaped her lips said otherwise. "Poor little waif!"

He remembered the terrible tussle that had taken place earlier in the afternoon and wondered just what part this young woman had in it. Certainly she had fought like a wild animal. The unfortunate man who was taken away must have meant a great deal to her.

"Dear, dear, dear." Well, he couldn't just leave her lying there. No doubt the runners would be after her. How tragic if she ended up in Newgate. He didn't want that. No, indeed, he didn't. "The Madam puts such stock in the girl," he said aloud as if to make excuses for picking her up in his arms. "She will be desolate if anything happens to her." Carrying Dawn towards the house, he was surprised to feel that what he was doing was precisely right, that somehow she belonged there.

II

The Mysterious Lady
WEST SIDE OF LONDON

What's in a name? That which we call a rose
By any other name would smell as sweet. . . .

Shakespeare,
Romeo and Juliet,
Act II, Scene 2

21

Sitting on the velvet-cushioned window seat in her bedroom, Dawn watched as rain drops gently spattered the window. Autumn had come. Periods of rain, days of fog and muddy streets made life extremely unpleasant. Winter was just around the corner. Dawn found that people in fine houses had a better time of it. In poorer areas of the city people were jammed together in cold, damp, cramped spaces like sheep seeking comfort and warmth. Summer with its clear sunny mornings, the days she'd spent with her brother, seemed a lifetime ago.

Robbie. Dear, dear Robbie.

There was not one day that went by that she didn't think of him. She missed him desperately and feared he'd met his death at Newgate.

In desperation she had turned to the woman who had befriended her, revealing only bits and pieces about her life on the London streets. Insisting that her brother was a good lad at heart, she had enlisted Margaret Pembrooke's help. But all efforts to intercede and free Rob had been to no avail. Dawn feared she would never see her brother again. And yet it was Rob's misfortune that had changed her own circumstances so dramatically for the better. Since the day he'd been carted off by the runners, she had lived with Margaret Pembrooke.

Like the metamorphosis of a caterpillar to a butterfly, she was slowly shedding her old ways and becoming a lady, thanks to the elder woman's tutelage. Dawn Leighton had all but disappeared and in her place was a refined young woman who had begun to fulfill the promise that Margaret Pembrooke had glimpsed in Rosemary Lane.

It was a transformation that had threatened to snuff out Dawn's patience. Yet slowly and surely her stumbling and stuttering tongue had ceased tripping over new words and pronunciations. With carefully placed lips and tongue she now formed her consonants and vowels correctly and in well-modulated tones.

"It's not so much what you say, my dear," Margaret Pembrooke had told her with a wry smile, "but *how* you say it. We English put great stock in grammar and intonation."

She learned when to listen attentively and when to voice an opinion, how to nod her head politely in agreement or to shake it slowly when she disagreed. It seemed the nobs abhorred argument of any kind; thus it was important for her to remember never to raise her voice. A show of temper was a sign of ill-breeding.

"The voice, my dear, is so important."

Even Dawn's laughter had been the object of a lesson. Less guttural now, it had a melodious ring to it. She had even been given lessons in how to sing, after Douglas heard her humming at her dusting. He had drawn Margaret Pembrooke's attention to the pleasant sound. Now á cherubic-looking tenor trained Dawn to practice scales and sing madrigals twice a week. Dubbing her a soprano, he had invited Margaret Pembrooke to add a breathy alto harmony while Douglas took the bass part and he the tenor line.

Margaret Pembrooke introduced Dawn to the finest music. Every Friday five musicians arrived for a concert. Listening to them play their stringed instruments, Dawn was certain such perfection could only come from heaven. There were Haydn's intricate symphonies, and Mozart's delightful works, and then there was the explosive music of the man Margaret Pembrooke called "that heathen German," Beethoven. All were names Dawn had never heard before, but they were names whispered in proper circles and Margaret Pembrooke said Dawn must know them.

A board had been strapped to Dawn's back to remind her to stand up tall, shoulders thrust back. Now her walk was graceful, her posture stately, her poise commendable and unshakable in most instances. In addition she had learned how to curtsy and pirouette. Margaret Pembrooke had been tireless in her efforts to transform Dawn into a lady. Dawn had learned a great deal, but she was always aware of how much further she had to go.

"You must learn to dance, my dear. It is the mark of a lady to be graceful."

"Dance?" The only dances Dawn had seen were sailors' jigs.

"Yes, dance—a glorious creation of intricate steps that you make as your partner whirls you round and round. Quite romantic, I daresay." Dawn saw the sudden gleam in her benefactress's eyes but didn't question her.

"Then I shall learn to dance, Mrs. Pembroke." Dawn was always very careful to treat her benefactress with the utmost respect.

"Margaret. Call me Margaret, my dear. It makes me feel a bit less like a fossil." The woman's smile held just a hint of sadness.

"Margaret. . . ." Dawn said the name tentatively at first, feeling far more comfortable addressing the woman formally. But if it would please her to be

called by her given name then she would oblige.
"Margaret!"

The days had settled into an established routine.
Breakfast was precisely at seven, for Margaret Pembrooke would not abide loitering in bed. Then Dawn
would busy herself with the light household chores,
aiding Marietta, at her own insistence. She could
take advantage of Mrs. Pembroke's hospitality without earning her keep. Lunch was always an elaborate
affair. Dawn's once scrawny figure had acquired vo-
luptuous curves. Now she feared that if she didn't
have more willpower, she'd soon be as plump as the
maid.

The afternoon was spent in lessons. Often Dawn
read to her companion, which gave her a perfect
chance to practice her speech. Discovering Dawn's
skill at numbers, Margaret Pembrooke soon enlisted
her aid with the household financial records. One
ledger had a name all its own. *Oliver.*

"Just who might that be," Dawn asked. She was
met with a scowl.

"My good-for-nothing nephew, that's who. A wastrel, a scoundrel. A gambling rake. You'll meet him
soon enough when he comes to pester me for a loan.
Humph!"

"He gambles?"

"Incessantly!"

Robbie had often lost money at cards or dice. How
she missed him! Her brother should be sharing her
good fortune, not languishing in a prison cell. Or
worse! Oh, where was he? She would have no peace
until she knew. Nor could she put Taddie, Arien, Farley, Jamie, or the others out of her mind. She had
wanted to go back to them, but Margaret Pembrooke
had been most adamant.

"The runners may still be looking for you," she had
exclaimed protectively. "Stay here and be safe."

What young woman in her right mind would throw herself to the wolves? The runners *were* most probably searching for her at this very minute.

"You might lead them to your . . . uh . . . companions, my dear. Would you want that?"

Dawn knew that she did not. Danger lurked out on the streets, while here she had a safe nest, She might put the past behind her, but she would never turn her back on her friends. Someday, when it was safe, she would seek them out. If she made her own fortune, she would help them. In the meantime, Dawn felt Margaret really needed her; she sensed the deep loneliness in the older woman. Perhaps they were both lonely souls, she thought, succumbing to the melancholy of the day.

Encircling trees rustled in the wind, casting eerie shadows. Nearby a rabbit bounded about, searching for food. The animal made a few aimless circlings, then settled itself by a bush, gnawing at bits of greenery left untouched by the cold. Just like Jamie, Farley, and the others, it was a survivor. As a dog suddenly gave chase, Dawn leaned forward keeping her eyes fixed on the rabbit until it disappeared into the safety of a hole at the side of the carriage house. It reminded her of her own circumstances. Here she too would be safe from any pursuers.

I wanted to be a lady and now I have my chance, she thought, turning from the window to stare into the dying embers of the hearth fire.

She owed a great deal to Margaret Pembrooke. She could never fully repay her. The woman had patiently, tenaciously molded her until she became that which she had so wanted to be. Besides, she really did want to stay. For the first time since she was a child, she had her own room, and that privacy was a blessing she cherished.

Clad in a thin linen nightgown, her hair falling

loose about her shoulders, Dawn sat with her arms folded about her knees and her legs drawn up to her chest. It was an unladylike position and had Margaret seen, she would have scolded her, but Dawn found it extremely comfortable.

Slowly her eyes settled on the blue satin canopy over her bed. A dressing table covered in the same shade of blue stood in one corner bearing elegant silver implements of beautification. There was even a lamp with a lovely round globe by which she could read whenever the urge struck her. So many comforts and luxuries she had once dreamed about were now reality.

The house was enormous and beautifully decorated with crystal chandeliers and rich wood paneling. Graceful windows held diamond-shaped panes of leaded glass. There were flights and flights of stairs, all fully carpeted. Dawn remembered how she had first wandered through each room, admiring the furniture, running her hands over the smooth velvets and intricately carved woods. Pembrooke House had twenty rooms including a library, with its walls lined with leather-bound books. Someday when she had the time she was going to read every one!

The front lawns stretched out on both sides of a cobbled drive, artfully landscaped with shrubbery and a checkerboard of flower beds. There was a small, separate house for the servants, a livery stable, a carriage house, a gazebo, a guest house, a gardener's shed. There were houses for everything. At times it was difficult for Dawn to come to terms with such wealth when she was so keenly aware of London's poverty. At times she felt guilty to think she slept on a soft bed while so many had no beds at all. And what of her brother? Where was he sleeping? Had Robbie's misfortune paid for her own success?

Rising to her feet, Dawn padded across the room

on bare feet to look in the dressing table mirror. Was she expecting to see a stranger looking back at her? Yes. But the eyes, the nose, the mouth were still the same, though Margaret Pembrooke insisted that the new fullness of her face made her look even prettier.

I'm still me! But now the days spent stealing handkerchiefs seemed unreal and she had to force herself to remember. She would never allow herself to become some haughty snob, mindless of the suffering that went on around her. Oh, no!

Opening a small drawer, she stared at two objects that she kept as reminders. The handkerchief and the watch. She wanted never to forget.

Robbie had given her the watch for her birthday. She would always treasure it. And the handkerchief? She had used it to wrap the watch, to keep it safe from scratches and to remind her how wrong she had been in once judging a man to be kind. She would not allow herself to lapse into foolish dreams of what might have been.

"Dawn!" It was Margaret Pembrooke's voice, accompanied by a soft knocking. "Are you in there, dear?"

"Just a moment." Closing the drawer, Dawn eyed the bracket clock as she moved quickly to the door. It was much later than she had realized. Her musing had caused her to "doddle," as Margaret called it. Trying to maintain her poise and keep the guilty flush from her face, she opened the door wide and Margaret Pembrooke wheeled her chair into the room.

"You're not dressed! Are you ill?"

"No, I was sitting by the window, reflecting on how my life has changed, and time got away from me," Dawn said truthfully. "I'm sorry if I've displeased you." She met the woman's eyes unflinchingly, expecting a scolding but receiving a smile instead.

"Good. Good. That you are not suffering the va-
pors, that is." She gazed intently at her. "I think it's
time you mingled with society, my dear."

"Mingled?" Dawn put her hand to her throat, shaking her head. The word "society" conjured up memories of the snubs she'd received for years. "I'm . . .
I'm not . . ."

"Ah, but you are ready. Relax. It is just my nephew
that I have in mind."

"Your nephew? The gambling wastrel?" Dawn remembered that he was the young man prone to lascivious behavior about whom Mrs. Pembrooke always spoke so scathingly.

"Aye, the gambling wastrel." Throwing back her
head, Margaret Pembrooke gave in to her laughter.
There was a refreshing honesty about this child despite a history of thievery. Margaret Pembrooke had
known from the first that Dawn had been forced into
a most unfortunate occupation. Even so she had decided to take a chance. She had yet to be sorry. There
was something about the girl that always delighted
her. Dawn was poised, intelligent, mannerly, and so
straightforward about what she thought that it was
refreshing. "I've decided to give him another
chance."

"I'm glad." Though she didn't understand, Dawn
was glad to see Margaret laugh. "He is your only family, or so you've said. It's only right that you should
be together." The ties of kinship meant a great deal to
her, especially after suffering the loss of three of her
own loved ones.

"Yes. Yes. I suppose it is." Squinting her eyes, Margaret Pembrooke let her gaze sweep from the top of
Dawn's head to the toes poking out beneath her
nightgown. The child was a marvel. In such a short
amount of time she had come such a long way. Oliver
would be intrigued. Certainly if he had an eye in his

head he would be attracted by Dawn's beauty. If everything worked out as she planned, this young woman would soon be her niece. As a member of a very influential family Dawn would be safe from anyone who might wish to harm her. Whatever she might have done in the past, it didn't matter.

"Perhaps I should leave the two of you alone. . . ." Self-consciously Dawn put her hands behind her back. In truth she didn't really want to meet Margaret Pembrooke's nephew. She was content in her newfound isolation and still a bit unsure of herself. Time. She needed far more time to feel really at ease.

"Oh, pooh! The truth is his whining bores me." Margaret Pembrooke had in fact begun to look upon Dawn as the daughter she'd wanted but never had. "You're grateful. He's a thankless ninny! You're a wise woman; he doesn't seem to have a brain in his head. All he wants is more, more, more. But perhaps with the right woman . . ." She said no more lest she give her well-laid plans away. "But we'll speak not a jot more about it. Just be certain to take a nap, dear. Sleep does wonders for a woman's beauty. In the meantime I have some matters that must be attended to before tonight."

Before Dawn could say a word, Margaret Pembrooke was gone, maneuvering her wheelchair down the hall as skillfully as a hackney driver guided the coach in his charge.

22

"What a wet, dreary morning!" Oliver drummed his fingers against the office window in abject annoyance. "Miserable day. Quite!"

"Not a good day for an open carriage ride in the park, I would say." Garrick looked up from his drawings, voicing his thoughts aloud. "But then perhaps that is really a blessing. Perhaps now you will give your undivided attention to that large sheet of paper lying on your desk. Eh?" Oliver had been quite unproductive of late. Had it not been for their long friendship, Garrick would never have put up with it. "Have you any new ideas for Southwark Bridge?"

Oliver shook his head. "I can't concentrate. My head seems to be full of pudding or some such thing." Leaving the window, Oliver paced up and down, back and forth.

"What's wrong, Ollie?" As if he really had to ask. It was always the same. Money. Garrick tried to keep the scolding tone out of his voice. "Have you incurred some new debts?"

"Yes. By God, yes! And don't say 'I told you so.' I don't want to hear it!" As if to ward off the lecture he knew must be brewing, Oliver put his hands over his ears.

"Ollie . . ." Garrick studied his friend and partner very critically. There seemed to be much more on

Ollie's mind than just unpaid gambling notes. Well, if he was really in trouble, he'd renege on his vow not to give him another penny. So thinking, he put down his pencil, rose from his chair, and made his way to the large landscape painting on the wall behind which a safe was hidden. Fumbling with the lock he soon had it open and reached inside for the money box he knew was within.

"Garrick . . . don't . . ."

"Fie! I'll show you I'm not the stingy ogre you think me to be." The metal box, fastened with a large iron lock, was heavy and took both hands to manage. "I've been gruff and stubborn with you these past weeks, but I'm not blind. You have the look of a mouse cornered by a cat. I want to help." The lid of the strongbox creaked as he opened it.

"There's no way you can. I'm ruined!" Moving quickly to Garrick's side, Ollie seemed loath to have him look inside. "Please, by the friendship we share, put it back!"

"Put it back?" Garrick would have had to be a simpleton not to suspect what was wrong. "Ollie, what have you done?"

"No . . . nothing!" Oliver grabbed the money box, but Garrick would not ease his hold. The result was that money, ledgers, and stocks went flying. "Oh, dear. Oh, dear." Falling to his knees Oliver began picking up the scattered papers and coins.

"If you've ruined both of us, I'll never forgive you!" Garrick's jaw ticked with anger. Finding the ledgers, he examined them. Everything seemed to be in order. Quickly he made a tally of the money that should have been inside the strongbox. Nothing seemed to be missing. Perhaps Oliver was merely overdramatizing.

"I didn't take any money. I swear by my mother's

hat, I didn't, but . . ." His hands shook as he covered his face. "I . . . I sold some of our stocks."

"You *what?*" Garrick was thunderstruck. It was as if Oliver had punched him in the face. A blow might have caused less pain. More precious to him than gold, those stocks represented ownership of the business he and Oliver had so painstakingly built.

"I had to. But at a devastating cost to my conscience. I've lived in fear these past three weeks. I knew you would find out eventually. But I had to, Garrick." He smiled sadly. "You see, in a way I was worse than a mouse. Circumstance forced me to be a rat! And you . . ."

"I am the cat you feared. And well you should." Springing to his feet, Garrick hoisted Oliver up by his shirt front. "I ought to shake you until your teeth rattle. And I would if I thought it would put some sense into your thick head. God's pocket watch! You've ruined me, and all for a stupid game of cards."

"I'm sorry, Garrick. I am! I am! I'll never do anything so foolish again." Tears stung Oliver's eyes. "Hate me! You have every right. I don't blame you," he sobbed.

"I don't hate you." A shudder convulsed Garrick as he pushed Oliver away from him with disgust. "But don't blubber. I won't have it. If you've—as they say in Bloomsbury—done us in, then at least face it like a man." Giving Oliver a not-too-gentle nudge, he forced him to sit down and tell him the whole story.

It was just as he might have supposed. Feeling certain that he could surely recoup his gambling losses, Oliver had run up a tremendous bill at his club. Instead of winning, however, he had lost miserably. There had been nowhere to turn. His aunt Margaret had refused to give him a shilling; Garrick, too, had been adamant.

"They threatened me with debtor's prison!" Oliver's shoulders shook. "Prison! Me, Oliver Howard Chambers. Oh, the horror of it all." He buried his face in his hands. "I couldn't bear it! I couldn't. Dear God, I could never forget the stench and horrid filth of that prison we visited. It was bad enough to be a visitor. But an inmate? I would have done anything."

"Even rob a friend?"

"I was desperate." Pulling out his handkerchief, Oliver blew his nose. "But then, just like an answer to a prayer, I was approached by a short, balding, bespectacled man who seemed to know everything about you and me. He offered to pay me a good price for only a small portion of ownership of our company. How could I refuse?"

"How could you?" Garrick said sarcastically.

"So . . . I sold him some stock. My bills were paid. All I had to fear was you! And I did fear you. Nearly as much as I had feared that awful prison." He smiled sheepishly. "But not quite. But . . . but, it will be all right. And . . . and they were *my* shares that I sold."

"When we started this venture we agreed there would be no outsiders. You have gone against your word. How can I trust you now, Ollie?"

"I won't sell any more. And . . . and I'll buy those stocks back. You'll see! You'll see!" Folding his arms across his chest, he seemed to have a resurgence of his confidence. "Auntie Margaret seems to be speaking to me again. She's invited me to dinner tonight. To meet some young woman she's taken under her wing." Putting a hand to his lips he said softly, as if there were someone there who might hear, "Most likely some spinster with ice-cold hands. But anything to please her."

"By God, if you have to marry some pinch-faced prune to get your butt out of hock, it would serve you

right! For once don't argue with your aunt, Ollie. If
courting some woman will help you get that stock
back then, good God, man, do it!"

Oliver was indignant. "I will! I will! It's what I intended to do in the first place without you scolding."
His brows drew together in a frown that was quickly
wiped away. "Oh, why am I raging at you? It's my
own fault I'm in a pickle. But do come with me tonight. Will you, old sport?"

"No!" Since that night he'd tussled with the young
thief on the lawn, he'd avoided Margaret Pembrooke's house. Perhaps it was because he didn't
want to remember the look of stark fear he'd read on
the young man's face when the runners took him. Or
the heartrending wails of grief from the girl who had
fought to pull him free. His pride had been avenged,
but at what cost? A man's freedom. He had been
judge and he had been jury, demanding that the lad
be brought to justice. Why then did the memory of
that night bother him so?

"No?" Oliver tugged at his sleeve. "You must.
Please, Garrick. Please! I always feel more at ease
when you're there to spar with the old dragon. I'm
certain she won't mind. She always has Cook put
enough food on the stove to feed Napoleon's army."
He stifled a giggle with the back of his hand. "You
can play matchmaker for me with the 'prune' if you'd
like. That way you'll be sure I get my comeuppance."

"By God, you're right!" Garrick cocked a brow.
"And it would serve you right. All right, I'll come!"
Striding back to his desk, he took a seat. "Now, for
the love of God, Ollie, get back to work!"

"Aye, aye, sir." Mimicking a soldier, Ollie saluted,
then, sprawling in his leather-upholstered chair, he
too picked up a pencil.

23

A light rain fell softly filling the night sky with a gentle haze. Dawn watched the rain from her bedroom window. Trying to take her mind off the evening to come, she stood a long time at the window, thus catching sight of the trim black carriage that rolled up the road and turned in at the carriage house.

"Mrs. Pembrooke's nephew!" What would he be like? Fat or thin? Tall or short? Dark-haired or of light hair and complexion? Leaning against the window, she tried to catch sight of him, but all she could see was two dark forms alighting from the carriage and approaching the house.

It was obvious that Margaret Pembrooke intended her nephew and Dawn to meet and become attracted to each other, but Dawn wasn't interested. Not after her disappointment with love. She would be pleasant, she would be polite, but she did not want him to be interested in her. Matters of the heart caused too much turmoil. And yet perhaps tonight would be a good test of her accomplishments. She would see if Oliver Chambers believed her to be a proper lady or if she gave herself away.

Opening the door of her bedroom, Dawn listened to the sounds below. To bolster her lagging self-confidence she made a quick accounting of all she had accomplished in the last few months. She doubted

Oliver Chambers could have done as well, and that made her feel better.

What on earth will I talk to them about? she thought anxiously, moving to her dresser mirror. She approved of the image that stared back at her. Her dark hair was done in classical style, with a curled fringe in front and ringlets behind. The mass of curls was pinned up at the back to form a chignon. A bandeau of parchment-colored silk held the curls in place. Dawn decided she approved of this new coiffure. Here and there a curl escaped its restraint, brushing the nape of her neck, tickling her skin, and feathering around her face.

She looked most fashionable. Her high-waisted gown was also of parchment-colored silk striped in forest green. Its short sleeves were caught up at the shoulders. A narrow black velvet edging outlined the oval décolletage, framing the unblemished skin of her throat. The skirt, which formed a small train at the back, swept the ground, rustling as she walked across the floor to the door. A necklace of gold and emeralds, loaned to her by Margaret Pembrooke, completed the outfit. Reaching up, Dawn assured herself that it was still safely there, then smiled ruefully as she slipped out of her room and descended the stairs.

Garrick shook the rain off his umbrella, closed it and stamped his feet before stepping inside the door. He was hardly in the mood for dinnertime chatter. He was still incensed by what Oliver had done. Having gotten himself into this predicament, Ollie was the only one who could extricate himself. That included learning how to manage his aunt and stay in her good graces, a most valuable lesson.

"You look as if we were going to a hanging. Smile, Garrick. I'm the one who is about to be skewered,"

Oliver grumbled. He forced a smile as he handed his coat to the butler. "Good evening, Douglas. I hope my aunt is in a pleasant mood."

"She is, as we all are of late."

Garrick was amazed by the servant's smile. What had thawed the man's icy hauteur? "Well, whatever the reason, Douglas, I assure you I heartily approve."

"Come this way."

Douglas led them to the drawing room, where Margaret Pembrooke waited. Leaning down, Garrick kissed her cheek. "Good evening, Margaret. I hope it's all right that I've come."

"Quite! You're always welcome, Garrick, as well you know."

"Thank you. I must say you look lovely tonight in that peach-hued gown. Surely one of the most attractive women in all London."

Under the scrutiny of his gaze she blushed. "You, dear sir, are a flatterer. But since I want to believe you, I will."

"As well you should."

Margaret turned her attention to her nephew, wishing with all her heart that he could be more like his friend. Steady. Dependable. Utterly charming. "Good evening, Oliver."

"Good evening, auntie." His eyes darted searchingly about the room. "Just where is this young woman you are dying to introduce me to?"

"She'll be down shortly."

"I can hardly wait," Oliver said snidely, casting Garrick a wry smile and looking towards heaven as if he sincerely needed help from that direction.

"Here she comes!"

"Oh, wonderful. I . . ." Oliver turned, speechless as a stunning young woman glided down the stairs. Any sarcastic remark he might have made died on his lips as he moved forward. Garrick too was staring, but unlike Oliver he stood his ground, too entranced to do anything but feast his eyes as the young woman gave them a charming smile.

"Dawn! Come and meet my nephew Oliver and his good friend."

Dawn paused in midstride. It was not Margaret Pembrooke's nephew she was staring at, however, but the man who stood behind him. Her eyes opened wide, her hands started to tremble as her mouth formed a perfect O of surprise. Garrick Seton here? After all the heartache he had caused, he was the last man on earth she ever wanted to see again.

No! It could not be. Not *he*! The world was much smaller than one could ever imagine.

"This is my nephew's friend, Garrick Seton, Dawn, my dear. Garrick, may I introduce you to Miss Dawn *Landon*." Catching Dawn's eye, Margaret Pembrooke winked as she said the last name, but Dawn barely saw the gesture—she was staring too intently at the devastatingly handsome man whose face had haunted her for so long. His light brown hair was a bit longer than it had been and it brushed against the strong column of his neck as he turned his head.

"Beautiful," he breathed.

"She's exquisite, auntie."

Dawn opened her mouth, but words of polite greeting would not come. Flee! That was her first instinct. She did not have the courage to face *him* just now. This man was responsible for Robbie's ill fortune, and somehow he would be her ruination too. He would recognize her, and then she would be taken away to languish in Newgate.

"I am very pleased to make your acquaintance."

Truly Garrick was overwhelmed. No prune-faced spinster, this one, but the most ravishingly lovely woman he had ever beheld. He judged her to be about eighteen, beautifully fresh like a rose just coming to bloom. Never had he seen such soft, unblemished skin, lips so perfectly shaped, or eyes that shone so like jewels in the light. And yet she seemed unaffected. There was no false coyness in the way she stared at him, no seductive lowering of her lashes. Fascinated, he took her hand, his lips lingering on the soft flesh as he kissed it.

Dawn took a deep breath. He didn't recognize her. Not as the child waif, nor as the woman at the docks —but then why was that so surprising? The day he gave her back the filched purse he did not realize her double identity. Perhaps now that she spoke correctly and dressed fashionably he would take her for a lady of quality. It seemed that he already had.

Dawn touched her tongue lightly to her lips to ease the dryness, unaware of the provocativeness of her action. "How do you do," she said slowly, trying to keep her voice from quivering. She must be careful in her choice of words for more than embarrassment would be her punishment if she made a careless slip.

"I'm doing quite well. Especially now . . ." She captivated him just as surely as if she had woven a spell. Indeed, perhaps she had, he thought, for at that moment he wanted her more than he had ever before desired a woman. Moving to stand beside her, he breathed deeply of her delicate fragrance. "Violets."

"I beg your pardon?" Dawn was discomfited by his nearness. Every nerve of her body was vibrantly aware of him, his strength, his good looks. The faint, pleasant hint of musk and tobacco teased her nose, and she remembered the time she had huddled in his carriage. Even then he had held sway over her feelings. Oh, dear God, how could she still be so overwhelmingly attracted to him after what he did? Robbie. She must not forget that this man had coldly and callously called the runners on her brother.

"You smell like violets, my favorite flower."

"I see." Her heart thundered so frantically she thought it would surely burst, but as their eyes met she suddenly felt relieved. The worst was over. They were face to face and so far she had not given herself away.

"Hmm." Sensing the current that seemed to flow between his aunt's companion and his friend, Oliver tried to regain the attention of those in the room. "I say, Aunt Margaret. What do you think about our dear king? It's said he's quite mad, that he has lapsed into lunacy again."

"I think it's tragic!"

"Why, I've even heard rumors that he has been put into a straitjacket. The whole city is buzzing with the news."

"Then the whole city should still their gossiping tongues. As should you, young man." Margaret Pembrooke was irate. George had been on the throne for fifty years, succeeding his grandfather, George II, when she was just a child. He was the only king she could remember well. "A king deserves the respect of his subjects, not their twittering. Besides, I'd rather have George as king, be he mad as a hatter, than that pleasure-loving, emotional flibberty-gibbet of a son of his."

Oliver was contrite. "I'm sorry. I didn't mean to offend you, only to keep you up on the latest news."

"Well, now you've told me."

Slowly Garrick drew his gaze away from Dawn's face as he overheard the squabbling between aunt and nephew. "Hush, you two," he said good-naturedly. "There's no need to argue on such a fine night."

"Fine night?" Oliver cast his friend a sideways glance. "By God, it's pouring rain outside." He darted a worried look at Garrick. Oh, the young woman was certainly lovely, but it was the first time he'd seen such a look on his friend's face. He wasn't sure that he liked it. One thing was plain. Garrick was totally entranced. Well, if he could see himself now, looking like a love-sick calf, he'd be appalled. He'd chide him merrily tomorrow at the office. Indeed he would. Besides, his aunt had invited *him* here to meet the young woman, and Garrick had merely tagged along. She was meant for *him*.

"Dinner is served."

"Oh, it is?" Garrick offered Margaret Pembrooke's houseguest his arm, but Oliver obstinately placed himself in his path. Oliver took her hand and placed it in the crook of his elbow.

"We'll talk about prunes tomorrow, shall we, Garrick, old boy?"

"Prunes?" Margaret Pembrooke looked puzzled as Garrick wheeled her into the dining room. "Indeed!"

Oliver cast Garrick a triumphant smile as he successfully contrived to seat his aunt's pretty young ward beside him. "Where are you from Miss . . . Miss . . ."

"Landon. Dawn Landon, and she is from Norfolk. The daughter of a very dear friend of mine." Margaret Pembrooke caught Dawn's eye and smiled. "It is her first time in London."

"Her first time?" Garrick raised his eyebrows. Why did she seem totally new, a revelation, yet vaguely familiar? Something flickered at the edge of his memory, but he couldn't grasp it and finally shrugged it off altogether. If it was her first time in London, then it was impossible for him to have seen her anywhere. *Except, perhaps, in my dreams,* he thought with a smile. She was just the kind of woman he had always dreamed of meeting someday. Now he had.

"Norfolk, auntie? I don't remember that you had

any acquaintances there." Oliver shrugged his shoulders.

"Then you don't have a very accurate memory!" She sniffed indignantly. "But that doesn't matter. I expect you to show Miss Landon every courtesy. London is an exciting city. Show her the sights. A successful architect like yourself will know just where to take her."

"And if he doesn't, I do!" Garrick placed himself strategically across the table. His eyes caressed Dawn with a heat that stirred her blood and set her heart racing.

"That would be most gracious of you, sir." Dawn smiled sweetly, at last managing to regain her poise completely. How many times had she dreamed that Garrick Seton had fallen in love with her? More than she could count. And now suddenly it did not seem to be such an impossible imagining. He did seem interested in her. *In my dreams I surrendered to him,* she thought. *But not now. Never! Not after what happened to Robbie.*

Revenge for Robbie's tragic fate? The idea appealed to her. It was exactly what she wanted. She would make this coldhearted man fall in love with her, and then she would break his heart. Just as callously as he had called in the runners to arrest her brother.

24

The air was fresh as it can be only after a cleansing rain. Garrick breathed in deeply and walked briskly. For the first time in a long while he felt light of heart. Happy.

Oliver hurried to catch up with his friend as they made their way to the carriage house.

Thrusting his hands in the pockets of his overcoat, Garrick paused for a moment to gaze into the night. Strange, but it was as if he were looking at the world through different eyes, viewing it less critically and seeing only its calm and beauty.

"Brrrrrr! It's abominably cold for this time of year. For the love of God, Garrick, why are you stopping? Let's hurry to the carriage before I freeze my tail." Flinging his scarf about his neck, Oliver broke into a run. Opening the door to the carriage house, he quickly summoned Garrick's driver. "Hurry and hitch up the horses, man! Be quick about it."

"Yes, sir! Immediately, sir." Opening the door, the carriage driver bowed.

Oliver hurled himself inside, bundling under the thick lap robe in an effort to get warm. "All I want is a hot toddy and the warmth of my own fire. Do you want to come to my house, Garrick?"

"No, not tonight, Ollie." Garrick stepped up and took a seat beside his friend, shutting the door behind him. He was immersed in his own thoughts and anxious for his own bed. Tonight he knew he would have very pleasant dreams of a dark-haired beauty with the most fascinating eyes. Dawn Landon. The name suited her, for surely she was as breathtaking as a sunrise.

"She told me *no*, Garrick. Oh, I knew she would. The heartless old witch. All she could do was scold." Oliver expelled his breath in a sigh. "She'd watch them cart me away to debtor's prison and never lift a finger to help. Oh, I am the most miserable wretch. I suppose this will be the end of our friendship, for I will not be able to buy those stocks back, at least for the moment. Garrick? Garrick?"

"What?" Garrick shrugged in apology. "I'm sorry, I didn't hear you. My thoughts were elsewhere."

"So I noticed," Oliver grumbled. "I said Aunt Margaret turned me down. She said that the only way I'll learn my lesson is to pay the piper. Ha! I wouldn't put it past *her* to have been the one to put that fat little squirrel up to buying the stock. Just to teach me. Do you suppose?"

"It's possible, but I doubt it. One of our competitors is a more likely prospect. John Rennie, perhaps. He has his eye on developing Marylebone Park, but I think we are going to be called to do it. We'll just have to wait and see. I have a feeling our new partner will soon reveal himself."

"I'm sorry, Garrick. I suppose you'll never forgive me! Since Aunt Margaret won't loan me the money, the stock will just have to stay in unknown hands. I don't know what else I can do."

"You can work, Ollie. W-o-r-k! Just as I did when I didn't have two shillings to rub together. It will mean long hours, dedication, and new clients, but it can be done."

"Ugh! It sounds depressing. Couldn't you perhaps give me just a small sum and I could try . . ."

"Oliver!" Garrick's exclamation snapped like a shot.

"All right. Starting tomorrow I'll become a slave to my pencil, ruler, and paper. I'll work myself to the bone if that's what you and Aunt Margaret insist upon." He pouted like a little child. "Garrick?"

"I don't want to talk about it just now, Ollie. I want to indulge in more pleasant thoughts."

"And I know just what of." Oliver pulled the lap robe up to his chin, taking Garrick's portion. "No wonder you want me to be preoccupied with those silly old drawings. That way you won't have any competition. I'm not a fool."

"I know. I'll give you fair warning. I intend to woo and win the fair Miss Landon from Norfolk."

"From Norfolk? Something is not right, Garrick. I tell you my aunt doesn't have a friend in Norfolk. And . . . and did you notice the way this Miss Landon talked? So precise and measured. Too perfect, as if she were trying to cover up an accent or something."

"You're trying to find fault, Ollie, where there is none. I thought she was witty, bright and beautiful. . . ."

"She totally charmed you!"

"Indeed she did." Garrick slapped Oliver on the back. "Cheer up, old chum, and stop being a bad loser. Just because she agreed to go to the theatre with *me* doesn't mean she's one of Napoleon's spies. And even if she were, I'm not certain I would care."

Putting his head back on the seat Garrick closed his eyes, recalling Dawn Landon's enchantingly lovely face. He'd met a lot of women in his twenty-six years but never one of her incomparable beauty. And yet it was her aura of innocence that had touched him even more deeply. Guileless in this age of jaded coquettes, she brought out a protectiveness in him, a gentleness that he'd never felt before. Oh, yes, he intended to woo her, all right. As a matter of fact, he could hardly wait until tomorrow night.

Standing at the drawing room window, Dawn watched the carriage disappear down the road, still astounded that Garrick Seton was an acquaintance of Margaret Pembrooke's. What a ghastly joke! Once she might have been elated, but now that revelation only saddened her. What might have happened had they met under different circumstances? She would never know.

"A handsome man, isn't he?" Margaret Pembrooke had not been blind to the looks that had passed between her young ward and her nephew's friend.

"Yes, he is," Dawn answered stiffly.

"Ah, well, so much for good intentions. Besides, my nephew has done it again. Perhaps he is a totally unsuitable man for you. Put himself in debt to poor Garrick's detriment. I don't know why he puts up with the boy. Certainly Garrick has a good business head. If he didn't . . ." Touching her throat, Margaret Pembrooke laughed. "But I won't go on and on so. At least not until I compliment you, dear. You were perfection tonight."

"Thank you."

All in all everything had gone well. She was pleased. Garrick had been captivated, and she sensed her nephew had been interested as well. Oh, what an interesting little triangle this was going to be, but it would do Dawn a world of good to have two men fighting over her.

"Two young eligible bachelors vying for you the very first night you come out of your cocoon. Quite an accomplishment."

"You're the one who deserves the praise. I couldn't have done it without you." Dawn bent down and hugged the woman affectionately. "I am grateful."

Margaret Pembrooke's eyes misted. "Oh, pooh! I've learned far more from you than you could ever learn from me. You've made me feel alive again, child. Why, even Douglas has taken to smiling now and again. He is, if you have not noticed, your staunchest admirer."

"I know. I couldn't have two more loyal and loving friends." Dawn's smile was melancholy. "I'm very, very happy."

Margaret Pembrooke read through Dawn's words. "No, you are not. Why, Dawn? What happened tonight?" She bristled. "Did my nephew say anything to hurt your feelings? If he did, I swear I will cut him off without a farthing. Oh, well, I already have but I'll . . . I'll take him out of my will. I'll . . ."

"It wasn't Oliver."

"Garrick? Why, I don't believe it. He was totally smitten."

"It's not what he said, but who he is." Dawn couldn't hide her bitterness.

"Who he is?" Margaret Pembrooke was puzzled. "And just who is that, my dear?"

"The bloke who brought the runners down on my Robbie." In her anger Dawn let the word slip out. "Gentleman!" she amended quickly.

"Oh dear!"

"It's his fault I lost my brother." Dawn tightened her lips, remembering.

"You don't know that until you hear his side of the story. Give him a chance to tell you what happened. There was so much confusion, what with everyone running this way and that . . ."

"I know beyond a doubt what he did." Dawn tilted her chin stubbornly. "And as if that were not bad enough he was also the principle witness against my brother."

"You mean Garrick is the young *nob*, as you call him, who sent your brother to Newgate?" Margaret Pembrooke was aghast. Usually she kept up on the news of London. How had this bit of information slipped by her?

Dawn nodded her head in confirmation. "Cruelly and callously, he condemned Robbie to prison."

Mrs. Pembrooke was stunned. "I . . . I didn't realize that it . . . it was Garrick. You were so distraught that day that I hardly took note of anything. To tell the truth, I don't really remember what happened. Except that your brother was taken away. And that you were the most mournful little soul I had ever seen."

Dawn scarcely heard her, she was much too occupied with her own thoughts. "Oh, I have wondered how he happened to be here that day," she said more to herself than to her companion. "But I put it out of my mind. Now I know. Robbie followed me here, undoubtedly worried about my safety. Little did he know that there was someone waiting to pounce. Just like a cat on a mouse. Someone who would delight to trap him and see him put in a cage."

"Why . . . why I can hardly believe that. It doesn't sound like Garrick." Mrs. Pembrooke shook her head, not wanting to believe ill of the man she respected. "He is always the most noble and sympathetic of men. You should hear his tirades about how appallingly the poor in the city are treated. Why, he is the only man I know who treats his servants with unswerving respect."

"He is the man. I know it beyond a doubt. And I will never forgive him." There was much about her past that Dawn had not confided even to Margaret Pembrooke. "He has done me an ill turn, that is all I will say. And as for my being attracted to him, why I wouldn't want him if he were the last man in London."

"Well, all right then." Gently touching her arm the older woman tried to sooth Dawn's disquiet. "I won't ask him here again if he is going to upset you."

Dawn thought about the matter for a long, drawn out moment, then said softly. "On the contrary, I want him to be a frequent guest." Her eyes glittered brightly.

"Dawn, what are you planning?" A flicker of fear swept through Margaret Pembrooke. "The fewer people who know of your . . . your er . . . prior circumstances the better. I think the world of Garrick, but men can be such pompous prigs when crossed. Don't goad him. I warn you. He is not a man to trifle with."

"You are right. He'd more likely than not turn me in to the runners if he knew who I was, without even so much as a wink of his eye. But he'll not learn from me that I was a street sparrow before basking in your kindness."

"It will be a secret between us. Hmm? That's my good dear. There is no tempting fate."

"Let him go on believing I am the daughter of your friend from Norfolk, for I do intend to let him woo me. I intend to be a most charming companion, and when I have his heart within my grasp . . ."

Margaret Pembrooke was taken aback. It was so unlike Dawn to show such hostility, and yet perhaps it was deserved. "Then so be it. I will not involve myself in Garrick's defense if you are convinced he has done you such a wrong. I will urge you to caution, however. Vengeance is a two-edged sword. Be careful, Dawn, my dear, that in your attempt to wound you are not the victim."

25

The new Covent Garden Theatre was filled to capacity. The new building had been built by Smirke only last year to replace the theatre that had burned down. Even though it had been enlarged and modified it appeared there would hardly be room enough for all those who wanted to see the night's performance.

"John Gay's Beggar's Opera has always been one of my favorites. I thought perhaps you would enjoy it too," Garrick was saying.

"Beggar's Opera?" For just a moment Dawn stiffened. A strange selection. Why had he chosen something about beggars? Was he on to her? Had he seen through her pretense after all?

"Good. You haven't seen it before." Garrick chuckled. "It's a rather harsh satire on Walpole and Townshend. Clever. The melodies will undoubtedly be familiar to you. Sweet, simple, singable airs. You should enjoy it."

"I'm certain that I will." Taking a deep breath, Dawn relaxed.

"It should be worth fighting even this ungodly throng to enjoy."

It was as unruly a mob as she had ever seen, Dawn thought, narrowly escaping the elbow of a well-dressed gentleman ahead of them. Money was being taken at the gate. Standing in line, people were pushing and shoving, waiting for the doors to open. As they made their way through the excited crowd, Garrick held Dawn against him, imprisoning her in his strong arms as he gazed smilingly down at her upturned face. She was all too aware of the hardness of his body, searing her through her cloak and the silk of her gown.

Be careful, she told herself, remembering Margaret Pembrooke's warning. Harden your heart. *Don't let yourself care for him again.*

It was much easier said than done. Her feelings ran far deeper than she had suspected. Shivers danced up her spine whenever he touched her. An awareness of him that she could not ignore. His masculinity ignited a longing that touched her heart and craved an outlet. He was certainly the wrong man for her. Why then was it so difficult to think rationally when he was near?

I fell in love with a dream, a man who doesn't really exist, she thought sadly. He was cold and calculating as all men of his social position were. She knew that now. And yet her heart had a mind of its own and it was proving to be stubborn. She must get control of her emotions or all was lost. Taking a deep breath, shifting her position, she managed to maintain her calm, but even so she was immensely relieved when he loosened his hold.

"Come this way." His smile was dazzling. "I helped design this theatre. I know a secret way." He led her away from the jostling crowd to a darkened doorway. They entered and were soon winding their way up a broad staircase.

Inside, the theatre was richly ornamented. Dawn stared in awe at the gilt pilasters and latticed boxes, then quickly remembered herself. She didn't want to give herself away.

The theatre smelled of tallow, glue and a mixture of the fragrances from ladies' perfumes. As she looked down she could see those of lesser rank filling the middle gallery. Simply dressed but they were evidently bursting with high spirits. Indeed when a song or character did not please them, they often threw things to show their disapproval, or so Arien had said.

Dawn knew that pickpockets roamed through the audience, looking for prey. Oh, how Robbie would have eyed the men she was now rubbing elbows with. The rings, heavy watches and fobs, the seals hanging singly or in pairs from waistcoat pockets would have made his fingers itch. *Robbie.* Her brother's name haunted her.

Garrick led her to a private box and Dawn forgot all else in the excitement of the moment, staring in amazement at society's elite. Of course, she and Garrick were every bit as fashionable. He in black coat and buff-colored breeches, she in a dress of maroon silk. Margaret Pembrooke had been emphatic: a well-dressed woman or man never went out without their gloves, thus Dawn wore a pair that went all the way up to her elbows. She plucked them off now as she made herself comfortable on the soft padded seat, looking avidly about her.

Garrick was pleasantly amused by her wide-eyed interest. It was as if he were seeing the theatre for the first time through her eyes. "Well, what do you think?" he asked.

The stage was lit by fixed strips of candles behind the proscenium arch. The candlelight gave off a special glow. "I think it's grand!"

"I hate to admit it, but most of the people gathered here do not share your enthusiasm for the opera. The object is to be seen and to see others, not, I'm afraid, to watch the performers." Again he smiled. "Indeed, I would say that they come to view each other in their finery and to instigate gossip." Leaning over, he nuzzled her ear. She felt his breath ruffle her hair, felt the sensation continue down the whole length of her spine. Her eyelids felt heavy as if she had had too much wine.

Danger, she thought. *Remember what Margaret Pembrooke warned.* She was poised on the brink of a dangerous precipice, balancing precariously. What was happening to her? She couldn't look away. Couldn't move. She felt a warmth flow over her body like a tide.

"There, I do believe we've just caused a bit of scandal." Their eyes met and held and for just a moment the thrill that rushed through her threatened to melt her resolve. "By tomorrow all of London will be wondering who you are." Sheer excitement swept over her, radiating to her very core, but once again she urged herself to caution. Hastily she looked away, concentrating on the scene below.

There was an expectant hum as the audience settled in their seats. Garrick took the seat beside her, peering at the stage to see just what held her rapt attention. The curtains were still drawn but she seemed to be fascinated by the musicians who plucked and tooted as they tuned their instruments and prepared for the overture. She was a strange one, he thought, acting as if she had never seen an opera before. But, then, in Norfolk she might not have. It was possible. Perhaps she'd just never been to a large city before. Undoubtedly she was so lovely that her parents had sheltered her. Well, so much the better.

Dawn's eyes darted this way and that as she watched the procession of glittering women and fashionable men who filled the boxes. One woman in particular caught her eye, a bejeweled, blond who kept glancing angrily over at their box.

"Garrick, that woman. . ." Forgetting herself for a moment she pointed, a gesture which would have horrified Margaret Pembrooke.

"An acquaintance of mine. Think no more about it." So, Stephanie was here tonight. Dreadful timing on his part, but there was nothing to be done about it. Besides, he had a perfect right to choose his own company. Shrugging his shoulders, he turned away.

The murmur of conversation died away, a stillness settled over the scarlet and gold room as the orchestra struck up the first strains of the overture. The curtain was down but the music that suddenly filled the enormous room made Dawn shiver. She felt as well as heard it as each vibration touched her soul. The music reached out to her, soothing her pain, relaxing her. Slowly she closed her eyes.

"You're a music lover, I see." Garrick's voice was low, in harmony with the music as he spoke.

"Yes, I am."

"As am I. We already have something in common."

He was caught up in a web of enchantment and could not take his eyes off her. There was such a hungry intensity in the smile that lit her face, the exuberance with which she enjoyed the melodies. It spoke of a passionate nature, though she seemed to him to be a young woman who had never been kissed. The way she flushed each time he was bold in his appraisal of her confirmed his feeling. It was said that the eyes were windows of the soul, and he saw in hers an innocence that deeply drew him, a vulnerability that he didn't want to bruise.

He was consumed by a desire to kiss her, to be the first to touch her lips, but decided to take it slow. Above all he didn't want to frighten her. Dawn Landon was not the kind of woman he usually kept company with. Her heart was not hardened but fragile. Besides, now was not the place or time. The feelings taking root in his heart were of a private nature that he did not want to exhibit to the elite of London just yet.

Drawing his eyes away he forced himself to focus on the musicians. "I think the *Beggar's Opera* will always be one of my favorites." At least it would be now.

"I *have* heard these melodies before," she whispered. One or two had been her mother's favorites in a time long since gone by. The music was entrancing, weaving a magical spell.

"They are popular English, Scottish, Irish and Welsh ballads. Gay engaged John Christopher Pepusch, a composer of German origin, to mix the sauce and orchestrate the songs. There will be sixty-nine in all." Garrick made no secret of his intent to impress her with his knowledge of the work. "There's an element of romance in it which should please you."

Glancing at him out of the corner of her eye Dawn took note of his strong profile, the firm jut of his chin, the thickness of his rich brown hair as it waved at his temples. His lips looked so very pleasing when he smiled, making him look far less formidable and threatening. Somehow she just couldn't look away. She could have spent every minute of every day just looking at him.

"All ladies I'm told adore such tales."

"They do . . ." Oh, how was it possible that despite all her resolve he was so quickly entangling himself in her heart? She should run away. Take to her heels and speed back to the Dials. What had ever made her believe she could live in his world? Somehow, today, tomorrow or the next she would give herself away and then all would be lost.

The overture ended, the curtain slowly parted. Dawn focused her gaze on the stage, fighting against the gasp which rose in her throat. She had been expecting bright costumes but instead what she saw was like glimpsing a part of her past. Two figures held on to the curtain, one of them dirty and disheveled, his stockings filled with holes, his coat tattered, his three-cornered hat pulled down low upon his ears. By contrast the other man was dressed in foppish splendor, carrying a velvet cocked hat under his arm.

"The beggar insists that he wrote this story. From his point of view. You'll find this ballad opera devilishly amusing," Garrick was whispering in her ear. "It implies that the rogues and thieves of Newgate operate in much the same way as those who run the government. Peculation, bribery and treachery. But then I won't spoil it . . ."

"Newgate!" For just a moment Dawn panicked. It was all she could do to remain in her seat. Newgate. The very name conjured up frightening thoughts.

"It's set in Newgate Prison for the most part. It concerns the criminal underworld of London. The cast of characters is made up of the motliest collection of strumpets, bawds, jades, cutpurses and highwaymen ever assembled on an English stage."

Just the sort of people Dawn had lived among. "Those who circumstance has forced into a dismal life," she breathed. How smug he must feel. How superior. "I feel sorry for such as they."

Garrick cocked his head, taking note of her tone of voice, the look of compassion on her face. "So, you have a kind and sympathetic heart. A good quality in a woman." Quickly he informed her of his own empathy for those unfortunates. "Gay is right in the moral he brings forth in the story. He insists that the rich have all the vices of the poor, but that the poor alone are punished for them."

"Punished so very cruelly," she replied, thinking

about Robbie. Even so she was swept up in the story, completely entranced. It concerned Peachum, a receiver of stolen goods who improved his living by informing on his clients. A man a great deal like Black John Dunn. Seated with his account book, Peachum sang of his confirmed belief in the dishonesty of everyone, setting the tone of the play.

It was a strange kind of love story for Polly, Peachum's daughter had fallen in love with MacHeath, a gentleman-highwayman and the hero of the story. Her marriage to the highwayman so outraged her father that he decided to inform on his son-in-law and thereby make of his daughter a widow. The first act ended as Polly went to her husband's side to warn him of the danger.

"Do you like it so far?" The sets were being changed for the second act, slid into place as the audience watched.

"Yes. . ."

There was a growing sense of intimacy sitting there beside him. She sensed his presence beside her with every fiber of her being. It was dark, with only the stagelights casting a soft, golden glow over them and Garrick's knee was touching hers. She was very much aware of him. And yet knowing the danger didn't make it any easier to pull away.

The dancing light played across his long lashes, nose, and high cheekbones, highlighting the perfection of his face. She had never thought a man could be beautiful, but in his way, Garrick Seton was. Flawlessly handsome. Oh, how she loved his face—the arch of his eyebrows, the strength of his jaw. She wanted to reach out and touch the thick hair where it waved at his temples. It was an impulse she carefully controlled. Fearing he might sense her attraction to him, she turned her attention back to the stage.

"Did you know your hair shines with magenta fire

in the candlelight? Such lovely tresses. The darkest shade of brown I've ever seen. In the shadows it's nearly as dark as a raven's wing." Even his voice drew her, rumbling with its low-pitched masculinity each time he spoke.

She was aware that his total attention was focused on her, but she didn't answer. His eyes were caressing, moving from her head to her neck and lingering on the rise and fall of her bosom. How could she keep from blushing? How dare he be so bold! Her mouth tightened indignantly. She wanted to be angry with him. Perhaps then these other feelings would go away.

"Something is troubling you. What?" he asked, seeing her sudden frown.

"I do not like Peachum," she said quickly, trying to hide her real thoughts.

"Nor do I. Unfortunately there are far too many like him. And not just among thieves." Garrick took her hand, stroking her palm with his thumb as they turned their attention back to the stage.

Act Two opened with MacHeath's gang assembled in a tavern near Newgate, determined to thwart Peachum. With clever dialogue and song MacHeath was arrested, sent to Newgate Prison to await execution only to be freed by Lucy, the jailor's daughter, who had also fallen in love with him.

The rascals reminded Dawn of some of her friends. There was Filch, a young pickpocket who plied his art with all the professional pride of a surgeon, Jemmy Twitcher, Crook-fingered Jack, and Ben Budge, all members of MacHeath's gang. She found herself laughing more than once over their bawdy words and antics.

"See how cleverly Gay has set eight women of the London demimonde to satirize the ladies of high society, their dress, their manners and conversation. The names are monuments to Gay's ingenious wit."

The stage was like a bright oasis, each hue intensified by the brilliant candlelight. The air hummed with music and Dawn found herself trilling along softly. She was enjoying herself immensely. "I hope it has a happy ending," she said at last.

"It has to end on a joyful note. A love story must end thus, you see." *Love,* the word caused a flutter in the pit of Dawn's stomach. It was such a potent word when he said it.

"Most operas are love stories, aren't they."

"Yes, because it is love that really rules our lives if we only stop to think about it." He squeezed her hand affectionately, unleashing a maelstrom of sensations. A quiver danced down Dawn's spine as all her senses came alive.

Oh, how she wished it were possible for her to have a happy ending but such a thing was impossible. Even so a reckless tide of feelings surged through her. She was afraid to speak lest her words flow out in a torrent of emotion. She dare not tell him what was in her heart. Never.

I've embarrassed her, Garrick thought, taking her silence for shyness. Definitely a country girl, he thought with a smile. But in her naïveté was a great deal of charm. She was like a balm to his soul. Perhaps a young woman like Dawn Landon could soften his heart. Or had he grown too cynical? Was there hope for him? As if to seek reassurance he entangled his fingers with hers, pressing lightly.

Dawn thrilled to the touch of his warm hand. Her blood quickened as his arm tightened possessively about her shoulder and she saw the flaring passion in his dark blue eyes. He caught and held her gaze. Their eyes conveyed the attraction without any need for words, but then the thought of Robbie rose like a wall between them and she turned away. If only she didn't enjoy being with him so. It was one thing to pretend, another to allow herself to really care for him. Robbie. Once again she willed herself to remember her brother and the pain this man had caused him. Tears stung her eyes at the thought, and this time she managed to shield her heart and keep her thoughts on the stage.

The evening progressed much too quickly for Garrick's liking. Act Two was concluded and the last act had begun. What did it matter? He hadn't seen one moment of the opera. He had been entirely intrigued with *her*. Indeed, he could have spent every minute of every day just looking at Dawn Landon. Oh, how grateful he was that Margaret Pembrooke had a friend in Norfolk and that that friend had borne a daughter. One thing he knew for certain. He wanted very much to see her again.

"You were right. It did have a happy ending," Dawn said as they joined the throng of people leaving the theatre. "I'm so glad that MacHeath was freed." Somehow it gave her hope as she walked along. At least in stories love always conquered all.

"Dawn . . ." Garrick found himself tongue-tied for the first time in his life when at last they were alone together in his carriage. All he could think of was how much he wanted to kiss her. That he did not was a triumph of discipline.

"Yes, Garrick?" She turned to him, wondering what was going to happen now that they were alone. Strange how the half-light of the street lanterns made his a stranger's face. It made it easier for her to pretend she did not know him.

His eyes moved tenderly over her thick dark lashes, her wide eyes. She must be at least six years younger than he. Innocent and vulnerable. Unspoiled and unpretentious. So different from the type of woman one found in the London social circles. Refreshing and lovely. She was just the kind of woman he had been searching for, a woman who very possibly could share his life and his bed. What would she do if she knew what he was thinking, that he wanted to hold her in his arms and never let her go, to make love to her? He looked at her for a long moment before he spoke. "I cannot tell you when I have enjoyed an evening as much as this one."

"Nor I." She had enjoyed herself far too much. Was she playing with fire? Should she end this dangerous game? Tell him goodnight and never see him again? Though she knew the answer to be yes, she couldn't put her feelings into words.

"I want to see you again and again and again . . ." The words came from his heart. All this time he had been so lonely and he hadn't even realized it until he'd looked into her green eyes and envisioned how love was meant to be.

"I . . . I don't know." It was a perfect chance to tell him a permanent good-bye, but she couldn't say the words. Instead she took the coward's way out. "Mrs. Pembrooke has so many things planned for me . . ." She shifted her position, moving away from him, but as she moved the material of her dress tightened against the firm flesh of her bosom, emphasizing the ample cleavage there. She had beautiful breasts, as Garrick couldn't help noticing.

"I know Margaret very well. She would never deny me your company." *Unless she can read my mind,* he thought. Dawn's bodice was laced in front with maroon ribbons, and his fingers trembled as he thought how much he would like to untie them. "Tomorrow at the same time. Vauxhall Gardens." Compulsively he took her hand again, his fingers closing firmly around hers. Then, bending his head, he pressed his warm lips against the upturned palm of her hand.

Now she couldn't bring herself to say good-bye if she were forced to say the words.

One more time, Dawn thought. *What could be the harm in that . . . ?* Perhaps she might even be able to draw him out, find out what he knew about her brother's fate. Anxious to find an excuse for her weakness, she would agree to see him again. She would go with him, for Robbie. For *Robbie*.

"Tomorrow," she sighed. There, that was that. She'd made her decision. She ignored the voice, whispering in her ear, that knowingly said she wouldn't change her mind even if she could.

26

~~~~~

The setting sun was a great orange disk, hovering like a coin in the sky. It was an unseasonably warm night for November without rain, wind or fog. London had been kissed by cupid's warm breath just to make a special evening for lovers. The weather, Garrick thought, could not have been more perfect if he had planned it. His timing was perfect. Tomorrow Vauxhall Gardens would be closing for the season.

Though the streets surrounding Vauxhall Gardens were clogged with carriages, he was in a most tranquil mood. He was with a beautiful woman, there was magic in the air, and he had a feeling everything was going to work out just the way he intended it to. He'd made up his mind to kiss Miss Dawn Landon. Tonight.

Vauxhall was a perfect place to begin a seduction. The grounds were spacious, and lovers could usually find a quiet place beneath the tall trees on one of the walks that led away from the bright lantern light and the noise of the orchestra. For those who were hungry or thirsty there was generally a vacant booth where they could enjoy a bottle of wine, a cup of tea, or a glass of Vauxhall punch. On special occasions there were fancy dress balls with dancing all through the night, something to keep in mind for the future.

The contagious high spirits of those brightly

dressed Londoners bound for the pleasure garden,
passing by in open curricles and closed carriages, increased his feeling of euphoria. Even the air had a
heady intoxicating aroma. Edging closer to Dawn's
side of the carriage, he took her hand.

"I told you earlier that you look fashionably radi-
ant, but I'll tell you again." She was dressed in a
white linen dress decorated with emerald-green
leaves, a most interesting rigid-brimmed bonnet, and
matching brown cloak. "I'm so glad that you agreed
to come."

"So am I." She had come so very close to telling
him she had a headache, but something had compelled her to come tonight. Well, so be it. "I am anxious to see these famous gardens of yours." She did
not reveal that this was one of her old haunts. Let
him believe she was enthralled.

"Vauxhall Gardens is a most popular and pleasant
retreat, laid out here in Lambeth in 1661. Now it is
undoubtedly as famous as the Garden of Eden." And
just as many sins had been committed here, he supposed. Everyone from the Prince of Wales and his
friends to shop boys, apprentices, pickpockets, and
highwaymen frequented it. The price of admission
was only a shilling, thus it attracted every class. As
naïve as she was, he would have to keep a very keen
eye on her to make certain she didn't come to harm.

The gardens were usually crowded and tonight was
no exception. Leaving Vinnie, his carriage driver, to
park the carriage, Garrick guided Dawn through the
pleasure-loving throng of Londoners. A great crowd
had congregated around a small building that reminded Dawn of an open temple. It was a place she
had always avoided before, for the area was well-
lighted and thus a pickpocket's lament, but now, taking hold of his arm, she was free to satisfy her curiosity.

As they strolled closer they could hear the trilling voice of a soprano who was entertaining the onlookers with an aria. Applause greeted her as she ended the song.

"Margaret tells me you have the voice of an angel. I'd like to hear you sing sometime."

Dawn smiled demurely. "Perhaps that can be arranged. My music teacher comes on Wednesdays and Fridays at two in the afternoon. Margaret, Douglas, and I join him for a quartet."

Hand in hand they strolled along the broad gravel walks. It was an unseasonably warm night. Dressed in winter finery, young men and women, as well as those comfortably along in years, were laughing, chattering, and embracing.

"All of London has decided to stroll tonight." Garrick was anxious to be alone with her. Ah, well, he must not rush the moment. "Tell me all about yourself. We've seldom spoken about *you*."

Dawn tensed. "There's very little to tell. I'm afraid you would be frightfully bored."

"I want to know."

Thinking quickly, she repeated the story she had practiced with her benefactress. "Well, as Mrs. Pembrooke told you, I am from Norfolk. I'm a country girl, really."

A country girl. He'd thought as much. That would explain her delightful naïveté. "From a small town?" His upraised eyebrows asked her which one.

"Woodbury!" It was a name that popped out of her mouth before she even thought. *Dear God, let there be such a place*, she thought.

"Everyone has his own private fantasy. Since I was a boy I've always wanted to live on a country estate. That comes from living one's entire life in the city, I suppose. But the grass is always greener. I would suspect that on the contrary you always had dreams of coming to the city."

"Yes, I've had my dreams. . . ." How could she reveal to him that they had all been of him until he spoiled them? Love. The greatest fantasy of all. She'd given her heart to a shadow, a man who didn't exist. That man had proved himself to be cold, judgmental, and heartless. If he ever found out who she was, if her true identity as a "sparrow" was ever revealed, he would no doubt turn on her, too.

The crowd promenaded the gardens in every direction. In the distance a well-shadowed avenue of trees attracted lovers to a private place where the night air was tinged with romance. A bubbling fountain could be heard nearby.

Following the sound, they soon reached the bank of a pond graced by a gigantic statue of Neptune with eight white sea horses. To the left, another avenue led straight to a statue of "Fate," then on to "The Hermit" and the Temple of Pythia, where a woman in the guise of a Gypsy reclined on a soft bed of hay under a straw-roofed shed. "Palm reading," Garrick said. "Would you like to have her read your future?"

The woman held out her hands, beckoning. "Readings. Only sixpence. You, my fine sir?" The Gypsy, a comely woman with dark olive skin and black hair, eyed Garrick eagerly.

"No!" Dawn was afraid to know the future and afraid that the woman might also be able to see into her past.

"You don't want to know what awaits you?" Garrick shrugged his shoulders. "You are probably wise. Sometimes it is ultimately more interesting to be surprised. Come, let's move on."

The dwelling of the sage-hermit was their next stop, but no one was permitted to enter. They stood on the threshold, admiring the scenery—mountains, valleys, precipices—all worked in canvas and pasteboard. The old man with a white beard, long robe, and wooden staff looked as if he had walked straight out of the Bible.

"The stars are clear tonight. Step forward and I will guide you to your destiny. Will you be wealthy or doomed to poverty? Happy or meet a tragic ending? Will there be a great love in your life or will you spend this life and eternity alone?" He pointed at Dawn, who cautiously stepped past him as Garrick moved forward.

"I know it's probably foolish, but I'm curious. Let's just see what he says." His wink was conspiratorial.

The white-haired man asked Garrick a few questions, disappeared, and then in a few minutes returned to hand Garrick a carefully copied written prophecy of what was to come.

"It says 'things are not always as they seem,' an astute philosophy." Garrick laughed. "It says that I will travel to a far country. That I will never know true need. Mmm. He also prophesies a beautiful woman, one who will join me on my path through life. All in verses, written most colorfully."

Dawn took the paper from his hand, remembering what Arien had told her. He had once gotten a job copying such verses by the dozen. With a toss of her head she crumpled the paper and threw it away.

"Why did you do that?" Cocking his head, he studied her. She seemed to be a young woman of thoughtful intelligence. "Ah . . . I have it. You are the practical type. Margaret Pembrooke has influenced your thoughts with her stoic principles."

"No one can really see into the future. It is folly to think one can." She'd gone to a fortune-teller with her father once, and he had promised them a long life and prosperity. A week later her father was dead and she one step closer to a life on the London streets.

He threw back his head and laughed. "You *do* sound like Margaret! Egad!"

"Margaret Pembrooke has been very kind to me." Dawn scowled defensively.

"I'm certain that she has." Taking her hand, he looped it through his arm. "I meant no offense. Margaret is a fine woman. One of the finest I've ever known. It's just that she has let a disappointment in youth color her views. But enough." A quartet of strolling musicians walked by and he hailed them. "Come, play us a tune. The one about the maiden with hair like the night and eyes like the sky."

A scarlet-clothed musician stepped forward, eyeing Dawn appreciatively. "I would be honored." Strumming his guitar, he broke into a song about a soldier's daughter, ending with the verse:

"Her hair hung down like waves of night,
    They called her the fairest of fair.
She was my fondness, my delight,
    The lass with the long raven hair.
On the green, green grass she laid her head,
    I gave her my heart and my soul.
We made sweet love on the earth's fine bed,
    And now I will ne'er live alone."

With a well-practiced flourish, the musician ended his song and swept his feathered hat from his head as he bowed. Garrick rewarded him with a handful of coins, feeling immensely generous.

All around them amorous couples sought secluded corners. Taking Dawn's hand, Garrick pulled her down upon a stone bench before a splashing fountain. Her beauty moved him deeply. Emotions stabbed his chest like a sharp knife. Just as in the song, he wanted to lie on the grass, to be alone with her.

"Now, where were we? Ah, yes. You were telling me about yourself. That you come from Woodbury. I will bless that town forever in my heart because it nurtured you."

Feeling the treacherous warmth of her attraction to him, Dawn shifted slightly away. *He* was supposed to fall in love with *her*, not the other way around.

"Your parents?" he was asking. "Are they anxious for you to return?"

"No . . ." Tears misted Dawn's eyes as she spoke the truth. "My parents are dead."

"I'm sorry." He felt her pain. "How . . . how did they die?"

"An accident. One that changed my life so very drastically. A family is so important. Without loved ones, life is empty."

She drew herself up, conscious of the tears that wet her face, but it was Robbie she was thinking of, not her mother and father. The last of her family, now he was lost to her.

"Here." He searched in his pocket, found a handkerchief, and dried her tears with the end of it. It was a strangely intimate moment. "I won't ask you any more about it if it is so painful to you."

"It is . . ." Strange that it was the second handkerchief he had given her, she thought. If only he knew. She accepted it, blotted her cheeks, then handed it back.

A few feet away from them a musician began to play a lute, a sad, dissonant song that was no less pleasing to the ears. "Life is full of sadness," the tenor sang. "Life passes by all too quickly. Nothing is forever. Catch your happiness where you can before the moment flies away forever."

"Don't look so sad. Please . . ." Garrick's voice was

soft. The next thing she knew she was in his arms. Dawn's stomach churned in delicious anticipation. *Catch happiness before it flies away.* He could be her happiness, if only . . . *Reach out for it. Forget about the past and begin anew.* She could with him.

Something was happening over which she had no control. Her heart raced with emotion whenever he was near. It was as if they were bound by an invisible thread that kept drawing them together. Was there such a thing as fate? Was it only coincidence, or was it something more?

The moment was right, the magic of the evening mesmerized them. Wrapped in each other's arms, they watched the water spewing from the fountain, mingling with flecks of moonlight. He held her so tightly, so fiercely that she could not break free. Dawn realized that she did not want to as she buried her face in the hollow of his neck.

Before she could speak, his mouth was upon hers, his firm lips parting her softer ones. The kiss was incredibly gentle at first, a mere touching of lips. Then his mouth fused with hers in a searing caress that left her trembling from head to toe as delirious sensations swept through her body. Dawn's only experience with men had been wet kisses and groping hands in the dark. Nothing had prepared her for the jolt of sweet fire that filled her at Garrick's kiss. Engulfed in a whirlpool of sensations, she somehow found herself reaching up to draw him closer, wanting to savor this tender assault. Shyly at first, then with increasing boldness, her tongue moved to meet the heated exploration of his.

She couldn't think, couldn't breathe. Her ears filled with a soundless rushing. She was melting under his touch as her heart pounded, then seemed to stop beating entirely. Dear God, she had never realized that kissing him could be anything like this. Under his intoxicating exploration, she forgot everything. This was the moment she had dreamed about.

Garrick sensed her response and continued kissing her. His lips parted hers, searching out the honey of her mouth. The fragrance of violets engulfed his senses. It seemed that his skin flamed where they touched. His passion, his fierce hunger shook him. Though he was not a ladies' man, he had been with enough women to know that this was something very special.

Taking his lips from hers, he gazed longingly into her face. "Dawn . . ."

A warmth deep within her flowered instinctively at the sound of his voice. It was as if she had been only half alive, waiting for his kiss. "Mmm?"

"I have a confession," he said softly. "I brought you here tonight in hopes that you would grant me a kiss." He untied the lacing of her bonnet and pulled it off. Slowly, languorously, his hand traced the curve of her cheek.

"And as you see, I have . . ."

Her hair was held atop her head by three pearl combs, but he pulled them loose. Entwining his long fingers in the thick strands of her hair, he sent her dark tresses tumbling down her back.

"Lovely hair. I'd wondered at its length." For just a moment he gave himself up to the hungry desire that swept through his body, then stiffened as he regained his self-control. "You are lovely. I thought that from the first moment I saw you." His mouth swept across her cheek to her hair. Burying his face in that soft treasure, he whispered her name again. Suddenly fireworks burst across the sky. Dawn jumped, startled.

"I'm sorry, I should have warned you."

She clung to him, remembering the feel of his lips touching hers. "It's . . . it's all right." It was as if the

heat of their embrace had sparked the explosion, a
most dazzling, brilliant exhibition.

The gardens were bathed in a bluish light. The lanterns looked suddenly pale and dreamlike. Fountains
sprayed, reflecting the glittering light of the fireworks above. For a moment it was as if they were the
only two people in the world, but dimly Dawn became aware of other lovers kissing and gazing up
into the sky. From far away she heard a girl's laughter.

Garrick could not take his eyes from her. With
hungry intensity he watched the way her smile
played upon her lips, the way her green eyes widened
with each spark that lit the night. He was absolutely
mesmerized.

The fireworks ended with a final incandescence
that trailed sparks of red, blue, yellow, and green
across the sky. His response to her nearness was almost as powerful, Garrick thought. The moment his
lips touched hers, his body exploded with a surge of
desire. Even so, there was much more. He felt a
yearning to give, to share, and, yes, to possess. Her
mouth was achingly soft against his, and for one instant he had nearly lost his head completely. The
question was, what to do about it?

He prided himself on being an honorable man, a
sensible man, and yet one kiss had unleashed feelings he had never thought possible. An all-consuming
tenderness tempered his passion now. She was not
some bawd to be tumbled on the grass. He pulled
away, surprised by the thoughts that pummeled his
brain. It was a longing that intensified as the night
progressed. Being with her made him happy. He
wanted her. Not for an hour, a night, but forever.

Later that night after they had danced, kissed
again, and strolled the garden until their feet ached,
she nestled in his arms as the carriage jostled and

jiggled. Dawn's eyes were closed as she leaned her cheek against the muscles of his chest, and he watched her sleep. This lovely, enchanting young woman, touched by innocence yet passion too, was the living, breathing answer to his prayers. Was anything important compared to the exhilaration he felt just holding her? Yes, he wanted her, wanted to marry her. At that moment it seemed to be the only answer, and the only thing in all the world that truly mattered.

27

Garrick lay in bed, staring up at the moonlight dancing on his ceiling. Slowly his thoughts gained coherence as he sorted out his emotions. He was totally and unabashedly smitten with Margaret Pembrooke's ward. He was entertaining thoughts of marriage. Marriage! The very word had once caused every muscle in his body to stiffen, his throat to go dry. Now the thought of spending the rest of his life with Dawn Landon was an enthralling obsession.

Every night since he'd first seen her he'd fantasized about holding her, warm and naked in his arms, giving vent to the hunger her nearness inspired. And so tonight he had kissed her, not realizing what a soul-stirring experience it would be. The moment his lips had touched hers he had known. Dawn Landon was the woman he had waited for, the woman he wanted to take as his wife.

She was a woman with whom he could share his life, his soul, his heart, without fear of betrayal. Unlike some other women he had known, she was not socially ambitious, looking to him to further her position in society. In fact she didn't really seem to care about such things. She was clearly just a shy, beautiful, beguiling country girl. Oh, how she drew his love. Not just that she was pretty. No, it was much more. It was as if his soul cried out to her. He was happy just being near her. She'd give a purpose to his very existence. Indeed, he'd be eager to come home just to find her waiting.

Putting his hands behind his head, Garrick reflected on his life. He was a man who seldom believed in dreams, who held few illusions, knew all too well mankind's faults and so guarded himself accordingly. Success and security were all he'd thought of—until now. Now he wanted someone to share his good fortune, someone to open his heart to, who would love him in return.

Clad in a thin pink negligee, her hair loose about her shoulders, Dawn sat huddled in a chair by the fire, her eyes fixed on the fading embers. How long she sat staring into the hearth she didn't know. Minutes? Hours? She was as still as stone yet the world seemed to quake around her. Touching her fingers to her mouth, she remembered Garrick Seton's kiss and gently licked her lips as if to experience it again. A sweet ache coiled in her stomach. His warm caress had ignited a host of sensations. Desire. Something she had never really felt until she'd met him.

Trembling, she glanced towards her turned-down bed, but her mind was too active, too troubled to permit sleep. Leaning her head back, she tried to quench the flame in her blood that the memory of him evoked, but the thought of his hot exploring mouth and husky voice tormented her with yearning. She imagined his strong arms holding her, caressing her, thoughts that sent tickling shivers up her spine. He'd held her so tenderly as if she were precious to him.

"No!" She didn't want to feel this way. She wouldn't. The feelings that stirred inside her breast for Garrick Seton were certain to plunge her into treacherous waters. *You must never see him again,* she counseled herself, yet feared as soon as the whisper escaped her mouth that it would be impossible to keep such a promise.

Seeking the safe haven of her bed, she pulled the covers up to her chin to bring warmth to her chilled body. Again she tried to push all thoughts of Garrick Seton from her mind but could not. Her mind, her heart, the very core of her being longed for him. Her body, lying warm and yearning, rebelled against common sense. Desire was all too primitive and powerful a feeling.

Tossing and turning on her feather mattress, she pictured every detail of the evening they had spent together. Immersed in a cocoon of blankets where everything was soft and safe, Dawn stared up at the ceiling of her bedroom. Beams of moonlight danced through the windows, casting figured shadows on the ceiling overhead. Two entwined silhouettes conjured up memories of the embraces they had shared. For several long, tormented hours, she lay awake trying to exert her will over her fevered, longing body. She closed her eyes. Wrapping her arms around her knees, she curled up in a ball, envisioning again the face of the man who haunted her now. At last she gave in to the blissfulness of sleep and dreams.

She was in a ballroom where dozens of crystal prisms glittered from the ceiling. Twirling and whirling, brightly clothed figures came within arm's reach. Faces sped by her. She glimpsed her mother and father, but though she tried to touch them, they eluded her, fading away in a cloud of light.

"Dance, my dear." Darting from shadow to shadow she sought the source of the voice.

"Mrs. Pembrooke!"

"Dance." Margaret Pembrooke was on her feet, joining the others with a lilting laugh as she moved across the floor.

"I will dance. I will . . ." Dawn tried to join in, but

the music was faster, louder. Colors blended into each other until the features on the faces were indistinguishable from one another.

"Dance, Dawn!" A chorus of voices cajoled, but she couldn't remember the steps. It was as if she were on a treadmill, trying to join the others before they vanished, but falling short again and again.

"I can't." Waving her arms frantically, trying to keep her balance, she turned just as the floor dropped out from under her feet. She was falling down, down into a great gaping hole.

"No!"

Hands reached out to grasp her. "Dawn . . ." A voice whispering her name.

"Garrick?" She reached out to him as he steadied her. "Oh, Garrick!" She sought the safe shelter of his arms, but he turned away, moving through a cloud of translucent people. Running, she tried to catch up with him just as another figure beckoned.

"Shame, shame on yer, Dawnie. 'Ow could yer e'en gi' 'im the time o' daiy after wot he done?"

"Robbie!" Mists of fog enfolded her and she tried to fight free. "Robbie! But there is such magic when he touches me."

"Because o' him I got me neck stretched, I did. The *steps and the string.* Aye, 'at's wot 'e bought me. 'E killed me, sister dear." Grabbing his neck, he stuck out his tongue in a gruesome mockery of a hanged man. "And 'e'll do yer in as well."

"Oh, Rob, please understand." She tossed her head from side to side as visions swirled madly through her mind.

"There she is! Catch her. She's a thief too!" Black John Dunn pointed accusingly.

"The runners!" She had to find a place to hide. "Garrick!" He was up ahead, beckoning her to come to him. "Help me!"

"She's a thief!" A chorus of voices gave warning. "Hang her!"

"Not now! Please. I'm not! I'm not . . ."

"Hang her!"

"I'm not! I'm not a thief." Bright daylight played across her face, teasing her eyelids awake. Rubbing her sleep-filled eyes, Dawn propped herself shakily up on one elbow and looked around her. *Dear God! A dream. Just a silly dream after all. And yet . . .*

She remembered bits and pieces of the dream and shivered. *Robbie.* How easily she had put him out of her mind. She had been determined to wrest some information about her brother from her aristocratic beau but the spell of the evening had wiped all thought of Robbie from her mind. Was it any wonder then that he had intruded into her dreams to rebuke her?

She could hear the thin tinkling of the watchman's bell in the distance and the Charley's loud voice calling out "all is well."

"For him perhaps but not for me," she whispered forlornly. She'd made a terrible mistake. Nothing in the world could have prepared her for this desperate longing to belong to Garrick Seton, to forget all else but the warmth of his arms. How could she have been so foolish as to be drawn up into the whirlpool of his masculine charm? *The architect and the sparrow,* she thought bitterly.

She sat up so quickly it made her head spin. How could she have done it? She had so cleverly prepared her trap, but she was the one who had been ensnared, just as Margaret Pembrooke warned. She'd fallen hopelessly, helplessly in love and would have followed Garrick to the ends of the earth just to see him smile. She wanted to forget the past and begin anew. But it wasn't possible. She knew that now with a frightening clarity. Sooner or later the truth of who she was and what she had been would be revealed. Would he then look so lovingly into her eyes? No! He'd feel cheated. All her dreams would tumble to earth like apples from an overturned fruit vendor's cart.

She couldn't let it happen. She couldn't allow her heart to be broken. She was a survivor. She had no intention of taking such a chance.

At long last the first light of the sunrise painted the room with a rosy glow. Shivering she slipped on a robe. She could hear the members of the household stirring below. "I should go!" She should pack up her belongings and flee. And yet she could not leave. Not after Margaret Pembrooke had been so very kind to her. She was trapped between two worlds. She had lifted herself from the streets and alleyways of Soho to walk halls trod by satin-slippered feet. How could she be happy among the pickpockets now?

Her predicament played on her mind as she hurriedly donned a russet-colored dress and hurried down the stairs to join her benefactress at the breakfast table.

Margaret Pembrooke was just finishing her pork-and-kidney pie when Dawn entered the dining room. She was thirty minutes late. Margaret frowned and gave a pointed look in the direction of the tall case clock which stood against the wall.

"Good morning." Margaret Pembrooke picked at the remains of her pie with a fork. "I would assume by your tardiness that you had a pleasant time."

"The gardens were beautiful." Nodding to Molly, Dawn turned over her cup. "A half cup of tea and an omelet, please." The girl hurried into the kitchen and returned with a fluffy yellow concoction. The savory aroma of onions and peppers filled the air.

"And Garrick? How was he? Did you enjoy his company? Do you wish to see him again?" Margaret Pembrooke suddenly had the countenance of a smiling cupid.

"He was very polite. I had a wonderful time. But no. I do not wish to see him again." Dawn's tone was emphatic. "We're ill suited to one another for more reasons than I had supposed."

Mrs. Pembrooke regarded her thoughtfully, her gray eyes sharpening their gaze. "You're trying to convince yourself, but you can't fool me, my dear, nor can you fool yourself."

Silently Dawn took several small bites, averting her eyes. "All right. I'll tell you the truth. I love him!" There, it was said. "But there can never be anything between us."

"Your brother?"

"That and other things." A frown etched two vertical lines between Dawn's well-shaped eyebrows.

"Your unfortunate past." Margaret Pembrooke touched her mouth with the corner of her napkin. "You fear he will find out? I can assure you that I will go to great lengths to make certain that he does not." She had already instigated such a process.

"I know you would, and for that I thank you but . . . you see, you were right when you warned me. So much for vengeance." Dawn forced herself to eat a bite of the omelet, washing it down with a gulp of tea. She had lost her appetite. "Your nephew has asked me repeatedly to let him call, and I have decided to agree."

"I see, though I can not applaud your wisdom. Trading Garrick for Oliver is a bit like trading a stallion for a goose." Nevertheless she smiled. "But we will see what happens. Indeed we will see. It may very well increase the stakes in this game and make it far more interesting."

"It is not a game. Not now." Indeed she recognized with agonizing clarity that it was not. She had let a tiger out of its cage, and now she wasn't quite sure how to get it back in. How was she going to stop caring about Garrick Seton? Perhaps it was impossible. But above and beyond all she had to try.

28

❧❧ ❧

The late morning sun gilded the muddy waters of the Thames. Thick smoke belched forth from smokestacks and chimneys, obscuring the horizon. The bewildering clamor of human voices, rattling wheels, and horses' hooves filled the air. An ordinary day, yet somehow Garrick saw the city through different eyes, occupying himself with reading signboards as the carriage made its way through the melee.

Deciding to walk, Garrick alit from his carriage, and hastened down the cobbled streets towards his office, pausing only to buy an apple tart temptingly displayed on a tin at the pastry cook's door. He'd slept late, an unusual occurrence in his well-ordered and disciplined life. The enticing erotic visions he'd savored last night and early this morning were surely responsible, pleasant dreams in which he made passionate love to Dawn Landon.

Walking behind two middle-aged men who plodded steadily along with no object in view but the countinghouse, he was aware of just how dull his life had become. Indeed, as he watched the men walk without stopping to exchange even a hurried salutation, he was doubly thankful that Dawn Landon had come into his life. Just thinking about her, about last night, lightened his mood and gave him a feeling of elation. For the first time in years he saw the possibility of filling the aching void in his heart.

Bond Street had an unmistakable character. It was a quieter, truly "businesslike" street. The large white beautiful flagstones that lined the roadway were a touch Garrick's architectural hand had lent to the area. Passing the shops with their plate glass windows, his jaunty step carried him up the steps and through the door to his office.

"Good morning, Ollie!" he said merrily, taking off his hat, scarf, and coat and depositing them on the brass rack beside the door.

"*Afternoon,* don't you mean." Oliver sat at the far desk, his sleeves rolled up to his elbows, his shirt front jutting open. There was a peevish expression on his face as he looked up from his drawing. "Gad, how I remember the tongue-lashings I received when I sauntered in at such a late hour. My, my, my, how times do change."

"Don't be grouchy, Oll. Not when I'm in such high spirits." Clasping his hands behind his back, Garrick walked nonchalantly over to Oliver's desk. "What are you working on?"

"What does it look like?" Oliver's voice was husky with laryngitis.

It was an intricate drawing that displayed terraces, villas, markets, roadways, and canals. Oliver had even sketched in a landscape of trees and shrubs. "Marylebone Park. Impressive, Ollie."

"I'm glad you approve, since I've worked my posterior off doing it. Why, would you believe I've been here since six thirty this morning?"

"No."

"Well, I have. It was so bloody early, in fact, that I witnessed a sky free of the hideous gray smoke that usually enshrouds it. And yet just like a swarm of ants there were people milling about, grubby souls going about the drudgery of their daily lives. It made me realize a few things." Wrinkling up his nose he sneezed. "Excuse me."

Rolling up his own shirtsleeves, Garrick sat down at the other desk and picked up his pencil and drawing scale. "Such as?"

"That money is not a thing to be thrown away. Without it a man is in a sorry hell. You are right to be so diligent, Gar. I see that now. Though I do wish there was an easier way to wealth. Aunt Margaret, for example. My uncle left her enough money to share."

"Perhaps she will be more generous with you if you prove yourself reliable." Thinking of Margaret Pembrooke brought Dawn Landon to mind and he smiled. "I'm exceedingly fond of your aunt, as you know. Particularly now."

Oliver sighed, his petulant frown giving in to a smile. "All right, out with it. I know you're just dying to tell me about last night. Oh, no, you haven't fooled me for a moment. I know why you have been grinning like a buffoon and looking so buoyant since you came through that door. You're veritably floating on air. Did you kiss her?"

"Indeed I did." Just the memory ignited his desires anew, and he took a deep breath to cool his ardor. Her mouth had been achingly soft against his. The moment their lips touched he'd known something very special was happening between them.

"And?" Ollie raised his brows suggestively, expecting more. "Did you . . ."

"No! Perish the thought. She is every inch a lady." Garrick laughed softly. "But I would be lying if I didn't confess I wanted to. Last night I spent a torturous night alone in bed."

"Oh? So Garrick Seton has succumbed to love. Delightful. I never thought I'd see the day." Throwing back his head, Oliver merrily gurgled an insinuating giggle. "Sleeping alone, but not for long, hmm, Gar?"

"No. I intend to do something about it. I intend to ask Miss Dawn Landon for her hand in marriage." London was a frivolous, flippant, venal, and villainous city. Was it any wonder then that he wanted to offer Dawn Landon the protection of his name? She was like a newly blossoming flower whose perfection he didn't want marred by society's scandalous sins.

Oliver's laughter quickly sobered. "You intend to do what?" He was incredulous. "No!"

"I want to marry her, Ollie. It is as simple as that."

"Marry a woman you have just met?" Bolting from his chair, he grabbed Garrick's arm, then let go. "No! I won't let you do it. You've given me some good advice over the years, and now I'll give you some. *Don't do it!*"

"Ollie, I knew it was what I wanted the moment I kissed her." Garrick smiled as he remembered that moment very vividly. "How can I make you understand? I've never experienced anything like the feelings that surged through me when our lips met."

Oliver broke out in a tirade. "So you kissed her. A kiss is a kiss. I daresay, if you married all the young women you've kissed, you'd be a bigamist." He paced round and round Garrick's chair like a dog chasing its tail. "You know nothing about her. Three evenings, that's all the time you've spent with her."

"Ollie, stop circling about. You're making me dizzy." Rising to his feet, Garrick blocked Oliver's path. "I'm not an impulsive man, as you well know, but there are times when a man just senses some things. I want to protect her."

"Then get her a bloodhound, old chap! But don't let her put a collar on you."

"It's time I took a wife, Ollie. I want a home and children. What's more, she's everything I could want in a woman. She's beautiful, delightfully charming, innocent . . ."

"Stop right there!" Crossing his arms, Oliver leaned against the desk. "She's lovely, it's true, but I would hardly imagine she is the innocent you have conjured up in your mind." Taking out his handkerchief, he blew his nose. "Dreadful cold. The chill the other night did me in, old fellow. As I was saying, she is amusingly naïve, but a woman after all. No saint, Garrick. They are all the same, bless their deceiving little hearts. Undoubtedly she has come to London intent on nabbing a rich and proper husband. For the love of God, at least wait a proper spell before you offer yourself up on a platter."

"You're wrong about her, Ollie. I know all about deceiving women. My mother is a prime example." He would never be able to forget the parade of men his mother had taken to her bed. She had used various men like rungs on a ladder to climb to the top and secure her future, and then proceeded to amuse herself with any male who took her fancy. "I loathe that kind of woman. But Miss Dawn Landon is not like that. She is as fresh and unspoiled as country air, the kind of woman I've been waiting to meet."

"Balderdash, as my aunt loves to say to me. There is something very strange and mysterious about that young lady. She's too perfect to be believed." Putting a finger to his nose, he warded off a sneeze. "In the meantime, I've set some inquiries in motion. To quell my own curiosity, I might say. I want to find out all about the Landons of Norfolk."

"Spying on her, Ollie?" Garrick's voice trembled with suppressed anger. "That isn't like you. You're usually such a devil-may-care sort."

"My sudden reversals have changed all that. I've seen what sort of life the uh . . . uh . . . unfortunate endure in this city, and I want no part of it. I've decided it's about time I used my head. I'm not certain I am comfortable with this young woman who suddenly shows such devotion to my aunt. I will not be cheated out of my rightful due."

Garrick glowered at his friend and partner. "You can be certain you won't be cheated by Miss Landon."

"Tut, tut, tut! Just give me two weeks and I will prove to you that your fantasy is but a vision you've conjured up in your mind. A woman is a woman, after all." Returning to his desk, Oliver picked up a notepad and began scrawling with a pencil. "Two weeks, that's all I ask."

29

Garrick didn't know what had possessed him to come to the East End of London when he found himself looking up at the sign of the Red Feather Inn. It was the only tie he had to the little beggar girl, his only hope of finding her. For some undefinable reason she'd been on his mind a great deal of late. Perhaps because of the happy future he now envisioned for himself. He wanted to share at least a pittance of his good fortune. With that thought in mind, he was determined to find the mobcapped child, to ascertain that she was safe and offer his friendship to her once again.

Before him lay the badly lit alleys, the rundown, narrow houses. He shuddered to think that it was here the poor child was condemned to live out her days. Why hadn't he acted sooner? Taken her under his wing? Because he had been too concerned with himself, he thought in self-condemnation. Well, he would find her and when he did he'd do all he could to give her the chance to lift herself out of her poverty.

Dressed in a plain forest-green dress, one of the rain hats she had created, and leather shoes, Dawn wrapped herself in a thick woolen shawl, and braved the damp, dreary day. It was time to visit Soho and see how Jamie, Farley, Taddie, and the others were faring. She had been selfishly cautious long enough. Besides, they might have gotten word about Robbie since last she had seen them.

Picking up a basket filled with day-old rolls, bread, a large slab of ham, some cheese, and fruit that Cook had granted her from the kitchen, she slipped out the front door. They'd have a bit of lunch while her friends filled her in on what had been happening in the East End.

"West End, East End . . ." It was all too easy to forget that she really was a merchant's daughter whose mother had died in debtor's prison, a reformed street sparrow who through the kindness of an elderly woman had been lifted out of the depths of poverty and despair. She was not one of the *ton* no matter how correctly she spoke or what fine dresses she now wore. She was Dawn *Leighton,* not Dawn Landon. Above all she must remember so that when this dream ended she would not be inconsolable. All good things must come to an end sooner or later, or so Robbie had often said.

Fearful of taking the Pembrooke carriage to her destination, Dawn trudged on foot, pausing to catch her breath. The good life was making her soft. Once she would not have thought a thing of walking a mile or two; now her feet and legs ached after several blocks and she was tired. Most of the streets in London's fashionable area were paved but there were many thoroughfares which were little more than tracks, a haphazard jumble of round stones and cobbles placed outside shops by individual shopkeepers and householders. She was careful to watch her step as she moved along.

Carriages with trunks and bandboxes between the drivers' legs and outside the apron rattled briskly up and down the streets. Stepping into the street, Dawn hailed a hackney and peeked out through the window as the vehicle rumbled along, leaving the pillars and brick of the West End for the pot holes and wooden walls of the East.

The cobbles were strewn with decayed cabbage leaves, broken hay bands, and all sorts of litter from the vegetable carts. Here and there an apprentice or laborer, with his day's dinner tied up in a handkerchief, walked briskly to his work. Men, women, and children shoved and fought their way through the crowded streets. Those dressed in rags struck a pang of grief in Dawn's heart. When the cold of winter took over the city, they would have little protection against the raw winter winds.

"Driver, stop here!" Paying him his fare, she quickly alighted and made her way to the house she had once shared with her pickpocket friends. A young boy, aged seven or eight, purposefully jostled against her, his hands lightly skimming her body in search of valuables. Seeing Dawn's knowing look, he quickly bounded away.

"Boy! Boy!" Though Dawn meant him no harm, indeed had it in mind to offer him one of Cook's rolls, he fled.

Dear God, she thought, *was it really so very long ago that I had that same tormented look?* Closing her eyes for just a moment, she remembered Black John Dunn and his school of crime, where a coat had been suspended from the wall with a bell attached to it. Dawn and the others had made attempts to take a handkerchief or purse from the pocket without ringing the bell. Over and over she had practiced this skill until she could do it adroitly. Now thanks to Margaret Pembrooke she would never have to steal again.

After the many weeks spent in Pembrooke House, she felt the squalor of the streets was even more shocking. She remembered those days all too vividly. Days of hunger, days of fear. This was what she had left. In that moment Dawn knew beyond a doubt that she could never return to her former life. Never! Even so it was good to lay eyes on Taddie as she appeared in the doorway of her old room.

"Who are yer and wot . . . Dawn!" With a squeal of delighted surprise Taddie ran forward. Her newly enlarged stomach got in the way as she hugged Dawn to her. "I didn't think we'd e'er see yer again, I didn't. And don't yer look fine . . . Yer didn't forget me."

"I couldn't forget you, Taddie. Are you well?" Dawn was worried about the dark circles under the young woman's eyes.

"Well enough. Got me a young one on the way, as you can see. Thought I'd rue my carelessness but I . . . I . . . well, I want the child. It will gi' me company."

"Company? Are you living here alone, Taddie?" Dawn's gaze searched for the others.

"Farley, Jamie, Arien and the others 'ave gone. They were in a state of confusion after Robbie . . . well . . . Farley, 'e joined with ole Tweezer. Jamie's on 'is own. Arien is writing plaiys for the theatre. But I've joined wi' another gang, I 'ave." Touching her stomach, she looked down at her toeless shoes. "My baby's father lives 'ere."

Dawn set down the basket, doubly thankful now that she had brought food. "I've brought a few things. We can sup while you tell me what's been happening." Since there were no chairs or table, they sat on the floor.

"We was all panicked after Robbie was cornered and sent to . . . to that place," Taddie said between mouthfuls of bread and cheese. "Then, when yer didn't come back, we was all sure someone 'ad done yer in."

"Has . . . has there been any word on my brother's fate? I've tried to find out, but it's as if he just disappeared." Taking a deep breath, Dawn shivered as she asked, "Was he . . . was he hanged?"

"Jamie doesn't think so. He paid someone wot could read to scan the lists. Even went so far as to view several of the 'angings from afar. No, he's still behind Newgaite's wall if yer ask me."

"But Mrs. Pembrooke said he wasn't there and . . ." Dawn shook her head. "Never mind. I'd much rather believe he's still alive. It gives me hope." She'd ask Margaret Pembrooke once again to use her influence to search for him.

"God 'elp 'im if 'es been taiken to the hulks. Or transported. Poor Robbie. . . ." All criminals feared the unseaworthy ships that had been converted into prisons nearly as much as they feared the gallows. Conditions in the hulks were unspeakably horrible. Criminals were packed together very closely on three decks. At night the hatches were simply screwed down, leaving the convicts to fight among themselves and suffocate in the fetid darkness. Or if they were fortunate they had candlelight. Hell on earth, it had been called.

"I've got to find out!" Reaching out, Dawn grasped Taddie by the shoulders. "Please help. If you hear any word, see anything, send a message to this address." Hastily she scribbled the street name on a piece of discarded newspaper with a piece of charcoal. "If . . . if Robbie is still alive, I've got to free him. Somehow . . ." Her eyes misted with tears. "If he's dead, I want to see him put in a proper grave."

"I'll do all that I can to 'elp. Keep me eyes and ears open, I will." Licking her fingers, Taddie smiled sadly. Though she didn't say anything, Dawn knew what she was thinking, that it was very possible he had been hanged and his body given to the surgeons who dissected them in their quest to find out how the body worked. "In the meantime, taike care o' yerself."

They talked of many things before the church bell struck three. Rising to her feet, Dawn said a tearful good-bye. Taking the shawl from around her shoulders, she draped it around the young woman. "This is for you, to keep you and the baby warm. Be careful, Taddie. And . . . and if you're ever in need, don't be afraid to send for me. I'll never be too busy to help a friend. . . ."

"I'll keep that in mind, but I'm doing just fine. Jack has nimble fingers. He taikes care o' me, 'e does." She kissed Dawn on the cheek. "I'll tell Jamie and Farley yer was 'ere if I see 'em. And . . . and be careful yerself."

"I will. Be happy, Taddie." Dawn started for the door but Taddie called her back. "You remembered something about Rob?"

The young woman shook her head. "No. About ye. Right after Robbie was taken there was a man asking about a young girl in a mobcap. Seemed desperate to find 'er 'e did. Jamie and Farley thought he was askin' after ye and I began to think so too."

"A man? What did he look like?"

"Tall. 'Andsome as an angel. Offered up a reward 'e did, but none o' us would turn yer in even for a fortune."

"I know, Taddie." Garrick Seton had been asking about the girl in the mobcap. Because he had finally realized that she and the woman who had ensnared him at the docks were one and the same? The thought chilled Dawn to the bone. How long would it be before he suddenly realized just where he had seen her before?

30

It was a tranquil afternoon despite a chill in the breeze that rippled through the air. Garrick stood before the gate of Margaret Pembrooke's huge house with hat in hand, feeling much like a schoolboy. Damned if his stomach wasn't a bit queasy. Ah, yes, he was nervous, he who always took such pride in his self-assurance.

On impulse he had stopped by the estate on his way home from the office, hoping he could persuade Miss Dawn Landon to go for a carriage ride with him. Now that he was here he had second thoughts. He didn't want to appear too bold by showing up out of thin air and yet he needed to see her, if just for an instant.

Coward! he scolded himself. He was losing his nerve. She was only a woman, albeit a lovely one, and he was certainly experienced in dealing with the fairer sex. He willed his feet to move.

Catching his reflection in a pane of the parlor window, he hurriedly ran his fingers through his tousled brown waves. Leaning casually against the door frame, he crossed his arms over his chest and rapped with the large brass knocker. To his surprise it was not Douglas but Dawn who opened the door.

"Hello!" he said jauntily. His mouth curved up in a lopsided grin that would have melted the heart of the most prudent, hard-hearted spinster. His blue eyes gazed at her in a mesmerizing stare. One of his strong hands rested lightly on the railing.

Dawn eyed him warily, her heart doing somersaults in her chest. The mere sight of him was nearly enough to make her throw all caution to the wind. What was he doing here?

Garrick read the question in her eyes. "I just came by on the hope that perhaps I could show you a bit more of London before the sun sets." He nodded towards his waiting carriage.

His white linen shirt and cuffed wrists and the buff breeches that clung to his lower body like a second skin emphasized his muscular body. The memory of his lips molded to her own came unbidden to her mind. She wanted to go with him, wanted to be with him.

"A carriage ride?" She started to smile but remembered Taddie's warning. Garrick Seton was searching for the girl she knew to be herself. What if this were naught but a game? What if he knew at this very moment exactly who she was but was merely toying with her? It was entirely possible.

"There's a chill in the air, but it will be warm inside. There's a lap robe and . . ."

"No," she said all too quickly. Every muscle in her body stiffened. She met his eyes steadily, unsmiling.

Her reserve stunned him. After the kiss they had shared he was expecting a far different greeting but reasoned that after all it was daylight and they were in view of others' prying eyes.

"No? Not even to watch the sun being swallowed by the Thames?"

Dawn swept an agitated hand across her brow. This was going to be much more difficult than she had imagined. Garrick Seton was not the kind of man to take no for an answer. But she had made up her mind and had to maintain her resolve. "I can't, Garrick. Not even to watch the sunset. But thank you for your invitation . . ."

In the silence that fell between them she found it difficult to breathe. Her breasts rose and fell sharply, drawing his gaze. His eyes dropped to the soft mounds shrouded in white muslin and lingered there for a long-drawn-out moment before moving back to her face.

"I dreamed about you last night," he said softly, reaching out to touch the soft curve of her cheek with his thumb then trailing it down the graceful length of her throat.

Dawn flushed to the roots of her hair. "You shouldn't have," she said, quickly pulling away. Oh, dear God. Loving him seemed to be the most natural thing in the world when she was with him. She was helpless to deny the effect he had on her. She opened her mouth to speak, but her words were lost as her eyes met his heated gaze.

"Ah, but I couldn't help dreaming about you nevertheless. You have enchanted me most thoroughly, you see." Had there ever been a more romantic figure than this handsome young man? Dancing beams of sunlight played across his face emphasizing his appeal. A lock of thick hair had fallen across his forehead and she felt the urge to brush it back.

"Garrick, I . . . I . . ." Her heart surged with hope as she stretched out her hand to him, but just as suddenly she pulled it back. Loving him and giving in to that emotion might very well be the most dangerous thing she had ever done in her life.

"If I have my way, I'll be with you every moment that I can. That is what I wish, Dawn. To be together . . ."

With the greatest effort Dawn tore her eyes from his face. Despite all her protestations to the contrary she had as much backbone as a titmouse. One smile from him and she turned to jelly. Fighting against her emotions as she was, her voice held a reproachful tone.

"You take much for granted, sir."

Her reaction stung Garrick. He was not expecting rebuff, nor was he accustomed to it. He couldn't be mistaken. Surely she was attracted to him. Even now he could read it in her eyes. Why then was she refusing? It was very simple. He *had* taken her too much for granted. Being a young woman unused to such attentions, she would undoubtedly feel apprehensive until she knew his intentions were noble.

"I assure you that I do not," he said, but he had. Because he was so smitten with her, he had just assumed that his feelings would be returned. It was as simple as that. But Dawn Landon was a woman who would have to be wooed, he thought. "And I will prove it to you, madam." This said, he turned around and walked to his carriage without once looking back. Her heart was a prize that had to be won. Well, let the wooing begin.

Dawn awakened to the sweet fragrance of flowers. Sitting up in bed, she scanned the room and thought for just a moment she'd been transported back to Covent Garden. "Roses!" White, pink, and red flowers met her eyes.

"Aye. Roses, mum." Mrs. Pembrooke's grinning young maid was skillfully arranging the bouquets. "Not one, but four dozen of them. My, my, my. It seems Mr. Seton is quite smitten."

"Oh, dear!"

"And yesterday the bonbons! A whole basket full of them. Your young man is quite attentive. Oh, how I wish . . ." Blushing, she turned her face away from

Dawn's avid stare. "I mean, he's . . . you're so fortunate, you are!"

Fortunate, Dawn thought. *Hardly that. Just the opposite in fact.* Garrick Seton was playing havoc with her life and her emotions. *Stay away from Garrick Seton, forget him.* It was much easier said than done. Obviously he had no intention of letting her elude him. In the three days that followed his visit to the house to invite her for a carriage ride he had wooed her with a vengeance, making it all the more difficult for her to be firm in her resolve. And yet she had to. Succumbing to his charm would only bring heartache and possibly more dire consequences.

"Bonbons are certain to make one quite fat. And . . . and as for roses, they make me sneeze. Take them away, Agnes. I don't want them in here."

"Take them away?" Agnes looked at Dawn as if she had suddenly lost her mind. "But . . . but, mum." The young maid fondled the soft petals lovingly. "They are so beautiful."

"Please!" Dawn's voice was sharp and she regretted her peevishness. She was hardly one to give orders to this poor girl. "Put them in your own room if you'd like, Agnes," she said in a gentler tone. "I give them to you. Someone should appreciate them."

"Put them in my room, miss?" The maid's blue eyes opened wide in disbelief. "They're mine? Truly?"

"Yes, I give them to you."

"Oh, thank you!" With a squeal of delight the young woman quickly gathered them up and carried them from the room, as if fearful Dawn would change her mind. The door closed with a soft thud.

Well, I've gotten my wish, Dawn thought sadly. She'd wanted Garrick's affections, had dreamed about it night after night. Now that dream had turned sour, for she was caught in her own trap and wasn't quite sure what to do about it. Pulling the covers up to her chin, she sought the haven of her pillows and thought of all the reasons she should hate Garrick Seton. He was responsible for Robbie's sorry fate. That alone made any affection for him out of the question. He was heartless to have done such a thing. And was he still trying to locate the young girl in the mobcap? To put her in Newgate too? He was an unfeeling monster.

The only reason Garrick Seton is sending me flowers and such is because he believes me to be acceptable. Being Margaret Pembrooke's friend makes me eligible. He would have turned up his nose in an instant, come to retrieve every one of his flowers, had he known who she really was. Just like all the others of his class, he was a snob! Cold and unfeeling. Deaf, dumb, and blind to the suffering going on right beneath his nose.

Closing her eyes, Dawn tried to forget him, but his face stayed in her mind's eye. The way his hair brushed his forehead, the shape of his nose, the width of his shoulders, the way he walked and talked all haunted her. And his mouth . . . full and artfully chiseled, possessing a sensual curve when he smiled. Touching her lips, she remembered his kiss and felt a warm glow flicker through her.

No . . . I won't let him bother me this way, she told herself. *I won't let him turn me into a lovesick ninny!* In aggravation she threw back the covers and rose from her bed only to discover that Agnes, in her hurry, had forgotten one solitary red rose. Lying all alone on the carpeted floor, it beckoned her touch, and though she knew she should ignore it, she bent to pick it up. It was too fragile, too lovely to be crushed underfoot. With trembling fingers she touched the velvety petals and sighed. It was then she saw the note Agnes had left behind.

"I will never forget our kiss nor your sweetness,"

the note said. "I want very much to see you again. Love, Garrick."

And she wanted to see him again too. Dear God, but she did. No matter how stubbornly she might try to convince herself that she hated Garrick Seton, she never would, never could.

Robbie. Remember Robbie! Her mind screamed a warning that was answered by her heart. She tried to tell herself again and again that Garrick Seton was a cruel, unfeeling man, yet how could she forget the kindness he had shown that first day in the carriage? There had been genuine concern in his deep blue eyes. He hadn't given her away, though he well might have. Instead he had been kind, had even insisted on taking her home, and she nothing but a little waif. And then again the day he had given her back the stolen purse. He had been worried about her, he said. Not a heartless snob, then, but a compassionate man. Nor in truth had he sought Robbie out unjustly. In all fairness she had to admit that Robbie had stolen from him. Had she not interceded, her brother would have been guilty of conspiring to murder him.

"I want very much to see you again," she read again. Oh, if only she could confide in him. Tell him the truth. Perhaps he would understand the circumstances that had put her out on the street with Black John's band. She had been only a child when she embarked on her life of crime. All that had changed now. With Margaret Pembrooke's help she was trying to make something of herself. Surely she deserved a chance. Tell him! Perhaps there was a chance for happiness after all if she were honest with him.

No! The memory of the night in the warehouse came back to haunt her. He might forgive the child, but not the woman he thought a whore. She had tried to reason with him then, but he had shown his loathing, had even accused her of trying to kill him. "Your sweetness," he had written. How disillusioned he would be if he knew the truth. She was a thief, not some blushing country miss. She couldn't tell him. Seeing that look of disgust again on his face would be her undoing. And he would look at her like that again when he found out.

Dawn viewed the rose through a mist of tears knowing what had to be done. There was really only one answer. She had to cool Garrick Seton's desire by making him believe she was interested in another man.

Ollie greeted Garrick with a triumphant grin as he walked through the office door. "Good morning, Gar!"

"Good morning, Ollie. My, but you look quite like the cat that has swallowed the proverbial canary. Care to tell me what is up your well-tailored sleeve?"

"Oh, let's just say that I'm contemplating my success. Remember our talk about your new ladylove?"

Garrick's brow furled in irritation. "Yes." He didn't like Oliver's smug look. "Have you found out something about her?"

"I think I just might. You see, I have some acquaintances who have a country estate in Norfolk. It seems there are only three families with the name Landon in the entire area. Care to make a little wager as to whether your Miss Landon is among them?"

"A wager? You know I don't gamble, Ollie."

"Mmm? I say this oh-so-proper young woman is an actress, hired by someone out to nab my aunt's fortune. A Drury Lane darling."

"An actress? Preposterous!"

"If you don't think so, then as they say at the track,

'put your money on it.' I say she is not from Norfolk and her name is not Landon. Will you make a bet?"

"All right, I will! But you really are going too far, Ollie. Just because you can be devious on occasion is no reason to see such perfidy in others. Really! You bloody well can be a trial at times."

"Trial or not, I'm going to prove just what a fine friend I can be by stopping you from making a ghastly mistake, old boy. Marriage to Dawn Landon, indeed!" Scribbling with his pencil, Oliver made a few calculations, grinning all the while. "You say you are brave enough to wager, eh?"

"If that will prove something to you about my trust in the young woman, then yes. I believe her to be exactly who she says she is." Flinging his hat across the room, Garrick sprawled in his chair. "But you are hardly in a position to put up any money for so foolish a venture as a bet, I would say. You have very little money left."

"Ah, but I have my matched pair of bays. Beautiful horses. Against your carriage?"

"Are you serious? You must be mad, Ollie. But to make you see the foolishness of your ways, I'll agree. I've always wanted two such splendid horses."

"And I have always had my eye on that leather-padded vehicle of yours. It would be perfect for seductions. Agreed?" He held out his hand and Garrick took hold of it in a firm handshake.

"Agreed. Though I hate to fleece a friend. But if losing will teach you a lesson . . ." Unrolling a current drawing, Garrick bent his head to work, trying to put the matter out of his mind. Ollie was just a bit jealous, that was all. Were Dawn Landon batting her eyelashes at Ollie, it would be a far different story. And perhaps he was afraid that a woman would disturb their camaraderie. Oliver was always espousing the advantages of bachelorhood and the pitfalls of being wed, but there were also benefits to matrimony.

Smiling, Garrick thought how pleasant it would be to return home at day's end to find Dawn waiting in the doorway to greet him. After they were married he'd send her flowers every day, just as he had this morning. And tonight he'd invite her to the theatre again, *The Beaux Stratagem* was playing at the Lyceum, a delightful tale he was certain she would enjoy. He hadn't been with her for six days. Six days! It seemed a lifetime. Certainly that was a sign of how much he cared. He'd never longed for a woman's company so fervently before. He ached to be with her, to savor her lovely smile, to touch her again. The very anticipation made him feel like a young boy again. Perhaps love did make one ageless.

A soft tap on the door interrupted Garrick's musings and he rose to answer the knock. A young boy he recognized as being from Margaret Pembrooke's house stood in the doorway. Hope soared in his heart. It was a message from her. No doubt she was thanking him for the roses.

"I'll take that, Dickon," he said, rewarding the lad with a shilling for his trouble. With trembling fingers he turned the envelope over only to feel a jolt of disappointment when he saw it was for Oliver instead. "For you, Ollie. Although it doesn't look like your aunt's handwriting."

"Let me see!" Oliver tore the note from Garrick's hand. Loosening the wax seal with his pencil, he opened it with a flourish. "My, my, my, my. It appears my invitation has been accepted." He patted Garrick on the arm with an air of bravado. "My condolences, old chum. It appears you have a bit of competition for your lady fair, whoever she turns out to be. Ah, this should prove interesting."

"What do you mean?" Garrick's brows shot up as he snapped the question.

"Why, it seems Your Miss Dawn Landon may not be yours after all. You see, she has just accepted my invitation to Lady Ashley's ball!"

31

∽∾

The crystal prisms in the mammoth chandeliers glittered like a thousand diamonds, giving off a rainbow of shimmering hues. The ballroom was a dazzling array of splendor. The flames of a hundred or more candles shone down on polished white marble, and Dawn realized that she could see her reflection in the smooth surface of the floor. Though she had become accustomed to the grandeur of Pembrooke House, still she stood in awe.

Looking about her, Dawn's eyes took in the elegance of the room. Blue brocade couches had been strategically pushed against the wall to enlarge the dance floor and give those who didn't want to exert themselves a place to rest. There were so many potted plants placed about the ballroom, that one might almost forget the chill of the oncoming winter season.

"Lady Ashley certainly knows how to give a party, eh what?" Her escort was saying.

"Yes, she certainly does." Everything was perfect except that Dawn was with the wrong man. Oh, he was pleasant enough, this smiling nephew of Mrs. Pembrooke's, but he wasn't the man she longed for. That man was standing across the ballroom alone, looking so forlorn that she felt a twinge of regret for what she had done. No matter what she might have planned, she knew now she never could hurt him.

"Well, well, well. Let's introduce you to the *ton*, shall we?" With a nod, Oliver pushed her gently along. She suffered through a maze of faces and handshakes as strangers scrutinized her, anxious to judge her by speech and appearance. Once these same people would have turned up their noses at her, but now they were greeting her warmly, prying so politely into the wheres and whens and hows of her life.

"So you are a friend of Margaret Pembrooke's. Such a dear, dear woman. Tragic, though, the accident that left her crippled. How distressing it must be to be helpless."

"She isn't helpless at all. I've never seen a more independent woman." Dawn quickly came to her friend's defense. Certainly they wouldn't have felt pity if they could see the way the woman managed her household, wheeling herself about and taking charge of every detail. "Margaret Pembrooke is amazing. There isn't anything she can't do."

"Mmm? Well, yes . . ." The gray-haired dowager looked skeptically at Dawn through her lorgnette, then flounced off, her large bosom bouncing with every step.

Dawn felt tense and ill at ease, but she managed the rest of the introductions with skill and poise. Tonight she was going to enjoy herself. She would dance, laugh, and be gay and put from her mind all thought of Garrick Seton. And yet, if only he hadn't been there to taunt her with his presence, it would have been so much easier. As it was, her eyes seemed compelled to seek out his tall, handsome form, and she had to glance quickly away when he returned her gaze.

"Shall we indulge in a dance or two?"

In the great hall the dancing had begun. Dawn recognized the music as a polka. Hopefully her lessons would stand her in good stead, enabling her to move about with ease. Before she could think more about it, however, Oliver had caught her in his arms and was whirling her onto the floor. Just as in her dream she twirled faster and faster as faces sped by and colors blended into one another. Only this time she was part of the dancing throng.

When the polka ended, Dawn found herself held within the warmth of another pair of masculine arms. Then another and another man claimed her, each vying for her attention. She should have been ecstatic, but she wasn't. She could feel Garrick's piercing blue eyes and knew that he watched her. In those moments she felt the pain of her longing to be with *him.* What was the use of dancing? She only wished it were his arms around her. How could she laugh when it was his smile she wanted to see? She struggled against the love in her heart, but she was powerless. When he was near her for even the briefest of moments, all was lost. Even so she forced herself to laugh and act as if she hadn't a care in the world.

Garrick watched her solemnly. Even in a room full of people she caught his eye over and over again. *Beautiful!*

Her long, dark, shining hair was swept up into an artfully arranged composition of curls, held in place by a double strand of pearls. Only a few tendrils of hair were permitted to escape, at her temples, forehead, and in front of her earlobes, framing her lovely face to perfection. Her dress was high-waisted, a filmy white satin, hemmed with a rainbow of brightly colored threads. The neckline was less than reckless yet revealed the twin mounds of her full breasts enticingly. Unlike the other ladies in the room who flaunted their jewels, she wore only the pearls in her hair and pearl eardrops.

She was a charming combination of virginity and sensuality. The most beautiful woman Garrick had ever seen or probably ever would, he thought, eyeing her jealously. Every man there was certain to covet her. Every man including himself. And she was with *Ollie*. Dear God, how that hurt. Oliver of all people. His friend. An attractive man, to be sure, but a philandering rogue and a wastrel.

"Well, well, well. If it isn't Garrick Seton. I thought you had disappeared from the face of the earth." Laying a white-gloved hand on his shoulder, Stephanie Creighton positioned herself in his arms. Her diamonds gleamed like stars in the candlelight. "Let's dance, darling."

Though he really wasn't in the mood for the mazurka, he didn't refuse. He would maneuver himself so that he could take a turn at dancing with Dawn. He needed to talk with her, to find out why she had been avoiding him so blatantly tonight. Something was wrong, and he intended to find out just what it was. He wouldn't give her up to Oliver without a fight. She'd responded to his kiss with passion, had not been immune to the magic that passed between them. Why then had she accepted Oliver's invitation? It was only one of the questions that demanded answers.

"Smile, Garrick. This isn't a funeral, after all. Oh, but it is good to see you again. I assume you have been busy at the office and that is why I haven't heard even a peep from you?" Stephanie smiled at him, looking up through her lashes.

"Yes, I've been very busy. There have been a few problems."

"Yes, I know." She pirouetted, swirling in a turquoise rustle of skirts. "Do you approve of my dress?" Without missing a beat she came back into his arms.

"It's quite dazzling."

"Have you ever seen anything quite as exquisite as this gown? It came all the way from Paris just for the occasion. Lady Ashley always dresses so . . . so elaborately that I hoped to outdo her at least this time. But as you were saying . . . about your little problems. I know exactly what has been going on."

"What do you mean?" Garrick didn't like her knowing smile, it made him uneasy.

"Why, I know that your dear partner was at a loss for money. Because you are so very dear to me and because I wanted to protect you, I interceded." As the music came to an end, she took his hand and led him to one of the brocaded settees. "You see, I invested in your firm, my dear. It is *I* who own those stocks, in case you wondered."

"You?" Garrick couldn't have been more stunned if she had slapped him. "You bought them?" He was unsettled by that knowledge. Stephanie Creighton was not the type of woman who did anyone a favor. There was a reason for her buying into his architectural firm that had nothing to do with kindness. To get him in her power, he thought. She knew how much his work meant to him, how diligently he had striven to make a success of himself.

"Yes. I bought them." Her eyes strayed to where Dawn now stood in conversation with Oliver. "Why, isn't that the young woman I saw you with at the opera? I've heard it said that she is a guest of Margaret Pembrooke's. Certainly the tongues are wagging. I thought . . ." Her laughter was soft. "Oh, darling, of course. You were escorting her as a favor to Oliver and Margaret Pembrooke." She touched him on the tip of the nose with her finger. "Then you are quite

forgiven. Though I must admit I plotted my revenge."
Throwing back her head, she laughed huskily.

The laughter caught Dawn's attention. Disturbed,
she looked at Garrick and immediately recognized
the stunning blond woman as the one who had
glared at her from the velvet-draped box at the theatre. From the expression on the woman's face she
adored Garrick Seton, and why not? He was everything a woman could ever want. The feeling that shot
through Dawn as she watched them sitting side by
side was torturous, and yet by her own decision she
had pushed him into another woman's arms. A
woman of his own kind, a woman without a past to
hide. Even so, the thought gave her cold comfort.

"One more dance, and then we'll have a glass of
champagne. Properly chilled, of course," Oliver was
saying.

Once more Margaret Pembrooke's nephew led her
onto the floor. Usually Dawn loved music, but now it
thundered in her ears, making her cringe. She
wanted to be far away from here, away from the
sight of Garrick in that blond beauty's company. Oh,
if only. If only!

"My, my, you are stunning. My aunt obviously has
ideas in mind for me and for you." His cold, clammy
hand squeezed hers tightly. "Not that I mind her
playing Cupid, mind you. I'm intrigued and more
than a little grateful."

"Your aunt has been very kind to me."

"And now to me." Skillfully he led her towards the
shadows. "Your coming here with me tonight gave
me hope that I have a chance of winning your heart.
Do I?" As if to tempt her, he lightly kissed her throat,
but instead of sending shivers up her spine, it only
made her blood run cold. "Well? Do I have a chance?"

Dawn didn't have time to answer. Suddenly she
was yanked from her partner's arms and found her-

self gazing up into a face as recognizable as her own. "Garrick!"

"If ever a lady needed rescuing, it seems to be now. Excuse me, Ollie, I believe a dance with this very beautiful lady is long overdue. Shall we?" His voice was low, a deep rumble, and held a tone that sent a quiver dancing up her spine.

"Yes . . . yes, of course . . ." His eyes were compelling, robbing her of her will, her reason.

For a long moment they stood just looking at each other as he held her hand. One could have heard a pin drop, a clock tick, the world spin, it was so silent. As if all of the other people in the room had disappeared and she was alone in the room with him. At first he simply held her, then his strength moved her across the floor.

He was a wonderful dancer, graceful despite his strength. Her feet barely touched the floor. It was as if she danced on air. She felt the strength of his chest against her breasts, the muscles of his thighs burning through her gown, the heat of his body enveloping her. The contact was searing, evoking memories of the embrace they had shared at Vauxhall. Being so close to him, with his arm around her waist, his mouth brushing her cheek, sent her senses spinning with a mingled feeling of pleasure and alarm. She was lost. All her resolve had flown as quickly as leaves in the wind.

Being so near Garrick made Dawn feel dizzy, so much so that she clutched at his shoulder for balance. Slowly, vibrantly, she was bound by the music's spell, a fragile silken thread that wove about them. For an instant she allowed herself to forget who he was, what she had been, what could happen if she allowed herself to love him, and gave herself up to the moment. The look of passion in his eyes made her believe herself to be all the things she'd longed to be. Beautiful. Proper. Alluring. Desired. The kind of woman a man like Garrick Seton could love.

His chin touched the top of her head. She was so petite, he thought. Fragile yet with an inner sense of strength about her. He wanted to sweep her up in his arms, carry her off, and never let her go. Protect her from Ollie? Yes. And from the rest of the world he knew to be so cruel. She was out of her element here. These shallow people were not her kind but selfish and calculating. What did she know of the games they played?

"Dawn . . ." There were so many questions he wanted to ask but suddenly felt tongue-tied. "Did you . . . did you like the roses?"

"Yes. Thank you." What would he think, she wondered, if he found out she had given them to the maid? "They were beautiful."

He heard the fabric of her gown rustle against her skin and felt a familiar flash of desire surge through him. Just being near her fired his passion. To Oliver she would be just one of many. To him she was unique. He had to make her understand.

"Why? Why did you come here tonight with Oliver?" His brows quirked up as he asked the question and his voice betrayed his annoyance. *And yet I don't own her,* he reasoned. *She had every right to accept the attentions of another man.*

"Oliver?" She lifted her head breathing a deep sigh. *Because I had to, can't you see?* she thought. She had hoped that by being with Garrick's friend, she could dissuade him from his affections. That would have made it so much easier for her. If only she could have made him think she preferred Oliver to him, then perhaps he would vanish from her life. But Garrick was far more sure of himself than she had supposed. Or perhaps he did not give up his women quite so easily.

"Not that I want you to misunderstand." Garrick's eyes moved tenderly over her face, pausing at her lips. "I have no claim. Yet, when we kissed . . ."

"Nor do I want you to think . . ."

"Oliver can be very charming. It's just that I believed that our being together had touched you as deeply as it had me."

And you are right in that assumption. I love you, so desperately, and yet you can never love me. Not the person I really am, Dawn thought. How could she make him understand? "I . . . I like him. Oliver. He's a most amiable fellow."

"And what am I?" His face was shadowed, but she could feel the heat of his gaze. His head bent, tempting her as his lips brushed against her own as if to remind her of what had passed between them.

My life, my love, she thought. For the moment all she knew was the feel of his lips, the current of expectation that swept through her. She could feel her heart beating so loudly she was certain he could hear. She couldn't think, couldn't breathe. *Tell him you love him,* an inner voice whispered. *Take a chance. Let him love you and give him your love in return. Grasp happiness with both fists and hope that you'll have a happy ending. Fairy tales can come true!*

"What am *I*?" he asked again. Their gazes locked and she couldn't look away. An irresistible tide, the warmth of her feelings for him, drew her. How could she lie to him?

"I've never met a man like you. You are the kind of man I've dreamed of, but you frighten me too."

"Frighten you?" Of all the things she might have said that was the last he had ever expected her to say. "Frighten you?" Her words wounded him. Gathering her close against his chest he whispered, "I'd never do anything to harm you. Never."

"Never?" She trembled against him. Never was a strong word. He had already harmed her. But he didn't know that? How could he? And what would he think if he did know? Would he be sorry? Would he still be gentle and smiling? *Tell him the truth. Trust him and all will be well. Margaret Pembrooke knows about your past and she still cares about you,* she thought. *Perhaps he can too. Perhaps all is not lost after all.*

"Something is bothering you." He traced the pucker of her frown with his fingertip. "Tell me what it is." A wisp of curls had fallen into her eyes and he brushed it away. "Perhaps I can help."

"I'm . . . I'm not . . . not . . ." Dawn swallowed hard, preparing herself to begin the tale. Would he understand? Would he believe her when she told him that her days of thievery were behind her? Warily her eyes searched out the terrace, and seeing it to be deserted, she took his hand and led him there. "Come with me."

If she was going to confide in him, they needed privacy. Margaret Pembrooke would be her witness. She would corroborate what Dawn was going to tell him now. Somehow Dawn felt Margaret could make Garrick understand even if she herself couldn't. She had to take the chance or turn her back forever on whatever happiness she might have. One thing she knew for certain—ignoring Garrick Seton just wouldn't work. Nor could she hide her love by hanging on to Oliver's coattails. Oliver was a pleasant lad, but he could never measure up to Garrick.

Cool wisps of wind brushed against Dawn's face as she neared the terrace. She tried to sort out her jumbled thoughts, to prepare herself to use the right words. Coolly, logically, her mind took command.

Just begin at the beginning and tell him the truth. Her mother had always told her that truth won out over lies every time.

"Garrick, there's something I must tell you . . ." she began.

"Miss Dawn Landon. I'm looking for a Miss Landon." A shrill, boyish voice pierced the air. "I have an urgent message!"

"A message?" Garrick reacted before Dawn did. Raising his arm, he beckoned the boy over to where they stood. "This is Miss Dawn Landon."

The grim expression on the boy's face alarmed Dawn. "What is it?"

"I have been sent to find you. You are to come with me right away. Mrs. Pembrooke has been taken ill and is asking for you. Hurry!"

"Margaret?" Dawn was stunned.

"My aunt?" Oliver's voice shook as he came up behind them. "But she is in perfect health. The doctor said so the last time he visited. Strong as a Yorkshire-bred cow."

"All I know is that I was sent to fetch Miss Landon, as well as yourself, sir."

"Oh, bother it all! I'll have Douglas boiled in oil if she has fallen again. Drat the man!" Wrenching Dawn's hand from Garrick's, he said, "Come. Come. Let's not waste a minute."

32

The physician's face was grim as he took Oliver and Dawn aside. "There's not much I can do. Just make her as comfortable as I can and hope for the best. Sometimes a patient gets well, but then at other times . . ."

"But what is wrong?" Dawn gasped to see the pale, haggard face of the woman in the bed. "She had a bit of indigestion a few days ago at breakfast. Nothing more."

"Ah, yes. Dyspepsia. Mmm. A common complaint in these times. But that is not what she is suffering from, I fear."

"Then what?" Oliver's tone was as shrill as Dawn's. "Speak up, man. What is ailing my aunt? Why . . . why, she is usually as healthy as a veritable horse, I'll have you know. By your own words!"

"Something to do with her stomach." The doctor shook his head. "We know very little about such things, I'm afraid."

"You know very little. You're a doctor, for God's sake." A moan and a stir from the direction of the bed caused him to lower his voice. "You bloody well better know."

Clearing his throat, the physician was defensive. "Why, I daresay that despite all the dissections those blasted surgeons engage in, we're still barely out of the Dark Ages when it comes to knowing about the body. If you want my opinion, I would wager a guess. It quite possibly could be peritonitis."

"Periwhatis?" Oliver shrugged his shoulders in confusion.

"Peritonitis. A kind of poison."

"Poison!" Clutching at his throat, Oliver grimaced. "Poison?"

"An inflammation of the peritoneum, the membrane that lines the cavity of the abdomen. The result of a burst appendix, I daresay. Of course, in the early stages, an inflamed appendix usually causes a great deal of pain but since your aunt has no feeling below the waist, it's possible . . . It's altogether possible . . ." He turned towards Dawn. "Tell me about her complaint. How it started."

"Well, she thought she might have come upon a bit of bad food. She had a spell of nausea, then vomiting. But it went away. I asked her if she wanted something for the midday meal, but she wasn't hungry. She told me she had lost her appetite and said jokingly that she would soon get back her girlish figure if she continued in such a manner." Dawn felt a twinge of guilt. She had been so filled with her own thoughts of Garrick, the ball, and her decision to go with Oliver, that she had taken little notice of Margaret Pembrooke's complaint. "Now that I think back on it, she did seem a bit feverish. Her face was flushed. Oh, I should have called you."

"Ah, yes, and I would have bled her immediately. As it is I'm afraid the poison has gathered. But I have bled her now and given her a castor oil, a mild laxative, and syrup of pale roses. That should relieve some of the poison and hopefully correct the problem." He stuffed his remedies one by one back in his leather bag. "She should get better. If not, summon me immediately."

Dawn and Oliver hovered anxiously over Margaret's bedside, but instead of improving she got steadily worse. Murmuring incoherently, she finally drifted off into a fitful sleep.

"Trust a physician. Ha! The farther away one stays from such quacks the better, I always say," Oliver mumbled. "Trying to move in proper social circles as if they were aristocratic. Ha! Their overblown vocabulary is spiced with Latin words and such, but their Oxford education is all for naught. Charlatans, that's what they are. Why, they are little better than surgeons, if you ask me, though they think themselves above them."

Dawn remembered her father had held much the same view. He had regarded all doctors with skepticism. "The safest thing to do when ill is to keep well away from doctors' remedies and rely on your mother's healing herbs," he had always said. "Hospitals are for the destitute, the fever ridden, and the insane. No one in their right mind would enter one." Certainly neither the doctors nor the surgeons had been able to save him after the carriage accident. And her mother had died as well, though there had been a physician at the prison. Oliver was right in calling them quacks.

"And yet he was very kind, and is certainly trying to do all that he can," Dawn whispered, trying to soothe the disgruntled man at her side.

Oliver wrung his hands. "Well, if *he* knows what is good for him he'll save my aunt. Or he will rue it! That I swear."

He really does care, Dawn thought, looking over at the worried young man who now had his face in his hands. If only Margaret Pembrooke would open her eyes and witness her nephew's devotion. So many times she had bemoaned to Dawn that her nephew cared little for her, that only her money drew his attention. Surely his worry now was not feigned, nor his anger.

"He has done all that he can. The rest is up to God."

"God? Then I beg him to spare her." Tears misted the young man's eyes, and he wiped them away with his lace handkerchief, then blew his nose. "I've been a selfish dolt. Too concerned with my own pleasures. It's just that Aunt Margaret seemed so formidable. I . . . I thought she would always be here. A veritable landmark, as it were. I never thought . . ."

"She understood." Dawn lied to spare his feelings. "Really, she did. You are very dear to her. And . . . and she will get well. You will see." How was she to know then how wrong she was or how quickly life could take a bitter turn?

The flame in the oil lamp flickered and sputtered, casting eerie shadows on the wall. In the bedroom all was silent as the physician resumed his place at his patient's side. Dawn began to fear that Margaret Pembrooke was going to die. She had come to love the old woman, to admire her strength and tenacity, to trust her as she did few people. Who else would have taken her into her own home, shown her as much kindness as a mother did a daughter? To teach her, pamper her, and help her attain her dreams? Now the pale face, the cold hands, the ragged breathing all gave warning that Margaret Pembrooke's life was in danger.

"Is she in any pain?"

"Not now. I gave her quite a large dose of laudanum."

"Dawn . . ." The voice was a whispered croak, but Dawn crept nearer. Taking the old woman's hand, she held on tightly, as if by clinging to her she could keep her in the world of the living.

"I'm here. And Oliver is here too. We both love you very much."

"Not . . . worried . . . about . . . Oliver . . . but you."

"I don't want you to worry, just to get well. Oh, I'm going to tell Cook never to give you steak-and-kidney pie again!" Reaching out, Dawn brushed back the gray curls that clung to Margaret's dampened brow. "Oh, if only I'd known you were so very ill. I never would have gone tonight. I would have stayed with you and . . ."

"Hush! Not . . . your . . . fault. Stubborness. Mine. Like . . . to . . . think . . . I'm invincible." The grandam's eyelids fluttered as she breathed a deep sigh.

"Doctor!"

"She's just resting."

Putting his finger and thumb on Margaret Pembrooke's wrist, the doctor clucked his tongue with worry, nevertheless. "Her pulse rate has increased dangerously despite my efforts. It's racing. I must bleed her yet again."

"Bleed her? You've already taken half her blood. By God, you had better know what you are doing, old man." Raising his fist, Oliver made a threatening gesture, then once more hung his head.

"Her pulse?" Dawn asked, feeling utterly helpless. "Is there anything we can do?" Her own heart thundered in the silent room as she looked down at her benefactress's still form.

"No. It is just as I feared. The poison has spread and there is nothing I can do to stop its flow. It is only a matter of time. All we can do is to make her comfortable."

"You mean she is going to die?" Oliver bolted to his feet, his eyes desperately searching the doctor's face. The man's expression answered the question.

"No-o-o!" Dawn's lament was a soleful wail. Closing her eyes, she prayed fervently. "Spare her, dear merciful God. Please. Oh, please . . ."

"She *is* going to die!" Angrily Oliver struck the wall. "So much for your puttering. But then I'm certain you'll require your *fee.* Those in your profession always do, even when you've failed. You incompetent ass!" Losing all control of his temper he grabbed hold of the doctor's coat and pulled him to his feet. "Get out of here! And take your bag of tricks with you."

"Oliver, please! This is not the time . . ." Only Dawn's interference kept Oliver from aiming a kick at the physician's behind as he shoved him out the door. "Let your aunt have a measure of peace." Hurrying towards a china basin she poured some cool water from a pitcher, grabbed a cloth, and returned to the patient's side. "She won't die. She can't. She can't." Bending down, she spent a long, long while at the bedside, moistening the cloth and wiping Margaret Pembrooke's fevered brow. Grasping her friend's hand, she held vigil long into the night, offering what little comfort she could. "I have grown to love you so, I have. You've been like me mum. So very dear."

If only Margaret Pembrooke would get well. She wanted to hear her laugh again, to bask in her praise. "Very good, Dawn, my dear. Your *h*'s. You have mastered them. Now your *a*'s. Oh, the world will be yours once you've learned. You'll see . . . You'll make every man's head turn tonight at the ball. . . . I think of you as the daughter I might have had and didn't. . . . Above all, my dear, be happy. Life is but a fleeting sneeze when all is said and done. Too short for trivialities, I daresay. Be happy."

The tick of the clock on the bedside table marked off the passing hours. Reneging on his vow never to allow the physician to set foot in the house again,

Oliver frantically sought out his aid. But it was as the man said. Too late.

Dawn's face was wet with tears as she watched the doctor close the once gleaming eyes and cover the still form with a sheet. "Be happy," Margaret Pembrooke had said. How could she be happy? She had no one in the world who really cared about her now. Suddenly the bright embers of her world had turned to ash, and she couldn't help wondering what was to become of her.

33

Dawn clasped her hands tightly together as Mr. Cambridge, the solicitor, read the last will and testament of Margaret Anne Harrington Pembrooke in a low, droning voice. Her baggage was packed with the few possessions she had brought to Pembrooke House, and she was fully prepared to leave, if that was what Oliver wanted as the estate's new owner. Certainly she could not stay.

I'll go share a room with Taddie, she thought. Taddie would have need of her now, with the baby on its way.

"I, Margaret Pembrooke, being of sound mind, do hereby put forth my last will and testimony." The man read on, using a string of long difficult words Dawn didn't understand.

"The Pembrooke fortune is rumored to be at least seven hundred thousand pounds. Maybe more," a primly coiffed lady whispered behind her fan.

"I've heard it is considerably more. Someone will be unreasonably wealthy after today," a bespectacled man answered.

Seven hundred thousand pounds, Dawn thought. She'd never realized there was so much money in the entire world, and yet not even such vast riches had been able to grant Margaret Pembrooke her life. Money, then, could not buy everything!

"To my sister I bequeath the amount of one thousand pounds annually and all my hats." All eyes focused on that fashionably coiffed lady, who sat dabbing at her eyes with a handkerchief as she sniffled.

"To my brother-in-law I leave two shillings, the exact amount he owned when he married into my family." A muffled oath answered.

"To my loyal butler Douglas I declare Pembrooke House his home as long as he wishes. I have set aside a sum that will pay him his regular salary for the rest of his life."

Meeting Douglas's eye, Dawn smiled, glad that the man who had been so devoted to Margaret Pembrooke would be secure now that she was gone. Perhaps all was not lost. Maybe she too could stay there. As a maid. Douglas had proved himself a friend and had always complimented her on her chores. With a house as large as this there was always work to be done. And yet without Mrs. Pembrooke's deep, throaty laughter it would be such a lonely place.

I have to pinch myself to believe that she is really gone, Dawn thought with a sigh. And yet the memory of Margaret Pembrooke lying so still in the coffin at the funeral was all too real. Oliver had been lavish in choosing a headstone. A white marble angel playing a trumpet, heralding his aunt to heaven, he had said.

Dawn listened as the list of bequests went on and on, covering the servants who had been so very loyal to the matron of Pembrooke House. Poor Oliver, she thought, he had grieved so for his aunt, though now he seemed to be recovering. From beneath her lashes she looked his way, not at all surprised to see Garrick sitting by his side. A pillar of strength, that's what her handsome gentleman had proved to be. She knew Oliver would have fallen to pieces if *he* had not been there to take charge. She wondered what they were talking about now as they bent their heads together.

"Garrick, my friend, I'll most certainly have no more need for those silly little drawings again, once this is over." Oliver smiled smugly. "I'm certain that my aunt will not overlook me when all is said and done. Besides my parents, whom she abhorred for their greed, I'm the old woman's only heir." Counting on his fingers, he tried to calculate just the net sum he would be granted.

"Ahem . . ." Looking over the rim of his spectacles, the solicitor challenged Oliver to silence.

"Oh, all right, my good man. I'll be quiet, but do get on with it."

"Ollie, you are incorrigible. Grant your aunt a measure of respect," Garrick scolded.

"I did! I mourned her for three solid days," Oliver muttered in his ear. "But life is for the living, not the dead. Aunt Margaret is gone and I wish her a safe journey to heaven but . . ." As the solicitor turned his way again, Oliver quieted down.

The rest of the will's reading progressed rapidly as all the servants were named along with the amounts they were to receive. Margaret Pembrooke was taking care of everyone who had been near and dear to her. Suddenly, however, the tempo slowed. It was obvious that the list was coming to an end, and the mood of anticipation heightened.

"To my nephew I leave my carriage and six matched horses, with the stipulation that they not be used for racing purposes nor disposed of. My house in Devonshire, which may not be sold nor credited to pay any debts. A sum of ten thousand pounds to be used for his education and for that alone. In addition I leave him a trust fund that shall be strictly administered over a monthly period. That trust to total forty pounds a month."

"Forty pounds?" Oliver stamped his foot. " 'Tis a pittance. I will starve."

"I doubt that, Ollie." Garrick pounded his friend on the back reassuringly.

"But the rest of the fortune? Who? Or what?" Crossing his arms angrily, Oliver waited. "Probably to one of her silly charities."

"The bulk of my estate, including the house I have loved so dearly, and my jewels, I leave to Miss Dawn Landon, my companion, friend, and surrogate daughter." Those words were met with an amazed gasp as all eyes turned Dawn's direction.

"What? To *her*?" Oliver bounded to his feet. "I protest! I protest! She is no kin of my aunt's." He waved his fist accusingly at Dawn, glaring all the while. "There is villainy at work here, sir. That woman . . ."

"Silence!" The solicitor went on with the terms of the will, verifying that what he had said was indeed correct. Margaret Pembrooke had been diligent in making certain the document was quite legal and binding.

Dawn sat silent, too stunned to speak. She, once a merchant's daughter, then a beggar, then forced to become a thief, was now just as rich as she had once been poor. So very unexpectedly, she found herself to be a woman of means.

34

Dawn felt like Saint Nicholas as the carriage rolled down the streets headed for Soho. Today would be Christmas for her friends. Beside her on the padded seat were boxes of every shape and size as well as a large iron box filled with coins. She had rummaged through the finest shops in the West End for presents of coats, dresses, scarves, hats, and shoes. Jamie, Farley, Arien, Taddie, and the others would never have to endure poverty again. There would be no more cold nights fearing there would be no coal for the fire, no torn and patched clothes, no nights of going to bed hungry.

Although Dawn had been cautioned, she had been stubborn on the matter. "If a person can't share their good fortune, then of what good is it?" she had defiantly said, calmly asking the solicitor to arrange for a large sum to be apportioned from her inheritance. Certainly she was not of a mind to be greedy or selfish. Those who had stuck by her through thick and thin, who had shared her misery but still given her loyalty and kindness, would now get their due.

"I'll give Arien enough money to get his poems published. Leather-bound volumes just like those of Shakespeare I read in Mrs. Pembrooke's library. He'll be known all over England." She was certain that if Margaret Pembrooke was looking down from heaven right now she would approve. "I'll set Taddie up in her own flower shop, and I'll see that Doris is well coached as an actress."

She would do the same for Jamie, Murdock, and Farley, a business of their choosing, perhaps as costermongers. No more would any of them be thieves —they would all be respectable citizens of London. All they had ever really needed was a chance.

"Driver, stop here, please." Stepping from the coach, she struggled with the burden of her purchases as she ascended the dark flight of stairs.

"Ooh, lookee 'ere, Ned. Ain't she a nice one, eh? Can I 'elp yer, lovely laidy?" Two men accosted Dawn with smiles that scarcely hid their sly intent.

"Go awaiy, yer blokes, or I'll knock yer ears from yer 'eads! Yer won't steal from me, yer won't. I'm not o' a mind ter bother wi' the loikes of ye," Dawn quickly retorted, reverting to the way of speech she'd fought so hard to forget. Now it came to her aid. "Well, don't stand there staring. Git, or ye will rue it." She fumbled in her pocket, making a pretense of retrieving her knife. "I'll carve yer up, I will. Move yer blinkin' arses!"

Startled to hear such a well-dressed woman swear at them, and fearing she just might make good on her threat, the men turned tail and fled down the street. From the safety of an old rain barrel they looked back, but before they had time to give her any further trouble, Dawn had reached the top of the stairs. The smell of stew grew stronger with each step she took. She'd come just in time for supper.

"Taddie! Jamie!" She called out as she pushed open the door to the main room, the "drawing room," Taddie had once laughingly called it. The cookstove's fire was blazing, making the lid of the tin saucepan rattle up and down as steam gushed out. Wooden bowls and spoons cluttered the area, a harsh contrast to

Cook's well-organized kitchen. Overhead, on a string that stretched from wall to wall, hung a pair of lady's stockings, two shirts, a shawl, and a patched pair of trousers. During the cold days of winter every bit of heat was well utilized.

"You there, wot are yer doing in 'ere?" As she turned around, Jamie's eyes opened wide in surprise. "Dawn! Wot a sight fer sore eyes yer be."

"I've brought presents, Jamie. We'll pretend it's Christmas already." Dawn's eyes shone with exuberance as she dropped the bundles on the faded and tattered couch. Opening one of the boxes, she brought forth a blue coat with long lapels and held it up for the little man's inspection. "You said you've always wanted a double-breasted coat; now you have one, Jamie. Here, take it."

"For me?" The dwarf's fingers shook as he took hold of the fine cloth.

"Put it on." Dawn watched as he pulled it over his arms, then fastened the buttons one by one. Strutting before the chipped and cracked mirror, he smiled with gratitude. As others of the little family came meandering in, they likewise were given their gifts of clothing. Soon they were all prancing about exhibiting their finery.

"Yer be a bloomin' saint, Dawnie, dear."

"As generous as anyone could be. Aye, yer are." Procuring several chipped glasses and a bottle of gin, Farley proposed a toast. "Ter our princess 'ere."

"Ter our own dear Dawn," they all chorused. Tugging on her sleeves and the skirt of her dress, they all made inquiry as to how she had been able to manage such luxuries. Sipping her gin, Dawn told them of Margaret Pembrooke's kindness, her sorrow at her friend's death and her astonishment to be named heiress.

"You would have loved her as much as I. I will miss

her more than you can ever know, but I know she would have wanted me to share my newfound wealth with all of you. So . . ." Opening the iron chest, Dawn revealed another surprise. "I want you to share this equally. It is but the beginning of your boon, but it must be spent wisely. Not for gin or gambling, but to make something of yourselves."

"Lord love a duck, ain't that a grand sight!" Jamie caressed the coins in disbelief. "Are they real?"

"Very real."

"And they're ours?" Laughing merrily, Farley scooped up a handful of shillings and let them trickle through his fingers.

"They're yours to set yourselves up in business. No more stealing. Promise?" She'd been afraid that eventually all of them would end up in Newgate, but now she need worry no more.

"Well!"

"Farley!"

He wiggled his fingers. "I guess I can put these to a different skill. I promise."

Laughter permeated the room, giving it a warm glow. For just a moment Dawn forgot the smoke that polluted the room, the broken panes of glass stuffed with brown paper, the patches in the wall, the leaking roof, to enjoy her visit with her old friends. Only one thing spoiled the moment. Robbie was not there to join in her good fortune. Robbie. She would have used some of her newfound fortune to send him to school, perhaps even Oxford eventually. Oh, what a fine lawyer he would have made, for he could argue the devil out of his horns, or so he'd boasted often enough.

Taddie read her thoughts. "Rob, ain't it, that look of sadness in yer eyes?"

"Yes. He's always in my thoughts. Oh, Taddie, what could have happened to him? How could he have just disappeared like that? I tried so hard to find out where he was. . . ." Dawn hung her head.

"*I* know where he is." Lifting his head from his tally of the money, Jamie met her eye.

"Where, Jamie?"

"In the swells section of Newgate. He's alive, or so I just found out from a turnkey who's in Weasel's paiy."

"He's alive?" Dawn's breath caught in her throat. Her hands trembled.

"Aye, alive. Seems for some reason or other one of the nobs thought fit to keep him from an 'angin'. There's been more than a few shillings changed 'ands to keep him from the gallows."

"Someone has paid to keep him alive?" Gratitude flowed through her, for she knew well who that someone must be. Garrick Seton. "Bless him! Bless him!"

"Strainge thing about it though is that this particular swell not only didn't want 'is or 'er identity revealed, but also didn't want it known just where our Robbie was cloistered awaiy. Strainge, wouldn't yer saiy . . ."

Dawn barely heard Jamie. "Robbie is *alive*. Alive!" As long as he was alive, there was always hope of getting him free. Somehow! So Garrick Seton was a worthy man, a compassionate man. Never had she loved him more than she did at this moment.

"Ole Rob, or so I'm told, is living loike a king. Not loike some o' the other blokes. Oh, no. 'E plays at dice and cards wi' the guards, eats the finest food, drinks only the best whiskey, beer, and gin, even 'as himself a bed with a feather mattress. Probably better off than we was 'ere, until yer caime, Dawnie dear."

"Nevertheless, I must get him out. But it will take time." Although she was anxious to approach Garrick Seton, to free Robbie, she had to work slowly. A new trial perhaps, this time with a barrister of her choosing. Mrs. Pembrooke's solicitor had recommended John Barrister. In the meantime, at least she knew her brother was alive and living in relative comfort.

It was cold outside the tenement. A brisk wind whipped at Dawn's hair as she walked along clutching her cloak. Still she stubbornly refused to hire a carriage. She wanted to walk, to let her feet skim over the cobblestones. She knew just where she was going—to Garrick Seton's office to give him a proper thank you. It was late, about six o'clock, but she thought perhaps he would still be at his desk.

One lone lamp shone in the window, silhouetting Garrick's splendidly masculine form as he bent over his drawing board. Taking a deep breath, Dawn gathered up her courage, moved to the door, and knocked loudly. She could hear his steady footsteps as he came to answer the door.

"Dawn! What a pleasant surprise."

There had been so much confusion, first with Mrs. Pembrooke's death, then with the settlement of the estate, that he had hardly had a moment alone with her. He opened the door wide and beckoned her inside, thankful Oliver had already gone. Ollie's resentment and dislike for Dawn Landon now knew no bounds. He was more determined than ever to prove that Miss Dawn Landon was a fraud. His obsession bordered on insanity.

Dawn looked around her. Somehow it looked just as she had imagined it would, from the upholstered chairs to the shelves of drawings that lined the walls. Masculine. Elegant. Just like Garrick himself.

"To what do I owe the pleasure of this visit?" he was saying, allowing his smoldering gaze to run lingeringly over her. With her wind-whipped hair she looked a bit wild. *Like a Gypsy*, he thought with a smile.

"I wanted to see you." At another time she would have felt brazen to come here, but now she was so grateful, so elated that she was beyond rational thought. "Oh, Garrick!" Impetuously she reached out for him, her hand resting on the firm hardness of his chest. Standing on tiptoe, her eyes riveted on his mouth, she initiated a kiss.

"Mmm," he groaned, pulling her into his arms. A hungry desire that clamored for release swept through his body as he caressed her lips. If she only knew how he'd longed to be with her. Now his mouth closed on hers, engulfing her in a maelstrom of delicious sensations.

Passionately Dawn yielded to him as her lips and teeth parted to allow his exploration. Her hands slid up to lock around his neck, her fingers tangling in the thickness of his thick brown hair. She sighed against his mouth, trembling with pleasure. This, this was what she had wanted to experience again, to be in his arms and have him kiss her. Now that she knew he had not seriously harmed her brother, she allowed herself to relax and enjoy the sensations he always aroused.

The feel of him, strong, warm, and loving, was all Dawn wanted in the world. She didn't fully understand everything that was happening to her—she knew only that he alone could arouse such an urgent need within her. He was the source of every comfort, every beautiful thing she could imagine at this moment.

Garrick forgot everything but the sweet, soft lips beneath his. All caution fled as the hungry desire he had tried to put from his mind sprang free. He was aware of nothing but his intense driving need for her. He tightened his arms around her, and his kiss deepened in intensity as he explored the moist sweetness of her mouth, craving her kiss as others might crave brandy. He didn't know why she had come, only that she was here.

Garrick inhaled her fragrance. Violets. A sweet yet heady aroma. Desire bubbled like a powerful tide, hot and sweet, as he continued to kiss her. He had always kept a cool head in matters of the heart, but whenever she was near he was all but overwhelmed by his emotions. He knew he should stop this blessed assault but he couldn't. She was too tempting. The hot ache of desire coiled within him and made him overbold. His hand crept up the velvet covering her rib cage to close over the shapely curve of her breast, seeking an entranceway into her bodice. Just as he'd supposed, her breasts were softly enticing.

Dawn was stunned to feel warm seeking fingers on her naked breast, yet she didn't push his hands away. She thrilled to his touch, surprised that his fingers could rouse in her such rapturous feelings. As he stroked and caressed her, she moaned low in her throat and leaned against him. It was such an intimate act and yet she felt no shame. Somehow it didn't seem wrong for Garrick to touch her like this.

Dawn wasn't aware of the leather-upholstered settee until she felt it beneath her. Without disrupting their embrace, Garrick slid slowly to its padded softness with her cradled in his arms, rolling her over until they were lying side by side. Sensually his mouth traveled from her mouth to her throat, across her chest to the soft flesh he had bared. His tongue savored the peak lightly, and Dawn felt every nerve she possessed quiver, then tighten in response. She found herself mimicking his caress as she explored the hard strength of his chest. Her heart hammered frantically. His heart answered in an echoing rhythm.

"I want you, Dawn Landon," he said at last, his eyes glazed with an expression she had never seen before. "You can't have any idea of what you do to me." The words were spoken low, nearly in a growl as his hand caressed her breast. His gaze hovered on the smooth golden flesh that he had exposed. "Beautiful . . ."

Dawn watched the expressions that played across his face, recognizing the passion so clearly revealed. Even in her dreams he had never looked at her like this. That look alone fired her blood, and the thought occurred to her that she wanted him to go on touching her like this forever. She wanted him to make love to her, to make her cry out in the night as she'd heard the others do in Seven Dials night after night. Oh, no, she was not so naïve that she didn't know what would happen now, and yet she'd never before wanted a man to possess her. No matter what happened in the future, she would have this night to remember, and possibly many nights to come. Therefore, she was surprised when he pulled away from her.

"What am I doing?" Cold reason flooded over him as he looked into her eyes. She didn't understand. She couldn't. His body was one hard, long ache of desire, but he held himself away from her. She was a lady. "Tumbling you like some Soho whore. I'm sorry, Dawn."

She wasn't. Moving towards him, she sought to have him hold her again, but he pushed away. "Garrick . . ."

He forced his eyes away from her tantalizing breasts, fighting his urge to touch her. The expression on his face was a mixture of sensual longing and stern control. "How could you understand? You are not a man." He kissed her nose lightly, then, taking her hands, pulled her to her feet. He spoke more to himself than to her. "I don't know why you came here tonight, but I am glad to see you. However, I assure you I won't let my volatile emotions run away with me." His hands touched her bodice again, but this time to rearrange it more modestly.

"I . . . I was in the area and I remembered Mrs. Pembrooke mentioning where your office was. I wanted to see you to thank you for being a very compassionate man. That's all." That was all she dared say for the moment. She blushed as she recalled the intimacy they had shared only a moment ago.

"To thank me with a kiss. A most pleasant way to be about it. Quite! But I'm afraid I lost my head." He felt the overwhelming need to protect her. How ironic that it was from himself that he sought to defend her honor. Reverently his finger traveled over her features, lingering on her mouth. He longed to kiss her again but knew where that might lead. "Well, I'm just shutting up shop. Suppose I get my carriage and give you a ride home." He quirked his brow. "There are some matters we need to attend to, such as what happened between us, or at least nearly did, tonight." He kissed her lightly on the cheek. "Come . . ." It was time that he spoke his mind. Honestly and from the heart.

35

It was late when Garrick at last arrived back at his town house, a residence in which he spent very little time, if truth be told. Tonight he'd spent hours driving about London with Dawn at his side, just talking to her, enjoying the warmth of her presence beside him, and responding unguardedly to her natural charm. He'd listened to her as she had talked about her family and childhood years, giving him a glimpse of her life to which he had never been privy before. She had obviously been very close to her father, had adored her mother, and still doted on her brother. How tragic she was now all alone.

Garrick thought of the smile that lit her face when she talked about those she held so dear, yet she had been strangely guarded when he had asked too many questions. She had stumbled once or twice, putting her hand to her mouth as if holding back imprudent words. Undoubtedly the loss of her family had caused her so much pain that she dreaded talking about certain details. He could understand. Certainly there was much about his own early years he was loath to discuss. How as a child he had stumbled upon his mother and her lovers all too frequently; the loneliness and isolation he had suffered because of his mother's indifference. Strange how he had thought the past was behind him, and yet just thinking about it brought pain again. Memories he'd successfully buried now came flooding back.

Garrick had been seven years old when his love for his mother had turned to disgust. It had been a summer's day and he had awakened from a nap and gone in search of his mother. The bedroom door was wide open, and there on the bed were two moaning figures, lost in their frantic movements.

"Maman?" His shrill voice startled the occupants of the bed.

"Who is that snooping little brat?" Garrick recognized the voice as belonging to a neighboring lord.

"Only my son. An annoyance, to be certain, except that his upcoming birth snared my wedding ring."

"He'll tell what he saw. I have no liking for scandal. My wife . . ."

"He won't say a thing if he doesn't want to have his nose cut off. Do you hear me, Garrick? If you mention this to anyone I will get a knife and slice off your . . ."

"No!" Turning from the door he had fled, but her threat haunted him and kept him silent. His fear made him a party to her deception, and for that he had never forgiven himself. Coward! That was what he had been, emboldening his mother to bring her lovers openly into the house again and again. And though he had not fully understood what he had witnessed, it later became clear to him when as a young man he developed an interest in such things. A whore, that was what his mother was then and now and perhaps would always be. From the day he realized what she was about, he had loathed all women who freely gave their bodies. No, not freely, really. For a price, whatever that proved to be.

But thank God for Dawn! She was as different from his mother's kind of woman as day from night. Passionate, yes, for what man would want to make love to a frigid stick of clay? *But with a heart filled with love only for me.* She made him feel as if he were the only man in the world.

"Marry me," he had said tonight.

"What?" Her head, resting so comfortably on his shoulder, had turned abruptly.

"Marry me." He had pulled her gently to him, resting her pliant softness against his strength. "I love you, Dawn." For the moment there had been no passion between them, only an all-engulfing sensation of tenderness, a sweet promise of what awaited them if they molded their lives together.

"We're home, sir."

Garrick was brought out of his reverie by the voice of his coachman.

"Yes, Vinnie, I can see that." Because it was one of the better neighborhoods, a gas light was placed at every tenth house. Thus Garrick could see his town house clearly as it came into view. Garrick wondered why he had ever settled upon a place so large, three stories in all, a rectangular structure without wings or courtyards, constructed of magenta-hued stone. Now he was glad that he had chosen it. It would make a good place to raise a family.

Like every English house of consequence it had an ostentatiously high fence, an iron-stockaded enclosure, and a doorway bridge. The thick wooden door had a brass knocker. Stepping down from the carriage, he tried that door now and was surprised to find it unlocked.

With a grumble he pushed the door open and entered. "I'll have to speak to Edward." It was not unknown for houses to be burglarized, even in this area.

The small space between the street door and the stairs was carpeted. Garrick called it a hall, though to his clients that word had a more grandiose meaning.

Two mahogany chairs, potted plants, polished brass wall sconces, statuettes of cupids aiming their bows, and a painting or two here and there decorated the foyer. Visual evidence of his success. Even so, it was a starkly lonely house, despite a staff of servants that included a scullery maid, a cook, a housekeeper, his coachman, Vinnie, and his valet. Not a home, for that, by his definition, was a place one wished to return to, but rather a place to take off his hat and shoes, to bathe and to sleep. Now perhaps it would become a home, a place he longed to return to, with someone waiting for him here.

Pausing to light a lamp, he passed through the parlor with its tasteful array of matched Chippendale furniture and pushed through the large folding doors to his den. He was surprised to find a fire already crackling in the fireplace, but supposed Edward, his valet, had seen his carriage coming up the drive and thus had thought to take the chill from the room for his return. So thinking, he stepped into the room to discover that he was not alone.

"Who the devil?" A trespasser? No intruder—Oliver. The dancing firelight shadowed the circles beneath his eyes, the hollows in his cheeks, his winsome grin. His rowdy chuckle clearly told Garrick that once again his friend was inebriated. "Ollie, what are you doing here?"

"Why, I came to see you, of course. I returned to the office once or twice, but you most certainly were not there." His words were slurred but intelligible. "I've bounced about from here to there and everywhere in between, then decided if I remained here you'd have to return *eventually*. Gad, where have you been?"

Garrick knew Oliver's bitter resentment on the subject of Dawn Landon, but he said nevertheless, "I was riding around in my carriage with a most beautiful lady, the one of whom you voice such abject disapproval."

"*That* woman?"

"Yes, *that* woman." He braced himself for a tirade. He would face the devil himself for the woman he loved. "I asked her to marry me tonight and she accepted." Closing his eyes, Garrick remembered that moment very well. They were enshrouded in a web of enchantment. He watched her intently as he asked the question and was rewarded by the soft glow in her eyes when she whispered "yes" without hesitation.

"You did *what*?"

"I asked her to marry me."

"You fool." Oliver was sitting with his feet propped up on a stool. Now he kicked that unfortunate three-legged object over. "You besotted, blind fool. She's nothing but a scheming, conniving little bit of baggage."

"Ollie!" Garrick's jaw ticked warningly. "I will not allow you to say such things about my future bride." Clasping his hands behind his back, he paced before the fire. "I can understand how you must feel since your aunt chose to grant Dawn the share of fortune you thought should be yours. Had you offered your aunt more consideration, it would not have happened. But to constantly malign another human being as you have been doing borders on . . ."

"I have proof! That's why I came tonight." Oliver was unsteady on his feet as he rose from the settee. "I told you! I told you! Well, now I have documented it. I don't know who your lovely paramour is, but she is not a *Landon*. I wonder if she is even from Norfolk, as she claims. I have my doubts."

"Not a Landon." Only by the greatest of effort was Garrick able to maintain his temper. "Don't ensnare yourself in lies just for revenge, Ollie. It doesn't become you."

"I'm not lying, as this affidavit will attest. Sworn statements from the heads of the Landon households in Norfolk. Witnessed by a magistrate, I might add. You see, I hired several men to scour the countryside from Norwich to Thetford, Wisbech to Wickhampton. Alas, the Landons have been most unfortunate in their progeny." As Garrick took a step closer, Ollie playfully held the paper just out of reach. "Aha! I thought you would be interested." By the light of the fire he read the pertinent information. "An outbreak of fever all but wiped out the Landons of Swaffham, leaving but one son." He grinned at Oliver. "He's now twelve years old."

"What of the other Landons?"

"The family living in Happisburgh has been proven to be involved in smuggling. Our dear King George has taken revenge on them all by sending them to Botany Bay! Others of their blood have been hanged. Sons all!" Cupping his hand to his mouth he whispered, "They say Happisburgh is haunted by the ghosts of those who have swung. A hideous ghost of a legless smuggler for one, whose head hangs backward between his shoulders on a strip of skin from his neck. Grisley, eh what?"

Garrick ignored the remark. "Perhaps Dawn has the stigma of illegitimacy to her name. If so, I don't care." Certainly he himself had been sired before the marriage vows.

"Oh, Gar, you poor, poor fellow. To be so ensnared. You, who have always been such a brilliant gentleman. Ah, well . . . It happens to the best of us, I suppose. Illegitimacy? Hardly. She lied about who she is. It cannot be anything else."

"I won't believe that!" Garrick clenched his jaw as he inquired, "The last family of Landons?"

"An old couple living in Grimston. Childless. When they die out, they will take their name with them. No *Dawn* Landon, Garrick, old chum."

"There must be some explanation!"

"Of course, and I know what it is." Oliver sniggered behind his hand. "She's a fraud. Don't be a sore loser, Gar."

"Loser be damned!"

"You wagered your carriage and now it's mine. You lost. She isn't who she said she is."

"I don't care what her name is. In case you haven't heard, Ollie, Shakespeare said, 'a rose by any other name would smell as sweet.'"

The smile died on Oliver's face. He swore violently, "Bloody damn! Somehow she managed to make a fool of my poor aunt, and now she's making a fool of you as well." As Garrick started to answer, Ollie held up his hand. "One other point. Cambridge, the solicitor, tells me that no sooner had my aunt's will been read than your ladylove began withdrawing large sums of money. A small fortune, which she bristled about when he asked her to explain. And then to-night, I had her followed. Where do you suppose she went?"

"She came to the office." How could he ever forget? Her kiss had precipitated his proposal.

"But before that!"

Garrick shrugged. "I have no idea."

"She came from *Soho. Soho,* of all places. Hardly a spot for a quiet country girl. She was seen going in and coming out of one of the shabbiest tenements about."

"I don't believe you, Ollie."

"Ask your own carriage driver. Vinnie will tell you. I paid him to follow her because I know how stubborn you can be. Vinnie has no reason to lie. . . ."

Garrick paused before the fire, staring at the flick-

ering flames. "I don't know what you are up to, but it
won't work. I love that girl, and therefore I trust her.
I won't believe the worst of her when she is not here
to defend herself. You're not being fair, Ollie."

"Then ask her to explain and watch her squirm.
She bilked my aunt out of her fortune, and I intend
to see her brought to justice for it." Oliver's eyes were
slits of anger. "I wouldn't even be surprised but what
she poisoned the old girl. The physician said that
auntie died because poison had spread throughout
her body. Indigestion? Ha!"

Anger coursed through Garrick's veins. Putting up
his fists he eyed Oliver squarely. "Get out of my
house, Ollie. Get out, I say. I don't want to hurt you
but, by God, I will if you say another word."

"Get out?" Something in Garrick's expression
warned Oliver that if he didn't want a black eye he
should leave. "All right, I will." Picking up the damaging piece of paper, he scurried through the door.

Garrick was overcome by his emotions, but later,
when his logical mind took over, he began to see
things differently. He'd asked Dawn Landon to
marry him, but before he went through with the ceremony he would have to do a bit of investigating on
his own.

36

Rain pattered steadily upon the windowpane, yet as Dawn stretched lazily and opened her eyes, she thought it a lovely morning. Every day is beautiful when one is in love. From the leaping fire on the stone hearth to the downy, velvet-covered quilt on her bed, the room welcomed her like a friendly smile. Humming a tune, she slipped out of bed.

"Are you ready for breakfast, mum?" Peeping through the doorway Agnes made inquiry.

"Toast and tea." Her stomach was still queasy just thinking about last night.

"That's all? Why, you'll waste away, mum."

"I'll have something later. Besides, we're having a guest for the midday meal. Garrick Seton. Tell Cook to fix something very special." Dawn felt proud just saying his name.

"Garrick Seton!" The girl's blush gave her thoughts away, and Dawn suspected Agnes had a secret yearning for him. Well, why not, he was a handsome man, one who would soon be her husband. Hugging her arms about her body, she thought how unbelievable that was. Even in her wildest dreams she had never imagined that.

"I'll tell you a secret, Agnes. He's asked me to marry him!" Her voice was breathless for she could hardly believe it to be true.

"To marry him? Oh, mum! I'd be telling a fib if I said I wasn't envious." Agnes clasped her hands together. "What a handsome gent. In truth he is."

"I know. I have to pinch myself to be sure I'm not dreaming." Garrick was coming for lunch to discuss details of their wedding. She wanted everything to be perfect.

Immersed in a warm, hazy glow, Dawn drifted dreamily through the morning hours, remembering last night. If Garrick had not pulled away from her when he did, she would have given herself freely to him. What would it be like to be naked in his arms, to feel his caress all over her body, from neck to toes? As Agnes prepared her bath she wondered.

The water in the brass tub felt warm and wonderful. Dawn lingered over her bath, sponging herself, imagining the cloth to be Garrick's caress. Recalling his love for violets, she asked Agnes for a bar of soap that held that fragrance. Leaning back, she closed her eyes and luxuriated, sighing with pleasure.

Stepping from the tub, wrapping herself in a large towel, she dried herself, then set about finding just the right dress to wear. She chose a simple lawn-green dress of linen with a neckline just high enough to be decent but low enough to be interesting. Around her neck she tied a ribbon with a cameo that had been one of Margaret Pembrooke's gifts. She couldn't help wondering what the grandam would think of her upcoming marriage. Surely she would have heartily approved.

Always one to scorn corsets, Dawn had a change of heart, allowing Agnes to lace her up tightly. As to her hair, she remembered Garrick's comment about its length and decided to let it hang free. To make certain the dark waves were shiny, she brushed it a hundred times. Viewing herself in the mirror, she smiled, pleased with her decisions.

"Your gentleman is here!" Agnes couldn't hide her breathless excitement.

"Tell him I will be right down."

As she slowly descended the stairs, Dawn was a vision of loveliness, so breathtaking that Garrick could only stare. Ollie was wrong, he kept thinking. How could anyone with such a winsome smile be a liar? A poisoner? A cheat? And yet wasn't his mother capable of putting on an innocent air now and again?

Watching her closely as they walked to the dining room, he tried to judge her objectively. Could he bear it if she proved to be a fraud? What if by his own efforts he learned she was not who she professed to be? What then? If she were false and treacherous, could he just walk away? No. He didn't think he could. With a frightening intensity he realized that Dawn meant more to him than anything else in the whole world. Strange, how quickly she had gotten into his blood.

"I've had Cook prepare sturgeon with wine sauce. I remember Mrs. Pembrooke telling me that it is your favorite fish."

Garrick winced at the mention of the wealthy dowager. Imagine Oliver being so hateful as to accuse this lovely young woman of poisoning her! It was slander and he really should have beaten the daylights out of the young pup.

"I do much prefer sturgeon to beef. I guess that makes me very un-English," he said with a forced laugh.

Now he, too, was having Dawn watched. It bothered his conscience. One of her own servants was now in his pay, with instructions to watch her comings and goings. So much for trust. It was all to prove Oliver wrong—and yet, what would he have thought if she had him watched and followed? He would have been insulted, even outraged.

Like a practiced and most gracious hostess, Dawn
saw that Garrick's plate was filled with succulent
pieces of fish, small onions, carrots, and potatoes.
Sherry, port and claret were served continuously
through the meal, leading Garrick to remark that if
he indulged himself he would be too much in his
cups to return to the office. And all the while Dawn's
wide green eyes held him captive.

He was conscious of a fierce urge to throw caution
to the four winds, sweep her up in his arms, and
elope with her. Ollie be damned! His feelings for her
were all that mattered. Ollie was wrong! He was playing some sort of silly, childish game which would
backfire. Looking at her, he prayed it was so.

The intensity of Garrick's look unnerved Dawn
slightly. There was something forced in his smile.
The sparkle in his eyes had turned to a pensive glow.
Something was wrong, but she was uncertain just
what it might be.

"Is everything all right?"

"Fine. Everything is delicious."

He thought to test her. "Margaret never told me
what part of Norfolk you came from," he said, sipping at his port.

Dawn laughed nervously, wishing she could tell
him everything but still feeling the need to keep her
secrets. "The middle section," she blurted, not being
familiar with Norfolk at all.

"The middle?" It was a strange answer. "What
town?" His eyes narrowed, her nervousness not going unnoticed.

Dawn thought quickly. "No town, really. We . . .
we had an . . . an estate."

"An estate. Mmm. But where?"

She couldn't look him in the eye. How she hated to
lie. Why had she and Margaret Pembrooke fabri-
cated a false identity for her in the first place? Ah,

yes, because of Robbie and the fear that somehow she might be connected with him. Remembering a rhyme her father had once told her so long ago about a peddler named John Chapman who had come to London to earn his fortune as a shopkeeper she blurted, "Swaffham," the town where that man was from.

"Swaffham. Then no doubt you heard about the suspected treasure said to be buried there."

"Treasure?"

Garrick laughed. "When I was a child I was told about the Swaffham peddler who dreamed that if he stood on London Bridge, a man would tell him how he might become rich. He walked to London and stood on the bridge for hours but no rich man came by. At last he fell into conversation with a shopkeeper and told him how he had been led on a fool's errand by a dream. The shopkeeper replied that he too had had a curious dream, in which he saw treasure being buried in the garden of a gentleman in far-off Swaffham."

"John Chapman!" Dawn remembered the story very vividly now.

"Yes! Chapman returned home and began digging." Garrick's suspicion died. He was letting Ollie's jealousy and foolish accusations get to him.

"And there were two enormous pots of gold buried beneath a tree. As a thanksgiving offering, the peddler built the north aisle and tower of a church."

"Yes." Garrick put all of Oliver's tattlings out of his mind. Arm in arm they walked slowly back to the drawing room.

They talked of many things, settling on the subject of the wedding as they retired to the drawing room. Garrick was anxious to set the date, wanting the ceremony to take place as soon as could be arranged.

"The pounding in my blood tells me we had best set the date for our wedding very quickly."

He pulled her into the warmth of his embrace and she put her head on his shoulder just as she had last night. Mesmerized, he kissed her with all the tenderness and gentleness in his soul.

"The sooner the better. . . ." he whispered at last.

"I was afraid you might have changed your mind," she teased.

"Changed my mind?" As he thought of Ollie and his accusations he frowned. "No. Never."

"I'm glad. All I could think about today was you." There was no cunning in her voice, no coquetry in her smile.

He laughed softly. "I don't know how much longer I can act the proper gentleman." Pulling her into the shadows, away from Douglas's watchful eyes, he pulled her up against him, his mouth hungrily finding hers again. His kiss was urgent, his lips hard and demanding against hers.

Dawn pressed tightly against him, kissing him back eagerly as their bodies strained together. It was heaven to have her in his embrace. As her arms wound around his neck, all Garrick's doubts and suspicions melted away.

37

The ugly gray walls of Newgate loomed before Dawn's eyes like a fearsome monolith. The doors seemed to grin at her maliciously with their iron-plated teeth. She shivered as John Barrister led her towards the entrance. *Newgate!* Oh, how that very name used to fill her with dread. Now she was coming here of her own free will to see about freeing her brother.

"It will take quite a sum of money, Miss Landon, to free this young man. Are you prepared to pay the fee?" John Barrister regarded her quizzically.

"Money is no object, I assure you," she answered, laying her hand on his sleeve. Dawn had kept the truth of Robbie's relationship to her from the barrister for safety's sake. Somehow anyone who represented the law still seemed suspect. She had spent too many years running from those who professed to uphold the law while they took bribes and switched their loyalties this way and that to suit their advantage. All too many solicitors, barristers, magistrates, turnkeys, and parish beadles were corrupt. One never really knew whom to trust.

"Then let us be on our way, though I warn you this will not be pleasant." The tall, balding man grimaced as he withdrew a snowy white linen handkerchief from the inside pocket of his dun-colored coat. "Take this, my dear; no doubt you will have need of it." At her questioning look he said, "You will find the stench nearly unbearable, at least until we get beyond the common prisoners."

The heavy spiked doors swung open with a groan and Dawn followed the barrister inside. From where they stood behind the wicket she could see prisoners being admitted and watched in fascinated horror as tattered individuals were transported to their cells in prison carts.

"Poor souls!"

"Hardly, my dear. Criminals, every last one, or they would not be here." John Barrister patted her arm. "But I assure you this is a very secure prison. No one has ever escaped nor will."

Silently she traversed the endless corridors and descended the steeply winding staircases into a place that reminded her of hell. *This is the place where Robbie has spent his days while you have been living with Margaret Pembrooke in splendor*, she thought. Dear God, if she had only known, but even her worst nightmares paled beside the hideous reality. The Fleet, where she and Robbie had spent some time, was luxurious in comparison.

As she walked along, her eyes searched in the dim light, staring through the grates for a glimpse of Robbie's face, but all she could see were clutching hands as the gaolers rationed out their moldy bread and unappetizing food.

"Disgusting animals. Savages," John Barrister mumbled into his handkerchief. "I don't know why I chose such an occupation. Better to have been a merchant, I daresay."

"My father was a merchant," Dawn murmured, touched by the deprivation that she saw. The gaunt faces and wild, hopeless eyes of those who somehow managed to push their faces against the grating gave her a glimpse of their suffering. She could feel their misery and mourned for them, remembering her mother and how prison had so devastatingly changed her.

"A merchant? Is that so?" As Dawn paused, he put his hand in the small of her back and gave her a nudge. "Come along. The prisoner you seek has been lodged in far more comfortable quarters."

"Different quarters?" Dawn breathed a sigh of relief. Jamie had said that Robbie was living as comfortably as was possible in a place like this. "Yes, I believe Garrick Seton made the arrangements."

"Garrick Seton?" The lawyer paused in midstride, shaking his head. "No, no, no. Mrs. Pembrooke is the one who set up the fund to pay for the unfortunate man's keep."

"Mrs. Pembrooke?" Margaret Pembrooke had said that she could find no trace of Robbie, had made Dawn believe that he had disappeared. Why had she told such a vile lie? The betrayal stung Dawn.

Why hadn't Mrs. Pembrooke set Robbie free if she knew where he was? How could she have dried Dawn's tears, calmed her worries, and spoken such soothing words, all the time knowing Robbie was behind the bars of Newgate? Because she knew Dawn would return with him to St. Giles. Perhaps in her way she had meant to protect Dawn, and yet it was such a treacherous deceit.

She wanted to ask John Barrister what he knew but thought better of it. Instead she made a pretense of knowing all about the situation. "Yes, yes, of course, Mrs. Pembrooke. It is because of her wishes that I am here. She would have wanted to have the young man set free."

"Upon my soul, I can't fathom why." The lawyer grimaced his disapproval. "By all I've heard he's a scoundrel!"

"Nevertheless I want him out of here!" Margaret Pembrooke might have broken Dawn's trust, but now her money would at last help set Robbie free.

"As you wish." John Barrister resumed his stride, not stopping until they approached a big burly guard. "The pickpocket Robert Leighton. We are here to see him," Barrister annouced.

The guard was surly. "Wot do yer want wi' 'im?"

"It's not for *you* to question. Just unlock the door!"

Without another word the turnkey obeyed, slamming the door behind him. In a matter of minutes Robbie's beloved face appeared at the grate. "Dawnie, me dear! If yer ain't a sight fer sore eyes." His eyes twinkled merrily. "And blimey if yer don't look grand. Like a queen or such."

"Oh, Rob! Rob! I thought I'd never see you again!" Putting her fingers through the grate she touched his hand and squeezed it affectionately. Tears flooded her eyes and coursed down her cheeks. "But I'll get you out of here, I promise. Mr. Barrister, who has accompanied me, is a barrister. He's going to see that you have another trial, one that will prove you innocent."

It would be a simple matter, John Barrister said, if only Garrick Seton would cooperate. Dawn had been so certain that he would. But now that she knew the truth of the matter, she had her doubts. Mrs. Pembrooke had been the one. It was still hard to believe.

"A new trial? 'Pon me word, I ne'er thought ter 'ave such luck, though it 'asn't been all that 'orrible 'ere. A warm bed, enough food, and pleasant enough company to while awaiy the toime. But there ain't no substitute for a man's freedom, that's all I can saiy, Dawnie. I'll be looking forward to walking through 'at door, all roight!"

"And soon you will. Trust me, Rob. But you'll have to be patient." Again she squeezed his hand.

"Patience ain't one o' me virtues, but I will try, me dear."

John Barrister's scrutiny made Dawn afraid to say more. Something about the man cautioned her to be wary. Too much said might be dangerous. What was important now was that Robbie knew she would soon set him free. But oh, how she wished she could throw her arms about him, hug him, kiss him, and tell him how much she had missed him and still loved him. As it was, she could do no more than touch his hand. She had to be satisfied with a mumbled farewell.

"We'll return, Rob, just as soon as possible with the proper papers. Until then, good-bye . . ." Dawn looked back several times as John Barrister led her back the way they had come. Then, at last, the suffocating depths of Newgate were behind her.

38

〜⁓ ⁓〜

Garrick fidgeted nervously as he sat on the edge of his carriage seat looking out the window. Ducks, swans, and geese glided over the Serpentine in Hyde Park, taking advantage of a rare bit of sun, and he passed his time watching them. A flock of sheep grazed peacefully, competing with the cows for rare greenery. The London butchers had been given grazing rights in the park with the double purpose of fattening their animals and fertilizing the land, but Garrick thought it was an abominable inconvenience when one wanted to take a walk. Better to stay inside the carriage and wait until the individual who had sent him the message showed himself.

I wish I'd never put Henry in my employ. I have no liking for this spying business, he grumbled to himself, feeling uneasy, much like a man awaiting his own sentencing. Would what he was about to learn shatter his dreams?

The minutes dragged by into a quarter hour. In summer, London's four public parks usually bustled with activity but today, Hyde Park was all but deserted. He spotted the dark-cloaked figure immediately, as it moved closer to the carriage. A woman! He watched as she daintily lifted up her skirts to avoid the mud puddles. Perhaps Henry's paramour, then.

Opening the door, Garrick offered his hand, helping the young woman up. "I don't want anyone to see
me," she gasped, looking cautiously behind her. "Oh,
I feel like such a traitor. She's been very kind to me.
But Henry said . . ."

"We'll have privacy inside." The only one who
might overhear was Vinnie, and Garrick trusted the
young man implicitly. "You're . . ."

"Agnes." The young woman blushed under the heat
of his stare. "I was 'ired by Margaret Pembrooke to
be Miss Landon's personal maid. And I've taken good
care of her. Until now . . ." She looked down at her
shoes, concentrating on the large buckles.

"I thought for a moment you weren't coming after
all."

"I 'ad to wait til she was gone." She punctuated her
words with a long-drawn-out sigh.

"I presume you know something that might interest me, concerning your mistress's identity?" Somehow he didn't want to know. Did it really matter who
Dawn really was? And yet he could not build his marriage on a lie. "Who is she?"

"I don't know 'o she is, only what I heard from
some of the other servants when I first came, that
Margaret Pembrooke 'ad taken her in. Oh, the money
that woman lavished on her. Why, you might've
thought she was 'er daughter or something." She
sprawled in the seat next to Garrick.

"Her daughter?" A surge of relief flooded through
him. Was it possible that the old dowager had comit-
ted an indiscretion in her youth? Perhaps Dawn was
her illegitimate daughter. That would answer so
many questions and put all Ollie's arguments to rest.
"Perhaps she *is* . . ."

"Oh no! Mrs. Pembrooke took her in off the streets,
or so I'm told. She 'oused her and clothed her and
taught her to speak proper."

"Why, I can scarce believe it. Her diction is flaw-less. . . ."

"Mrs. Pembrooke's tutoring." Agnes clasped her hands so tightly together that her knuckles turned white. "Which I guess does prove that you can turn a sow's ear into a silk purse. Oh, that I 'ad been so fortunate, for she lives like a princess now, she 'o used to walk the streets."

Garrick shook his head. "I don't believe you. I don't know why you're telling me this ghastly tale. It just won't do. I won't give you a farthing without proof. That is what I asked for. God knows if I wanted to hear a silly story I'd listen to Ollie. He has enough of them." He opened the door as if dismissing her, but she didn't budge.

"I need the money you promised. That's the only reason I came. That and the fact that you are so 'and-some. I don't think I could deny you anything." She looked at him hopefully.

Garrick's whole body tensed. So that was it. She thought to discredit Dawn and take her place. His tone was scathing. "And just why should I believe you?"

"Not just me. Several of the servants can testify to the fact that I speak the truth. And . . . and Mrs. Pembrooke's solicitor, Mr. Cambridge, he'll tell you. 'E was the one who rewrote the will. Or Mr. Barris-ter. He knows." Her voice lowered conspiratorially. "As a matter of fact he accompanied Miss Landon this morning. And where do you think they were go-ing?"

"I have no idea."

"Newgate Prison, that's where. And why do you suppose they went there?" When he didn't answer she said, "To try and set one of the prisoners free. A young man. A thief! I listened at the door." She took off her bonnet, toying with the ties. "Now why do you suppose a decent young woman would care what 'appened to the likes of 'im?"

"Why do *you* suppose?" Garrick sat on the edge of his seat.

"Well . . . there's been talk. But I'd say at one time he must have been her lover! It makes sense if you think about it. Oh!" She shrieked as Garrick moved away so swiftly that she tumbled backward in the seat.

"You are wasting my time! I'm a busy man. I have no liking for the direction this conversation is going. I'm beginning to think Oliver has put you up to this. Well, you can tell him I'm not amused." He nodded with his head towards the open door. "Now, if you don't mind . . ." Was it Ollie? Or was this young woman so filled with jealousy that she was willing to fabricate the most outrageous stories? Newgate indeed! An inmate as a lover! "Ridiculous!"

"Oh? I don't know." She positioned herself farther back on the seat, refusing to be so rudely dismissed. "I brought you something of interest. It bears your initials, yet I know she had it long before she met you that night Mrs. Pembrooke's nephew brought you to dinner."

"My initials?" He was puzzled.

"What roused my suspicions is the way she always keeps it locked up in a drawer, as if she's afraid someone might see it. And . . . and I've seen her take it out and look at it as if it were covered with diamonds. Once when I came in behind her and she was eyeing it, she jumped as if I'd frightened her half to death and hid it behind her back. I ask you why?" Taking it out of her pocket, she dangled it tauntingly before his nose, then pulled it away. "A timepiece! Now what do you suppose she wants with this?"

Garrick's eyes followed the swinging motion for a moment. The watch looked all too familiar. "Give it

to me! By God, girl, I won't stand for any teasing!"
Reaching out, he grabbed it, turning it over in his
fingers. His initials danced before his eyes. G.F.S.
There could be no mistaking. It was his watch, the
one that had been stolen at the docks. He'd had it
specially made. There wasn't another one like it.

"You see, I told you I had something that would
pique your interest." She laughed softly. "Now will
you give me the money you told Henry would be the
reward for any information on our mysterious lady?"

"Lady!" Two images hovered before Garrick's eyes,
one of a proper young miss, the other of a painted
face. The images switched back and forth, merging
into each other. No, it couldn't be! He would have
known, would have suspected. And yet, finding *that*
woman in Margaret Pembrooke's house would have
been the last thing he would have expected.

"Am I right? Did she steal it from you?" Agnes
licked her lips. Lord, but he was acting strangely.

"No! No . . . you . . . you see, I gave it to her."
Even with his mounting anger, he thought to protect
her.

There was no masking her disappointment. "Gave
it to her?"

"Yes, so you see where your meddling has taken
you. I will have to tell Miss Landon that you have
been spying on her and searching through her things.
I'm certain she will dismiss you immediately." Garrick suddenly remembered that it had been in front
of Margaret Pembrooke's house that he had finally
apprehended the young rogue who had robbed him.
Coincidence? He knew the answer.

"Oh, no! Please, sir. I thought to help. I . . . I
thought . . . well . . . well, you can see why I
might. She was acting so strange, hiding it and all. I
thought . . ."

"You thought wrong!" Only by the greatest effort

was he able to maintain his composure. His heart was hammering; he felt as if every drop of blood had been drained from him. The harlot! The dock whore! It was beyond belief. She and the demure, proper Miss Landon were one and the same. Beneath her elegance hovered the same young tart who had set him up to be robbed and nearly killed. How could he have ever been such a blind fool not to realize? Because he had been so taken by her beauty, her feigned innocence. He had assumed her to be exactly who she professed to be. A young woman from Norfolk!

Lie upon lie, deception upon deception! The dock whore and Dawn Landon! She had skillfully manipulated him. Had she so easily fooled Margaret Pembrooke as well? That poor woman had thought to help her, and where was she now? In her grave.

For a moment as he looked at the watch, his eyes narrowed to angry slits. How she must have been laughing at him all the while, knowing they had met before and under what circumstances. Oh, how he had courted her, the conniving little bitch. And all the while she had played her innocence to the hilt. Blistering fury took hold of him. She had nearly been the cause of his death! She and that tattered young thief. Her lover? Somehow all the pieces began to fit together. And poor Margaret Pembrooke had not known the type of woman she sheltered.

And yet even knowing caused him such pain! He had thought her the perfect woman, the woman he had been searching for all his life; a woman so completely different from his mother, one to give him the love he had never had. He had craved her but held himself back. She was too virtuous to be taken advantage of, he had thought. Virtuous! Ha! He remembered the passion she had displayed when she came to his office. Like tinder awaiting a spark. He should have given in to his desire there and then and taken her on the carpeted floor. But he had been obsessed with being a gentleman! Fool!

"Take this and put it back where you found it." He thrust the watch into Agnes's trembling hands. "Perhaps I may not tell on you if you promise not to say a word of this to anyone."

"You'll keep silent?" Taking his hand, Agnes kissed it gratefully. "Thank you, sir. You won't be sorry. I'll do you a good turn someday. I will. I promise!" She slid from the carriage and took to her heels without once looking back.

Garrick's anger fed upon itself until it was a fire raging out of control. He'd fallen in love with a scheming little *trull*. Allowed her to weave her silken web around him until he was helplessly trapped. He'd been completely besotted, just as Oliver had said, and oh, how she must have laughed all the while. Closing his eyes, he remembered the way her breasts had pushed against him when they danced, the soft touch of her hands. Marry her? Hardly. But he would claim what he had burned for all this while, *before* he flung the truth in her face.

39

Garrick pulled his carriage up to Oliver's house wearing a scowl that made him look like the very devil himself. Jumping down he bade Vinnie unhitch the horses.

"Are we going to be staying a long while, sir?" Vinnie looked down at him from atop his perch.

"I'm giving the carriage to Oliver Chambers, Vinnie. We won't be using it again." His disposition was not improved by the question. "Drive it around to the stables."

"Giving it to Mr. Chambers, sir?" The young driver looked totally baffled. "But . . . but why?"

"It's too long a story to tell, nor do I have the stomach for revealing my motives at the moment. But don't worry, I'll buy another so you will not be unemployed." Not wanting to take out his foul mood on the lad, he patted him on the shoulder. "Let me just say that to my regret a woman has something to do with it. Hopefully your own romance is running more smoothly."

"We're going to be married, sir. She's given in to my wooing." Vinnie blushed a shade to match his livery.

"Marriage. A noble institution," Garrick said dryly. "Well, carry on!" He paced back and forth in front of Oliver's front door, not at all anxious to hear Oliver's

"I told you so, old chum." He'd jolly well been duped. Tricked. Deceived. Was it any wonder he was in such a black mood? "Women be damned!" he whispered under his breath.

Devious, every last one of them. Whores at heart, using their charms, be they ample or wanting, to snag a husband, then damning the fellow with their every breath. From fishwife to aristocrat it was all the same. Stephanie Creighton, for example. He knew very well why she wanted him. Nor did a wedding band mean they were any less dishonest. Had a gold band kept his mother faithful? It was merely a symbol of security. Well, he would never marry. Not now. Particularly not some little baggage who had plied her trade at the docks.

"Garrick? Garrick, old boy!" Oliver spied him from the window and waved. Pushing open the front door, he bounded down the steps. "Whatever are you doing stalking about out here? I've got a fire blazing inside and I've opened a bottle of brandy. "I've a guest . . .""

"I feel the need to be out in the fresh air, Ollie. Do you mind?"

"But there is a chill . . . and the damp . . ." Oliver shrugged his shoulders. "It's freezing, but if you insist, let's at least sit here on the portico while you tell me what has you in such a snit. Or shall I guess?"

"I have instructed Vinnie to unhook my carriage and take it around to your stable. Does that answer your question?" Garrick cast him an icy glance; then, deciding it wasn't Oliver's fault that he had been made a fool, he extended his hand. "I'm making good on my bet, and I apologize for some of the things I've said. Fair?"

"Oh! It sounds as if you have been stung. So you found out I'm right, eh, Gar? Now you believe me when I tell you that she isn't from Norfolk." He motioned towards a chair. "Here. Sit. Sit and tell me all."

"Not only is she not from Norfolk, but she's a common little strumpet. And a thief! From London, no less." Though a voice deep inside urged him to use prudence in revealing the story, his anger goaded him on. While Oliver made himself comfortable, Garrick stood with one foot perched on the chair rung, telling his friend about the young maid's visit.

"The maid had your watch?"

"She confiscated it from our dear Miss Landon. No doubt it was given to *her* by that young scoundrel who came upon me at the docks. You remember, Ollie. I was there to meet with *your* client, after all. She came up swaying her hips and smiling seductively at me while he was hovering behind me with a club, ready to bash my head in. I woke up in an old warehouse to find her bending over me with a knife."

"Gad! It's even worse than I suspected! Poor Aunt Margaret!" Putting a hand to his throat, Oliver winced.

"Murder wasn't in her plan, at least that night, for I did get free. She tried to convince me she had come to help me. I wonder . . ." Somehow he couldn't believe that Dawn would kill anyone, no matter what else she had done. No, of that she was vindicated in his mind. As to her male companion, he wasn't so sure. "If you remember, I caught that young pickpocket near your aunt's house. Now I know what he was doing there. He was in league with her. Though what they had planned, we'll never know."

"Oh, my! And to think that now *she* has inherited Aunt Margaret's fortune. Something will have to be done at once. We'll call in the . . ."

"No!" Oliver's intentions were like a spray of cold water, dousing Garrick's anger. "I don't want to be hasty. Besides, we have no proof." He didn't want to see her thrown out on the street with nowhere to go, returning to her former lifestyle. Never that. He was neither a cruel nor a mercilessly vengeful man. Something of this magnitude would have to be thought out carefully.

"The watch! You told me . . ."

"I gave it back. It's in her possession, not in mine." Garrick grabbed hold of one of the colonnades that held up the porch. "I don't want to talk about it any further, Ollie. I need to think. Please try to understand. I loved her. I really loved her."

Oliver clucked his tongue in sympathy. "I'm sorry, Gar! Really I am. But women are women, after all. What can one say? Eve and all that, eh? Poor Adam. That's when it all began, I daresay." Rising to his feet, he patted his friend on the back. "But I have just what you need. Come inside. A good stiff drink will make you forget what has happened."

"And another and another." Garrick knew it would take more than just one. Dear God, how she haunted him still. Even now the very thought of her in his arms fired his blood.

What kind of fool was he? What the sweet, bloody hell had happened to him? Did it matter? She had been an illusion after all, he thought with bitter mockery. Her performance would have put any Drury Lane actress to shame. For a moment he had even thought she cared. Feeling a twinge of self-pity he followed Oliver inside and there succumbed to three fingers of brandy.

"She used me." That thought made him grind his teeth. And yet what had been her purpose? Had her passion been feigned? With the Pembrooke fortune at her disposal hadn't she had all that she could want? What had been her game? Letting the fiery liquid trickle down his throat, he knew there was only one way to find out for himself. To ask her.

40

The fire in the great hearth leaped and sparked, warding off the chill of the night. By the light of the Argand lamp, Dawn studied the documents John Barrister had given her, wishing she could really understand the details. There were so many words that they blurred before her eyes. Still, everything seemed to be in order. It made Robbie her ward and requested a retrial. *How strange*, she thought, *to be named as his guardian.* Yet the barrister had counseled her to this action. Well, to get Robbie out of that terrible place she would have done anything, even bargain with the devil himself if necessary. Dipping a pen into the ink bottle, she hastily scrawled her name to the papers spread out on the drawing room table, using the elaborate penmanship Margaret Pembrooke had insisted upon.

"We need to find witnesses who will testify to the young man's good character," the barrister had said, cocking a brow. "Upstanding men of consequence." Dawn wondered just who that could be, then remembered what Black John had always said, that enough money could make any bloke testify that a sheep was a cow. Well, if she had to resort to bribery to free her brother, she gladly would.

It was quiet in the large house. She had granted Douglas the night off. Agnes had been acting fidgety and had gone to bed early, and the others of the household had retired to their own quarters, thus Dawn was startled by the loud tapping at the door. Glancing at the mantle clock, she saw that it was nine o'clock. Rather late for a visitor. Perhaps it was John Barrister, anxious to retrieve his documents so that he could be about his work first thing in the morning.

Dawn waited for just a moment, but when the insistent knocking began again, she went to the door. To her surprise she found Garrick standing there, leaning against the doorframe. "Garrick!" The faint hint of brandy teased her nostrils as she stepped closer.

"Surprised to see me?" There was a sharp edge to his voice, and something in his smile that chilled her.

"Pleasantly surprised," she whispered, taking a step backward. Something was wrong, she knew it immediately.

"But not enough to invite me in?" There was a reckless glitter in the blue eyes staring back at her. "Shame, shame, shame. Where are your manners? A *proper* young lady, like you?" His hair fell forward across his forehead and into his eyes. Usually meticulously groomed, he looked shockingly disheveled. His cravat was missing and his shirt was open down the front, revealing the strength of his neck and a tuft of hair on his chest.

"I'm sorry. Please, come in. You are always welcome." Suppressing her disquiet, she moved out of the way.

He pushed past her with a predatory grace. Slowly, insolently, his eyes moved over her as he shut the door behind them. Walking towards her, he reached out and touched the hair falling at her temples, then closed his fingers in a fist. She was so very lovely. Looking at her now it was hard to believe she had led a life of crime and debauchery.

Against his will, he let his eyes stray over her, lingering with grim appreciation on the slim column of her neck and the full, tempting line of her breasts. He remembered the heat and warmth of her skin, the taste of her, her softness, and an intense, nearly painful surge of desire swept over him. Wanton or not, he had to have her. He was caught in her silken web.

"You really are a very beautiful woman."

"Thank you," she said softly confused by an undercurrent of anger she could not fathom.

"Beautiful . . ." As he spoke his lips barely moved, and she could see that his jaw was clenched. The firelight cast a sinister shadow across his face as he moved towards her.

"Garrick!" This was not the man who had charmed her at the theatre and won her heart. There was no gentleness in his face now. This man was a stranger, unpredictable and dangerous. "You've been drinking!" she scolded.

"Astute observation, my dear. But then, no doubt, you've seen enough men in their cups. Unfortunately, I'm not drunk. Or perhaps there's just not enough brandy in this whole world to get you out of my blood." His hand shot out at her and he tried to grab her arm, but she scurried around the end of the table, avoiding him.

"Garrick, please leave." Something was wrong. Very, very wrong. She was unnerved by the unyielding look in his eyes. "Come back tomorrow and we'll pretend this never happened."

"Pretend? Ah, yes. You are an expert at that, are you not?" This time when he reached for her she couldn't evade his hands. Drawing her towards him he held her unmercifully, clasping her chin in his rough hand and turning her face toward the light. "Who are you?" he asked suddenly. "For I know that Landon is not your name."

Her gaze flew to his, her face paled. "What do you mean?"

"There are no young ladies of your age or name in all of Norfolk." His smile was cynical, though he let her go. "Don't playact with me. I know you for what you are."

"All right. My name is not Landon. It's Leighton."

"Leighton?" She had a very expressive face. Her eyes were as wide as a hunted fawn's, her mouth tight and quivering. He almost felt sorry for her. "Well, whatever your name, you are a deceiving little bitch! Lovely but conniving."

She nearly strangled on the reply that sprang to her lips. Without even thinking, she slapped him hard. The sound of her palm striking his cheek reverberated through the room like a shot. An ominous silence fell as they stared at each other for a long aching moment.

Oh, what had she done? How had it all come to this? Her pulse beat violently at her throat as she said, "I don't know what you have learned or why you are so angry, but I will tell you the truth."

"The truth? I doubt you even know how. You, my dear are a liar, a thief, and a trollop!"

"No!" She clung to the table for support. How was it possible her world could so suddenly crumble around her? He hated her now. She could see it in his eyes, and it made her reel with pain. "I was a thief once, yes. My parents died when I was eight years old and I was condemned to the streets. My brother and I were taken in by a man named Black John Dunn who trained us to be thieves."

"So . . . a measure of truth at last. No lady at all, but a pickpocket!" He folded his arms across his chest and stood glaring.

"Yes, a thief." His tone angered her. He was so self-righteous, he who had never known what it was to miss his dinner. "It was either that or starve. Certainly the men and women of *your* class showed me no pity. Not one crust of bread, nor even a measure of kindness. I might have been a bug for all they cared." She took two deep breaths, trying to regain her poise. "Black John at least saw to it that we did not go hungry at night, albeit there was a price. I was taught to steal handkerchiefs in his nursery of crime. Soon it was the only life I knew."

"That and whoring!"

"No!" How she hated the word and what it implied. "I never sold my body. I've never let any man touch me in that way. Never!"

Her answer filled him with contempt. "Then let me refresh your memory. A dark night at the docks. A soiled white dress. A hat with a broken feather." The scene flashed before his eyes so vividly it was as if he were reliving it. "You sauntered up to me with your seductive invitation, hands on hips, mouth pouting. Am I to believe you merely wanted to know the time?" He grasped her by the wrist, pulling her face to within inches of his.

An anguished sob tore from her throat. So he remembered and now thought the worst. "It was a ploy. Rob and Black John coerced me into it, much to my regret. I was to play the trull so they could rob you." Her admission was so damning that she winced, regretting with every beat of her heart that she had ever consented to the deed. Because of that night Robbie was in Newgate and her own life on the brink of ruin.

"Rob me?" He threw back his head and laughed bitterly. "Ah yes, I remember all too well. My head throbbed painfully for weeks. A charming little career you established for yourself. Just see where it has taken you." With a show of disgust he released her arm and stepped back. "Though I can't for the life of me understand how you could have fooled Margaret Pembrooke for a moment."

"I didn't. She knew what I was and showed me kindness. She taught me how to talk and walk, helped me escape my mean surroundings. She gave me hope and love."

"And was rewarded with treachery."

"No! Never that. She was my friend. I would give anything in this world to have her back again but . . ."

"Liar! How can you expect me to believe you?"

"It's the truth. . . ."

A tight ball of pain coiled within Garrick's chest as he caught the expression in her eyes. He wanted to take the words back, give her a chance to explain, but stubborness overcame his reason. She had made a total fool of him with her pretense of virtue. He wanted to punish her. He thought of her lying naked in his arms and once again desire engulfed him. His eyes darkened with passion, his full mouth took on a cruel, sensual curve. He wanted her and could think of no reason why he shouldn't slake his passion. Now. Tonight!

With that thought, he closed his hands painfully around her shoulders. She was jerked unceremoniously up against the hardness of his chest as his mouth descended, taking hers with a savage intensity. He kissed her like a man with a fierce, insatiable hunger to appease. It was as if he wanted to hurt her, wanted to cause her pain, and yet she didn't fight him. The touch of his mouth, brutal as it was, evoked a fierce answering hunger within her. Love was a healing thing. Perhaps she could prove that what she felt for him was real. She knew she could prove she wasn't a whore. Always she had guarded her virtue most vehemently, despite her circumstances. Now she would give it up to him.

His lips were everywhere—her cheeks, her ear-lobes, her neck, and back to her mouth again, his tongue plunging deeply, insistently between her lips. Her hands moved restlessly over his chest, up to entangle her fingers in his hair. His hands answered her caress, sliding down her body. Then he was sweeping her up in his arms and carrying her towards the stairs.

41

Moonlight streamed through the open curtains, casting eerie shadows on the wall as Garrick made his way up the stairs with his beautiful bundle. Kicking open the door to Margaret Pembrooke's chamber, he made his way to the bed with Dawn in his arms.

"A woman like you doesn't understand gentleness. But you will understand this." His mouth was hungry as it took hers, plundering, urgent, as he explored her mouth's sweetness.

The pressure of the kiss should have hurt her but it didn't. Instead it drained her very soul, then poured it back again, filling her to overflowing. Despite his anger that kiss proved to her that he cared. It was not lust alone that fueled him, no matter what he might say to the contrary.

So thinking, she returned his kiss, her defenses devastated by her own craving. There was nothing in the world for her but his mouth. She surrendered to him completely without even a token resistance, wishing the kiss could go on forever. If he wanted to punish her he'd chosen the wrong penalty. Twining her hands around his neck, she clutched him to her, pressing her body eagerly against his chest. She could feel the heat and strength and growing desire of him with every breath. She loved him, and he wanted her.

Garrick pulled his mouth away, looking deep into her eyes. She looked artless and young, but he must remembered that she was a woman as false as Jezebel. No matter what happened tonight, he must not allow himself to forget. With a ruthless intensity he wanted to teach her a lesson she would never forget. She was a greedy little strumpet who had lied to him, baited him into a trap, and Lord knew what else.

His voice was low, with a strange throaty quality to it. "The moment of truth is at hand, my dear," he said with a wry smile. Depositing her unceremoniously on the huge bed, he slid down beside her. He reached for her and she found herself imprisoned on the feather mattress. She heard the soft rhythm of his breath as he spread her hair in a dark cloak about her shoulders.

"Beautiful. So bloody lovely."

With questing fingers he unfastened her gown and pulled the material away from her shoulders. She could feel his hands forcing her dress lower, felt the warmth of his fingers as they touched and caressed. She couldn't bring herself to utter a protest, even when he pinched the peaks of her breasts.

"Aren't you going to fight for your *virtue*?" he asked mockingly.

"I'm not going to fight you at all. I love you, Garrick. I always have, believe that or not."

"Love? Love!" The pain of his mother's rejection and her calculating heartlessness was like an ugly scar buried deep within him. He meant to hurt her as he slid his hands beneath her bodice to close over one temptingly full breast. Dawn moaned as she felt his palm cup her sensitive flesh, and that sound took away all his resolve.

"I do love you!"

Closing her eyes, she refused to think of anything that might bring her back to reality. He was the man

she loved. Her body had recognized that from the
very first moment she laid eyes on him. Garrick, her
Garrick. Her angel gentleman. She spent so many
nights dreaming that he would make love to her that
she wouldn't let his anger spoil it now. Somehow
she'd make him understand. She had to.

"Garrick . . ." Her voice was husky as she spoke
his name against his mouth. As his hands outlined
the swell of her breasts, she sank into the softness of
the feather mattress. She was vaguely aware of
where she was. Mrs. Pembrooke's room. The velvet
coverlet beneath her was warm and soft. It was red,
red, the color of passion, the old woman's favorite
color, she thought fleetingly. She was aware only of
Garrick.

"So much wasted time," he murmured. "But now
I'll make up for it." His head was bent low, his tongue
curling around the tips of her breast, sucking gently.
She gave a breathless murmur of surprise, and her
body flamed with desire. She ached to be naked
against him. Did that make her a wanton? Then so be
it.

Garrick breathed deeply, savoring the scent of violets. The enticing fragrance invaded his flaring nostrils, engulfing him. Bloody damn! What had she
done to him? He had meant only to take her, as he
might any Soho strumpet, and yet from the moment
he walked through that door, he had been swept
away by something stronger than mere lust, deeper
by far than just desire. He swore furiously to himself
that he didn't love her but knew that to be a lie, and it
was a galling admission.

Fool that he was, he could not make his brain connect with his heart. He didn't care who or what she
was; he knew only that whenever he was with her, it
seemed as if she had been made for him. Even now
her gentle curves fit into the length of his hard, mus-

cular body. His flesh felt as though it were on fire whenever it pressed against her yielding softness.

"Dawn . . ." Her name was a prayer on his lips. She was the answer to his loneliness, and yet she was his torment. *She's a woman, just like your mother,* he thought. But just touching her made him want to forget.

Raising himself up on one elbow, he looked down at her and at that moment knew he'd put his heart and soul in pawn. Removing his shirt, he pressed against her bare bosom, shivering as the sensation sent a flash of quicksilver through his veins.

There was no fire on the hearth, yet it was hot in the room. Slowly Garrick stripped Dawn's garments away, like the petals of a flower. His fingers lingered as they wandered down her stomach to explore the texture of her skin. Like velvet. He sought the indentation of her navel, then moved lower to tangle his fingers in the soft wisps of hair that joined at her legs. Moving back, he let his eyes enjoy what his hands had set free.

"Do you have any idea how much I want you? Do you?" he breathed. Then he laughed. "Of course you do. That's the point in being so beautiful, isn't it. To tempt men beyond endurance. Well, you've won." Swearing softly he took her hand and pressed it to the firm flesh of his arousal. She felt the throbbing strength of him as her eyes gazed into his. Then he bent to kiss her, keeping her mouth captive for what seemed an eternity.

The warmth and heat of his lips, the thought of her fingers touching that private part of him, sent a sweet ache flaring through Dawn's whole body. Growing bold, she allowed her hands to explore, to delight in the touch of the firm flesh that covered his ribs, the broad shoulders, the muscles of his arms, the lean length of his back. He so was perfectly formed. Beautiful for a man. With a soft sigh she curled her fingers in the thick, springy hair that furred his chest. Her fingers lightly circled in imitation of what he was doing to her.

"Blessed saints!" Oh, but she knew her trade well, he thought sourly.

Feeling encumbered by his clothes, Garrick pulled them off and flung them aside. Their bodies touched in breathtaking intimacy, and yet he took his time, lost in this world of sensual delight. She was in his arms and in his bed. It was where she belonged. She was his, he would never let her go. Not now.

"Dawn! Dawn!"

They lay together kissing, touching, rolling over and over on the soft bed. His hands were doing wondrous things to her, making her writhe and groan with pleasure. Every inch of her body caught fire as passion carried them into wild oblivion. He moved against her, sending waves of pleasure exploding along every nerve in her body. The swollen length of him brushed across her thigh. Then he was covering her, his manhood probing the entrance of her secret core.

"You'll see. I'm not what you think. . . ." she whispered.

His kisses stopped any further words she might have uttered. She felt his maleness linger at the fragile entry to her womanhood, then he pierced that delicate membrane with a sudden thrust. For one brief moment there was pain, but then Dawn's passion rallied. So this was why Taddie and the others cried out in the night. Wanting to relish this new feeling, she pushed upward.

"By God!" Only when he entered her did Garrick realize the truth. It couldn't be. A virgin? This woman who had tried to seduce him on the docks was a virgin! He had not believed her. Now too late he learned she had spoken the truth. But he could not pull away. She was so warm, so tight around him that he closed his eyes with agonized pleasure.

Burying his length deep within her, he moved with infinite care, not wanting to hurt her, wanting instead to initiate her fully into the depths of passion. And love. Yes, love, for that was what he felt. Like the currents of the sea that surrounded England, his body drew hers.

Tightening her thighs around his waist, Dawn arched up to him with sensual urgency. She was melting inside, merging with him into a single being. His lovemaking was like nothing she could ever have imagined. It filled her, flooded her. Clinging to him, she called out his name.

Garrick groaned as he felt the exquisite sensation of her warm flesh sheathing the long length of him. He wanted it never to end, wanted no suspicion to intrude on the rapture of the moment. She was silken fire beneath him. A fragile flower, blossoming at his touch. A tenderness welled within him that banished bitterness to the darkest recesses of his mind, as they were both borne up into the sweet blinding light of love's fulfillment.

42

The moon had set. The room was dark. Dawn could see the tip of Garrick's thin cigar shining like a tiny beacon as he sat in a chair by the bed. They did not speak, not knowing what to say. They had been swept away on a tide of longing neither one of them could deny. Where would they go from here?

I love him, Dawn thought, *but how does he feel about me?* Could he forget the past and give her a chance to make him happy? She was physically and emotionally drained, much too vulnerable to confront him with questions, thus she took refuge in the darkness and contented herself with the pleasant sound of his low, raspy breathing.

His lovemaking had deeply affected her. Her body would always remember every touch, every kiss, every caress. It had been the most beautiful moment of her life, a mindless delight of the senses and the heart. Nothing in the world could have prepared her for such joy. It was as if she had been starving all of her life and had only now discovered food. But only Garrick Seton could whet her appetite. Now she wanted to be with him forever, to walk beside him, to share his dreams.

A deep yearning rose in her heart, a hope that it was not too late for happiness. He had wanted to marry her once. Would he still want that now? Or would he think her too far beneath him? A tattered little pickpocket. Would he accept her now for the woman she had become? And if not, what then? Could she content herself to be merely his mistress?

She lay still as stone, watching him. Did he love her or had he simply assuaged his body's cravings? When he entered her, her heart had seemed to swell, full of him, full of love. She had felt like the richest woman in the world. But what of Garrick? What was he thinking now?

Garrick closed his eyes with a sigh. Never had he realized that love could be like this, an ecstasy so shattering it was almost pain. And yet what to do about it? Marriage? It was out of the question now. Or was it? He had proof she was not a whore, but there were other things to answer for. By her own admission she had been a thief.

He was dressed only in his breeches. He could so easily divest himself of his trousers and crawl into bed again. Yet he held himself back. He clamped the cheroot between his teeth and sprawled in his chair, stretching his long legs out in front of him. Sympathy warred with resentment. He could imagine what a beautiful child she must have been. Orphaned and walking the streets. She was right about the city's lack of compassion for homeless children. London was much like an anthill, too intent on industry to give thought to those in need. The poor, the sick, and the unfortunate were treated like so much refuse, to be discarded or ignored. He'd condemned such heartlessness. In her circumstances would he have done any differently? Was he then in any position to judge her?

Bloody damn! Bloody damn! he swore to himself. He put his foot up on a low chest at the foot of the bed. Why did she make him feel as if he were the one in the wrong? Whatever her circumstances, she had set him up to be robbed, that much he knew to be true. Even now her brother was serving time in Newgate for his part in the robbery. How could he hold her totally blameless?

And yet she had looked as gentle as a kitten as she stood before him tonight. Not once had she tried to escape him. She had felt his anger, sensed his thirst for revenge, yet she had returned each kiss, each caress "with love," he whispered.

He would never have made love to her tonight if he had really thought she spoke the truth about not being a whore. He wasn't the kind of man who enjoyed deflowering virgins. And yet he had! Before he penetrated her, she had never known another man. That put a whole different light on the matter, made him feel responsible for her. Despite his common sense, how could he just walk away?

"Dawn, are you awake?" He tried to temper his voice, to hide his frustration with himself.

"Yes. I never went to sleep. I couldn't." She suddenly felt the need to talk, to make him understand. "I would never go back to a life of thieving. I was miserably unhappy, only I didn't know it then. And whether you believe it or not, I saved your life that night at the warehouse. When I came back, it was to free you."

"Ssh. I really don't want to talk about that now." It took every ounce of resolve he had not to go to her and take her in his arms.

"Do you believe me?"

"I don't know what to believe. So much has happened tonight that my brain feels like pudding. I only know that you are not the young woman I thought you to be, either for good or for ill. I need to do some thinking, Dawn. Some deep, serious thinking. Until then I can't say anything or make any commitments. Please understand." He'd fallen in love with a shadow, a dream, a woman who didn't exist. What did he feel about the real woman?

"Garrick . . ." She loved him without question. Her senses were filled with wanting him. *Then go to him*, a voice inside her head whispered. Life was so short, so uncertain. One never knew what the future held in store. He was here with her now, and she wanted him to make love to her again.

Rising from the bed, Dawn crossed the polished wood floor on bare feet. Leaning towards him, she stroked his neck, tangling her fingers in the thick strands of his hair. Garrick snuffed out his cigar and closed his eyes, giving himself up to the rippling pleasure of her touch.

"Make love to me again. . . ." She leaned forward to brush his mouth with her lips. That simple gesture said all she wanted to say, that she loved him, desired him. Slowly his hands closed around her shoulders, pulling her to him, answering her shy kiss with a passion that made her gasp. Gathering her into his arms, he carried her back to the bed.

She gave herself up to the fierce emotions that raced through her, answering his touch with searching hands, returning his caresses. Closing her arms around his neck, she offered herself to him, writhing against him in a slow, delicate dance. She could feel the pulsating hardness of him through the fabric of his trousers and reached up to pull his breeches from him. If that was being overbold and brazen, she didn't care.

Sweet hot desire fused their bodies together as he leaned against her. His strength tenderly assaulted her softness, his hands moved up the curves of her hips and her waist to her full ripe breasts, warming her with his heat. Like a fire his lips burned a path from one breast to the other, bringing forth spirals of pulsating sensations that swept over her like a storm.

Garrick's mouth closed on hers, his kiss deepening as his touch grew bolder. Dawn luxuriated in the pleasure of his touch, stroking and kissing him back. He slid one hand between her warm, silken thighs, then he raised himself, holding himself poised above her. The tip of his maleness pressed thrillingly against her, then entered her in a strong, slow thrust. He kissed her as their bodies melted together, and from the depths of her soul Dawn's heart cried out in joy. If only they could forget her past . . . if only he could come to trust her, care for her! A flame of yearning ignited within her as he whispered her name. Tightening her thighs around his waist, she moved against him and he responded with a growing sensual urgency.

Garrick's passion left her breathless. It was like falling, falling endlessly in exquisite delight and never quite hitting the ground. Her arms locked around him as she arched to meet his body in a sensual dance, abandoning all inhibitions until the boundaries between them burst into rapturous oblivion.

Even when the sensual magic was over, they clung to each other, unwilling to have the moment end. Dawn was reluctant to have him leave her body. Surely the fire they had ignited tonight would join them together for eternity. Smiling, she lay curled in the crook of Garrick's arm. They were together. It was all she had for now. For the moment it had to be enough.

"Sleep now," he whispered, still holding her close. With a sigh she snuggled up against him, burying her face in the warmth of his chest, breathing in the manly scent of him. She didn't want to sleep, not now. She wanted to savor the moment, but as he caressed her back, tracing his fingers along her spine, she drifted off.

Only when she was fast asleep did Garrick get up. Gently disentangling himself from her arms, he rose from the bed and gathered his clothes. He had to get out of here now, before he succumbed to his heart's pleading. A long walk in the night air would help immensely. Tomorrow he would make some decisions. With agonizing clarity he knew something must be done. By coming here tonight he had unleashed a tiger, and he knew beyond a doubt there would be no taming it now. What was he to do? He had to get away before he was completely imprisoned by her beauty.

43

~∞⌒∞~

The bustle of servants going about their morning chores woke Dawn. Her eyes fluttered open and she stretched languorously. Sitting up, she felt the chill of the unheated room against her skin and realized that she was naked beneath the coverlet. She smiled and instinctively reached for Garrick, only to be disappointed when she found herself alone. He had left, then, sometime during the night or early this morning. Though she was disappointed not to find herself curled up in his arms, she thought that perhaps it was all for the best. Had he been found there this morning, her reputation would have been hopelessly compromised.

"My reputation," she whispered, stifling a laugh with the back of her hand. That was the least of her worries. How had he found out about her? What mistake had she made? It didn't matter. She felt actually relieved that he knew. The secret of her past was a burden that had been taken off her delicate shoulders. This morning she felt happy and blissfully carefree.

Dawn's mind relived the night, from the moment he swept her into his arms and carried her upstairs until the culmination of their lovemaking. Her breasts were tender from Garrick's caresses, and she felt an aching between her thighs, proof it had not been a dream. And yet she welcomed the sensations.

A flush of color stained her cheeks as she remembered how boldly she had come to his side and asked him to make love to her again, yet she had no regrets. She would never be sorry for one kiss, one sigh, one moment. Now she was Garrick's and he belonged to her.

Marriage? She pushed away the one thought that could cloud her happiness. She could only hope that once Garrick sorted everything out in his mind he would still want to marry her. Hadn't their hearts spoken for them? And yet, what would he say the next time she saw him? She resolved not to worry. Today was for rejoicing.

Turning her head against the pillow, she realized how deeply she loved him. There could never be any other man. Not for her. At first he had seemed like a figure out of a dream, so far away, so unobtainable. The gentleman and the ragged pickpocket—an impossible combination. True, for a time she had wanted revenge, but now she loved him for the man he was.

Kicking back the covers, she slid her feet to the floor and looked about her. They had made love in Margaret Pembrooke's bed. For a moment that gave her pause. Had the dear woman's ghost been watching? On second thought, it seemed strangely fitting, for it had been by Mrs. Pembrooke's hand that she had been made a lady, acceptable to a man like Garrick Seton. She remembered the twinkie in the dowager's eyes whenever she spoke about him, the smile when he was about to call for Dawn in his carriage. Margaret Pembrooke had known where it would all end, that the spark between Garrick and Dawn would have a happy ending.

Reluctantly Dawn picked up her undergown and

covered herself, just in case one of the servants might barge in. She would have liked to spend the entire morning in tender recollection, but it was late. The clock in the hallway was chiming nine. Dressing quickly, straightening out the coverlets on the bed, she sought the haven of her own room.

A while later, when she had bathed and dressed, she went downstairs for a breakfast of croissants and tea. "Good morning, Douglas. I hope you had a splendid day yesterday."

"A very fine morning." The butler grinned. "I went to the theatre last night with a young widow who works as a cook across the way. Had a deucedly good time. Though a fight broke out after the second act."

"A fight?" Dawn remembered the countless times she'd gone to the theatre with the express thought of nabbing a handkerchief. In those days the occasional drunken brawl had been her opportunity.

"A minor fisticuff. It didn't spoil my evening. I most thoroughly enjoyed myself." He did seem quite cheerful.

"I'm glad."

"I hope it was not too lonely for you here with me gone, mum."

Dawn blushed to the roots of her hair, wondering if her secret showed on her face. "No . . . no, I was just fine."

Making herself comfortable on the settee, she read the *Morning Post*, bringing herself up to date on the latest news and gossip. That Frenchman, Napoleon, was still causing trouble, denying most of Western Europe any British imports. The Tories, favoring the wealthy, were firmly in power. Beau Brummell was mentioned again and again. It seemed the wealthy had little to hold their attention beyond notions of fashion, a preoccupation with style and appearance carried to absurd lengths. Garrick wasn't like that.

No preening dandy with lace at his throat and a terror of grime on his coat. No, he was special, and he was hers.

Putting the newspaper down, Dawn finished the last of her tea. The weather was dreary and yet she felt impelled to make an outing to the shops and bazaars. She wanted to find something filmy and frilly to wear the next time she and Garrick made love. Certainly she had not cared for such extravagance before, but now it seemed a pressing matter. She had few undergarments: one undergown, a chemise, and two pair of stockings, having thought them unimportant since no one would see them. Now someone would and she found it strangely exciting to imagine Garrick slowly removing each fragile garment from her body.

Bundling up in a coat, hat, and muff, she braved the short distance to the carriage. Her breath hung like little clouds of smoke in the icy air. Charlie, a jolly old fellow who resembled pictures she had seen of Bacchus, had lighted a fire in the carriage house hearth, so she was comfortable the moment she stepped into the vehicle.

Dawn's senses were heightened. The carriage made its way through Fleet Street, passing St. Dunstan's at ten strikes. It was as if she were seeing the world through different eyes—the eyes of love. The colors were more vibrant, the sounds of the city more intense. Even the air seemed fresher and more pleasant as she drew it deep into her lungs. Love? Indeed last night had made her feel more fully alive.

Her visit to Margaret Pembrooke's seamstress, who lived near Whitechapel, took up most of the day. It was an endless parade of fabrics and lace. By the time they were done, Dawn had decided upon seven nightgowns—one for each day of the week, four chemises, and two undergowns.

The streets were filled with shoppers. There seemed to be something about cold weather that made one loosen one's purse strings. Dawn pushed through the throng of men and women: pretty and plain, young and old, smiling and frowning, simpering and scolding—she felt a wave of goodwill towards them all. The yelling, screeching, swearing, and laughing didn't offend her ears. Her thoughts were elsewhere.

On the way back to Pembrooke House she had the driver take her past Garrick's office, but her courage failed her. She could not pay him a visit. Not yet. Let him come to her. He would come, of that she had no doubt. No man could exhibit such tenderness without love in his heart.

It was still light when the carriage rounded the curve of the drive. An ornately decorated coach stood in front of the entry. A visitor? For a moment her heart fluttered erratically. Garrick? No, it was not his carriage. Who then? John Barrister, perhaps.

Moving towards the vehicle she felt a pang of disquiet. She wasn't really up to company. Whoever it was, she hoped they wouldn't stay long. Lifting her chin she made her way towards the front steps, feeling vaguely troubled. Why did that carriage look strangely familiar?

Suddenly it came to her. It was a magistrate's carriage. She and Robbie had dodged them many times in the past. What was it doing here?

"Excuse me, I'm looking for a young woman named Dawn Landon." A man in a dark suit and hat accosted her.

"I'm Dawn Landon," she said hesitantly.

"You?" As she nodded her head, two men in red waistcoats joined him. "Seize her!" he commanded.

"She is a swindler."

"A thief!"

Too late Dawn recognized the Bow Street Runners! Every nerve in her body urged her to flee, but it was too late. They had her by the arm.

"I beg your pardon. What is the meaning of this?" she asked, trying to appear calm. "There must be some mistake. . . ."

"You are under arrest for swindling and thievery!" None too gently they pushed her into the carriage and Dawn realized with horror that she was being taken into custody.

The sun was just setting when Garrick returned to his town house. Strange, but he didn't even remember telling Vinnie to drive him home, and yet here he was standing in his own hallway. It only proved how jumbled his thoughts were.

It had been a wretchedly hard day. Blast Ollie, he had not come into the office at all. Up to his old ways again, Garrick thought. He'd been certain that being so hard pressed for money, Oliver had learned the merits of discipline. Apparently not. Now that his anger had worn off, he regretted telling Ollie about Dawn's past. He didn't want her the target of gossip, no matter what she had done. Hopefully Oliver hadn't spent the day at his club spreading the story.

The house seemed empty except for the welcoming smells emanating from the kitchen. Agatha, his cook, made everything from a pinch of this and a pat of that, and yet she worked wonders. Well, he would enjoy his dinner, have a glass of port or sherry, and then think the matter out. He changed his clothes, carefully hanging the garments in the closet, put on a loose-fitting smoking jacket, then immediately returned downstairs. The fire was crackling in the library and he sat for a long while in front of its warm flames. Like a romantic fool he'd spent the day thinking about *her*. A bitter growl escaped his throat. He was completely, inescapably in love with Dawn Landon. Totally besotted, as Oliver had said.

The situation was rather ironic when he recalled their first meeting on the docks. He'd wanted to strangle her then; now he wanted to take her into a far different embrace, to hold her and never let her go. At the thought of a life without her he felt an aching emptiness deep within him, a loneliness for which there was no solace.

His lips twisted in a smile. He had always prided himself on being above emotional entanglements, but he had taken quite a tumble. It was a damning admission and yet an honest one. Damn, but he could hardly leave her alone. Even now it took all his self-control not to get back in the new curricle and have Vinnie drive him to her. But he would not.

"Dinner, sir."

Strange but he, who usually hastened to the dinner table, had no appetite. He found himself remembering what she had said about the callousness of his social class towards the poor. Certainly *he*, for all his talk, had done little to alleviate the poverty in the streets. He'd concentrated on designing buildings for the fashionable parts of London and shunned any projects for the poorer sections.

Walking to the fireplace, he picked up a decanter and poured himself a glass of sherry, swirling the amber liquid in the glass. Except for the kindness he had once shown a little beggar girl, he had no claim to sainthood. Tilting his head back, he drained his drink in a single gulp and threw the glass into the fire.

Bloody damn, but he had to admire Dawn Landon's spunk. To have worked so hard at her diction as to have fooled him must have taken a great deal of fortitude. She had raised herself up so high he had put her on a pedestal. Now that he thought about it clearly, perhaps that was where she belonged. Margaret Pembrooke had seen a diamond in the rough and given it polish. The creation was astounding.

But marry her? Somehow he still couldn't come to terms with what she had been, what she had done. "Allow me to introduce my wife, but please keep a firm hand on your watch," he mimicked wryly. He needed some time, he thought, pouring himself another glass of sherry. How easily a man could become a victim of his own heart. *Marry her? Ha!* With cool desperation and grim resolve he tried to keep his emotions in check, returning to the fireplace to stare into the dancing flames as if he would find the answer to his dilemma there.

44

The stale odor of rotting straw assailed Dawn's nostrils. She looked about her at the cold stone walls of her prison cell. Newgate. When last she'd been here, she had been on the other side of these cruel doors. Now she was a prisoner awaiting trial.

She remembered all too vividly the ride in the prison carriage. She had been shackled, treated most wretchedly. By the time they reached the prison she was completely distraught. Two Bow Street Runners had placed themselves on either side of her. They had to drag her from the carriage and thrust her up the stairs. Oh, she had been stubborn, a snarling, swearing, fighting wildcat, as they half carried, half pushed her towards the scarred doors.

In mortification she had watched the guard record her name in the large leather-bound prison book. Dawn Landon he had written until she had corrected him. Miss *Dawn Leighton*. The other name caused her too much heartache.

"So, you are Dawn Leighton, are ye? *Miss?*" The stocky guard had guffawed. "Yer won't be thinking yer be a lady now. There ain't no aristocracy here." His voice had lowered conspiratorially. "Unless yer got some money stashed away that you could give to ole Bill. I can prove ter be a good friend or a powerful enemy. I'll let ye choose which it's ter be." Dawn had heard Black John talk often enough to know just what the guard meant. Without bribery her life would be hell.

Dawn had been led along the dank, dimly lit stone passages. A thick iron-hinged door swung open and she was pushed into a stinking cell with a small barred window.

Now she sat forlornly in the far corner, hugging her knees to her chest, her hair falling into her eyes. She was still slightly dazed, barely capable of coherent thought. He'd turned her in! That was the one thing she did know. How else had she come to this? Garrick had gone to the Bow Street Runners and told them about her life as a pickpocket. That thought was like a knife twisting and turning in her stomach until she couldn't breathe. She had loved him so much that she would have done anything for him, but he had used her, then savagely betrayed her.

Her eyes were blank with pain and disbelief. How could he have done such a thing? He had held her, caressed her, made love to her with such a show of passion. "Why?" Her voice broke in a sob. Tears flooded her cheeks and she didn't even try to brush them away. She was beyond caring what happened to her. Tomorrow was her trial date and yet she didn't care. Let them lock her in here and throw away the key. She never wanted to see the outside world again. It was too cruel. Too brutal. Too full of deceit. Sagging against the cold stone wall, she put her face in her hands and wept.

The cell door cracked open and she jumped, hoping it was Garrick, that he had had second thoughts. He'd meant to frighten her, to punish her for having been a party to robbing him. But now he was here to take her away. Her heart thudded like an old bass drum as she waited, but it was only John Barrister.

"You've come to help me?"

He shook his head regretfully. "I'm . . . I'm sorry, Miss Landon, but Oliver Chambers, who now holds the estate, has cut you off without a penny. My services are not free, you know. I only came to tell you that I am sorry. The plans you had for your brother will now come to naught."

"I see." So she was not even to be allowed the luxury of an attorney. She was penniless. She knew all too well what that meant. She was doomed. There would be no way out for her now. But would she hang? The laws were strict enough. It wouldn't be the first time. There would be no Margaret Pembrooke to save her the way she had saved Robbie.

"Look at 'er, ain't she somethin', Teddie, me boy?"

"I always did like wenches wi' dark hair and green eyes. Like a cat. Mayhap we can 'ave a bit o' sport wi' her once she's consigned to this place permanent-like?"

"Could be."

Dawn listened dully, uncaring, as the turnkeys talked. She shivered convulsively. She'd die before she'd let them touch her. She'd kick and bite and give them trouble. She hadn't lived in St. Giles, in violence and bloodshed for nothing. She knew how to protect herself. She'd given herself in love once but no man would ever touch her again.

And she would have to protect herself. There was no one else to care what happened to her. Oh, Robbie would care, but his fate was now just as precarious as hers. With no possessions, nothing with which to bribe the gaolers, they were both as good as lost.

Dawn lay down on the thick covering of moldy straw and closed her eyes. *Be brave! Be strong! Don't let yourself give up, no matter what happens.* So cruel a man wasn't worthy of her tears, she told herself, and yet the thought didn't ease her pain.

All right, so you are all alone. It wasn't the first time

she'd been in prison. She was only eight years old when she'd first been confined behind stone walls. But she'd had Robbie and her mother then. Now she had no one.

She didn't know how long she lay there. Without a timepiece, the hours seemed to merge from night into day. She only knew her world was reeling and spinning. How could she have ever been such a fool as to think a nob could really love her? There was a gulf as wide as the English Channel between them. The rich never let the poor into their world, not really. Those who had money wanted to keep it for themselves. She had thought Garrick different, to have at least a measure of compassion running through his veins, but she had been so wrong. Now she'd have to pay the price. Loving him had destroyed her.

The pain will pass, she told herself. But saying it didn't make it so. Her head ached, her throat felt dry. Though her heart still beat in a steady rhythm, she felt as though it was no longer there. He hadn't even awakened her to say good-bye, or to give her a shilling for a night's use of her body, she thought in bitterness. And the worst was yet to come. She was numb, but all too soon she would fully realize what he had done.

She would never see Garrick again. She knew that to be a fact. With a surgeon's calculated skill he had severed their bond, caring little what it would do to her. She had loved him only to be left with an aching pain from a wound that would never heal.

The hours passed much too quickly. At dawn the turnkey came to unlock the door. Dawn stood up and walked unsteadily down the corridor. Now was the hour when she would be brought up before the magistrate. "Dear God, give me strength," she whispered. Lifting her head proudly she shrugged off the arms that held her and walked the long distance with as much dignity as she could muster.

It was cold. Garrick felt as if his nose would freeze on his face. The curricle he rode in was in no way as comfortable as his carriage had been. It was open, for one thing, and the seats were not thickly padded. Well, that was what he got for wagering, he supposed. He was especially susceptible to the splashing mud. Luckily it was early and there were few vehicles on the street.

The shops were open, the apprentices and shopmen busily engaged in cleaning and decking the windows for the day. He passed a bakery, a butcher shop, a haberdashery, a tailor's establishment on his familiar route to the office. Passing an apothecary shop he could see the large red, green, and yellow bottles in the window sparkling like rare jewels. Well-shaped gilt letters announced that he had arrived at the jewelers.

"Stop here, Vinnie." The words were out before he could even think. Taking his time, he stood before the shop window as he scanned the array of watches, the silver, and the rich jewelry.

The sound of footsteps alerted Garrick to the fact that he was being followed. Not two paces behind him a young wretch stared wistfully at the glittering heaps of baubles as if speculating on the possibility that a gold watch might bring enough to fill his hungry belly for quite a while. Or was the fellow contemplating a bold dash through the frail sheet of glass for a hasty try at snatching all the watches, rings, and bracelets lying within? Whatever his intent, the young rogue took to his heels when he noticed Garrick's eyes upon him.

"Does that young scoundrel hang about here often?" he asked the man inside the shop.

"He's there every morning about this time, but so far he hasn't given me any trouble. No doubt his real interest is the bakery next door."

"He's hungry?" Garrick remembered Dawn's remark that he could hardly understand hunger, he who had never missed his dinner.

"Aye . . ."

"What would it take to give him a job?"

"A job?" The balding man behind the counter looked horrified. "A tattered wretch like that would be bad for my business. I have a reputation to uphold. My clients have a great deal of money to spend. Let him take his woeful looks elsewhere."

"Then suppose I make it worth your while," Garrick found himself saying. Taking out his money pouch, he handed over a goodly sum. Didn't everyone deserve at least one opportunity to raise himself out of poverty? It was hunger and want that most often led to stealing. "If you don't give him a chance, you could well find you've lost some of your goods one day."

Eyeing him up and down, the jeweler grumbled but nodded. "I suppose I could use someone to sweep my floors first thing in the morning. We'll see." Drumming his fingers on the polished wood counter, he asked, "Is there something you were interested in seeing?"

"A ring!"

"For yourself?"

"For a lady." It wouldn't hurt to see what was available. He held up his little finger. "Her ring finger is about two sizes smaller than this. A diamond, if you please. Square cut if you have it."

"I don't, but I do have one shaped like an egg." Reaching beneath the counter, he pulled out a black velvet box filled to the brim with diamond rings, some of them gaudy, others too simple. There was one that looked perfect, however. Winking in the light, it seemed to say to Garrick that it had been fashioned just for Dawn's delicate, long-fingered hand.

"This one . . ."

"Why, Garrick, I hardly imagined I'd find you in a jeweler's shop. Are you after a stickpin or perhaps a new *watch*?" Stephanie Creighton crept up behind him, looking over his shoulder with a smug grin. "A diamond ring? Garrick, it's lovely." She held out her hand as if expecting it to be for her. "Every woman loves diamonds."

"So I've found." Something in her attitude goaded him. He started making comparisons. Stephanie Creighton had never known a day of hardship in her life. Her first bite of food had been from a silver spoon. Did he want to share his future with her? No. "I'm hoping one particular woman will find it pleasing."

"One woman?" Her brow furled into a sudden frown. "You can't mean . . . That is to say, Oliver told me all about your uh . . . unfortunate experience. I can imagine how horrified you must have been. . . ."

"Oliver told you? Blast and damnation!" He should have known Oliver couldn't hold his tongue. Whom else had he told?

"Now Garrick dear, we've all made our little mistakes. I can understand how easily you might have been fooled, but that is over now. I have forgiven and forgotten." She took his arm with a self-assured familiarity.

"There is nothing to forget or forgive." Taking her hand, he disentangled it from his arm.

"I only meant that we could carry on as if the entire unpleasant incident hadn't even occurred. A man's eye wanders from time to time. I do understand. I think you have been punished quite enough. . . ." She eyed the diamond ring avidly.

"It wasn't an unpleasant incident, Stephanie, nor was I punished, as you put it. It might very well have been the greatest blessing of my life." His lips were tempted into a smile. "What would you say if I told you that my days of bachelorhood are over."

"You're marrying her?" A strange glitter came into her eyes. "I wouldn't count on that, Garrick. Life can be filled with little surprises." Handing an emerald-and-diamond bracelet to the jeweler, she announced haughtily that she wanted him to adjust the clasp.

"Surprises?" Something about her attitude struck a note of disquiet deep within him. Was she making veiled threats or merely making a statement? "What do you mean?"

She shrugged her shoulders. "Only that one should not take anything for granted. After all, I had intended to marry you!" She turned her back on him, and though he started after her, hoping to learn more, she closed the shop door firmly behind her, stepped into her carriage, and was gone.

45

The courtroom at the Old Bailey was filled with noisy, laughing, jeering people who seemed to view the sentencing of miscreants as entertainment. Jostling each other, they fought for seats that would give them a good view of the proceedings. Dawn stood wearily with ten other unfortunates, barely aware of what was going on. The judge and counsel in their intricately curled white wigs blended into the blur of the crowd.

She had been escorted with her companions past the cells, through the yards, and out through the heavy iron-studded door of Newgate into the waiting prison wagons. There, with several other frightened, dirty, and disheveled men and women, some who seemed nearly as apathetic as she, she had been brought to the Old Bailey for trial.

"Trial, they calls it. Ha, I says!" A ragged gray-haired woman standing next to her snorted her disdain. "Don't know why they bother, I don't."

"It's proper justice to 'ave a trial, that's wot," said another, looking beseechingly in the judge's direction.

"Justice? Ha! If we escape the 'angman, we'll be transported to New South Wales and go through 'ell in a convict ship. Is that justice? I 'ad five children to feed and nowhere to turn. 'At's why I gave in to temptation." In the hope of making herself more comfortable, the woman shifted her gaunt weight from one foot to the other.

"Five shillings. 'At's the amount we can be 'anged for stealing. Five lousy shillings!" The man kept muttering over and over. "Five shillings."

Hanged. Transported. Dawn's already sagging spirits dropped even lower. Lifting her eyes, she scanned the crowd, wondering if he would even show his face. Would he watch her humiliation? No, he was not here. She would be given no second chance.

"Bastard! You unfeeling, unforgiving bastard!" she whispered, her voice a harsh, broken croak. She could still hardly believe that angry though he had been at first, he would subject her to such degradation or punish her so ruthlessly. She had given herself to him in token of her love. Was that why she was being punished? Was this his way of running away? Her head ached so intolerably and her throat was so sore that she wondered if she would be able to make herself heard when it came time for her to speak.

Dawn's eyes swam with stinging tears. *I loved him,* she thought. *Still love him, no matter what he has done.* Strange that she could make that admission. At this moment she should hate him, and yet she couldn't find that dark emotion in her heart. Instead she felt strangely sorry for him. He had something so very precious within his grasp, and he had thrown it all away. Putting her hands to her throbbing forehead, she tried to keep her emotions under control.

The proceedings were conducted with calm indifference. There was a great deal of form, but no compassion; considerable interest, but no sympathy. Dawn watched through her tears, assessing the judge who sat pompously straight, the Lord Mayor, exhibiting an equal measure of dignity, and the barrister, who seemed anxious for the morning to be over.

The other prisoners were dealt with quickly and efficiently. A roar of laughter rose from the gallery when one unfortunate man insisted that he was innocent, that his twin brother had done the deed. In the end he was sentenced to a long term in Newgate. Three prisoners were condemned to the gallows, two to the pillory, one young lad was given the lesser penalty of the lash. Taking a deep breath, Dawn was determined to face her fate with dignity, to hide her deep all-consuming heartache.

"What is your name?" The judge eyed her sternly and Dawn wished she had a mirror and a comb. She hoped she did not look as unkempt as the two women standing beside her.

"Dawn Catherine Land—Leighton!"

The judge towered over her from the height of his bench, studying her critically. "Have you any witnesses to speak to your character, girl?"

Dawn hung her head. Margaret Pembrooke was dead, Garrick most certainly would not come to her aid. Agnes? Douglas? What could they say? "No!"

"No witnesses," the judge repeated, nodding to a clerk who scratched the information down on a long roll of paper.

"The charge is stealing a watch. How do you plead?"

Stealing Garrick's watch? He knew very well she hadn't stolen it. A flash of anger made her defiant. "I didn't steal it! I am innocent, my lord."

The judge raised his brows, obviously annoyed and anxious to get the matter over and done with. "I have a signed affidavit that says you did."

So Garrick did not even have the courage to face her with his traitorous accusation. He had merely written it down in a document and signed away her future with a flick of his pen. "I don't care what that paper says. I did not steal it."

"Then how did it come into your possession?"

She was cornered, forced to reveal a story which was just as damning as if she had really stolen the watch. Hastily she mumbled a brief account of that night at the docks. She was forced to leave out the part about saving Garrick's life for fear of condemning her brother. "Robbie had that watch in his possession and gave it to me for my birthday."

"Gave you something that was not his to give."

"Yes." A slight stir fluttered over the spectators like a brisk London breeze. One man, wholly engrossed in the morning paper, looked up at her with interest as if wondering how she was going to get herself out of this.

"And knowing that, you did not return it."

"No, I kept it!" *Because it meant so much to me to have something that had belonged to him*, she thought. But how could she ever make the judge understand?

"Kept it! Stolen property."

"Yes."

The prosecutor shrugged with a sly look in his eyes. "Then I would submit, my Lord, that the prisoner is convicted by her own admission. But perhaps it would be wise to show some clemency. I would agree to waiving the gallows in favor of the ships."

"Mmm . . ." It was the first time that day the judge had smiled. "Ah, Philip, you are always so anxious to transport our problems to other shores. But the cells are overcrowded and the citizens seem to prefer sending our criminals over the sea. There are two ships now moored in the Thames. And I, like you, abhor seeing a lovely woman hang." He looked towards the jurors.

Dawn barely heard the judge's sentence. Her eyes

were drawn to the fashionable women of London, decked out in their feathered and beribboned hats, their velvets and linens, to witness the spectacle. Perhaps her greatest crime was to try and be like them. Was that what Garrick could not forgive? Well, she was every inch as much a lady as any of them. So thinking, she straightened her shoulders, lifted her chin, and matched them stare for stare as she was marched along. Only the sight of a haughtily smiling blonde caused her to falter as she remembered the woman. Garrick's friend, come to enjoy the day and give him a detailed account of the proceedings. Then she was swept from the dock, taken down the stairs, and hustled back to the prison wagon. Only then did the judge's words echo in her mind. She was going to be transported, sent away from England to New South Wales.

46

Garrick endured three sleepless nights, wanting to go to Dawn, to tell her that he loved her, to ask her to marry him, but stubborn pride held him back. Instinct told him that Dawn was not the wrong woman, that she was very right for him, could make him happy, but until now fear had counseled him. He wanted to be absolutely certain he was doing the right thing. Now he was.

Garrick walked to Pembrooke House, patting the diamond ring in his pocket that bounced against his chest as he walked. He knocked on the door, flushed with pleasure to imagine the look on her face when he offered up his treasure.

"Yes . . ." Douglas opened the door with his usually bored expression. "Mr. Seton, sir."

"Is Miss Landon in?" Placing his hat and cloak in the butler's hands, Garrick moved expectantly towards the staircase.

Douglas shook his head. "No sir. She's not in."

"Well, perhaps it is just as well. I'll wait until she returns." It would give him some time to compose himself. He was as nervous as a schoolboy. "In the meantime, I have some questions for you, Douglas." He had to put his mind to rest.

"Yes . . ."

"Did . . . did Mrs. Pembrooke know about Miss

Landon's past?" There was no use beating about the bush.

"I beg your pardon . . ."

"It's all right, Douglas. I know the whole story." Garrick smiled reassuringly. "I want to know if Mrs. Pembrooke did."

Douglas smiled fondly. "Oh, yes, but she didn't care. Right from the first. You see, she admired Miss Landon's honesty and spunk. Thought of her as a daughter, if truth be told. Took to her right away, she did. Bought all of her hats."

"Her hats?" Garrick listened as the butler related the story of that first meeting, when Dawn had kept the woman from being robbed.

"And so we bought her hats." He made a face. "They were ghastly, and yet Madam used them as an excuse to get her here. Against my advice, I might add. I didn't want the ragged little creature about. I was wary of anyone in her circumstances. Didn't trust her a bit. But I was wrong. She gave Madam a reason to live. And to smile." He flushed slightly. "And me as well. I think everyone here at Pembrooke House was in love with her."

So, no matter what Oliver thought, Dawn had been perfectly honest with his aunt. She had known all along just who and what Dawn was, but she hadn't let prejudice blind her. Unlike himself.

The clock in the drawing room ticked and ticked; the pendulum swung back and forth. Time seemed to drag on endlessly, and yet there was no sign of Dawn's return. Garrick was growing impatient. He was totally prepared to pour out his heart to the woman he loved, but first she must be present.

"Where is she?" he asked Douglas at last.

"That I don't quite know, sir. She went out a few days ago and hasn't returned." The butler was fidgety, as if he too questioned her whereabouts. "Of course, now I . . . I wouldn't want to be prying. It's not my place. Besides, she often visits her friends in the East End. One young woman was expecting a baby. Perhaps she decided to stay." It sounded logical, and yet there was a look of disquiet in his eyes that made Garrick apprehensive.

"You look worried."

"Well, it is rather puzzling, sir, what with young Master Oliver moving his belongings in." The butler studied the front of his coat, toying with a button. "Of course, Mrs. Pembrooke did once say that she hoped for a marriage between them."

A frightening premonition edged its way up Garrick's spine. He found it difficult to articulate his thoughts. "Ol . . . Oliver has been transferring his possessions?" No wonder he had not shown his face at the office.

Garrick stormed upstairs. Something strange was going on. Pushing open the door to each and every bedroom, he searched the house for any sign of the woman he loved. In the last chamber he saw a pile of dresses, underwear, and shoes, heaped upon a bed as if waiting to be disposed of. The maid, whom he remembered all too well, was going through the articles of clothing, separating them into two piles. She seemed to be laying claim to some of the garments, holding them up against her as if they suited her.

"Agnes!"

Agnes was startled by his harsh tone of voice. She dropped the petticoat she held in her hand. "I don't know anything! I haven't done anything!" By her very denial she looked guilty.

"Where is Miss Landon?"

"Miss Landon?"

"Don't speak the name as if you've never heard it before," he shouted. "Damn it, girl, where is she?" Grasping her by the shoulders he held his gaze steady, searching her eyes and not liking at all what he read in their hazel depths.

"Terrorizing the servants, Gar? That's not at all like you." Dragging a small trunk behind him, Oliver was climbing the stairs.

"Oliver! What in the bloody hell is going on?" Garrick cast Oliver a bone-chilling stare. "Where is Dawn?"

Oliver reached the landing, put the handle of the trunk down, and reached in his pocket. Holding forth a watch and a handkerchief, he smiled at Garrick. "Yours. I thought you'd want them back."

Garrick looked down at the watch and initialed handkerchief with a sick feeling churning inside his stomach. "Ollie . . ." Garrick took the handkerchief, his face a mask of amazement. He remembered the scene vividly. The child had been so frightened and he had given her the handkerchief as a gift. The little beggar girl, the one he'd been searching for so diligently. Dawn? His frown deepened. "Oliver, what is going on? Why are you moving in here?"

"This is my rightful home, Garrick." Oliver folded his arms. "You know yourself that a little pickpocket should never have cheated me out of my rightful due."

Garrick swore violently. "What have you done, Ollie?"

Oliver didn't answer, but his self-righteous expression told the story for him. Stubbornly he pursed his lips.

Garrick couldn't stem the murderous rage that consumed him. There was a roaring in his ears. Blindly he hurled himself at Oliver who fell backward. Together they rolled down the stairs to the bottom of the carpeted landing. "You stupid bastard! I'll kill you if you've done anything to harm her." A part of him was screaming in silent anguish. It was his fault, *his,* not Ollie's. He should never have told any-one about the docks. He had given Oliver just the ammunition he needed.

"I turned her in. She's at Newgate where she be-longs. With that other young rogue you had arrested. And I am justified in what I did. You know it! You know it! Why, stealing was undoubtedly the least of her crimes. I believe she poisoned Aunt Margaret, and she . . ."

A well-aimed punch connected with Oliver's jaw. "Oh! No, Gar, don't hit me again." Oliver rubbed the injured part, his eyes wide with apprehension. "You said she was a thief. You told me the story. Did you think I would just sit back and suffer while she had everything I wanted in her clutches?"

"My fault . . ." Garrick mumbled. He should have come here sooner, taken her in his arms, and wor-shiped her. Instead he had held back as if she weren't good enough for him. What a pompous ass he'd been! As if there could be any conditions to love. And now Dawn had been taken to Newgate! The thought tore at his very soul. She would think *he* had turned her in. Dear God! And yet wasn't he just as responsible as Oliver?

Garrick raced to his curricle, calling Vinnie's name at the top of his lungs. He had to hurry—there was no time to lose. He had to do everything in his power to free Dawn before it was too late.

III

Surrender the Heart
ON BOARD THE *SEA RAVEN* AND LONDON

The heart has its reasons
which reason does not know.
—Pascal, *Pensees, IV*

47

The icy December rains swept down in a silver curtain, drenching the city of London. Thunder boomed and lightning pierced the sky with its fiery ribbons. It was a furious rainstorm that pounded the decks of the ship waiting to sail. The *Sea Raven* was its name. A prison ship, it was bound for New South Wales as soon as the weather cleared.

It was cold. Cold and penetratingly damp. Dawn reached up to pull her threadbare blanket over her shivering body, only to be confused when her fingers came back empty. A slatternly woman with eyes like a cat's dared her to get it back. "Come on! Come on!" she taunted, holding her fists up.

"Keep it," Dawn said through swollen lips, remembering a time she had foolishly fought for one of her possessions only to suffer a beating.

Looking through the grille of the wooden door, she could see the shadow of the gaoler coming towards them, but she didn't shout out or make accusations. Let the woman keep the blanket if it was so important to her that she would steal. Dawn didn't wish her any harm. In truth, all of her fighting spirit was gone. Her green eyes held no sparkle, no fire. Hope was something she had long since discarded.

Dawn lay motionless, only vaguely aware of the chatter and the groans around her. The first night she had been unable to sleep. She had huddled in the corner, unseeing, her inner self refusing to accept her monstrous fate. It was like a terrible nightmare from which she could not awake. She had cursed Garrick, she had ranted at herself, and all the while the shrieking voices of the prisoners echoed and re-echoed throughout the enclosure of the thick wooden walls like the howls of lost souls.

Dawn's hair was matted, her garments dirty. She thought that the lack of a mirror was a blessing after all. Perhaps not seeing with her own eyes how low she had fallen made it easier to bear. And yet she was not as unfortunate as some. She had not succumbed to the fever that had taken others. She still had a measure of health. Some of the others were not so lucky. There was ague, the pox, and constant coughing. A number of the prisoners were disturbed by the constant rocking of the ship and vomited their protest on the straw-covered floor. Dawn buried her face in her hands, trying to escape the stench.

"I can't bear it anymore. I can't. I can't." But she knew that she could and would. There was a flicker of stubborness in all human beings that made them hold on to life no matter how dismal.

She remembered the first day she had been taken aboard the ship. She was certain that she could not survive, and yet she did. The fact that she was a new prisoner had caused quite a stir among those already imprisoned. There were lewd remarks and mocking laughter from the men who remarked on her beauty. The women regarded her with looks of envy, and Dawn's flesh crawled with a sense of her danger. The guard had brutally pushed the curious onlookers aside.

"Get back, yer 'ags. Move aside, yer gaping bastards! We got us another thief. And this one claims to be a lady." A thunderous cacophony of laughter had followed his remarks. "Shut yer mouths!" The guard had bowed politely. "Course now if yer 'ave a few spare shillings ter pay, I can make certain yer accommodations suit yer tastes. Well?" He waited expectantly.

"I have no money. Nothing of any value."

He pushed her away from him. "Then there is nothing I can do for yer. Ye'll 'ave ter take yer chances wi' the others." And she had, learning to elbow her way through the waving forest of arms for a crust of bread, wondering all the while what Margaret Pembrooke would say if she could see her now. When a person was going hungry, there was little time for manners.

A sudden shrieking, snarling fight broke out among three of the women over the ownership of a tattered piece of cloth. They had no fear of the gaoler as they flew at each other. Still when the guard put the key in the lock to open the door, the prisoners scattered like cockroaches disturbed by a sudden light.

"Argh . . . so we are privileged with a guest," one woman said with a snicker.

"Is it mealtime? Oh, how I relish the gruel yer gi' us."

"Aye, get back, yer dogs!" the guard growled testily. He was a burly man with frizzled brown hair, a bulbous nose, and a perpetual scowl.

"Mayhap he's going to take us for a walk." The woman who had stolen Dawn's blanket smiled sweetly.

"The only walk ye'll be granted is a hike up the gallows steps if ye don't shut yer mouth!"

"Better the gallows than this stinking hole!"

"Unappreciative yer be. Yer don't know how lucky yer be that ye've got a fine ship to take ye away. Always a shortage of ships but this one's nearly seaworthy." The guard guffawed. "Hopefully it will get yer to Botany Bay wi'out sinking. Why, this is a palace compared to most."

A palace, Dawn thought. *Hardly that.* Conditions aboard the convict hulks were unspeakably horrible, with unwashed criminals, both men and women, packed together in closed quarters on all three decks. Oh, what she wouldn't give for a walk on the deck, a breath of fresh air, or a bath. Things that were usually taken for granted now seemed a luxury to her.

Nor was there any hope of escape. Many prisoners thought it would have been better to hang. At night, the hatches were screwed down and the prisoners left to fight among themselves in the wretched candlelight or, when the tallow ran out, in the claustrophobic darkness.

And yet she had been granted a bit of good fortune. Usually newcomers were relegated to the lowest deck. If they had stamina and didn't succumb to gaol fever, they then progressed to the middle deck. She had been housed in the second deck from the beginning. Even so it had been "hell on earth," as one prisoner had aptly named it. Violent attacks from fellow prisoners were commonplace, and the slightest offense was swiftly punished by a whipping by the guards. One had to be constantly wary; no one could be trusted. Whatever remained of innocence or honesty was certain to be lost in the dark depths of the prison ship. Even death was not held sacred. Like vultures the other prisoners fluttered about to see if the "stiff" had anything at all of value on him.

Dawn's existence on the ship became even more precarious when she recognized a familiar face among the prisoners: Black John Dunn. His money for bribes had run out and he had been forced to take his punishment. Dawn hid her face during those rare moments when she was aboveboard, fearing his retaliation. She was fairly certain he would hold her responsible for his fate. Black John was a man who always got even.

From above the deck Dawn could hear a prisoner singing a bawdy song. Others joined in the chorus. As if in protest to the discord, a large rat ran across the floor and disappeared under a pile of wood. Dawn was used to rats. There had been plenty at Black John's tenement, but oh, how she wished she had Shadow with her now, just for protection.

"Rats, filth, and starvation," she whispered softly. She would never be free. Never feel the rain on her face or see the sun. Never hear the birds' songs in spring. She would be locked away forever. Even if she reached Botany Bay alive, she'd be forced to suffer such conditions. Oh, to be out of here, to be free!

As if somehow intruding on her own thoughts, she heard a man's voice whisper "freedom." Whispering, the men took up the chant. The whispers became a cry that was taken up by the women.

"The drunken sot o' a gaoler. He forgot to screw down the hatch and lock the holds when 'e left. It's our chance, yer blokes!"

"We're going ter break free!"

A prisoners' uprising!

"Perhaps we won't be going to Botany Bay after all."

The words jostled Dawn out of her lethargy. Since the first day she'd been incarcerated her head had begun to ache, and now the pain intensified, making it impossible to think. Frantically she urged herself to calm, remembering how she had stood on deck looking at the lights of London by night. She had felt an aching desperation at the thought of leaving her homeland. Now perhaps she would be able to stay if only she kept her wits.

Days of poor food had made Dawn weak. Her

knees trembled dangerously as she got to her feet
and she prayed she would not faint. Not now. She
had to get out of here, it was her only chance. Holding on to a wooden crossbeam for support, hugging
the side of the hulk, she fought to maintain her balance. She was pushed and shoved as the prisoners
fought their way through the narrow hatchway. Then
somehow she had made it to the upper deck.

All the prisoners were running to and fro, stealing
small boats, and pushing them into the sea. Others
were jumping overboard. The churning ocean offered two alternatives—freedom or death. Did she
want to take the chance? A gunshot behind her gave
her no choice. Pulling herself up, she was poised atop
the railing for only an instant. Then she was falling
. . . down, down, down, to be swallowed by the icy
waters. The turbulent sea tugged her under. Her ears
filled with a roar as the darkness enveloped her.

48

Dawn didn't know how to swim. Dear God, what had she been thinking of? She was going to drown! Her lungs were burning for want of air, and yet she held her breath. Kicking her legs furiously to propel her body upward, she was rewarded when she reached the surface. Gulping in the sweet nectar of air, she prepared herself for another assault.

The waves were furious, throwing her back and forth like two gigantic hands. Several feet away she could see four other forms struggling against the sea. She heard their shrieks of fright and watched helplessly as they were sucked under. Then she was struggling in the icy darkness alone.

"Help me! Oh, God, help me!" she sputtered when her head came up again. The water was so cold that it drained what meager strength she had, and yet she wouldn't give in to death. Strange, she thought, but the less she fought the water the fewer times it took hold of her. With this thought in mind she ceased kicking and thrashing her arms about and tried to work with the rhythm of the rolling water.

She wanted to survive so desperately. It wasn't her time to die, she vowed. She was needed! Taddie would be having her baby soon, and Dawn wanted to be there. The thought of being helpful to someone gave her renewed strength. But how long could she survive in the icy waters? The shore seemed to be miles away.

Up and down, rising and falling, she let herself drift with the waves, saving what strength she could. Could she somehow maneuver herself towards land? She doubted it. Her only hope lay in attracting the attention of one of the fishing boats that skimmed the harbor.

"Help me! Help! Help!" She cried over and over. Her voice, drowned out by thunder, sounded weak and pitiful to her own ears. Still she persisted. She hadn't survived Black John Dunn, the prison's stench, and the ocean's depths without reason. "Help me!"

The shadowy form of a boat loomed more than a hundred feet ahead. She could see its stern hugging the ocean. Taking a deep breath, she opened her mouth to scream, but a wave sent a froth of water into her face. She went down and came up choking. For an agonizing moment she feared she would die, that the waters would claim her. But no! She wouldn't give in. Gathering all her strength, Dawn tried again, and this time a loud shriek rent the darkness.

"What's that, Ian? Did ye hear a scream?"

"A scream? If I did, it would hae had to come from a mermaid! How much of that whiskey hae ye been drinking?"

"Ssh! Listen, I heard it again."

"A mermaid, singing to lull us beneath the waves? I didna hear anything."

Somewhere in the darkness a woman was crying aloud, her voice frantic but clear. "Help! Help me."

"There. Ye see! Follow that sound. Pull wi' the oars, Ian."

Dawn's watery prison seemed endless. Having swallowed so much water, she felt nauseous and had to choke back the bile that rose in her throat. But the boat was moving closer! If she could just hold on to her strength a little longer . . .

"Ye're safe!" A deep voice was speaking as strong hands pulled her from the water. She felt a mixture of joy and relief to feel solid wood beneath her. Lying in an exhausted sprawl of arms and legs, she closed her eyes.

"What on earth is a lassie doing out here?" A round cherubic face peered down at Dawn. "Are ye a mermaid?"

"Yes!" she gasped, hoping that might put an end to his questioning.

"Well, I'll be a tinker's ass."

"She *isn't* a mermaid. Must hae been on a boat that capsized, or on that prison ship." A lantern was thrust into Dawn's face. "She's a bonny one, she is."

"What if she was on the *Raven*. What then? Shall we take her back? They'll be looking for her."

"No! Please!" Opening her eyes wide with fear, she pleaded shamelessly. She couldn't bear to be aboard that ship again. Better by far to let the ocean claim her. "I didn't . . . I didn't . . ." Dawn tried to sit up but a strong hand kept her down. "No!" Her brave pretense of courage was shattered and tears overwhelmed her.

"Dunna cry, lassie. Dunna fash yerself. If ye are from the *Raven* we willna take ye back. The magistrates o' London hae no' dealt wi' us fairly. I hae no loyalty to them."

Two Scotsmen, their brogues soothing. She had no choice but to trust them. Dawn closed her eyes once again. She was shivering from the chill, but she was covered with a soft piece of canvas. The waves rocked the fishing boat back and forth, back and forth. Dawn lost all track of time as she lay huddled and quaking on the hard wooden boat bottom. She barely noticed her discomfort, she was so tired. So weary.

"Lie back and save yer strength," a deep voice said.

Wisps of darkness reached out to touch her, enveloping her in a merciful cloud of sleep.

49

Garrick's face paled as he read *The Times*. There had been a riot on the *Sea Raven*. Fifty or more inmates had escaped the confines of the ship; twenty or more had jumped overboard and supposedly been drowned. Every newsboy on every corner was shouting out the story. It was all over London. Mouthing a foul oath, Garrick crushed the newspaper in his fist, put it in his pocket, practically flew out his front door, and without even waiting for Vinnie, drove the curricle himself to the Old Bailey.

Walking up the steps, he swore like a madman, causing passersby to give him a wide berth as they stared. Once inside, he demanded to see the judge for the seventeenth time that week.

The judge was sitting at a desk with piles of documents in front of him. Hunched over the papers, he was scribbling something with his pen. The same pen that he had used to send Dawn to the *Sea Raven*? Garrick wondered then answered his own question. Undoubtedly.

Garrick stepped forward and the judge grimaced. "Gad, not you again, sir."

"Yes, me again. And I will continue to come here until Dawn Landon . . . or . . . Leighton, is released. You have my signed statement that she did not steal the watch, that it was all a mistake. What more do you need?" Garrick thrust the newspaper in front of the judge's nose. "I read this only this morning. Am I to assume Miss Leighton is safe, that she is still on board the prison ship?" His manner was one of icy calm, but inside he was trembling.

"I would assume, sir, that she is right where the court put her."

"I want to make certain." His temper was barely in control. If something had happened to Dawn because of this stubborn old goat's pride, he would make certain that heads rolled. "You've already bungled the deuced matter once. I wouldn't want to find that another mistake has been made. I want you to assure me that all is well with her."

He had been trying desperately to get Dawn released, but the bureaucracy thwarted him at every turn. It would take time, he was told. The judge seemed loath to admit he might have made a mistake in sentencing an innocent party. Garrick had begun to wonder if someone was purposefully foiling his efforts. Not Ollie, surely, for since their argument at Pembrooke House the young man had been quite contrite, even sorry for what he had done.

"When you sold those stocks to Stephanie Creighton to pay off your gambling debts, you signed my name," Garrick reminded him. Garrick had resolved to buy the stocks back from Stephanie as soon as possible, but there was no reason to tell Oliver that now. "Need I remind you, Ollie, that forgery, like so many crimes, is a hanging offense?"

"Why . . . that's barbarous!" Oliver had sputtered, but the truth had hit its target.

"But a fact nevertheless. The merchants, bankers, and property owners are very formidable and have the Tories in their pocket when it comes to protecting what is theirs." Did someone also have *this* judge in his pocket? Was there a reason he was being so dreadfully slow in having Dawn released?

"I will ascertain her whereabouts," the judge was answering in an exasperated voice. "I will then give you a written document, if that will keep you out of this office."

"Only a pardon will do that." Garrick pounded the desk with his fist. "By God, sir, you know what it is like inside the prisoners' quarters. Hardened criminals in the same cells with those whose only offense was stealing a loaf of bread. That is bad enough, but when an innocent party is involved, I must urge haste."

A shiver stole over Garrick as he remembered his visit to Newgate. The women were mixed together—young and old, the beginner with the experienced offender, the accused with the condemned, the transports with those under sentence of death—all crowded together in one explosive assemblage; a noisy, idle, clamorous throng, banging at the cell bars with spoons attached to the ends of sticks or fighting wretchedly among themselves. Some of the women were particularly vicious. He had seen a look of savagery in some of the eyes staring back at him, could feel their hatred as they had glared at him. Dawn would be helpless in their midst.

"Be that as it may, sir. These things take time. . . ."

"And in the meantime Miss Landon has been taken aboard that rat-infested ship. Well, Your Honor, I will hold you responsible if anything disastrous happens."

Garrick was about to walk away when a tall, cadaverously thin gaoler pushed him aside. "We've apprehended some of those responsible for the uprising," he blurted, "and we have a list o' those missing. Most likely in Davy Jones's locker now they be." Taking off his cap he showed a grudging display of respect, putting it to his breast as if at a funeral.

The judge was not as quick to pity. "I want the penalty for those who led the escape to be especially harsh. Twenty lashes might suffice to teach them a lesson. To the others give twelve and have them confined to the brig in irons for the rest of the week."

"Irons. The brig." The gaoler, obviously used to shipboard command saluted. "Yes, sir."

"And Ronaldson . . ." The judge rapped his fingers on the desk.

"Yes, sir!"

"Give the blasted fool who forgot to screw down the hatches the same. Twelve lashes."

"Yes, sir . . ." With an awkward bow the gaoler retraced his steps, leaving Garrick alone with the judge.

"Fools! I am perpetually surrounded by fools who cannot manage the simplest of tasks." Remembering Garrick, the judge regarded him with annoyance. "Well, you've had your say. Be off with you," he said impatiently. "I am a busy man."

"That list—the guard just said he had the names of those who are missing." As he spoke, Garrick's voice was steady, his eyes watching the court justice intently. "If you please, Your Honor. Knowing that Miss Leighton's name is *not* there would at least allow me a measure of calm."

His request had the desired effect. Retrieving the piece of paper from one of the piles before him, the judge hastily scanned the names. "I ought to have you thrown into prison yourself, sir, for showing such a lack of respect. I will. I will, upon my word, if you . . ." There was no mistaking his astonished expression.

"What is it?"

"Miss Leighton . . . she is listed. She was last seen jumping over the ship's railing, and . . ."

"And?" Garrick called upon every ounce of self-control he possessed.

Shaking his head, the judge seemed sympathetic for the first time. "She has not been found. It appears, my good man, that she has drowned."

Garrick stared at the judge, his eyes burning. "Dear merciful God!" Bitter despair enveloped him. She was gone! Dead! "Damn you! Damn you to hell!" he cried. "You and all the other self-righteous . . ." All this time he had managed to keep his hope alive, to believe that he would hold her in his arms again. He had so stubbornly clung to the belief that justice would prevail. But there was no justice! Only blind, stubborn fools like himself.

Love. It had come so easily to him that he had not treasured it until it was gone. He had fought against it, defied his feelings. And all for what? Because Dawn had once been a child of the streets? The image of her lovely face hovered before his eyes. There was no point to his life if she did not share it! No joy in the days that stretched ahead. No point in anything.

And yet, how could she be dead? He wouldn't believe it. Dawn was a survivor. No matter what that dratted piece of paper said, he would find her. And when he did, he would never let her out of his arms again.

50

Dawn wandered like a wondering child through the streets she had thought never to see again, caressing every building, every tree, every turn in the road with her eyes. She was battered, tattered, and ragged, but she was free! True to their word, the fishermen had rowed her to shore without even so much as a blink at the River Police. They had not turned her in. Free! Breathing in the misty cold air, she reveled in that knowledge. For the moment it didn't matter that she hadn't two ha'pennies to rub together; at least she could come and go as she pleased without the threat of shackles or locked doors.

Somewhere a clock chimed the hour. Five o'clock. The sounds of the costermongers and tradesmen hawking their wares from nearby market stalls was pleasant music to her ears, though a reminder of her return to poverty. She had no money, and it was nearing suppertime. She had not had a bite to eat since the fishermen had shared their catch with her. Oysters and a bit of turbot. Her stomach rumbled with hunger.

"Chestnuts, all 'ot, a penny a score."

"Hot spiced gingerbread. Buy me gingerbread! Smo-o-oking hot. If one'll warm you, wha-at'll a pound do? Wha-a-a-t'll a pound do?"

"Mussels, a penny a quart! Ni-ew mackerel, six a

shilling. Had . . . had . . . haddick, all fresh and good."

"Chestnuts, all 'ot, a penny a score!"

Dawn's bedraggled appearance drew wary looks from the vendors. Not even one "good day" came her way. Still, heady with her newfound freedom, she scarcely noticed this lack of civility. Life was what one made of it, she reflected. Perhaps happiness was not as elusive as it had appeared to be a few days ago. She had been given another chance. And somehow she would find a way to earn her keep.

"Shoes. New shoes. Old shoes. Pick 'em out cheap 'ere! Three pair for a shilling."

"Laces. Bootlaces. Penny a lot!"

"Hats! Who'll buy a bonnet for fourpence? Hats!"

Of course! The young woman peddling straw and ribboned creations was a reminder. Dawn would sell hats again in Rosemary Lane. Taddie could help her. "Before I met Margaret Pembrooke I did quite well," she reflected aloud proudly. "I'll sell hats to make my way." It was a creative and honest way to make a living.

Dawn hurried through the streets, anxious to find Taddie. It would be her first visit to Soho in weeks. Taddie, Jamie, and the others were her only haven now, for she had no other place to go. The thought of a warm bed, a bath, and a bowl of stew made her quicken her steps. Strange, she thought, how everything in life was relative to something else. Once she had cursed her impoverished surroundings, comparing her life to those of the upper classes. She had been full of dreams then. After the prison stench and deprivation, however, the rooms in Soho seemed a luxury.

Perhaps I'll have time to warm some of the water in the kettle for my bath, she thought. It would be good to wash away the river stink, to change into some clean clothing. Surely Taddie would have something she could wear. Even more important, Jamie, Farley, and Taddie would lend her a sympathetic ear.

Ahead of her the crowd was thinning, returning to their homes before the sun sank below the horizon. Dawn's eyes noted familiar landmarks—the sign of the Red Boar Tavern, the wall with six bricks missing, the second fork in the pockmarked street. It would not be much longer until her nightmare would really be over. She would be safe among her own. With a last surge of strength she pushed ahead. It was then that she saw *him*.

He was far away, but the way he walked, the way he held his head, told her it was Garrick. Desperately she glanced about her for a place to hide, ducking into the shadows of a nearby alleyway, pressing herself against the butcher shop wall. What was he doing here? Was he looking for her? She froze, standing perfectly still, hardly daring to breath as she watched from her hiding place. He was poised before a group of children, asking a lot of questions, rewarding the young ones with a handful of coins. Dawn had thought herself safe in Soho and yet *he* was here. And he was walking in her direction.

She had to get away! Once Dawn had associated Garrick Seton with roses and rainbows, but now he reminded her of the tortured days aboard the prison ship. Well, he wouldn't put her there again. Damn him! Picking up her skirts, Dawn headed in the opposite direction.

"You there! Stop! Please . . ." To her mortification he sounded as if he recognized her.

Bounding over barrels, darting in and out between buildings, taking care not to slip on the ice of frozen puddles, she sought to put as great a distance as she could between them. The devil himself couldn't have held more terror for her. Garrick Seton had cruelly

and callously sent her to prison, and for that she
could never forgive him.

For the next hour she darted in and out of the shadows, stumbling, then picking herself up, forcing herself to run on. Her knees were scraped, her elbows
bruised, the cobblestones had torn her already ragged skirt to shreds. At last, when she could run no
more, she found haven in an archway between two
stone buildings. A lumpy pile of old rags served as
her bed as she fell in an exhausted heap. Warily she
looked around her, listening for sounds of pursuit.
There were none. For the moment, at least, she was
safe.

51

Garrick ascended a dark flight of stairs, his impatience growing with each step he took. This had to be the place young Robbie Leighton had told him about. The slant-roofed building with scraps of brown paper and material stuffed into the broken windowpanes was the one the children had confirmed. Had he imagined it, or was it Dawn who had taken to her heels upon sight of him? He would soon find out. Raising his fist, he knocked three times.

The door opened slowly to reveal a girl with wide hazel eyes. "Wot yer want?"

He stared at the pale young woman in the doorway. "Are you Taddie?" he asked. The question brought fear to her eyes.

"I didn't do nothin', I didn't. I'm a good girl, I am."

Obviously she was unnerved to see a well-dressed stranger standing at her door. Garrick hardly looked as if he came from Soho, in his dun-colored breeches, white shirt, and dark brown tailcoat. "I'm sure that you are. I'm not here to bring you any trouble."

A gleam of suspicion hardened her gaze. "Then wha' are yer doin' 'ere?"

"Some children in the neighborhood told me that you and a young woman named Dawn Leighton are friends. I was hoping you might be able to help me

locate her. Please, it's most important." Before she
could stop him, he took a step inside. The room was
filled with smoke that curled in the candlelight, making everything so indistinct that he could barely see
the other inhabitants of the dwelling.

"I don't know 'er. I ain't never 'eard that naime
afore. No, indeed, I ain't." A stiff mask of imperti-
nence crept over her face, daring him to say she was
telling a lie.

"Would it help to loosen your tongue were I to say
that I know otherwise?"

"It might and then again it might not," she answered cautiously.

"I've just come from a visit with Dawn's brother,
Robbie. I've secured his release, as well as a retrial
for Dawn, that is, if she survived the Channel waters." His expression was imploring. "I've got to
know! Did she? I think she did. I believe she is alive!
Just a few hours ago I saw a young woman who
looked incredibly like her coming this way. When
she saw me she ran."

"And why wouldn't she? Eh?" Jamie grumbled,
coming up to stand behind Taddie at the door.
"Blokes loike yer mean trouble."

"I've come to help her. You must believe me." He
wondered how much they knew about Dawn's imprisonment. "It was a ghastly mistake that she was
accused in the first place. An error for which I have
very dearly paid with every minute that passes by
without her. But I had nothing to do with it." Leaning
against the doorpost, Garrick related the story of
Oliver's effort to reclaim his inheritance, his betrayal
of Garrick's trust. "She must think that it was I who
sent her to that horrible place. I've spent every minute of every day trying to get her free."

Taddie's expression softened. "Somehow I believe
yer. There's somethin' in yer eyes that tells me yer

ain't a bad bloke, but it won't do a bit o' good. I 'aven't seen 'er since she came sweeping in 'ere with presents and money for the lot o' us a while back. Just loike a bloomin' angel, she was. She's a dear one, she is. But I 'aven't seen 'er. Really." Her voice lowered warningly. "If I did see 'er I'd 'ave a word o' warning, I would. Black John Dunn escaped when the *Sea Raven*'s prisoners mutinied. 'E 'as a memory loike an elephant, 'e does. Comes bargin' in 'ere askin' questions. Trying ter find 'er, 'e is. For vengeance saike."

"Vengeance?"

"Seems a while back 'e and Robbie got it inter their 'eads to do a gent in. Stole 'is watch and satchel, they did. When 'e put up a fight it frightened ole Black John inter thinking 'e might cause trouble. John 'ired a man who robs graives to rub the blighter out."

"Rub him out? And . . . and did the man do the job?"

"Naw . . . Dawnie overheard wot was bein' planned, returned to the warehouse where 'e was tied, and set 'im free. Later ole Johnnie was taiken ter Newgate. 'E blames *er*. Now 'e's thundering about, saiyin' 'e'll be gettin' even wi' 'er. Lookin' all over the city, 'e is."

"Then there is another reason I must find her. Give me any hints as to where she might have gone." Now Garrick's every sense was alive to the danger. He knew he had to find her before Black John did.

52

Snow covered the ground in a blanket of white. It was Christmas Eve, a time of celebration. Dawn might have forgotten except for the carolers walking in fours down the muddied cobbled streets, going from house to house. Christmas Eve and she was all alone, afraid to seek out Taddie, Jamie, and the others for fear of crossing paths with Garrick Seton again. It was much too risky. Better to be a little bit hungry and without company than to take the chance of imprisonment again. Undoubtedly this time if she were caught she'd end her days on the gallows for having been so brazen as to escape. The "steps and the string," the term her brother used. Over and over it echoed in her brain, urging her to caution.

There was an air of wistful solitude about the frozen streets, Dawn thought as she walked along. Except for the carolers she was one of the few making her way about. The shops were shut, the vendors gone, the streets deserted. All those with family, friends, or a place to hang their hats had sought the comfort of a roaring fire and were watching the flickering flames of a yule log that would burn steadily through the twelve days of Christmas. Dawn paused to take a brief look into the windows of each dwelling she passed, remembering other Christmases.

"Help me hang the mistletoe, ivy, and holly, Poppet. It will bring us good luck throughout the following year," she remembered her father saying. "What a feast we'll have. Roast beef, stuffing, a bit of plum pudding. Your mother is a marvelous cook and a very beautiful woman. . . ."

A bit of plum pudding, Dawn thought. Oh, how good it would be to have even one taste of something good to eat. With that in mind she tagged along with the carolers, singing a Christmas song that she remembered. As she had hoped, she shared in their reward, a mug of hot spiced cider and a bit of Yorkshire pudding, batter baked in meat drippings. It soothed her hunger and made her realize that at least at this time, Londoners were men and women of goodwill.

Just as in ancient times there would be merriment all over England until the Twelfth Day, the sixth of January. When she was just a little girl there had been a present for her on each of those days and the same for Robbie.

Robbie. How she wished she could be with him. Where was he now? Was he safe? Was he happy? Was he remembering too? When they were children they had played a Christmas game called "king of the bean," in which a bean was hidden in a cake or loaf and the person who found it became king of the feast. Oh, how angry Robbie had been when she was accorded that honor again and again. The memory made her smile. Christmas always brought family to mind.

The narrow streets and alleyways were festive, made beautiful with colored paper and ribbons. Twinkling candles in doors and windows lit up the night. Children, their faces bright with anticipation, rivaled the candles in their radiance. Somehow their joy was infectious, making Dawn forget her sadness for the moment. When she thought about it, she realized she had much to be thankful for. She was free to roam about, she had her health, and she'd found an old abandoned wine cellar that gave her shelter from the cold. Picking up a stick of old wood, she decided it would be perfect for her own yule log. With that thought in mind she retraced her steps and headed for her makeshift home, humming the refrain of a carol.

The night air chilled her face and Dawn tugged her torn shawl around her thin body. Oh, yes, a fire would be ever so pleasant. Taking a turn into the dark alleyway, she was startled when a silhouetted form stepped forward to block her way. "Excuse me," she said politely, trying to sidestep the human obstacle.

"Watch that yer don't get in people's waiy. . . ." a voice answered. The man held a thick cigar between his teeth. As he reached up and lighted it with a match, his face was illuminated. It was Black John Dunn! At the same moment, he recognized her. "Dawnie! 'Ow nice ter see old chums."

"Yes. Pleasant." Dear God, of all the people she had hoped never to see again! Picking up her skirts, she tried to act as if nothing was wrong. "Have a prosperous Christmas, John."

"Now, not so hasty, wench!" When she moved to the left, he did so too; when she moved to the right, he mimicked her, putting himself in her path.

"I must be going. I'm already late. I will be missed," she bluffed, turning her back and walking quickly away.

"If yer know wot's good fer ye, ye'll 'ightaile it back 'ere, yer will. Little Miss Snitch!" John's voice thundered in the silence of the night.

"I never told on you, John," Dawn said evenly. "But

I did keep you from killing a man who had done you no wrong. For that I'm not sorry."

His growl was that of a wild beast. "Yer 'ad ter free the bleedin' toff against me orders. Well, yer conscience cost me precious days o' me life, dear girl. Now yer goin' ter paiy. . . ." He shook his fist at her back.

She spun to face him. "I'm not afraid of you, Black John," she said, but she was. Terrifyingly so. There was a savage fury etched on his face that warned her he meant serious harm. His face was pale; there were hollows beneath his eyes. Life in prison had taken its toll. A muscle twitched in his face, a nervous tick he'd never had before. Knowing she had to escape him, she took to her heels.

Breaking into a run, he caught up with her. With talonlike fingers he caught her shoulders and gave her a vicious shake. "Not afraid o' me? You should be. Yer don't know 'ow long I've wanted ter wring yer scrawny neck."

She tried to pull away, but his fingers only dug deeper into her flesh. "Leave me be. I'm warning you . . ." she gasped, feigning bravado.

In answer he dragged her over the broken cobblestones with menacing purpose. "Yer peached on me, Dawnie, and for that yer will paiy. No one what does Black John Dunn in doesn't get 'is due." He jerked her arm viciously, dragging her into the darkness.

"Get your bleedin' hands off me!" Desperation tinged with anger made her act instinctively. Doubling up her fist, she swung at his jaw. A loud grunt proved she'd caused him pain, but instead of cowing him it only made him angrier. Black John rubbed at his jaw for a moment or two, then, with a blow that took her completely by surprise, caught her on the face with his open palm. The blow momentarily stunned her.

"If yer loikes it rough, I can give yer blow fer blow. . . ." Like a tomcat stalking a mouse, he moved stealthily forward, taking a step at a time, moving round and round her in slow pantomime.

Dawn shook her head to clear her ears of their ringing. She knew she had to get away. Black John would kill her. Frantically her eyes darted from side to side, seeking an escape route, but found none.

"Oh, no! Now that I 'ave yer cornered ye won't be gettin' awaiy." Once again he reached out to seize her, his hands grabbing her arms and pinioning them behind her back. Agonizing pain tore through her body as he pulled tighter and tighter. Dawn screamed, certain he was going to pull her arms from their sockets. His knee slammed into her back as he said, "Another peep from ye and I'll snap yer in 'alf loike a lobster-tail, I will." John's weasel eyes glittered maliciously at her.

Dawn struggled to get free, but he hurled his bulky weight against her, pinning her to the ground. His hands were bruising as he clutched at her throat, squeezing until she couldn't breathe. Dawn pressed her eyes shut so she wouldn't have to see his leering face. She tried to keep her mind clear, to focus through her pain, but all she could concentrate on were the hands around her neck. He was going to kill her, and there was nothing she could do. And all the while his harsh laughter rang in her ears. The laughter of the devil himself.

Dawn imagined she heard footsteps. A dark figure hurtled through the air like a demon. She felt Black John's weight lessen as he was pulled away. She tried to adjust her eyes to the darkness, but all she could see was the outline of powerful shoulders tapering down into lean hips. The man was much taller than Black John, more agile, fighting with a furious intensity. Raising up on her elbow she tried to regain the strength her tussle with Black John had drained.

Rage exploded before Garrick's eyes. Striking out with his fist, he caught the black-bearded thief on the chin. Black John staggered back but did not fall. He maintained his balance, whipping a knife out of his boot and holding it out threateningly. "Come on! I'll cut out yer 'eart and eat it for tomorrow's breakfast."

Garrick was unarmed, but he remembered a trick he had learned while serving aboard ship. Taking off his coat, he wound it around his arm, using it as a shield against his opponent's slashing weapon. Sidestepping Black John again and again, he waited for a chance to turn the other man's anger against him and was rewarded to hear the knife clatter to the ground as he snapped his coat at his adversary's wrist.

Remembering his boxing training, Garrick controlled his breathing and clenched his hands into tight fists. Moving his hands in circular motions, he jabbed out again and again. He sized up his opponent and found him to be a man quick to blind surges of temper. That would work against him.

Overconfidence made Black John careless. Like a cornered, enraged bull, he struck out blindly again and again, missing his target. Eyeing the knife which lay on the cobblestones, he inched his way back, but Garrick sensed his intentions and blocked his path. They fell to the ground, rolling over and over as they fought with deadly determination to grasp the weapon. Black John reached out and grasped the handle, holding it between them menacingly, trying desperately to position it so it could do its lethal work. But Garrick was driven by a greater fury than Black John could imagine. He was fighting not only for himself but for the woman he loved. The thought of protecting her gave him added strength. Slowly, surely, he forced the knife from the other man's fingers. Then with a final well-aimed blow, he knocked Black John unconscious.

Then he was leaning over Dawn, his face looming before her eyes. The sight was all too familiar, filling Dawn not with gratitude but with fear. "It's *you*!" She shrank back from him. "No! Please . . . I won't go back to Newgate. I'll die first. . . ."

"Go back to Newgate? It is the last place you will go. You're safe now, Dawn, my love." He touched her neck, his fingers hauntingly tender. "Let me make certain he hasn't harmed you." Gently he moved his hands over her face and body, then slipped a hand around her waist, helping her to her feet.

Dawn, my love? Was that what he said? Dawn eyed him warily, wondering what game he was playing now. "Safe?" she asked despairingly. "You turned me in once. You betrayed me in a manner that is unforgivable. I can only fear that you might again. . . ." She leveled a cold stare at him. "Leave me alone. For the love of God, you've done enough."

He held her at arm's length, looking deep into her eyes. "On my word I did not turn you in. I love you, Dawn. I might have been a stubborn ass, but I would never be so cruel. I made the dastardly mistake of telling Oliver about your past, and it was he, not I, who summoned the runners. He wanted to claim his inheritance, but now the estate will be yours again, as Oliver's aunt intended." Choosing his words with care, he told her the whole story. "If you want to hold me to account, let it be for not realizing that you were the most precious gift I have ever been given. I want to marry you if you will have me. Will you?"

"Marry you?" It was the last thing she had ever expected to hear from Garrick.

For the moment the unconscious form of Black John was forgotten as they stared silently at each

other. Dawn swallowed with difficulty, not certain
what to say. Once she had wanted to marry him,
once she had loved him so much, and yet now she
could not get the words past her lips, words that
would tell him she loved him still. Time. Perhaps she
needed time. There were so many painful memories.
"Garrick . . ."

She felt his arms around her, lifting her up, holding her to him in a haven of warmth. Her body
screamed with exhaustion. What should she do, what
could she say? She would think of it all later. For the
moment the security of his arms seemed so welcome.
Closing her eyes, she burrowed her head against his
shoulder as he carried her down the streets of the
Seven Dials.

53

The flickering flames of the yule log seemed to pulsate with the rhythm of music, mirth, and merriment echoing throughout Garrick's house as he and Dawn stepped into the drawing room. Holly and mistletoe hung from every bower, and candles twinkled along the tables, illuminating the veritable feast laid upon them.

"What is this?" Dawn looked about her, unable to believe her eyes. There, sitting around one table were Jamie, Taddie, Arien, Farley, Murdock, and a face so dear to her Dawn gasped in delighted surprise. "Robbie! Oh, Robbie!" Her feet took flight as she ran to him, throwing her arms about his neck. "I thought never to see you again. I thought . . ."

"I'm a free man, I am. Thanks to a fine, upstanding bloke." Playfully he tweaked her nose, not wanting the others to know how deeply he was touched by the reunion. "Aye, but it is good ter see ye again, sister dear. When I 'eard what 'ad 'appened and all, yer being sent to 'the stone jug,' saime as me was, well, I . . . I . . ." His eyes sparkled with unshed tears.

"But we're all together now. Thanks to Garrick," Taddie said, coming to Robbie's rescue. "And oh, he really is a fine one, 'e is, Dawn. A gent for all that. A wonderful, wonderful gen'leman. Why, 'e insisted we all come 'ere and spend Christmas wi' 'im. Said 'e was going ter find yer if 'e had to search the 'ole of London, 'e did, and bring yer 'ere."

"He said that?" Dawn's gaze softened as she looked into Garrick's eyes, loving him so much at that moment that she thought her heart would surely burst.

Garrick was a bit embarrassed by Taddie's praise. "I wanted to give you a special Christmas, my love. Have I?" His eyes were on hers as he waited for her answer.

Looking at Garrick, then at Robbie, then at Garrick again, she smiled. "You have. You have given me the best Christmas gift of all. You've given me my brother back again." And love, she thought. How could she doubt him now?

"And am I forgiven?" The expression on his face was somber as he handed Dawn a tiny package. For a long time she stared at the little box, then she opened it with trembling fingers to find a diamond ring inside. Placing it on her finger, she watched as the stone reflected the sparkling lights of the yuletide flames. The ring was beautiful and told her how very much Garrick really did love her.

"Forgive him. Dawnie, I saiy, let bargains be bargains. I've put me anger behind me, I 'ave. 'Ere's me 'and on it." Sticking out his hand, Robbie took Garrick's in a firm handshake, then pulling him closer, patted him on the back. "All in all, 'e seems ter be a mighty fine bloke, for a toff, that is."

"Mmm, well . . ." Garrick eyed the young man warily, but decided it was the beginning of a tremulous truce. If Dawn said she would marry him, Robbie would soon be his brother-in-law and that meant they had to get along. The tension between the two men eased as he returned the pressure of Robbie's hand. "I hope we can be friends, Robbie."

Robbie grinned. "So do I, maite. So do I. I'm thinkin' ter become a gen'leman. If Dawnie 'ere can teach me the proper waiy to talk, that is." Putting his hands in his pockets, he sauntered across the room.

"Robbie!" Dawn's voice was stern as she came up behind her brother. "Give back the watch!"

"Wot?"

"I said, give back the watch." She sighed in exasperation. "I know what you did!"

Throwing up his hands Robbie pretended innocence until Dawn's search of his pockets produced the timepiece. He smiled sheepishly at Garrick. "I was only tryin' to see if I was rusty for lack of practice. No 'arm done. I would 'ave given it back. I *would*."

"It was a watch that got us all into trouble in the first place, Rob." Folding her arms across her chest, Dawn scolded, "Won't you ever learn?"

"I'm sorry, really I am. No 'arm meant." He put his hands out and wiggled his fingers. "But I proved to meself that I still got me dexterity. Indeed I 'ave. Eh, Garrick, old chum?"

Garrick laughed and turned his gaze to Dawn again. "It looks like you just might have your hands full, my dear. We both will. Your brother seems a bit set in his ways. But perhaps I can put his talents to use. I'll think of a way."

"A job?" Robbie shrugged his shoulders. "I suppose it's time I became an 'onest bloke."

"But there is a price to be paid." Smiling, Garrick swept Dawn into his arms in an ardent kiss. At last when they broke apart he asked her again. "That you marry me. Will you?"

She didn't even have to think before she gave her answer. "Yes. Oh, yes!" The words came easily. Tears of happiness slid unheeded down her cheeks. Her heart ached with sweet joy. She was going to be Garrick's wife, belong to him forever. She felt an overwhelming sense of peace and happiness. She had everything she had ever hoped and dreamed of.

"I love you, Dawn. With all my heart. . . ." They made plans for a life together, as the others politely turned their backs, pretending interest in the fire. Oh, but they did make a fine-looking couple, Robbie whispered behind his hand, and everyone raised their glasses in a toast.

All the uncertainties of the past were forgotten. Truly it was a wonderful Christmas. Garrick and Dawn basked in the warmth of their love as Christmas bells began to peal throughout London. Goodwill towards men. For the moment, at least, there was peace and joy in the city.